ANGEL
FIRE

A NOVEL BY
RON FRANSCELL

Laughing Owl Publishing
Grand Bay, Alabama

ANGEL FIRE

Library of Congress Cataloging-in Publication Data

Franscell, Ron, 1957-
    Angel Fire : a novel / by Ron Franscell. - 1st ed.
        p.   cm.
    ISBN 0-9659701-2-4
    I. Title.
PS3556.R35189A84   1998
813'. 54—dc21   98-6937
                                                    CIP

FIRST EDITION First Printing, 1998

Cover art and design: David Howlett

Laughing Owl Publishing, Inc.
12610 Hwy 90 West
Grand Bay, AL 36541
www.laughingowl.com

To Ann
My angel
And my fire

ACKNOWLEDGEMENTS

Any writer is lucky to find just one reader who is touched by his story. Throughout this journey, I have made many friends who returned their faith in *Angel Fire* by helping it find its way to your hands. In that way, I am most fortunate to have known them, but knowing them would have enhanced my life in any case. I wish to acknowledge and thank:

Dr. Tom Walsh, (Colonel, U.S. Army, Retired), a searcher.
Drs. Suzanne Witterholt and **Emily Keram,** who helped put me inside the minds of my characters.
Phu Mai Thuc Trinh, an angel who made an awfully long trip just to give me a few words.
Deb Holbert, Mark Whittington, Arlene Larson, Warren Adler and **Candace Hoffmann,** who gave free advice and moral support when it was most needed. And to my friend, **Mike Smith,** who works in a gas station.
Kathleen Dougherty and **John Ruemmler,** who knew how the words should fit together, and **Betty Kennedy** and **Suzanne Weakly,** whose eyes for detail were unerring.
My agent, **Linda Allen,** whose singular enthusiasm for this story made it a reality, and to **Heather Wilkinson** and **Hamilton Boudreaux** at Laughing Owl Publishing, who took a big risk on an unknown writer. They'll never be repaid fully for what they've done.
My wife, **Ann,** who gave me the passion and the inspiration to tell a good story; and my children, **Ashley** and **Matthew,** from whom I stole the most time as I wrote it. *Angel Fire* would have been meaningless if they weren't here to share it.
And, finally, The Old Ones, the storytellers who went before: Homer, Hemingway, Bill Nye, Kerouac, London, Steinbeck, Hugo and all the rest. I lay on the cairn one more rock.

-- **R.F.**
February 1998

"And when they saw him afar off, even
before he came near unto them,
they conspired to slay him.
And they said one to another,
Behold this dreamer cometh.
Come now therefore and let us slay him,
and cast him into some pit, and
we will say some evil beast hath
devoured him: And we shall see
what will become of his dreams."

GENESIS
37:18-20

"Just so did Odysseus lie while
Athene shed down sleep upon his eyes,
to sooner deliver him
from the pains of his weakness."

HOMER
The Odyssey

SOURCE
WEST CANAAN, WYOMING, JUNE 17, 1957

Mount Pisgah, the town cemetery, was only a few blocks from their father's newspaper office.

For Daniel and Cassidy McLeod, the route was every boy's idea of a proper path to the graveyard: a shortcut to the Dairy Freez corner window, past the balky back door of the Wigwam movie house, across the freshly sprinkled outfield grass, around the pond bank where flat rocks grew, racing at last through the wrought-iron gates of Heaven's own parking lot.

And on summer Wednesdays, the West Canaan *Republican-Rustler* was a hellish sweatbox. The overheated Linotype clacked and clamored like a caged beast in the basement, simmering lead fumes up through the floor. By suppertime, when the old letterpress was fired up and the sun braised the broad brick facade of the building, the heat was almost unbearable.

And the fires of press day were the genesis of their secret plan.

While his father worked, Cassidy hunted for the coolest spot in the place. He rolled a swivel chair to the front door, propped open with a pig, one of the printer's lead ingots, to air the place out.

He was only eight and his summer haircut had grown out into a soft, sun-bleached thatch. His thin arms were still red and peeling with the first sun of summer. Skinned kneecaps peeked through his ripped jeans, but his bony legs were barely long enough to keep him twirling in a lazy circle like a leaf in the stream of air trickling through the newspaper shop and out the back door.

The hot breeze off the street tickled the nape of Cassidy's neck like a big black dog breathing on him. He watched his father working at his steadfast Royal typewriter, an enormous black contraption that clattered like two, maybe three, sticks on a picket fence.

Archie McLeod's reading glasses had slipped down on his nose, exposing little creases at the corners of his eyes. Cassidy saw such things. He knew people sometimes died before they got old, like his mother. But he also knew that growing old was another way to die, and he didn't want his father, who was only thirty-seven, to grow old, ever.

Cassidy swiveled away from the thought toward the open door that faced onto Main Street, the dog's breath in his face now. Across the way, in front of the Little Chief Diner, the ranchers' pickup trucks were parked in a rusty row like the addled mail boxes at the end of a county road. Half of them had brooms stuck in their sideboard slots.

The asphalt cooked in the midday heat, and only a few people passed by. But just around the corner from the newspaper, among the crackerbox houses kept up by the widow-ladies and the retired shopkeepers too poor to move away, Cassidy knew the smell of sweet lilacs masked the oily pungency of the blacktop in early summer.

Daniel sat on the front counter and dangled his feet. He was almost eleven, lean and tall. Days at the creek had burnished him brown, which only made his perpetual smile more appealing. His tanned arms were just beginning to show signs of coming manhood, smooth suggestions of young muscle against his white T-shirt. Already he could hit a baseball out of the sandlot, clean over the Johnsons' clapboard house, something the town boys never imagined possible. After the first time, when the high arc of the ball carried it over the peaked roof, when Daniel came to the plate, the outfielders backpedaled through the snake grass, the infielders shuffled out of harm's way and the catcher just sat in the dirt. Daniel was a sandlot god.

But to Cassidy, Daniel was also a little-boy prophet, a maker of myths and a master rock skipper who would never grow old. His dark eyes saw great cities where there were only clouds and sunlight. And he knew secrets about people that maybe they didn't know themselves. He saw into them.

Then again, there wasn't much else to see in a little town like West Canaan, where a good imagination was as precious as a thousand acres of this grassy, high plain known as the Powder River Basin. Cupped in the smooth palms of the Black Hills to the east and the Big Horn Mountains to the west, Cassidy could stand on Mount Pisgah—being the highest point in the municipality, site of the town's gravity-drawn water tank—and see the thin, blue line of mountains on two horizons. The cemetery took its name from the Biblical mountain slope where Moses first saw the Promised Land. The town's pioneers, the Old Ones, knew their Bible better than they knew the promise of this particular land.

Three roads led out of West Canaan, but one, amazing grace, just ended. So three signs marked the town limits without regard to where the roads began. All roads led to: West Canaan Pop. 3,312.

Still, the calm sea of the surrounding plains permitted the good townsfolk a roomy life, safely secluded from evils that are best kept distant: temptations, distractions and dilutions. In some places, men shape geography; in others, geography shapes men.

That's what Cassidy heard his father say from time to time. Archie McLeod had grown up in West Canaan, too, the only son of Darius McLeod, a feed store operator who dreamed of inventing something fantastic but never did. The only thing Darius McLeod ever created that was worth a tinker's damn was the son he named after the man he believed to be history's greatest thinker, Archimedes.

Young Archie McLeod grew up during the Depression, a time of dreamers. While his own father dreamed up fantastic new gizmos that nobody would buy even if they could, Archie earned a dollar a week as a printer's devil. Mucking out ink buckets and cleaning wooden type blocks at the weekly West Canaan *Rustler*, he dreamed, too: he wanted only to become a newspaperman.

And so he did. Except for the time he spent at the University of Wyoming wooing and marrying Annie MacKenzie—a luminous girl from the great basin on the other side of the mountains—and a few years as a Marine officer in the Pacific during World War II, Archie's heart never strayed very far from this place, even if his mind occasionally wandered far away. That's how the landscape of Wyoming shaped Archie McLeod: it held him close forever, and it made him dream.

In his weekly columns, Archie was the conscience of his town, as well as its clarion and curmudgeon. He was plain-spoken but erudite, a country philosopher who could outthink and outcuss—sometimes at the very same moment—almost anybody in town.

Cassidy watched his father from his circle of moving air. He knew better than to interrupt his furious two-fingered typing, especially on a Wednesday, when Archie McLeod and the *Republican-Rustler*'s deadlines grew short.

Cassidy wanted to control time. Every day would be a summer day. His two front teeth would come in quicker. He'd keep his father from growing old. Daniel's stories would never end. And he'd let his mother live forever.

Cassidy was only four when his mother died.

When Annie McLeod knew she wouldn't survive the cancer that was filling her body, she baked one pie every day. Apple, lemon meringue, pumpkin, blueberry, mincemeat, pecan, strawberry, plum, sweet potato, huckleberry, crabapple, rhubarb, sour cream and raisin, raspberry, peach... every one in six neat slices, one for her husband and two young sons at lunch and dinner.

She was thirty-three when she died. They buried her on the south side of Mount Pisgah, where the sun would keep her warm. Sometimes, Cassidy visited her there.

Cassidy remembered what every boy is born knowing about his mother: her touch, her kiss, the sound of her voice as she hugged him to her breast. And he came to know the smell of her pies.

The talk about her cancer was beyond him, even now. Cassidy only knew that something had consumed her. Maybe it was him. Maybe, he thought, he'd needed her too much and his dependence ate her away.

Not long after she died, Archie took her pie tins out to the tool shed, unable either to part with them or see them every day. Sometimes, the boys sneaked out there at night and Cassidy would sit in the dark listening to his brother tell stories about her, among the tools and scrap lumber and dusty Mason jars.

Daniel felt her presence, but Cassidy bore the burden of her absence. So it was, always, between them: one searching for something that wasn't there, the other always a little empty.

Often Cassidy wished that home would smell like home again, like baking pies and his mother's dresses in the back closet. Cassidy never wanted to lose someone close to him again, nor to be so close that he might consume another loved one. He was not a sad little boy, but by his eighth summer, he'd grown quiet and sometimes distant.

That's when Daniel started telling stories.

And they were fantastic stories about faraway places and adventurers and magical times. From them, Daniel fashioned his own solace in a world that wasn't beyond his control, and Cassidy listened.

Their life was best when they were with their father, the master storyteller himself, playing checkers on a Saturday afternoon or fishing on Dead Horse Creek or sharing jokes around his cluttered desk at the newspaper. Sometimes they helped him till the clay soil in the garden, where they grew huge tomatoes despite Wyoming's ephemeral growing season.

That's when the circle was mended—perhaps only with a single, frail stitch—and they were almost whole again.

Miss Oneida Overstreet, their housekeeper after Annie died, cooked two meals every weekday and did their laundry for a paltry wage. Archie rarely missed one of Miss Oneida's country suppers with the boys.

Secretly, Cassidy studied his father's hands at the supper table almost every night. He saw tiny lines where black ink could never be scrubbed off, and they were growing deeper and longer.

Many nights his father would get up from the table and walk back down to the newspaper, where he could write. When he was writing, he wasn't sad. He was dreaming.

The Royal's rapid thwacking stopped, and Cassidy's daydream was interrupted by the sudden quiet.

Archie tilted back in his chair and peered over his glasses at his two sons. His jowls were taut, his lips thin. He rolled a mossy cigar stump between his teeth, and a blue haze encircled him, curling gracefully toward the lazy blades of the ceiling fan.

Whatever he'd been writing had him mildly agitated, so Cassidy guessed it was about the Damned Mayor, as he was known in the McLeod house. Cassidy didn't even know his real name. Hizzoner was just a stuffy banker who seldom failed either to provoke his father or to provide plenty of copy for every week's new edition, one way or another.

"Boys, never wrestle with a pig," Archie said in his most fatherly tone. "You both get dirty and the pig likes it."

They all laughed. Cassidy settled back into the squeaky chair, relieved. But only for a moment.

"So what trouble are you stirring up today?" Archie asked as he shuffled toward the backshop with his fresh copy.

Cassidy bolted upright. The swivel chair rocked a little more vigorously. He fixed his eyes on the floor as he scooted forward on the leather seat.

His father knew everything that happened in West Canaan. Cassidy feared for a moment he knew about the secret plan, too. He glanced nervously at Daniel, who hopped from the counter and stood ramrod straight as his father passed in the close quarters of the *Republican-Rustler's* front shop.

"We're going to wrestle a pig," Daniel said.

Archie stopped in the doorway to the smelly backshop and turned toward them. His pants hung loosely on him, cinched up by a belt he'd taken in a couple notches since Annie died. The tails of his wrinkled shirt, now two sizes too big, bloused around him, threatening to float free from his waistband at any moment.

He pushed his glasses onto the top of his head and pretended to be annoyed at Daniel, then smiled.

Then Archie glanced at his watch and grumbled. Cassidy watched another deadline ripple across his father's troubled forehead. He fished one of his inky hands in his gabardine workpants and produced a shiny Franklin half dollar. He flipped it to Daniel.

"Be home early," Archie told them. "We have a guest for dinner, a young writer from the East named Jack Lazarus, who's just passing through town. I expect you to be on your best behavior, understand?"

Before he finished, they were halfway out the door.

The half dollar, as always, was for Robbie, the sweet-faced, big-bosomed high school girl who wore red lipstick and dipped soft-serve in melted chocolate at the Dairy Freez. She was among the teen-agers who pursued clumsy romances on Friday nights on the far side of Pisgah, in the back seats of cars parked in the midnight shadow of the silvery water tower. Cassidy and Daniel had sneaked up there a few times to listen to the girls giggle and to throw pebbles through open backseat windows.

Now they waited impatiently in the hot sun while Robbie tittered about boys with two friends at the walk-up counter. Her pretty face glistened in the afternoon heat roiling off the sidewalk through her tiny screened opening.

Daniel sidled up so close Robbie either had to wait on him or include him in the conversation. She finally turned to him.

"Two dips, please," he told her.

Robbie spared a smile for the boys, who got a whiff of lavender as she leaned through the sliding screen window with a few napkins. Daniel handed her the fifty-cent piece.

"You boys stayin' out of trouble?" she asked.

"Yeah, we're going up to..." Cassidy blurted, before Danny stepped on his talkative little brother's left foot.

"Goin' to the pond to look for salamanders," Daniel said, grinding his heel into Cassidy's left "Chuck"—an age-darkened, hand-me-down, high-top sneaker ironically named not for a great basketball star, but a legendary shoe salesman named Chuck Taylor. Chucks were the only thing they wore in summer, their canvas nearly impervious to the everyday ordeals of little boys.

Cassidy flinched but kept his mouth shut.

"Thanks for the dips," Daniel said as they walked around the Dairy Freez's eye-aching white stucco wall toward Mount Pisgah.

"I wasn't gonna say nothin'," Cassidy defended himself. His voice was heavy.

"Yeah, like the time you accidentally snitched about the chickens in the suitcase?"

"That was different."

Daniel always told stories, but he seldom lied unless there was a good reason. Since climbing the water tower was an offense against both the town's and their father's laws, Daniel believed he had two good reasons.

They walked down the shady alley, past backyard gardens and coal-ash bins, to the ball field, looking for a little courage in melting vanilla ice cream.

They could see the water tower looming above the thick, old cottonwoods whose roots surely entangled what was left of the Old Ones. In the shade of Godbolt's Market billboard on the left field fence, they sat quietly and wiped their fingers in the cool grass.

"What do you think we'll see? Could we see our house from up there? Maybe we'll see Shadow, you think?" Cassidy chattered. He was fortifying himself for the delirious climb, painting a thin coat of eagerness over his dread.

"Maybe," Daniel reassured him, as he always did. He stood to size up the tower, shading his eyes against the afternoon sun glazing its shiny skin. "Hey, maybe we'll see Pledger Moon comin' in, who knows? C'mon, let's go."

Pledger Moon.

He was another daydream shared by two brothers. Daniel conjured Pledger Moon from a zephyr on the banks of the Crazy Woman and gave him life: a railroad gandy-dancer who enlisted to fight the Civil War and wandered from adventure to adventure on his endless road home. Someday, when other stories needed telling, Daniel would bring him home, but Cassidy hoped the story would never end. Moon was very real and precious to him, a gift.

Running through the cemetery, past the Old Ones' mottled headstones under the cottonwoods, they clambered over a fence around the base of the tower. They caught their breath and their courage on the rusty first step of the ladder, bolted precariously to one of the tower's four steel legs.

"You first. Hold tight and go slow," Daniel warned. "I'll be right behind you."

Cassidy looked straight up the dizzying steel stairway into the big afternoon sky. Beyond the narrow catwalk that girdled the tower's rotund belly, the clouds looked as if someone had stirred them with a spoon.

"Danny..." he whined.

"I mean it, I'll be here for you," Daniel said. "Just don't look down."

Cassidy took a deep breath and started up. The rusty handrails stained his trembling palms, still sticky with ice cream and sweat. He could hear Daniel behind him. Nothing bad could happen while he was with his brother.

They rose through the trees, above the roof lines of their squat little town. Creaky bolts and sagging steps only grudgingly forgave their trespass. They shimmied through a trap door and crawled onto the catwalk. They dangled their feet bravely through the railing, clinging white-knuckled to its dirty balusters.

The quiet, freshly mowed cemetery lay far below them. The gravedigger's sprinklers spurted in lazy pinwheels of light. They could see the newspaper's flat gray roof past the electric poles on Third Street. Their two-story white house on Ithaca Street was just two blocks farther, and Cassidy could see Daniel's bedroom window on the second floor.

They heard birds in the cemetery trees and the softly pulsing sprinklers below, but the little town made no other sound. They saw children riding bikes toward the park and a few cars rolling through the downtown, slowly and silently.

Beyond the trees, beyond Sheeran's junkyard at the edge of town, beyond the Crazy Woman Creek, a velvety brown bolt of prairie cloth unfurled west to the Big Horns, where storms lingered before they burst onto the flats. Billowing clouds grazed across an endless blue sky like a herd of white buffalo. The emptiness of the place fled away from the lonely little town in every direction.

Cassidy was thrilled by it. He imagined the breeze swirling to life in the distant mountains, sweeping over the snow that still capped the highest peaks, and drifting down to soothe his sweaty face.

"Whoa, you can see forever!" Cassidy marveled, resting his chin on the rusted rail, surveying the sweep of land he'd never seen quite this way. Maybe it was the Promised Land the Old Ones saw.

He saw far-off ranch houses, a web of washes and gulleys, dust chasing a truck on a dirt road, and off to the west, a lumpish outcropping where he and Daniel often hunted for arrowheads and horny toads.

"Look, that's the Pumpkin Butte, Danny!" Cassidy said excitedly, scrambling to his knees. "It doesn't look so big from here. Why do they call it that... Danny? Stand up and you can see the..."

The railing shrieked as it ripped free.

Cassidy had leaned too heavily upon the old baluster as he angled for a better view. The decrepit metal whined, a bolt popped, and Cassidy plunged forward into the empty sky.

It happened too fast to scream.

Daniel grabbed for him. Almost by luck, his left hand clasped a fold of Cassidy's T-shirt.

It tore away like wet paper.

His right hand—or three fingers of it—barely hooked the top of Cassidy's jeans. The dead weight of his little brother's body falling over the edge slammed Daniel's face into the grate walkway... but he held on.

"Don't move!" he screamed.

Sixty feet up, Cassidy flailed grotesquely, desperately. He hung face down, powerless to grasp the walkway above.

He was connected to this world, to life itself, only by Daniel's one-handed clutch. Below him, the dead of the earth.

"Goddammit, don't move!" Daniel half-grunted, half-yelled again.

Daniel flattened himself across the narrow catwalk, jamming his foot into a tight space against the tank itself, like an anchor. He tried again and again to grab Cassidy's arm with his free hand. He couldn't reach it.

"Reach back!" Daniel barked at Cassidy.

His little brother, beginning to panic, tried to feel Daniel's unseen hand in midair behind him. He couldn't.

Daniel was losing his grip.

Cassidy flung his left arm back. Daniel intercepted it, heaving him upward and back.

Cassidy felt his arm squirt-pop from its socket, like a drumstick yanked from an overcooked duck. The blue sky flashed in his face. His skinny little rib cage slammed into the railing, knocking the wind out of him.

Daniel grappled his frightened little brother onto the catwalk, to safety. Daniel had saved him, and at the moment, Cassidy thought of nothing else.

They hunkered on the catwalk, tight against the tank, for a long time. Both were afraid to move, afraid their perch might collapse under the weight of a sparrow now. Sparks of pain coruscated like St. Elmo's fire through Cassidy's dislocated shoulder. He was too shaken to move. He couldn't talk. He closed his eyes and trembled. Then he began to cry when he thought about the trouble they faced at home.

Daniel nursed a seeping, raw scrape on his arm and dawbed at his bleeding nose, where his face had smashed into the meshed steel of the catwalk. He didn't talk either, and his face was empty.

His eyes fixed on a distant place he could not have seen, even from the highest point on Mount Pisgah. He stared down through the old cottonwoods upon their mother's grave.

Then he said something that frightened his little brother, almost as much as the plunge off the tower. For the rest of his life, it would be as chilling to Cassidy as the sound of hurtling into the silent and immeasurable space between life and death.

"How far do you think it is to Heaven?"

Even then, so close, Cassidy didn't know.

NOCTURNE
SAN FRANCISCO, JUNE 21, 1995

Cassidy McLeod turned off his desk lamp and waited in the dark for the ghosts.

Rain tapped at the window sometime after three in the morning, a sotto reminder that another long night had almost passed and Pledger Moon was still out there somewhere.

His only beacon was a silent, blinking cursor on the empty green sea of a computer monitor, a tiny glimmer of light that so far had not pierced the fog. Pledger Moon was lost in the airless undertow of a synaptic squall, a wandering impulse adrift between treacherous neurons, one Scylla and one Charybdis.

The dark was real, even if Moon was not. Like the blackness inside a coffin, it seeped into every pore and filled the imperceptible spaces where there had been a laugh, a hope, a memory, maybe the taste of rain.

Perhaps it was better that he didn't watch his memories rot, Cassidy thought. They'd been green once, but now the only seasons that changed were his own: his colors were fading fast to middle age. All the words that clung to him now were turning brittle and pale yellow. In the dead of night, farthest from the light, his miasma shrouded his sad equinox from view.

Spring had started with a late frost. That's the day Barbara packed up and headed south to L.A. She'd been gone three months now, to the day. There was no other man, no midlife crisis, no haunting past: they simply grew distant from one another. Barbara's job with the ad agency was bicoastal and made her a darling of the frequent-flier set; Cassidy's writing helped him not to notice. They'd make love after her road trips, then roll over into their separate lives.

It was all over now, the marriage and the spring. The rain lingered and the nights grew longer, not shorter. The end came without a climax, no fights, no tears, just a frosty change in the air. He stopped writing shortly after she left, never quite sure if her departure was the reason or the excuse.

He still kept his favorite picture of Barbara on his desk.

His finger circled its black, oval frame, and he considered that perhaps it was really part of her, a dark border that defined her limits and hid her worn, unfocused margins. She was a pretty picture in a frame, Kodacolored right up to the edge, but sad and gray where you could not see.

It's easier for wives and husbands in their second marriages to inscribe cautious circles around themselves. In seven years, their circles had sometimes entwined passionately, sometimes tangled, sometimes deflected each other entirely. They had no children to be stranded outside their mostly impermeable borders, their frames.

But Pledger Moon, the itinerant figment of his imagination—no, his dead brother's imagination—was stranded, maybe as dead as Daniel, as the rain reminded him tonight.

The dampness rarely evaporated long enough for the smell to be fresh, to let him forget or to remember again. The coastal rain was stealthy, gentle. Barbara once called it feminine, as if it were a weightless lace scarf floating to earth. He wrote that down in his notebook, intending to use it in a book someday to describe the tender vapors of the Bay, although at this moment it described Barbara better: persistent, cool, temporary.

She was gone, the rain was not. On her way out three months back, she left the door open so all the blackness would seep in. There was no closing it, so it stood ajar every long night and Cassidy waited at the edge of his green sea, in the pathetic light of his flickering beacon, to rescue Moon.

Or to be rescued by his own ghosts.

After forty-six years, a writer's ghosts come and go as they please. They were welcome in his house on Russell Street, a reliquary where Cassidy—and they—were comfortable. His father's wretched Royal typewriter on a stand in the corner, all the old books, his first home run ball on the shelf, his mother's hope chest... his memories were well furnished and the old ghosts knew their way around.

Cassidy's memories, once the wellspring of his work, had become an anchor that dragged along behind him, sometimes stopping him altogether. His first two novels, both modestly successful, grew largely from the small town landscape where he grew up, and more importantly, from Daniel's extraordinary stories. Now they gathered dust somewhere among the untidy shelves that surrounded him.

The rain chilled him. Cassidy nestled deeper into his distraction and wondered where it all had come from, where it all had gone, like the black pup that followed Daniel home a long time ago. Daniel named her Shadow, not because she was black as printer's ink, but because at the first crack of daylight, she was gone. The first few times the boys chased her to the corner, but they soon learned she'd come home when her day's adventures were done.

On the sunlit morning of the Fourth of July, 1955, before the big town parade, she bolted out the kitchen door after breakfast, galumphed across the unmowed back lawn and their late mother's long-fallow garden, under the plank fence and into forever.

On summer nights the boys camped out in the backyard and Daniel would tell fabulous stories so Cassidy wouldn't think about dead mothers and lost dogs. Daniel would reassure his little brother that their mother was watching over them, and Shadow was somewhere out there, camouflaged in her blackness like a dying memory, *See, right over there beneath the lilac hedge...*

Cassidy squinted into the night, and the city lights eddied in the pool of his rain-splashed bedroom window. The dampness consorted with nightfall and conceived only a darkling fog. Even summer, like that old black dog with nowhere to go, cowered somewhere beyond the pane, always expected but reluctant. In the last hours of this dank spring, the rain had grown merely uncivil.

Nothing like the audacious, unladylike thunderheads that boiled out of the Big Horns back home in Wyoming, so pregnant with electricity you could taste them approaching. Their lightning was often so prolonged and furious the whole town of West Canaan was bathed in an ephemeral blue light bright enough to see faces in the neighbors' windows.

On such a night, Cassidy crept into Daniel's bed for comfort, and his brother told him a story about a little boy who could run between raindrops.

Now and then, when it rained, Cassidy still imagined his brother dashing through the downpour, a long-ago little boy who always turns back just once to smile and wave, then disappears into the mist and the blue light.

I wish you really could have run between the raindrops, Danny. Oh, God, I do. Can you help me do it? Please show me...

The rain stopped just before dawn, just before summer spilled its first light over the city. As the earliest gray light distilled through the fog, Cassidy lay down on the lonely side of his big, empty bed with a pillow over his face, a shield against the silent winking of his piercing electronic beacon.

His heart still measured time, murmuring in his ears every reckoned second of his life. Some nights, like this one, it counted backward to Wyoming, where he was a little boy again and hardly ever lonely. A place where rain was life, where seasons changed and little else. Where every boy's day ended with a nine o'clock whistle. A boundless place of light and sky where a man couldn't tell if he was looking back or ahead. Perhaps, he admitted to himself, a place that existed more in his memory than reality.

Sleep came quickly, but he couldn't dream.

The morning *San Francisco Chronicle* thudded heavily onto the front porch. All the old ghosts were gone and they'd taken his dreams with them.

Blackness seeped into those empty spaces, too.

CRUCIBLE
DAK PO KO RIVER VALLEY, VIETNAM, JUNE 21, 1971

"I'm gonna hate this movie," the moon-faced Spec. 4 said on another morning of war. "Shit's gonna happen."

The stinking jungle dripped with unremitting rain; the few hours of soggy sleep had only made the night more suffocating. Every breath sucked in a gulp of the apprehensive fever that hung in the liquid air. Already sweating under his poncho, Daniel ground a salt tablet between his teeth, grimacing as he choked it down without gagging. He took a swig from a canteen that belonged to the boyish Spec. 4 whose helmet bore his war name in government-issue black marker: "ARCHANGEL."

The Archangel's blue eyes were the color of a shadow across snow. They pierced the mud and sweat and rain, slicing right through Daniel, scanning the tree line as the gray light spread. The boy might never see Charlie, but maybe he'd glimpse the Elephant.

Fate.

Death.

Daniel knew he saw *something*.

The Archangel was maybe nineteen years old, his voice Southern and mellow, but he already had that haunted look of uncertain certainty: he didn't know what he was looking for, but he knew it was looking for him.

"You're Number One, man, I mean it," the Archangel said, hunkering further into his poncho to keep the rain from dribbling down the back of his neck. "No way I'd be here if I didn't have to. I can't believe you reporters volunteer for this crap. Man, if I was you, Danny Boy, I'd haul my chickenshit ass back to The World in a bug's blink and see my mama."

The Archangel spit into the wet grass and shifted under his pack. "What paper you with again?"

"The *San Francisco Chronicle.* Where's home to you?" Daniel asked, the caustic salt lingering on the back of his tongue. At twenty-four, he was an old man to these grunts, most of them just out of high school. That question always seemed a bit fatherly to him, but home was the only thing they all shared.

"Missourah. The Bootheel," he replied. "Little town called Kennett. My daddy's a preacher, no shit. I'll be home in thirty-two days, man, singing Sunday songs in my daddy's church and doin' boom-boom with all them girls that sit in the back row."

The Archangel reflected on that sweet image for a moment, and a grin broke across his face.

"Twelve more days, man, and I'm short. No more of *this* shit."

The kid still smiled broadly, and Daniel saw his mind drift off a hundred thousand miles, where the girls wore bright summer dresses to the Sunday box socials. Where the green landscape embraced you. Where the rain is a godsend. Daniel had been there, once upon a time.

"I went to college in Missouri, in Columbia," Daniel said. "But I grew up in Wyoming. A real little town, too. My dad is a newspaperman."

"No shit? A real-life cowboy!" the Archangel teased as Daniel handed his canteen back. "I gotta give it to you, man, you either got brass balls or you're fuckin' crazy."

Daniel wasn't crazy. He had just been too fresh and too adventuresome to stay in Saigon, where the war only occasionally intruded on the cocktail parties and exotic love affairs conducted with equal passion by his colleagues who stayed behind. He humped and hopped choppers upcountry to where the action was and took a tiny room in Danang, nearer the heat, closer to Heaven by way of Hell. For most of two years, he was in and out of ground combat, aroused by the simmering fear and the lunatic glamour of the job. He wore dog tags stamped *bao chi,* scant protection for a journalist. And at every firebase, the grunts sought out this strange motherfucker who *volunteered* for 'Nam when he could be safe and warm and whole back in The World. Daniel would share a joint with them, maybe some Jack, and tell war stories. In return, they told stories, too. He didn't have to be there and that made him Number One in their eviscerated view of life.

He was even wounded once, superficially, by ground fire while choppering near the Laotian border. His scar marked him as authentic, something better than the cadre of petulant hacks who copped a quick feel of Vietnam for the gentle readers back home, then retired nightly to the veranda at the Continental Hotel in Saigon.

But he hadn't gotten used to the permeating wetness of this place. It soaked below his skin, and like water in a wall, it rotted from the inside out.

Under the mud, the Archangel's face was no longer as soft as it once had been. It was haunted, old.

Daniel had first seen that look on grunts' faces up north in the I Corps, the hot zone they called Indian Country because it was on the frontier with the North. Up there, moods were like the monsoons: unpredictable, fluid, smothering.

"You tell it, man," the Archangel warned, his icy blue eyes fixed on Daniel. He screwed the cap back on his canteen, then dawbed his face with a long, black scarf.

"Shit's gonna happen here, man, and if you don't tell it, you ain't worth a crap," he said. "You gotta tell this shit the way it will be. See you on the other side, mo-fo."

The moon-faced boy tied the dirty scarf—a war souvenir from a dead VC, most likely—around his neck and stuffed its long tails into the top of his slicker. The Archangel unconsciously riffled his fingers across the left side of his chest, where Daniel presumed he'd taped one of his dog tags. The other was probably in his boot, in case he died in pieces.

The boy slung his drenched M-16 over his shoulder and fell in with the ragged column heading deeper into the jungle.

Then he was gone.

Archangel's final commandment hung in the hot, wet air.

Daniel inhaled.

It was Daniel's second monsoon in-country. This operation was to be just another "county fair," a routine search for Charlie in the patchwork of jungle, villages and farms that secreted the Ho Chi Minh Trail, the enemy's main supply line to the south.

But there was nothing routine about looking for Charlie in his own landscape, an alien place where one never knew who was a friend and who was an enemy. Innocent young American soldiers, certain at first they were saviors of an oppressed people, found these villages incomprehensible, impenetrable, hostile. And Charlie was a ghost.

The only ground they truly controlled was covered by the soles of their combat boots. They never understood anything they saw and never saw anything they could understand. So they just counted days backward from 365. *Short time* they could understand, but not this wet, green hallucination called Vietnam.

This time out, Daniel hooked up with an Army platoon assigned to sweep two villages near the Dak Po Ko River. A South Vietnamese intelligence officer was assigned to them as a guide and interrogator. The whole operation had a fancy name, but all Daniel knew is this story would likely cost him a week in the manic-depressive rain, an explosive case of diarrhea, foot rot and a few sleepless nights.

The company surrounded the first village, Song Be, before dawn and herded the groggy villagers into a cordon while they searched their huts and questioned a few of the farmers about VC presence in the area. The GIs passed out some rations and corpsmen tended to a few sick children, but they got no answers and found no sign of ghosts.

A claustrophobic jungle path led a couple klicks to the second village, Ba Troi. By the time they reached the perimeter, it was raining again and they dug in for a few hours of sleep.

Nobody slept. They waited, bug-eyed on Dexedrine tabs the docs passed around. Sometime after midnight, they strung out in a skirmish line along the edge of the jungle clearing, then moved in silently and quickly under the cover of the downpour.

Daniel knew a night raid on a Vietnamese village could be a cake walk or it could be a frenetic E-ticket phantasm.

Ba Troi started like every other village sweep, by the book: soldiers fanned out like rats' shadows in the dark. And waited.

Then the Archangel's movie flickered to life. Women howled over the unceasing static of the monsoon. Somebody shouted orders in a hash of Vietnamese and English. Babies cried. Pigs squealed. And flares threw otherworldly apparitions against the sheeting rain and the wall of jungle around them.

Unarmed, Daniel hung back until the operation was in full swing. He watched it unfold from twenty yards away, then moved quickly to a small clump of trees, a few yards behind some huts.

Suddenly, the night erupted.

One of the hootches was booby-trapped. Just as one of the grunts kicked in its bamboo door, it exploded, sucking oxygen out of the air. The concussion was so violent and so deafening, life stopped, even for the living.

The blast hurled Daniel backwards. Stunned, he lay in the wet grass, the rain spattering him. His head swam. For a moment, he wasn't sure where or who he was. He couldn't hear anything, except mysterious thumping and high-pitched screams somewhere, as if his head were under water.

Daniel cursed, but his voice made no sound, just a dull vibration in his skull. His sense of smell was not deadened: the air pulsed with the stink of raw fear and the burning hut.

The booby trap splashed them all, in some way. Already teetering on a razor's edge, Dexies boiling in their blood, the soldiers' nerves ruptured. Automatic-weapon bursts cackled. The volume of chaos cranked up, vibrating right through Daniel.

Somewhere off to his right, a GI was shrieking. Somebody was hollering for a corpsman. Amid the new spray of confusion, Daniel crawled for cover, still dazed. He watched as the movie unreeled.

Soldiers dragged peasants out of their beds to the center of the village, an ankle-deep quagmire where women and children clung to each other and wailed. Some of the huts began to burn and the whole village was illuminated in a violent orange glow. Staccato gunfire punctuated the shouting. Sulfurous smoke stung Daniel's nostrils.

But the wounded soldier's shrieking filled the night. Daniel rose unsteadily and ran crouching to where they had dragged the boy's body, away from the burning hut that Daniel knew would burn for many hours yet. A medic was working frantically.

Beneath him lay the moon-faced Archangel.

A chopped tangle of red bowels spilled into the bloody mud beside him. The hootch had been booby-trapped with a grenade, unzipping him from crotch to collarbone. The doc was just trying to pump enough morphine into him to make dying easier.

One of his buddies scooped handfuls of the Archangel's stinking, muddy guts back into the hole of his belly, where rainwater and blood surged together like hot and cold taps streaming into a basin.

It didn't take long for word to pass like a death-rattle among the thirty or so men in Archangel's platoon. It sucked them deeper into the airless depths of war until there was no breathing, no thinking, no feeling. The grisly rapture of Valhalla lured them down where the rain and the rage drowned them.

They started with the old men. Those who wouldn't or couldn't speak were shot on the spot, in front of their wives and children. Younger men were taken away one at a time by angry young soldiers and random bursts spat from the dark edges of the village.

Daniel had been in firefights. He'd walked through the corrosive, black aftermath of air strikes. He'd passed around the macabre snapshots of VC corpses. He knew the stench of pus. He'd seen human ears hanging in reeking necklaces around the necks of the

Lurp snake-eaters. But he'd never seen a whole platoon go insane. His mind convulsed.

The madness quickened.

A few yards away, three GIs grabbed a peasant girl, twelve or thirteen years old, and dragged her to a hut. Two waited outside, taking potshots at villagers while one, a pit-faced gunnery sergeant named Mastema, brutally fucked the girl just inside the doorway.

Then they traded off.

Daniel turned away as Mastema blew her face off with a discreet burst from an M-16. When her mother screamed in horror, he greased her, too. Their bodies, heaped together in a grotesque embrace, leaked blood and brains and semen into the warm, black mud.

Daniel couldn't stop them. It would have been suicide to try. His brain throbbed and he couldn't breathe. And he had shit his pants.

He scanned the inferno for the platoon leader, a young lieutenant from Idaho. When his eyes finally focused, he saw the LT setting fire to a hootch and laughing as he shot three old women who ran from their hiding places.

Our Father, Who art in Heaven... it gurgled in his deadened ears, welling up from deep inside somewhere, a tiny bubble of faith.

Sixty or more villagers huddled in a frightened clot, waiting to die in the fire and rain. Two soldiers tried to separate a man and his wife, but they clung so desperately to each other that one of the grunts just slit her throat. Her carotid spray spewed on all of them.

In his chest, Daniel felt the thumping rotors of a chopper somewhere close. Within moments, a medevac settled in a nearby clearing and a small detail shoved what was left of the Archangel aboard. They ignored half his entrails, laying like grisly atolls in a small lagoon of watery blood where he fell.

... Thy kingdom come...

The medevac bugged out, but Daniel felt the rotor-thump of another chopper coming out of the melting night sky. When it landed, he saw it was an ARVN chopper. The South Vietnamese lieutenant ran out to meet it. After a few seconds, he came back to the center of the village with two angry American soldiers flanking him. The ARVN officer unholstered his revolver and shoved it in the face of a peasant mother carrying a baby. She must have thought about running, but she hadn't even turned her face when he shot her in the forehead.

... forgive us our trespasses, oh dear God, forgive us ...

The officer pried the screaming child from her arms and trotted back to the Huey, followed by three more soldiers who had tied a farmer's elbows together behind his bare back. He collapsed into the mud several times as they pushed and kicked him toward the chopper.

The chopper blasted a hot gust of rain and wind over the village as it rose into the night sky, like a retreating dragon. It circled endlessly, all thunder and blinking lights, drowning out the pandemonium below. Daniel couldn't take his eyes off of it, nor stop the words throbbing through his brain: *shit's gonna happen, man.*

Even Daniel, the boy who once conjured dreams from prairie winds, could not have imagined the next horror.

The ARVN chopper drew tighter and tighter circles until it hovered a hundred feet above the terrified villagers. Then, in slow motion, a ball of blue and yellow fire tumbled from the gun bay.

... for Thine is the kingdom...

The flames trailed like delicate wings as the fiery bundle plummeted through the rain. It landed in a circle of wet earth among the villagers.

... and the power...

It looked like a wadded shirt on fire.

Except it squirmed.

The baby! Oh, Jesus God, the baby.

The ARVN chopper still hovered menacingly above the villagers. Though they must have known their own ends were near, none of them tried to put out the flames that licked the tiny body, which still convulsed. It threw off a black smudge as it smoldered.

The villagers wailed a horrific crescendo when the old farmer was shoved out of the gun bay. His body contorted in the air as he hurtled into them, crushing some.

A few tried to run. Daniel watched the soldiers kill them all in a final paroxysm of full-auto ferocity.

His whole body heaved. He'd lost any sense of time. He closed his eyes and prayed for dawn. No such horror was possible in the light.

Then he blacked out.

A blunt, violent force crashed into Daniel's ribs.

The force of it rolled him over in the tall grass, sucking for air. Broken gray clouds wheeled past his startled eyes. It felt like he'd been shot. Half-conscious, he wiped his hand down his side, expecting to stick it into a warm pile of his own guts or wash his fingers in the bright red, oxygen-filled blood from a chest wound.

A hulking grunt stood over him.

Mastema.

"Been huntin' for you, boy," he said. His voice was menacingly calm.

The morning light stung Daniel's eyes and he couldn't breathe. He rolled to his unwounded side, his head thrown back, struggling for air.

Mastema kicked him again, this time in the soft part of his belly. Pain flashed through him, contorting his face.

The gunny grabbed Daniel's wrists and dragged him through the grass, maybe twenty yards. Disoriented and in agony, Daniel couldn't fight him. He could barely breathe and he wasn't even sure where he was.

Mastema dumped him on a wet poncho spread across the mud. A corpsman nearby was packing up his gear for the hump out. He checked Daniel for wounds and lifted his drooping eyelids. He saw a little blood trickling from Daniel's ears.

"You got a concussion," the medic told Daniel. "You're a little fucked up, but you'll live."

Daniel's eyes burned and his throat was raw. A high pitched wail rang in his ears. An acrid whiff of burning grass and phosphorous coated his mouth and nostrils, like black rain seeping into him.

Had it been a dream?

He squinted against the light. White corpses of pigs lay in the grass, bloated bait for flies. The grotesque ARVN chopper was gone and the village was gone. Only a few dozen blotches of scorched earth marked its place. The jungle would reclaim it in a few months.

The soldiers now policed their mess like frat boys picking up after a wild party. They slogged through the killing ground as if they didn't know there were spirits in the mire. Real ghosts.

The horror was returning.

Daniel was too stunned to cry, too empty to think of a word for his revulsion. How would he write about it if he couldn't understand it... if he couldn't think?

He choked back a sob and breathed in deeply, hoping it would cleanse him, lift him up where he could float away.

It didn't. His crushed ribs ground against each other and he'd only sucked in the fumes of death.

Then he saw the graves at the edge of the jungle. A few mounds of sticky mud in a trampled clearing just a few yards away. Puddles of curdled blood matted the grass, thrashed flat by the burial detail. The air boiled with flies and mosquitoes.

Surely the monsoons will wash the burial dirt away, he thought.

Would the rains uncover that tiny blackened corpse? Would they even have the decency, after all this, to put it in the same hole as its mother?

Daniel wilted sideways and vomited into the muck.

A shadow fell across him. Mastema was back.

The gunny just stared at the medic, who wandered off without a word. Then he crouched in front of Daniel, close enough to whisper.

His breath was fetid. His front teeth were rotten and spit clabbered at the corner of his mouth. When he spoke, something dead inside him threw off a stench.

"LT says you blacked out when the hootch blew. Says you couldn't have seen the firefight with Charlie. We got a major fuckin' body count of dinks. He wants to see you ASAP, make sure you understand how this shit went down, how the fuckin' spooks greased all these here civilians. He just figures you want your story to be *accurate* down to the gnat's ass. You get my drift?"

Mastema's bug-eyes were evil. His bottomless pupils floated like poisonous black yolks in bloody whites.

Daniel couldn't answer.

Mastema stood. Without taking his eyes off Daniel, he pulled a forty-five from the back of his gun belt and chambered a round.

"I said, d'you get my drift, you little fuck?"

Daniel looked down at the ground between them. He saw dark bloodstains on the sergeant's boots.

The gunny shoved his gun barrel against the top of Daniel's skull.

He closed his eyes and imagined the bullet boring down through his brain, through his neck and shattering his heart before it tumbled through his guts. It felt like... deliverance. His neck tightened and jaw clenched as he waited for the blast to begin, wondering if he'd hear it end, or echo.

Or maybe he had already heard the echo of deliverance. Maybe he was already dead. The last pain, the baby tumbling to earth, had been too immense, the water too wide. There was no detouring around it, as he had avoided so many pains for so long. He summoned old memories before they were blown out of his skull... images candled like some old picture show he sneaked in to watch again and again, and though it never really ended, it replayed over and over with the same unfocused characters caught in a loop that was longer than a dream, but shorter than the time it takes to die.

Between death and dreaming, Daniel felt the steel burrowing into his scalp as Mastema squeezed the trigger. His little brother's face flickered across the screen.

The firing pin clanked.

Empty.

Mastema sniggered derisively, cursing Daniel: *Do ma. Motherfucker.*

The old movie glimmered and was gone. Even in his concussive fog, Daniel knew the truth about Ba Troi was to be erased like Ba Troi itself. He'd become the enemy because there was no Charlie. No body count. No place to run.

No words.

His head throbbed, blood chugged in his ears. He stood unsteadily and stumbled past Mastema into the hot morning air. He wandered toward the mass graves and fell to his knees. The razor grass sliced his palms, the mud sucked his wounds. Fat flies enshrouded him, like death-angels in search of fresh carrion. He heard Mastema laughing at him.

Daniel retched again and again, long after the sickening taste of salt and phosphorous washed in acid waves out of him. Even the sour bile wouldn't come up.

Intaglio is a printing technique in which words are engraved on a copper plate, creating, in effect, a shallow pool that retains ink. When the page is pressed upon the plate, the ink is absorbed from these depressions in direct proportion to their depth. The deeper the pool, the richer the tone of its impression.

Daniel was infinitely deep, and the imprint he left on Cassidy was indelible. Wherever their lives touched, some part of Daniel soaked in.

Cassidy had followed his brother, as his brother had followed their father. He'd worked at the *Republican-Rustler* after school, then went off to the University of Missouri to study journalism.

In the summer before his senior year, Daniel was killed. Now he was to be buried.

The rains came, intermittently at first, after Archie buried that small metal box, unopened, next to Annie McLeod's grave in Mount Pisgah.

Wyoming's fading summer was ashen, the color of death.

At the funeral, Cassidy tasted the piss-warm rain on his lips. More of it spilled into the dark hole in muddy runnels.

The waterlogged preacher read from Genesis, the part where God promised that rain would always be followed by sunlight, and a rainbow would be the token of the sacred covenant between Heaven and Earth. And from the Book of Daniel, he spoke of another prophet who dreamed, even if he did not always understand: "Go thy way,

Daniel, for the words are closed up and sealed till the time of the end... go thy way till the end, for thou shalt rest..."

Cassidy turned his face to Heaven. The Book of Daniel first captured his brother's imagination because he shared his name with the Old Testament prophet. But after he'd read the Scriptures, he came to know the ancient Daniel as a dreamer who saw cities rising from the sea. Blessed were the dreamers, at least in the Book of Daniel, the younger.

The water tower stood like a steeple above the old cottonwoods. Maybe sixty of the townfolk came to the graveside, and others sat in cars on the narrow asphalt road nearby. None looked up.

Daniel had known about rain, but he couldn't run between the raindrops, like the magical little boy he conjured in one of his childhood stories. No matter how hard he tried to avoid pain, and no matter how wide the gaps between raindrops, there was no way to avoid being splashed.

Three weeks after the *San Francisco Chronicle* broke his stories about the massacre at Ba Troi, while the wound of My Lai was suppurating back home, Daniel went out again with a Marine night patrol into the killing fields of the Ashau Valley.

The official report said they were ambushed in the dark by North Vietnamese regulars, leaving no time for the living to clear the dead in their frenzied retreat. The next morning, a dust-off crew flew in literally to pick up the pieces, bagging up as best they could the cold, loose meat that was scattered in the jungle.

No scrap of Daniel was big enough for a positive identification, according to the Marine action report, even if the Corps had cared much about finding the body parts of a back-stabbing reporter who'd betrayed the warrior class. But after a couple of months, a small, sealed box—an aluminum case no bigger than an apple crate—arrived at the Carlile Funeral Home in West Canaan anyway.

The rest was swallowed up by Vietnam.

A *Newsweek* photographer named Hollis Adams came to the funeral. As the mourners trudged through the rain toward the gravesite, he introduced himself quietly to Archie and Cassidy as they walked along, saying he'd humped all over Indian Country with Daniel.

It wasn't just his long hair or the jeans or the denim shirt or the wrinkled black tie that made him conspicuous among the proper mourners of West Canaan.

He wore no coat or hat. His clothes were sopping, his hair a drenched mop, and two spare cameras dangled in a dripping tangle from his neck. In the graveside downpour, Adams moved quietly among them, shooting pictures of Daniel's burial. Some of the mourners made no effort to hide their displeasure.

Archie sobbed aloud when the shiny box was lowered into the dark, wet hole. He'd held it together until now. Cassidy leaned against his father's shoulder and kissed him on the cheek.

The photographer, Adams, circled the hole in some grim ritual. The knees of his pants were wet and muddy where he'd knelt for a lower angle. He squinted against the gray light and the rain, composing every frame in his mind. He'd lift the camera briefly, then move off for another shot.

Circling.

Genuflecting.

Stopping time.

Later, the mourners gathered for white cake and coffee in the basement of the Presbyterian Church. Archie and Cassidy retreated to a pair of folding Sunday-school chairs beneath a faded painting of Jesus, two plates of uneaten cake on the long table beside them, a pair of shadows against a white wall as bright as Heaven.

A few old friends spoke to Archie and Cassidy, only briefly, because there would be other times to say what needed to be said. They were all afraid, in a way, of what it might mean: Daniel had ventured away from the safety of their circle. They feared what he might have found.

So they paid their respects cautiously, quietly.

Archie was numb. He hadn't slept for two days. His puffy eyes staring at the white walls, he cradled a coffee cup in his lap, sipping it without even knowing when he held the cup to his lips.

"He shouldn't have gone that way," Archie said. He closed his eyes, and his jaw tightened, fighting back the pain.

"If he could have chosen, Daniel wouldn't have gone any other way, Dad," Cassidy said. "He knew he was close to the flame. That's where he wanted to be."

"I'll miss him."

"I know, Dad. Me, too."

Archie closed his eyes.

"He was good company."

Cassidy touched his father's shoulder and slipped away from Archie's darkness, toward the auxiliary ladies' enormous coffee urn, the gurgling centerpiece of a thousand small-town weddings, funerals and baptisms.

As Cassidy filled his cup, Adams materialized in the basement doorway. He was dark and dragged the rain behind him, leaving a muddy trail in the bright room. He held out a manila envelope.

"I wanted you to have these," the photographer said.

Without a word, Cassidy sat down with him and opened it. It was a sheaf of black and white photos, maybe two dozen, of Daniel in Vietnam.

"I took 'em over there. Danny talked about this town, and it looks just like he said, God help him."

The photographer wiped a tea napkin through his damp hair. Adams smelled of whiskey and a faint whiff of pot. He'd been crying, and his red eyes aged him. To Cassidy, fresh from college, he *was* old, maybe twenty-nine or thirty.

The first photo showed Daniel astride an Indian motorcycle on some jungle road. His dog tags hung out of his shirt, his sleeves were rolled high, and his boonie cap couldn't shade his big smile.

"Danny. He was quicksilver, man," Adams said, cocking his head to admire the face in his picture.

Quicksilver.

Yeah, that was it, Cassidy thought. Daniel was that.

Mercury.

Now the alchemy of war had magically transformed quicksilver into a grotesque little box of meat. Cassidy put that haunting picture out of his mind as he thumbed through the other black-and-white images of his dead brother.

The first few were snapshots: Daniel hoisting a beer with some bare-chested, sunburned grunts outside a bunker; lolling in a street-side cafe in Danang; splashing in the surf at China Beach; walking down a dirt path through the jungle and glancing back to flip off the photographer, grinning impishly.

That was the boy Cassidy remembered, or the ghost of him.

Then the photos turned dark: Daniel, in a wild, unfocused shot, running headlong for cover on a burned-out city street; asleep against a sandbag with a blank page in his portable typewriter; reaching down to close the eyes of a dead soldier on the floor of a chopper's gun bay.

Cassidy choked back the rising ache in his chest. Adams watched him and took a long pull from a flask he yanked from his hip pocket.

"Man, you gotta know something," Adams said. His voice was grave.

Cassidy looked up from the photos.

"It wasn't Charlie that killed Danny," Adams said.

The photographer didn't whisper, didn't even try. Cassidy glanced quickly around to see where his father was, hoping he wasn't within earshot. He hadn't moved from his chair, where some of the church matrons were now fussing over him.

"What?"

"It wasn't Charlie, man," Adams repeated, still too loud. "Shit's bad over there, you can't begin to understand it. It's like a green inferno, unholy ground, and it's got everybody completely screwed up. Nobody knows who the bad guys are, and most of 'em don't give a shit."

Cassidy was confused, angry.

"Goddammit, this isn't the time or the place for some bullshit..." he warned Adams, but with every word, the photographer became louder, blacker.

"Man, it's fucked," Adams continued. "It's all fucked."

A few ladies pursed their lips and whispered to each other. Another stared in righteous contempt while she shuffled little paper plates of cake around her serving table.

Unperturbed, Adams took another hit on his flask.

"Danny got sucked down in a pool of shit, man, and they made sure he didn't come up for air."

"Hey, c'mon, you gotta keep it down," Cassidy told him. He glanced across the room to see his father was being comforted by some old fishing buddies, distracted. "Keep it down, for chrissakes. My dad doesn't need to hear any of this right now. Who are *they*?"

"Danny told me about you," Adams said, looking straight into Cassidy's eyes but avoiding the question.

It made Cassidy uncomfortable. He looked down at the pictures. If Daniel had shared so much with this guy, he deserved some slack, he thought. But if he's crazy, he'll just make it all worse.

"He talked about you. After Ba Troi. Like he knew something was going to happen..." Adams trailed off.

"Knew what?"

Adams stopped for a moment, hesitating. But his tone shifted.

"He told me you were gonna be a reporter, and he was real proud of that because you knew how to tell stories, man. He said you'd be a damn good one, and he said you'd tell all *his* stories someday. Except one. Maybe it was that one, fuck if I know. He didn't say anything after that and I didn't ask. I don't know what the hell he was talking about, but it sounded scary, man. Real scary."

"You're talking in circles here," Cassidy said. "What the hell is that supposed to mean?"

"Look, man, you ever hear of 'fragging'?" Adams asked.

The church sisters were busing crumbs and empty plates from the next table, eavesdropping. They couldn't have known what it meant. It was a word from a different world. Cassidy leaned forward to hear more, then Adams's message met him halfway and he recoiled.

"That's crap! We've got a letter from the lieutenant who was there, dammit!" Cassidy felt his face flush and his neck tighten. "Don't try to lay your anti-war crap on us now, not now. That's just paranoid bullshit."

"I'm sorry, man, but it's real. It's what happened. I just know it. He fucked 'em up good with that story about what happened at Ba Troi, and they got mad. Then they got even," Adams said, driving his finger against the table for emphasis.

Cassidy couldn't breathe. His jaws ground together. He reached across the table and grabbed Adams's shirt where it hung loose in the chest.

Adams was momentarily startled. Then he raised his hands in surrender and looked away. Not wanting to embarrass his father on this day, Cassidy shoved Adams backward in his seat.

"Danny once told me he didn't mind dying," Adams went on after a murmur in the room settled, "but he didn't want to go crazy, man. So they splashed his beautiful brain all over the fuckin' jungle. I'm sorry, man, but..."

Cassidy shoved the photos across the table and stood up. He slipped his hand under Adams's arm and dredged him off his seat.

"You'd better go now," Cassidy said.

Some of the ladies retreated toward the church's tiny, immaculate kitchen like a covey of murmuring quail in cheap cotton dresses and sensible shoes.

Adams stood there, numb. He tossed a wadded, wet napkin onto the table and shrugged his angular shoulders. He glanced down at the scattered photos on the table and touched Daniel's face in one of them.

Cassidy stepped aside to let the disheveled photographer pass. He felt sick to his stomach. His rage was clawing its way out.

"You shouldn't have said it, not here and not now," he told the photographer, who sloped toward the door.

There was no place and no moment that Cassidy wanted confirmation of Daniel's death, no matter how it came. The pain was too great. Once, they had learned to deal with the pain of death together, fused by their loss. Daniel had tried to show him how to avoid being splashed by it, how to run between raindrops.

Long after everyone left the church and hurried home in the warm early autumn rain, Cassidy sat in the dim sanctuary upstairs, where the rain couldn't touch him. He studied the photographs of Daniel again and remembered a little boy who wondered how far it was to Heaven.

Now he knew.

The storm lasted all afternoon.

I: CANTO, THE LAST
October 25, 1972

The autumn of Daniel's burial had hardly passed when the autumn of his father's death arrived.

In the fall of 1972, when he died, Archie was just 52, but he hadn't been whole for a long time.

Archie's end came on a Thursday, the morning after he put his last newspaper to bed. Cassidy, just twenty-three and as alone as he'd ever feared he would be, left San Francisco as soon as Miss Oneida called him with the sad news. He'd graduated with honors the previous spring, and took his first job at the *San Francisco Chronicle*, where Daniel was already a legend barely a year after he died in Vietnam. The old hacks had made room for the kid's memory, after all, he was good enough to die for the cause.

He drove all night and arrived in West Canaan after dark on a chill Friday night.

He parked on Main Street in front of the *Republican-Rustler's* darkened office. Someone had scrawled a note in deliberate hand-lettering and taped it in the window: "Death in the family. Will open Monday."

Carlile Funeral Home was only a few doors down and across the street from his father's newspaper office, close enough for Cassidy to walk. Emory Carlile, the mortician, let him in the side door and led him to a little room decorated in heavy but cheap gothic draperies where Archie's casket was propped open. Emory excused himself and closed the door behind him.

Archie's ink-stained hands were folded across his chest. Cassidy leaned over the oak casket and kissed his father's cool forehead. He wanted to speak but couldn't. What would he say? Maybe tell him about the day he almost died falling off the water tower, or reveal other secrets he'd long kept hidden? Words stuck in his heart, so he just held his father's hand and sobbed for a long time.

When he couldn't cry any longer, Cassidy left the funeral parlor and walked back across the street. He cut between the paper and the drug store into the alley behind the *Republican-Rustler*. A key was hidden behind a loose brick in an old chimney, and he let himself in. As he stepped inside, the familiar smell of ink embraced him, comforted him.

It was one of the few times he'd been in the place and not heard his father's typing or his voice. He ran his hand along the dark wall to the inky switch, and the light fell on the familiar disorder of the backshop. He lingered there a while, until the odor of ink was part of him again.

That night, he cleaned out Archie's desk and boxed up his father's beloved books. He'd take some with him and find space for the others on the bookshelves that lined no fewer than six walls of the house on Ithaca Street.

On his father's desk, beneath the clutter that accumulates within an arm's length of every small-town editor, he found what he would choose as Archie's epitaph. Just one word, a paperweight set in wooden-block type: *Newspaperman*.

Before he left, Cassidy sat at his father's desk one last time. He was a real newspaperman now, and it fell to him to write Archie's obituary for the next week's edition. He sat at the slack-keyed black Royal typewriter for a long time before he could put it on paper: Archimedes McLeod, son of a dreamer, husband of an angel, father of newspapermen, was dead.

Tears welled in his eyes, but he typed without seeing the words. He didn't want to see. Before he finished, he realized that Archie must have written the obituaries for both Annie and Daniel. He wheeled away from the desk in the squeaky old leather chair, and went downstairs to the *Republican-Rustler's* humid coal-furnace room, which did nothing to retard the disintegration of almost 100 years of yellowed newspapers in the wooden cabinet that served as the newspaper's morgue. He found the cumbersome bound volumes from 1953 and 1971 and took them back up to his father's well-lighted desk to read his mother's and brother's obituaries. The dry, prosaic idiom of a newspaper death notice didn't betray any hint of his father's twice-broken heart. Archie was, after all, a newspaperman.

And so was Cassidy. He took a deep breath and wrote his father's life on one clean sheet. Cassidy laid Archie's one-page obituary—he'd been tempted to write so much more—in the Linotype operator's basket and slipped out the back into the weedy alley and the night air.

He drove home for the first time in a year, back to the small, white house on tree-lined Ithaca Street, the street of his youth where now there would be one more ghost.

Archie's funeral was Saturday, and the whole town came to Mount Pisgah to say goodbye, even the Damned Mayor.

He was buried next to his young wife and whatever grim pieces remained of his eldest son, on the south side of Mount Pisgah, where the sun would keep them all warm together.

After the funeral, Cassidy slipped out of the reception in the church basement. He walked back to his father's house to sleep, but he couldn't.

At dusk, he was sitting on the darkening front porch when Miss Oneida padded up the walk with a foil-covered platter in her hands. Without speaking, she sat beside him on the long bench, the platter in her lap. Cassidy smelled fried chicken.

"We're losing the light," he said, watching the day slip behind the distant mountains. Miss Oneida knew what he really meant.

The autumn had turned cold, and the old housekeeper gathered the lapels of her corduroy jacket close. The leaves on all the maples and cottonwoods along Ithaca Street were already turning pale, and in this season, she always imagined they wanted to be neither the first nor last to fall.

"Your father was so proud of you both," Miss Oneida told him, wiping her eyes with a damp handkerchief. "You were newspapermen like he was, and that made him happy. He always showed me the stories you sent home. And Daniel's, too. He kept them all, you know, somewhere around here. Oh, it's all just so sad."

Cassidy squeezed her shoulders.

"He was good company," he said. "He's with Daniel and Mama now. They have each other..."

He fell silent, rocking.

Miss Oneida touched his hand and gently laid the warm platter of chicken on his lap. Then she rose and padded back down the walk, toward home.

Tired and hungry, Cassidy took the platter inside. He sat at the hand-made oak breakfast table, where every morning his father had sipped coffee in the first light that streamed through the window and watched birds scout for worms in the backyard grass.

Cassidy sat in his father's chair and stared out the window. The yard was declining, the old tool shed beginning to weather.

The tool shed.

He wiped his hands on a napkin and went out back. The shed door was unlocked, as always.

Cassidy rummaged around some old boxes until he found his mother's pie tins, hidden away in a wooden crate on a top shelf. He sat on a milk can, cradling then on his lap, touching them, remembering what he could about her.

He cried a little, and then he brought them back inside, returning them to their place on the pantry's empty shelves.

The next day, Cassidy arranged to sell the newspaper to a young editor in the next town. Until the sale was closed, his father's longtime typesetter promised he'd keep it going. Even writing his own father's obituary had not proven as difficult as selling the paper, for he knew that Archie had wanted his sons, someday, to come home to run the *Republican-Rustler*, though he never said so. Cassidy hated to let it go, but deep inside he knew he couldn't be his father.

He also hired a young lawyer, one of the older boys he knew from the old sandlot and a veteran of the junkyard wargames, to settle his father's uncomplicated affairs.

The circle had been reduced to its essence: a single, lonely point. Cassidy was determined to retrace its silhouette in the dust of three lives.

One task remained.

He would close up the house. He wanted to keep everything just as it was, so he boarded the windows and nailed the back door closed. After he was done inside, he'd seal up the front with a piece of plywood.

Except for the few memories he could pack in his Mercury, everything else belonged there. He'd simply lock up the place and drive away. Except in his dreams, he'd never return.

Standing before the back closet in his father's house, he gathered his mother's old cotton dresses gently in his arms. They were bright and unfaded by time. And after almost twenty years, he thought they still smelled like her, like the lilac scent she always wore. He slid them across the wooden rod and made room for his father's clothes, some musty flannel suits, a few shirts and slacks. He found a pair of inky gabardine pants in the back of Archie's haphazard closet, adrift in dust balls and long-lost socks.

As he folded them over a hanger, a shiny Franklin half dollar fell from one of the pockets.

It was as if Archie had been waiting all these years for his two boys to come by on a Wednesday afternoon, together again.

SHADOWS
SAN FRANCISCO, JUNE 22, 1995

In the house without words, the first morning of summer left no memory.

By the time Cassidy awoke, it was well past noon in the rest of The City. He would have slept longer had the phone been off the hook, as it often was when he was writing—and especially when he wasn't. Its ringing startled him from another empty sleep and the afternoon light disoriented him, even though he'd grown more accustomed in recent months to rising long after the lunch hour.

He was groggy and his left arm was dead numb. He pawed beneath some unpaid bills and wasted manuscript pages on his desk top, bumping the receiver from its cradle after the third or fourth ring. He spoke deliberately, trying to filter out any trace of a late-sleeper's cant.

"Hello... sorry," he said in half-hearted apology, hoping his caller would assume he was merely rushed, not sleeping in the middle of the day.

"Hello?" he repeated.

There was no answer, although someone was on the line.

"Hello? Barbara? Hey, c'mon, I'm busy here."

No answer.

He hung up and slouched into his writing chair. When he'd rescued this chair and the old Royal typewriter after his father's funeral, he didn't know the memories he was saving would only make life harder. The arm rests were cracked and dark with the ink and sweat of his father's hands. The seat sighed as he settled into it.

From where he sat, the writing desk in the upstairs bedroom of his unpretentious little place on Russian Hill, he could see The City was well into its day. The house at 29 Russell was a brown shingle on a gray, board-and-batten alley, quiet, hunkered down and shuttered against the outside world. A few cars wheezed past on Russell and a garbage truck was lumbering somewhere on the next block, banging cans. The Hyde Street cable car clanged breathlessly as it passed just a few doors down.

The geometric tide of afternoon sunlight through the window pane flowed inexorably toward its baseboard shores and, in a couple of hours, would flood the east wall.

So Cassidy McLeod's day began in the riptide between morning and evening, one flowing out to meet the other. Fortified by some coffee and habit, he read Herb Caen's column in the *San Francisco Chronicle*, then thumbed through the paper for the few bylines he still recognized from his old days in the newsroom. A few stories were worth more than their headlines: the Giants blew a four-run lead and lost to the Dodgers in the foggy ninth inning at Candlestick the night before. More diplomatic slow-dancing with Vietnam, even as a couple of developers announced plans to build a new multimillion-dollar resort on China Beach.

After an hour or so, he ate some toast and a frozen Baby Ruth bar, which is what passed for a late lunch on these lonely days. He circled his word processor for a few minutes, and finally settled across the room from it, sitting on the sill of the bay window, facing full upon the San Francisco afternoon. Just being around that machine now unnerved him.

The phone rang again.

Cassidy pushed up his reading glasses, and rubbed his eyes.

"Hello?"

Once again the line was quiet, but someone was there.

"Hello? Who are you calling for?"

Silence.

"Barbara, if that's you, I'm hanging up now. I'm right in the middle of something here," he warned, lingering on the line, secretly hoping to hear his wife's voice.

"Cass, don't hang up."

Barbara.

They hadn't spoken in two months, just a couple weeks after she'd left, and it was only to sort through their pied lives. They'd talked gingerly about a divorce, but left it hanging in the chilly air between them. They both knew they'd never be together again, although they balked at being apart so finally. So Barbara remained a cheerless advertising executive in Los Angeles and Cassidy a disconsolate writer in San Francisco, thrust across one another like the tectonic plates of the San Andreas, folding and faulting but never making a clean break.

"Hey, long time," Cassidy said.

"I've been very busy. How about you?"

"I'm doing all right," he lied. "Just going back over some things in the book, a few changes. Nothing big. I should be able to wrap it up, I don't know, maybe this summer."

"You're a bad liar, Cass," Barbara teased. "I know you better than that. You'll worry it to death. Besides, Tommy said you were late."

Tommy Matassa was his editor at Houghton Mifflin, a lifelong Brooklynite who shepherded Cassidy through his first manuscript eight years ago and another one since then. Cassidy had always been self-conscious about his small-town Wyoming roots, both a curiosity and an Achilles heel among his painfully cosmopolitan colleagues— but Tommy had never been west of Jersey City until he went to college. Both well into their forties now, they shared a childhood sense of comfortable confinement.

"Good ol' Tommy. *My* editor, *your* confidant. Just like family, huh?"

"Actually he was a little worried. Me, too, actually. He said you've stopped writing, Cass."

"Bullshit. Everything's fine," he shot back. "Is that what this is about? I don't hear from you in a couple months and you call to check on my writing habits?"

Barbara was right, he knew. The book was a memoir about his childhood in a small town, the son of a widower newspaperman and the brother of a brilliant little boy. Daniel's long-ago story about the wandering Pledger Moon was a colorful thread that sewed it all up, a yarn about leaving home and finding your way back, separation and salvation.

But the Moon story hung him up. Whether he'd forgotten or whether Daniel had never told him, Moon's fate was a mystery to him. It occupied him for days, then obsessed him. He wracked his brain trying to think of that last piece of the tale, unwilling to make something up in its stead. The damned thing wasn't supposed to have crashed his whole creative system.

"Look, I'm wondering... I mean, don't take this wrong or anything, but if you need some money or just need to get out of the house, I could use some solid copy for a new campaign for the Sierra Club. A little research, some face time with the marketing people, a couple calls. Never leave The City and make a thousand bucks. It'd be no sweat for you and..." she hesitated a moment, "and, well, what do you think?"

"I thought they spent all their money on whales or redwoods or something," Cassidy said, his finger tracing the outline of her photograph on his desk. "Hey, why don't you come up and do it yourself? Stay here. I'll cook. I'll even clean the place up. Maybe we could put it back together and save the whales, too. Sound like a plan?"

Barbara laughed, some of the old chill defrosted. "Been there. Done that."

"Oh, yeah, I keeping forgetting that was you I married. Hey, look, thanks for the offer, but I think it's not a good time to start a new project, you know. I'm a little distracted, that's all. Can I take a raincheck? Maybe I'll need it later."

"Sure, Cass. It's not like I can forget you."

They left it at that and said goodbye like the distant, old lovers they were. For the first time in three months, Cassidy realized how much he'd missed Barbara's voice.

And if Barbara missed him too, he knew she'd call again. He rooted around for their old answering machine in the coat closet and hooked it up to the hallway phone. He pressed the message button and heard the greeting they'd recorded together a couple years ago. He ran the tape forward and turned it over, just so he wouldn't erase her voice forever when he recorded his new message.

"Hello, this is Cassidy McLeod," he said into the microphone. "If you are my wife or my editor, you know I am probably doing something utterly and deliciously unproductive. If this is my life calling, please leave a message and I'll try to get back to you very soon."

It was almost seven. The sun had gone down behind The City. The air in the house was heavy and hot. Cassidy decided he might be ready for some real food for a change and some human contact.

He undressed to shower. As the steamy mist softened the edges of his nakedness, he glanced at himself in the full-length bathroom mirror: his stomach wasn't flat anymore, his unruly hair and his beard were more salt than pepper, and his skin looked worn. There in the mirror he saw more of his father than the star shortstop of the West Canaan American Legion team. He even saw a little of the loose-jointed, leathery old cowboys who stopped dreaming when they could no longer keep one leg on each side and their minds in the middle.

But Cassidy hadn't been thrown yet. Barbara's call buoyed his spirits. He slipped a James Taylor cassette into the stereo. In the middle of *Fire and Rain*, Cassidy searched for a clean shirt and his Giants cap.

The San Francisco dusk was clear and warm. He had planned to drive, then decided instead to walk. It was only five blocks or so to the Washington Square Bar & Grill, an old reporters' haunt in the North Beach. The hacks went there because it was a good place to eat and an even better place to drink. Cassidy didn't know much about wine, except that he liked it and that it always went well with night air.

Since his days at the *Chronicle*, the Washbag—as its coterie of harmlessly malevolent newspapermen once took up a collection of their meager affections and christened it—had become an upscale joint with pinstripe appeal, but a handful of reporters and writers still hung out there on off-nights.

Cassidy grabbed a stool at the brass-rail bar and ordered the house red, a pinot noir, while he eavesdropped on a gay couple at the end of the bar arguing about money. Like any other couple, Cassidy mused. Hell, like he and Barbara had argued on occasion.

After a while, an old newsroom colleague, still a beat reporter at the *Chronicle*, caught his eye and ambled over. He was fleshy, his eyes were rheumy. The odor of stale cigarette smoke draped on him like his threadbare sport coat. He was well over 60 now, Cassidy was certain. A web of tiny blood vessels mapped the terrain of his nose, and his jowls hung loose like some big, lovable dog's. Although it had been almost 15 years since Cassidy last saw him, only his frowzy mop of hair had changed much: it was white now.

Frank de Sales was among the handful of bylines Cassidy still recognized, and he was warmed by the propinquity of old reporters. They bought a bottle of wine, a thick merlot, and retired to a table, where they ordered steaks and talked about the bad old days.

Not too many of the hard-bitten, tough-fisted, old-school guys still around, the old reporter complained, "just a lot of whiny wise-asses who watch the clock and wear silk ties and think Woodward and Bernstein is the stock broker who manages their fuckin' trust funds."

"They're all goddamned thumb-suckers," de Sales grumbled.

Cassidy laughed. He thought about all the nights his father never left the acrid backshop at the *Republican-Rustler*, how the ink stains on his hands would never wash off, and how his own brother died for the sake of telling a story. Maybe some things *should* change, he figured.

"You were good, kid," de Sales said, swirling his wine as if he were rinsing the glass, then swigging it down. He wiped his chin with his tie. "Maybe you didn't know I was watching, but I was. They could have sent anybody on the road with Ronnie Reagan back in '80. And you wrote about the fuckin' AIDS before anybody knew what a fuckin' horror it was. I was watchin', kid."

"Frank, you covered Nixon in '68, didn't you?" Cassidy said. "You know how it goes. If you don't look busy enough, the editor gets you a ticket on the press bus."

"Bullshit, kid. You done good and they knew you could write, that's why they sent you. And eventually, when you figured it out for yourself, you became a fuckin' *author*."

De Sales didn't speak the word so much as he oozed it. Newspaper guys loathed and admired book writers in the same breath. For hard-bitten old beat reporters who summarized whole lives in twenty inches of copy, it wasn't so much that these so-called artists made long stories too long; they just made short stories too long.

Cassidy took the ribbing with good humor. His first two novels sold enough to support him for a few years, but he still considered himself a newspaperman, born and bred, like his father and his brother. Ink flowed in his veins.

Once, on a trip home from college, he sat with Archie on the front porch, sipping iced tea and talking dreamily about newspaper work. As he talked, he referred, just once, to himself as a "journalist." Archie bristled.

"Journalists are the soft-bellied sons-a-bitches who write supercilious pap for those ass-kissing magazines back East," Archie said, his cigar glowing angry orange in the night. "You are a *newspaperman*, son, and don't you ever forget it. You're a part of all those folks' lives out there."

Cassidy never forgot. Now, de Sales reminded him of his father, although he'd never seen his father drunk.

Before their second bottle of merlot was finished, the old reporter was in a drunken funk, pissed off at the world and "all the little turds with no lead in their pencils." In a fell swoop of his chubby fingers and the unlit cigarette jammed backwards between them, de Sales tried to swat away the demon that crept up on him: age. He just ran out of things to say and sat there staring into his empty glass.

After the busboy came around, taking even the empty glass, Cassidy paid the dinner tab and asked the waiter to call a cab for his friend. After a few minutes, the waiter signaled to Cassidy that the cab was waiting outside on Powell Street.

"You were good, Cass, like your brother. Why don't you come on back to the *Chron*?" the drunken old reporter said, bracing himself against the taxi's open door as he thrust his hammy palm toward Cassidy. Like most unhappy drunks, he just wanted to shake somebody's hand, anybody's hand, as a sign of reassurance.

"Thanks, but it sounds like you've got the place under control, Frank. You know what the man said: you can't go home again. Right? You just hang in there and don't let the bastards grind you down," Cassidy said, grasping the old man's hand. De Sales, he knew, wanted to connect with someone, anyone. "But, hey, you never know when they'll need somebody to cover the writer's-block beat."

"To hell with you," de Sales grumbled as he stood in the gutter. Cassidy slipped a five-dollar bill to the cabbie through the open passenger-side window. "Nothin' personal, but to hell with you."

Then Frank de Sales gently clasped Cassidy's shoulder and leaned close. He looked straight into Cassidy's tired eyes.

"I wrote a story once about a guy who stood on the same street corner for seventeen years waitin' for some girl he once loved, all because some guy told him if you stand in one place long enough, everybody in your life will pass by."

"What happened?" Cassidy humored him.

"She never came. Seventeen years, she never came. So one day, the guy gets a wild hair and walks across the street to the opposite corner. No shit. He pisses away seventeen years and starts all over again."

De Sales hooted, then belched, as he lolled against the open cab door.

"Can you fuckin' believe it? After seventeen years, son-of-a-bitch chucks it all and tries again. I didn't know whether to laugh or cry."

Cassidy smiled.

"Go home and sleep it off, Frank. I'll wait for you... right here on the corner."

"To hell with you, didn't I say?" de Sales groused. "Don't you see? She coulda walked by the next day. Probably did, goddammit. The guy said 'if you wait long enough' but maybe seventeen years wasn't long enough. Think about it. Don't give up, kid. Things'll come around."

The cab pulled away from the curb and darted into the night's traffic, submerging itself again in the stream of cars almost as abruptly as the old reporter's smudged faith had risen to the surface.

It was almost ten. As Cassidy walked back to Russell Street, he heard distant jazz and, after a few blocks, he stopped at the front window of Molly's Cafe on Delgado Place. While he stood there, hands in his pockets, an old Italian couple held hands and drank tea at Molly's counter.

He thought about Frank de Sales, tired and old and wondering if he'd wasted his life. Maybe there was a time to let go of the old stuff, he just wasn't sure when it was. Maybe there was a time to hold hands and drink tea with someone you loved. And maybe there was a time to change corners.

Cassidy wondered if Barbara had called while he was out. *Maybe that guy on the corner should have gotten an answering machine instead*, it occurred to him, and he smiled as he walked. He was conscious of the humor of it, and he thought maybe it was a good sign.

The tiny red message light on his answering machine was blinking when Cassidy opened the door into his dark house. Before he even turned on the hallway light, Cassidy touched the button. The machine stirred briefly, then clicked on.

There was a long pause, then an Asian man's voice he didn't recognize, words he couldn't comprehend.

"*Toi da tim ban*," the caller said, then after a few empty seconds, hung up. It wasn't as much a question as it was a statement. The machine beeped once and reset itself while Cassidy tried to sort out the muffled gibberish.

Curious, he pushed the message button again. Once more, a long pause preceded the peculiar words.

"*Toi da tim ban,*" it repeated, followed by the same lengthy silence, as if the caller wanted to say something else but couldn't.

Satisfied in the end that somebody in Chinatown had just dialed a wrong number, Cassidy went upstairs to his bedroom study. The infernal darkness of the night before was gone. He sat down at his cluttered desk and turned on his word processor. Its cursor awakened and began searching the dark corners of Cassidy's life.

Maybe it was the night air, or the wine, or a trick of the brilliant light that bathed the sidewalk outside Molly's Cafe, but Cassidy felt a strange presence.

Words stirred somewhere deep inside.

Moon, he thought.

SIRENS
WEST CANAAN, JUNE 23, 1995

The nine o'clock siren sang over West Canaan as it had almost every night for three generations.

Anyone who heard The Whistle instinctively marked the time. Maybe they glanced at their mantel clocks and wristwatches, or merely let fall to no one in particular, "Nine o'clock."

On summer nights like this one, the children of West Canaan knew the doleful wail mourned the end of another day. Their parents would be expecting them home soon. "Come home when you hear The Whistle," they were told as they abandoned supper tables all over town in a pastorale of squeaky screen doors slamming in evening harmony.

It was just as well. By the time The Whistle called them all home, the light was so dim a baseball became a moving chunk of the twilight sky. And the onrushing night made it hard to find the can, much less kick it. Darkness settled upon the children of West Canaan.

And upon a stranger, too.

When The Whistle blew this night, the old man crouched lower in the tall grass at the edge of the sandlot, watching the darkening sky. While the last children rummaged for their mitts behind the flagstone home plate, he warily searched the heavens. They were too big. He felt too exposed.

None of the children spoke to him, though they knew he was there. There were few places to hide in a small town's landscape.

As yellow porch lights flicked on, the cacaphony of play dwindled. The watcher had grown quite adept at hearing the sounds of darkness, and he heard, out there in the night, the screen doors banging for the last time.

The sirens that sang in the old stranger's dreams were the sirens of West Canaan.

For a long time, his nights had been horrific. The sky rained hot blood and vomit that seared his skin. A muffled drumbeat, like the slow rhythm of a clock's second hand sweeping not a second at a time but minutes, sometimes out of rhythm. The death angels came. The earth shrieked as he clawed at it, and the soil turned to entrails, to blood. Sometimes he wasn't even asleep when the dreams enveloped him.

But then he began to hear The Whistle above all the pandemonium of his nightmares. It started five moons before. Months and days didn't matter in that world, but moons could be counted through the trees because they could not conceal it. He was clever that way.

He didn't know what it was at first, the sound that came to his dreams. Just a low, guttural tone that started way off in the distance and came close and retreated. Background noise from another World, a soundtrack for his insanity. It wasn't always there in the beginning, then it was always there. It never changed, except to rise to a crescendo and fall away, as if it were coming back around the far side of the Earth.

Rise and fall.

Ebb and flow.

One night when he heard it, he knew, *he just knew* from somewhere in his soul, it was calling him home.

Then the angel came to him, but that was after the sirens sang. He heard them now, as clearly as he ever had, as close as he'd been in a thousand moons.

The sun sank behind the Big Horns. The stranger wandered to the white house on Ithaca Street where no porch light had burned in many years. The windows were boarded up and the dirty white paint was blistering badly. A fragrant hedge of lilacs, unpruned and unruly, had outgrown its small bed and hid the narrow concrete path that led to the backyard. He knew the way and he stayed to the dark corners to avoid being seen.

Out back, the old tool shed sloped west. A padlock hung open on double doors. The old man unhooked the padlock's loop from the latch and hung it on a crooked nail where a strand of rotten baling twine fluttered in the night breeze.

The shed was dark and musty, full of rusted garden tools and Mason jars full of nails and screws, cobwebs, hoses, an old tire swing, dried out lumber and greasy car parts in ratty cigar boxes.

There was room enough on the dirt floor for him to sleep, for it had been a very long journey.

Nothing escapes a small town's curious view. Certainly not the arrival of a vagrant.

A hundred eyes had seen him get off the four o'clock Trailways bus with a nondescript little gym bag and the clothes on his back: cheap brown slacks and a wrinkled, white shirt that looked as if it was ripped from its package and slept in. He wore the sleeves buttoned, even though the June day was hot.

Word of the old man's presence circulated quickly in the small town, the way a forest fire spreads underground through roots.

Curious eyes watched him trudge up Main Street toward the old elementary school and the nearby sandlot where the boys played ball. He kept his eyes on the ground in front of him as he ambled past all the storefronts, avoiding the panes that reflected him. Absorbed him.

From behind the glass, safely, the good folk of West Canaan watched.

They surveilled him while he skulked under the cover of night toward the old McLeod place. And when he sneaked to the back, undoubtedly trying to break in, two or three of them called Flashlight

Freddie Bascombe, the town marshal. But it was Friday night and Flashlight Freddie was upholding the law by shining his flashlight through the car windows of the horny and half-naked teen-agers who parked under the water tower at Mount Pisgah Cemetery.

Flashlight Freddie's wife took the calls and said she'd pass along the messages; she didn't.

The next morning, the formal investigation fell to Miss Oneida Overstreet, the old spinster on the next block who still tended Annie McLeod's small garden out back and a few beds of irises that heralded another summer's beginning. She was almost eighty now, with failing eyesight and a bonnet of bluish white hair. However, she took seriously her self-appointed role as caretaker of the old place.

Miss Oneida, who devoted every spare inch of her own yard's earth to her beloved flowers, had no vegetable garden of her own. In return for the McLeod's backyard plot, she did the best she could to keep up the appearance of the vacant house. Nobody had been inside since 1972, when Archie died, but she hated to see the place looking any sadder than it already did to her.

Armed with a rake handle and a pleasing cotton summer dress in case she came face to face with the intruder, she stood on the front sidewalk for a long time in the still morning, screwing up her courage. The purple bearded irises were up, she saw, and the peach irises—her sentimental favorite, transplanted from her own beds when she divided the rhizomes ten summers ago—were unfurling like little flags.

But the porch was empty. She saw nothing more unusual than a few daffodils erupting in yellow giggles, although it was late June and spring was only a memory.

So she padded toward the backyard across the clumpy, crabgrass-infested lawn, making a mental note to water it that evening. She wrestled aside the unruly lilacs that had grown well over her head and squeezed her matronly plump frame along the buckled sidewalk. She kept her rake handle at the ready.

The backyard was a profusion of her handiwork. A few daylilies were splashed along the alley fence, and white strawberry blooms polka-dotted the beds next to the house, where the ground was warmest. Irises poked up everywhere, and the garden plot was just beginning to send up tender green shoots of corn, zucchini, cucumbers and potatoes. With warm nights, even her tomatoes were beginning to bear tiny yellow blossoms.

The windows and back door were still boarded tight. The small back porch was vacant, too, except for her lawn chair, another transplant from her house. Everything looked in order.

Then Miss Oneida noticed the shed's padlock hanging on a nail. One of the two doors was wide open.

She'd lost the key long ago and never locked it up. Instead, she always looped the lock through the door handles when she finished her evening garden chores. Now her ample breast pounded faster than an eighty-year-old woman's heart should. She tried to convince herself that maybe she'd forgotten to close up properly the day before.

"Is somebody there?" she hollered politely toward the shed. She retreated a few steps and clutched her rake handle like a broadsword.

There was no answer. Nothing.

She stiffened her stance, tightened her grip on her weapon and smoothed her dress, just in case.

"I said, is somebody there?" Miss Oneida repeated a little louder. Her sweet little voice, although firm, almost apologized for any miscommunication.

Still nothing.

She inched toward the shed doors. When she got close enough, she stuck the end of her rake handle in the latch and flipped it open. It whined as one of the doors swung slowly toward her...

Nothing.

The old rusted garden tools and Mason jars full of nails and screws, cobwebs, hoses, an old tire swing, dried out lumber and greasy car parts in ratty cigar boxes were all as they had been yesterday, untouched. The intruder had either moved on or had been a figment of her neighbors' limited imaginations, she reckoned.

The old lady was relieved. She took a deep breath and pulled the double doors together. As she reached for the padlock hanging on the shed wall, she sensed something...

She wrenched her arthritic hip as she swiveled toward his hiding place in the weeds behind the open door: a grizzled old man, half gray, thin and unkempt, in a soiled white shirt.

Reflexively, her hands flew up to protect herself, knocking her glasses off her face. She was frozen, unable to run. A disjointed prayer jounced through her brain. She waited, unbreathing, for the blow that would kill her and she hoped it wouldn't hurt for long.

But the fatal blow was never struck. Never contemplated.

The man was crouched in a ball, leaning against the shed. He turned away from her, hiding his face against the weathered wall.

Miss Oneida fumbled in the dewy grass for her bifocals. The man never moved.

When she found her glasses, her trembling hands held them in place. She could see he wasn't really so old, except his eyes. They were ancient and full of pain—yet familiar. He was just a pathetic, pale apparition cowering in the wild morning glories and dandelions that thrived around the shed.

Her big, overtaxed heart was still rushing as she fumbled with her bent-up bifocals and moved closer for a better look. Her aging eyes, flooded with frightened tears, beheld a ghost.

Startled, Miss Oneida exhaled a huge gust from deep in her bosom.

"Jeezus Gawd!"

VIRGA
ON THE ROAD, JUNE 24, 1995

Nevada was a blur as Cassidy hurtled east on Interstate 80.

The ancient landscape flowed by him, like the wisps of distant rainstorms that reach longingly toward the ground but evaporate on their way to the desert floor, roots of rain the old Basque sheepherders called *virga*.

Miss Oneida's phone call flung him past the Sierras, past Reno, past the Humboldt Sink and Lovelock, way past Winnemucca and well into the afternoon, before he gathered himself. He looked down at his gas gauge for the first time since he left San Francisco, eight hours back, and it had sped with him toward empty.

The ringing phone had awakened him just after five-thirty that morning, a Saturday. Miss Oneida sputtered incoherently at first, something about her flowers and the old house and a prowler and... still half-asleep, Cassidy tried to calm her. He made her stop and take a breath before she went on.

"I went to the house this morning," Miss Oneida burbled. "Somebody seen somebody over there, but I didn't know it was *him*..."

"Did someone go into the house?" he asked her, worried that his hidden treasures and the old ghosts might be disturbed.

"No, no, no," she stammered. "It's him. He came to the house and he didn't know... I was... oh, can't you understand? It's him. He scared the bejeezus out of me just this morning. My God, he's... oh, it's him!"

"I'm sorry, Miss Oneida, I can't understand anything you're saying. Just, please calm down."

Cassidy heard a frustrated whimper at the other end of the line. He hadn't seen her in more than 20 years, though she always sent him a card at Christmas containing one delicately pressed flower from her summer beds. He imagined this little white-haired lady in her little white kitchen—such things never changed in West Canaan—wringing the phone cord in a knot as she struggled to speak. Except for his father's house, he couldn't fathom what might fluster her so much that she would call him in such a fit.

"I'm sorry, Miss Oneida, really I am. What's wrong? Is something wrong at the house?"

"Daniel... Daniel's back."

Cassidy thought he understood. He'd had those dreams, too.

A long time ago, almost every night, he dreamed about Daniel or his father, alive again. In each one, the cruel hoax of their deaths was always revealed, as if it had just been a joke, or maybe a misunderstanding.

In Cassidy's dreams, Daniel made up stories again and talked about the war and fly-fishing on the Middle Fork; Archie grumbled about dying and funerals and the Damned Mayor. They always laughed death off, just shed it. It was so easy to believe when Cassidy saw them smile again.

Night after night, they came and sat with him in the old places, never shadowy, night-wraith spirits, but always real to the touch in sunny places they loved: the banks of the Crazy Woman Creek, the old hunting camp in the Big Horns, the back porch on Ithaca Street. That their visits were always in the daytime—at least in Cassidy's dreams, the sun was always shining—made them more real to the dreamer, more painful to let go at dawn.

And after a while, Cassidy didn't want to wake up, for as surely as the nights were followed by mornings, he came to know he was only dreaming, even as he dreamed.

In the meantime, Cassidy grew old. The pain his dreams caused in his heart was more than he wanted to endure. Often, he'd wake up sobbing, his spirit aching. The dreams didn't stop. They simply evaporated, like ephemeral *virga*, before they reached dawn.

"It's okay, Miss Oneida, I know. I know. Sometimes the dreams seem very real," he comforted her, knowing she must have awakened from one and bolted to her phone.

But the old housekeeper turned insistent.

"Jeezus Gawd, Cass, he's here. As God is my witness, he's sitting right here watching a piece of huckleberry pie and he ain't said a word from *this world* yet," she said.

Cassidy swallowed hard. He couldn't focus his eyes yet.

"I don't... you can't be serious," he began to stutter, too. "Daniel is... he's *where*? What the hell is happening here?"

"He's here," she insisted. "In front of God and everybody. Cass, you gotta come home, now. Maybe he'll talk to you. Something's wrong with him, but it's Daniel, all right. I'm *not* crazy, you know."

Cassidy couldn't think straight.

"Can you put him on the phone?"

He tested her, but his disbelief was eroding. He listened intently as Miss Oneida handed the phone to someone and said loudly and deliberately in the background, as if she were talking to a child, "It's your brother."

There was only silence.

"Danny? Danny? Are you there?"

"*Toi da tim ban,*" a vacant voice said.

It was the same voice on the answering machine, calm and dispassionate.

"Danny, is it you? Is it you, for God sake? Talk to me."

A pause.

"*Toi da tim ban,*" the voice repeated, again without emotion.

Cassidy couldn't breathe.

Was this strange voice his dead brother? He couldn't tell. He wanted to believe it. He wouldn't allow himself to believe it.

Miss Oneida came back on the line.

"You've got to come home, Cass. Please come home now," she begged.

Then she began to cry and hung up.

The highways of the West were built for daydreams: straight and long and empty.

His conversation with Miss Oneida had looped through his mind so many times, Cassidy hadn't noticed until now that he was out of gas and hungry.

Battle Mountain was just ahead, a sign said. He found a little convenience store that would take his credit card because, in his rush to begin this irrational trip, he had forgotten to get cash and had only thirty dollars in his pocket. He loaded up his Taurus with unleaded gas, bought a bag of cinnamon sugar doughnuts and three cans of diet soda, then resumed his headlong journey toward Wyoming and whatever mystery waited for him there.

Daniel was dead, he was sure of that. Like the highway, reality was too straight and long and empty. Of them all, Daniel had gone the farthest down that road, fell off the edge of the Earth, and evaporated into the air.

The sun was behind Cassidy now, the long road ahead. The last time he'd been this way was when his father died, twenty-three years ago. The road was more painful then. Both lanes. The untorn black ribbon of asphalt led from San Francisco right up to his father's grave in Mount Pisgah. And then back again, in a car so heavy with memories that it mourned for twelve hundred miles in a low wail against the blacktop.

The landscape he traveled was primeval, unchanged, waiting. The distant mountains watched him pass, pointing him toward further basins and ranges, toward stopping places where nobody ever stopped, toward night, toward heartearth.

Toward home.

Night met Cassidy in Salt Lake City, where he ate alone in a sprawling booth at an empty pancake house on the eastern outskirts of the city. A pudgy waitress in her thirties named Callie, with false eyelashes and fresh lipstick, sat with him for a while, and he laughed politely at her threadbare jokes.

Callie had been a cheerleader in high school a long time ago, she told him, and he knew it must have been her proudest achievement. She was saving up to go to beauty college, or maybe secretarial school. She'd never been out of Utah, once briefly married, and revealed to him without prompting that she had a six-year-old daughter, whose picture she carried in a locket around her neck.

Then she asked if he was married.

"Barely," he said, feeling somehow that it was *almost* the answer she wanted to hear.

"I know how it is," she said. "I'm between divorces myself. Ain't found one I liked yet, I guess. Or who liked me enough to stay, I s'pose."

Cassidy heard her sadness, but she still smiled.

"What do you do? For a living, I mean?" she asked him.

"I'm not sure," he said, always a little embarrassed to admit that he was a writer, even when he was writing. To him, it still sounded pretentious. "I'm still trying to figure that out, too."

"You sure don't know much, do you? Here's an easy one for a travelin' man: where're you headed, then?"

Cassidy loosened up.

"Okay, okay. I'm sorry. I'm going home, somewhere I haven't been in a very long time."

Callie poked at a plastic creamer with her flame-red fingernails, staring down at the table.

"Salt Lake is a nice place, too, I suppose. Nice place to be *from*, they say around here. I wouldn't know since I never been anywhere *from* here," she paused. "That's a joke, you know."

Cassidy tossed a French fry at her and they laughed.

"You staying for a while?" she asked hopefully, glancing up at his face for any sign that he might linger just long enough.

"No, I'm just passing through tonight," Cassidy demurred, after a moment sorting through her dreams. "It might sound funny, but after twenty-three years, I'm in kind of a hurry to be where I'm going. I'm sorry."

She smiled in a way that told Cassidy she'd been unlucky with men who were always on a road to someplace else. She didn't say much else after that.

When he finished his burger and got up to leave, she turned a little despondent. Maybe she wanted a lover tonight, he thought, or maybe just a ride to some other place, far away from the cigarette smoke and the smell of grease that clung to her. He felt sorry for her and wanted to tell her she was pretty, but he knew he was a bad liar.

"You know, you're very nice," Cassidy said. "Be patient and the right guy will come through here to take you somewhere you dream about. I know he will. A friend of mine says if you just wait long enough in one place, everybody you know will walk by. Maybe a few others will, too, Callie. You'll be okay."

He signed his credit-card slip and gave the lonely waitress five bucks as a tip. He thanked her for sitting with him, then he went across the street to gas up. As he washed the desert dust from his windshield, he glanced back to the restaurant's bright front window. Callie waved goodbye with a sad little sweep of her palm. He smiled and waved back, hoping she'd find a way off her lonely little island.

His island lay ahead. Cassidy was only seventy miles from the Wyoming border, another four hundred from West Canaan.

Somewhere in Wyoming, in the middle of a night as still and warm as any morning, he pulled off the interstate onto a dirt frontage road to urinate. The Big Horn Mountains, a few miles to the west, rose into the night sky and disappeared in its blackness.

So far from city lights, the stars drifted and swirled over him like sawdust on a Saturday-night saloon floor. Crickets provided the music, while a meteor danced with the six sisters of the rain-bringing Hyades; the seventh, he knew because Daniel told him, was lost somewhere out there, waiting in the dark for the last dance.

Cassidy peed and stretched his legs. He couldn't see his hand in front of his face, only the stars. He hadn't seen a night sky like it since he was a child, sleeping out in the backyard on summer nights while Daniel told his stories under the light of a billion stars. Now, they guided him on a journey back in his own time, to a place he wasn't sure still existed.

He closed his eyes and the night carried him there.

Somewhere up high in the ice fields of Cloud Peak, the Crazy Woman weeps from the glacial snows of a hundred distant winters. She gathers herself below the tree line, trickling across wildflower meadows, cutting through deer trails and timberfalls, warming her icy blood in the early-morning sun that paints the eastern slope of the Big Horn Mountains.

The Big Horns were not born in violence, but in equanimity. Sixty million years ago, the crust beneath the great basin of the Sundance Sea compressed, bowing the earth upward slightly but inexorably. The basins to the east and west sagged and, over the next several million years, the husk of the Earth finally ruptured and the mountains sprang forth. During the uplift, antediluvian streams and rainstorms and the hot winds of prehistory stripped away sedimentary layers that had once been sea floor. The telltale bands of dissimilar colored stone remain visible where the steep flanks of the range now dip into deep, lonely canyons.

The Crazy Woman sneaks into Outlaw Hole on the western slope. There, the layers are exposed in great tumbling walls where the old-timers say Butch Cassidy and the Sundance Kid once holed up. The canyon bottom falls away and flattens out in shimmering pools of snow-water, luminous and aroused where it caressed the talus bed. Rainbow trout grow fat on stoneflies and mountain midges and move on downstream, never to return.

Warm air from the basin often seeps up the canyons and cools over the cold water, congealing in a "Cheyenne fog" that drapes the boulders and the trails and the trees and the graceful shadows of trout just below the surface. But not the sounds of the Crazy Woman weeping on her long, slow journey to dump her legends into the Powder River, the Missouri, and beyond, the Great Water.

Such are the habits of rivers.

The wake-up smell of coffee rose through the house long before dawn. Even at 10, Daniel sensed it before he awoke.

With Cassidy curled up beside him, he heard the back screen door slam twice. The wind-up clock on his dresser read four-fifteen, and he knew his father was loading the old Ford pickup with their fishing gear.

"Cass, wake up," he said, gently nudging his little brother.

Daniel rolled off the end of his bed, which was jammed sideways beneath the sloping eave. Cassidy often came up to his room in the middle of the night and crawled into bed, preferring the edge of the bed closest to the open window. The lace curtains hung still, pinned back on one side by Daniel's telescope. Outside, it was still dark and the morning sun hadn't yet stirred the air.

Daniel always rose early, even during the summer. He'd sit with his father at the breakfast table, sipping hot tea and eating toast made from Gunderman Bakery's day-old sourdough bread. Archie always teased him for getting up "at the crack of sparrow fart."

Cassidy turned toward the wall and burrowed deeper in his pillow.

"C'mon, Cass. Fishing's no good if you're late."

Half-asleep, Cassidy lolled upright in a limp heap, like an apprentice's marionette. He wore a wrinkled T-shirt, flannel shorts and one white sock. He rubbed his close-cropped head, then flopped backward on the rumpled bed while Daniel got dressed.

"Dad's going to be mad if we don't get our poles in the water by the time the sun's up. He's taking the cast-iron skillet," Daniel said, balancing on his left foot while he tugged a dirty canvas sneaker onto his right.

"I hate fish for breakfast," Cassidy mumbled, burying his head under a pillow.

"I bet I catch a bigger fish than you today," Daniel challenged him.

"You always catch a bigger fish than me."

Daniel changed his strategy.

"Okay, so bet me. Bet that perfect black arrowhead you found that I'll catch a bigger fish than you. I'll bet I don't."

Cassidy yawned. "You always catch the biggest fish and you always win the bets."

The screen door slammed again. Daniel heard the grumpy, mud-flecked Ford growl in the driveway as Archie backed it out of the garage. About the only time they drove the old truck was when they were going hunting or fishing. Old '46, as his father called it, was the first new truck Archie ever owned, having bought it for $1,100 on a note from the First National five months after he came home from the war. Daniel liked the oily leather smell of the cab, where the three of them jostled against each other on rutted back-country roads, ate box lunches of stale sandwiches and apples, and sometimes napped on rainy fishing afternoons.

But most of all, he loved being with his father and brother, anywhere. Those days were like open sky, fresh and deep.

"Dad's about ready, Cass. Let's get going."

Cassidy sighed and slid off the bed. He padded past Daniel to the stairs, rubbing his eyes. The night before, he'd set out his fishing clothes—a ball cap, sneakers, jeans and a long-sleeved shirt to protect his legs and arms from the thorns of mountain mahogany and currant bushes along the narrow trail.

Downstairs, Archie was filling a stainless steel Thermos with hot coffee. He wore a long-sleeved plaid shirt and paint-spattered Army fatigue pants, held up by the leather suspenders the boys gave him two Christmases ago. When Daniel came into the kitchen, he sipped his coffee and pointed to three jelly doughnuts piled on a saucer in the middle of the table.

"Good morning, Danny," his father said, leaning against the counter, where he'd just fixed and packed their sandwiches in waxed paper for lunch. "How about some milk?"

"Sure."

"Good fishing today. There was a ring around the moon last night, and the sky is clear. The Yellow Sallies are hatching. Maybe the Crazy Woman will smile on us, huh?"

Yellow Sallies, sand-colored stoneflies that emerged early on summer mornings, were Archie's harbingers of good fishing. A July day that began with Yellow Sallies would likely mean mayflies in the late morning, maybe caddisflies. If there were clouds, the afternoon air would be filled with little green stoneflies, launching themselves from high in the trees in a plunge toward the stream. They'd glide across the surface of the water, skipping like a stone to scatter their eggs. On the last glance, their life cycle is exhausted and they float there for a moment, quivering, until a trout rises from the depths in a glinting flash, like a sterling headsman's blade, to end it all.

Cassidy shuffled into the kitchen and plopped in a chair. His shoes were untied, his collar folded inside the neck of his sweatshirt. His eyes were half-open and puffy as he lay his head on the table.

"Can I just sleep on the way?" he asked.

"Fishermen have to get up early," Archie told him. "Those fish get smarter as the day goes on."

"So why do we wanna catch the dumb ones?"

Archie laughed. Daniel was warmed by his father's laugh, for he laughed far too little these days. And when it made Cassidy smile, time stood still.

"I'll have to get up a lot earlier to fool you, young man," Archie said, pouring the last swallow of coffee in the sink and rinsing his cup. "Let's hit the road."

The drive to Outlaw Hole was a little more than an hour. In the dull green glow of the dashboard, Archie kept them awake by telling the old legends about the place: how the Sioux hunting party once found a wailing squaw wandering in the canyon and, believing she was an angel touched by their Great Spirit, Tunkashila, left her to roam there forever; and how the train-robbing Wild Bunch hid themselves and their horses in a deep cave at the water's edge; and how Big Phil Gardner the Cannibal, a mountain man who once lived in the canyon, was said to prefer eating human flesh to venison. Archie warned the boys that nobody knows what happened to Big

Phil, a haunting caution that would keep them alert to timber rattlers on the trail, if not the occasional hungry cannibal.

By the time they reached the turnout where they parked the pickup, the sun was beginning to peek over the eastern horizon. They started down the trail toward the bottom of the canyon, more than a mile's walk, with canvas knapsacks strapped to their backs and their fly rods for walking sticks. The skunk bushes hid the trailhead, and in the dun light of morning, their steps were short and deliberate. Every fallen twig looked like a rattler coiled on a warm rock waiting to strike.

Almost halfway down the gorge, the trail came around a hillock and overlooked the length, east and west, of Outlaw Hole before the sunlight spilled over its rim and filled it. The mountains beyond glowed, rising up like an orange wall against morning. They sat beside a natural cairn of stones that marked what was the most wildly beautiful sight Daniel had ever beheld.

Daniel breathed in the morning. He could see a bend in the creek far below, where bright water gathered. Something inside him, some spirit of curiosity or adventure, willed his body to follow his eyes, to cast his line into the pool and feel beneath the surface of it.

Cassidy sat beside him, tossing rocks down the steep slope at the edge of the trail. Archie had wandered up ahead to relieve himself.

"The Crazy Woman still haunts this place," Daniel said, watching Cassidy out of the corner of his eye. His little brother rolled his eyes but stopped throwing stones down the hill.

"Yeah, sure, and there's a cannibal cowboy gonna eat us if we catch his fish."

Daniel kept on.

"She's here, I'm telling you. She's watching us right now. The Indians were smart enough to stay away from her. Maybe they were right. Maybe she was an angel sent to protect this canyon."

Cassidy leaned forward, peering down into the trees below. He listened intently but only heard the water rushing over the boulders toward the ancient buffalo wallows and, eventually, into the sea.

"Yeah, so what? We're not hurting anything. We've been down here a hundred times."

"Maybe she doesn't want us to catch any more of the fish. I dunno. I'm getting the willies," Daniel said, feigning a shiver.

Cassidy looked around for his father, who had gone around the next bend alone after his morning coffee hit bottom. Unwilling to admit being a little unnerved, he poured a half dozen pebbles out of his palm onto the trail.

"Hey, I've got an idea. Maybe the Crazy Woman wants a gift. A sacrifice. Maybe then she'd let us pass on the trail, maybe even give us good luck," Daniel suggested.

"A gift? Like what?" Cassidy tried to imagine what kind of offering would appease the spirit of an insane woman who lived among rocks and trees. A fishing pole? A dirty knapsack? A baseball cap? That's all he had.

"You. Maybe the Crazy Woman would like a plump little boy."

"Dad!" Cassidy hollered.

"Okay, okay! Relax! You're too sour anyway."

Looking around, Daniel stood and shoved his hands in his pockets, while Cassidy pouted. Something jingled as he dug deeper. Cassidy came closer as he opened his fist: two shiny dimes.

"I'll put these dimes under this pile of rocks. They'll be my gift to the Crazy Woman. What do you have?" Daniel teased. "Got to give her something..."

Cassidy was crestfallen. He had nothing to give and had hoped, however briefly, that Daniel would forego ten cents to save his little brother from an angry apparition.

"I don't have anything, Danny. Please..."

"I dunno..."

"Please!" Cassidy cocked his head and clasped his hands in a prayer to his big brother.

"Okay, but you'll have to do my weeding in the backyard for a week... and burn the trash."

Cassidy agreed, and they cleared a hollow in the outcropping. Blowing the dust off the surface of a flat piece of sandstone, Daniel put one of his dimes in Cassidy's dirty palm and together they laid the coins on it. They piled a few other rocks around them, then tossed a handful of mountain loam over them to make it look as it had, natural and untouched. Nobody would ever see their hiding place.

"Ladies like shiny things, and those were two fine dimes," Daniel said. "The Crazy Woman will smile on us today."

As they stood there, he put his arm around Cassidy. He understood the power of his yarns to move his brother.

"Don't worry, Cass," he said. "Nobody's going to hurt you while I'm here."

Archie returned, having defecated over a deadfall log to commune with nature in the manner of his ancestors. The three of them continued down the trail to the spot where they'd tied a rope around the trunk of a sturdy pine. Holding the rope and backing down through a thicket of wild currants, they came to the creek just as the morning sunlight kissed the water. The stream was rimmed with angular rocks and narrow shores where the spring torrents had flushed away the detritus. A rainbow rose to the surface of the restless pool in front of them, beckoning and taunting.

Daniel smiled like the morning, then rigged his bamboo rod. He felt Cassidy watching every loop and twist as he knotted a new hook on the leader, then he tied one for his brother, too.

Daniel was a graceful fisherman. He drew no distinctions between time and trout streams. Every summer day was more a place than a measure of a year, and every stream in his small world flowed through the days, through him. He knew fishing was about patience, which, like hope, was really just another way of describing the passage of time.

His casts were smooth, rhythmic and keen. He devoured all of Archie's fishing magazines, studying the tendencies that passionate humans attributed to the wily trout, but still he worked the water by intuition, even at ten. He knew the trout were less wary, more hungry, in the deep water. He knew that when the petals of the yellow monkeyflowers on the bank had fallen into the stream, the big trout would rise to dry flies more willingly. And he knew time was no more linear than the Crazy Woman Creek, which flowed effortlessly around any stone or sandbar that pained her. Such were the habits of little streams and little boys.

By a fair bank, he turned the first smooth stone of the day and captured a wriggling stonefly. In a few graceful sweeps of the long rod, slicing slow and perfect arcs over the stream, he lobbed the fly into a dark eddy where the easy water was full of promise. He tugged gently, imperceptibly on the line until it bolted upstream and the water boiled like molten silver. The first trout of the day was Daniel's, a brassy rainbow trout, more than a foot long, with a radiant scarlet stripe down its sides.

Between the three of them, they caught fourteen rainbows, eight keepers, before breakfast. Archie rummaged in his knapsack and produced an egg, a mushy stick of butter, some flour and a pouch of corn meal, which he used to bread the fish and fry them in his old black skillet. After they ate, they went back to the creek, where they caught their limits on Yellow Sallies and caddis nymphs they found hiding on the river bank.

When the sunlight began to seep out of the canyon again in late afternoon, it was the McLeods' custom for the fisherman with the fewest fish to take the last cast, which often was stretched into four or five last casts. While Daniel and Archie sat quietly on a boulder that jutted into the stream, watching little green stoneflies careen to their covenant with the Great Spirit, Cassidy laid his string in a pool beneath a willow clump. His nymph floated delicately downstream, swirling toward a cascade and the end of the day.

A resolute strike bent Cassidy's rod over. Daniel saw a surprised look glint across his face, then determination. Cassidy stumbled backward, trying to set the hook and take up the slack line without letting the fish run on him. The trout hit the tautness and crested.

"Keep the line tight!" Daniel shouted.

Cassidy held the tip high. He wound the reel close to his face as he watched his line slice the pool, back and forth, for seconds that seemed like minutes.

Daniel was standing now, leaning precariously over the edge of the rock. "Stay with her, Cass! You got her!"

Gradually, Cassidy drew her in to the shallows, and when he could see her colors, he reeled her in. In a twinkling, he was standing in the stream, holding his rod with one hand and hoisting a magnificent rainbow aloft with the other.

She was as long as his arm, the biggest of the day. Cassidy was filled with the thrill of deep water. His eyes smiled.

And Daniel cheered loudest of all.

With the Buck knife he carried only on their hunting and fishing trips, Archie gutted and washed the dozen pan-sized trout at streamside while the boys gathered wild mint leaves to pack around the fish in their creels. The wet leaves would save the rainbows' brilliant colors on the long ride home and mask the odor of their oils.

Father and sons clambered back up the steep slope with their rope and returned to the trail. Daniel followed Archie, and Cassidy followed Daniel.

And when they passed their makeshift altar to a ghost, Daniel winked at Cassidy, who broke into a toothless grin. It would be their secret forever.

That night, as the cantankerous old Ford lurched back down the mountain toward home, Cassidy fell asleep against Daniel's shoulder. Daniel put his arm around his little brother again and held him close, trying to allay the jostling of the ruts in the long road.

The Crazy Woman smiled.

It was almost dawn when Cassidy arrived in West Canaan. The slivers of light that went ahead of daybreak had slipped into town ahead of him to prepare for his arrival.

It was Sunday but too early for the church chimes. The streets were empty.

Aside from a new stoplight on Main and a few newer model ranch pick-ups parked in jaunty disarray in front of the Little Chief Diner—a few with ratty broomsticks poking out of their side-panel slots—little else seemed to have changed at first glance. Maybe his memory was playing tricks. After all, this whole trip seemed a thousand-mile riddle to him.

Time is a pool, and Cassidy waded into it. In his rear-view mirror he saw his own tired eyes, and twenty-three years fading away in the distance; ahead he saw the past, too.

The town was worn. As he drove past the *Republican-Rustler* office, Cassidy saw his father's ornate, hand-painted gold nameplate still in the window, reflecting the orange glow of morning's eastern horizon. In his mind, the edges had softened, and seeing it again after so many years sharpened the memory. The place was smaller than he remembered, and he wondered if the key was still hidden behind the chimney brick in back. A light shone somewhere inside, but the place looked empty.

The Dairy Freez on the next block, was now a hole-in-the-wall hamburger stand with a gravel lot and a few dowdy drive-up speakers under a tin awning.

The Wigwam Theater just around the corner, was showing second-run movies for a dollar-fifty. Cassidy tried to decode the skewed, misplaced and missing letters on the old marquee.

No wplayi g:
Forets G mp 7 & 9

Two things were apparent: movies still took a long time to get to West Canaan, and from the looks of the place, they were probably still too cheap to fix the busted back door where he and Daniel always sneaked into summer matinees.

And the old water tower stood above it all, even in its disrepair refracting the high rays of morning upon the town. A twinge fluttered deep inside his shoulder as he saw the tower looming over the trees, marking the immovable center of his circle of time.

Cassidy rolled down the window, turned off the electronic fuzz of too-distant radio voices. A meadowlark warbled, its welcoming lilt timed perfectly for a passing, open window. The morning smelled fresh, as if someone had run a sprinkler all night over new-mown summer grass.

And in that first pure light of day, saturated with dew and memories, Cassidy turned up Ithaca Street toward his father's house.

Downy seeds from the cottonwoods floated in a neap tide of morning air.

Time rippled again. A few of the dozen or so old houses wore different colors. Some were tumbling into middle age, like him, fading and unable to keep the climate at bay. He knew each of them all by different, long-ago names that almost surely would be unrecognizable in the neighborhood now, such as the Brantley place, the Winkies' and the Snake House. The homes of his childhood friends he remembered mostly by the kids' names: Amy's, Twin Tommy's and Bimbo's. But the old trees, mostly maples and the faithful cottonwoods whose seed floated on the breeze, were robust and tall, and the dawn caught them in a green summer splendor he'd once tried to write about.

Archie McLeod's sad house, in a state of mild decay with its paint peeling, windows boarded and yard in suspended animation, would have distressed him, had he really seen it as he drove up in front of it.

But he didn't see it.

Cassidy couldn't take his eyes off the gaunt, gray vagrant in a wrinkled white shirt, standing like a pitiful statue in the front yard.

The old man's lank arms hung at his sides, his fingers fiddling with the outseams of brown trousers so ill-fitting the cuffs rumpled generously around his ankles, nearly concealing his shoeless feet.

Transfixed, Cassidy bumped his Taurus up onto the sidewalk. The oddly familiar stranger didn't move, either to come closer or to retreat. He made no sign at all.

The man's face was like a torn piece of paper, blank and ragged around its edges. His dark, empty eyes just waited to be filled with some expression.

Cassidy stared at him.

If it was a dream, it was unlike any that had once comforted and tormented Cassidy, except for this:

The sun was up.

And Daniel was alive.

REVELATION
WEST CANAAN, JUNE 25, 1995

Miss Oneida took them back to her modest little house, where she served up two dozen homemade biscuits, some bacon and eggs, and a plump tureen of fatback gravy.

As Cassidy passed the platter of piping hot biscuits toward Daniel, his hand quaked. He felt chilled and light-headed, as if the blood had been plumbed from him.

Daniel sat sideways in his chair, facing away from them, toward the faded wallpaper of Miss Oneida's sunny little breakfast nook. He wouldn't take the platter, so Cassidy gently placed three biscuits on his plate for him.

Daniel had evaded Cassidy's embrace in the front yard of their childhood home more than two hours before, and he hadn't spoken a word yet. His eyes were vacant and red, as if the light behind them had nearly flickered away. But something deep inside still burned, Cassidy knew. Or maybe he just hoped.

Daniel merely stared at the little blue cornflowers on Miss Oneida's wallpaper as Cassidy opened the biscuits and slathered them in a creamy cascade of buckskin-colored gravy. Daniel glanced at the plate but didn't eat.

"Biscuits and gravy were always his favorite," Miss Oneida said. Daniel dipped a dirty finger in the gravy and as he opened his mouth to suck it off, Cassidy saw that his teeth were decaying and mossy brown.

"On his birthday, he'd ask me to cook them at every meal, breakfast, lunch and dinner, and serve him in bed," Miss Oneida said. "Do you remember that, Danny?"

Daniel looked away without acknowledging her. If he remembered anything, they couldn't be sure. His resurrection might have remained a mystery, until Miss Oneida remembered something.

In the middle of breakfast, she led Cassidy to her little sewing room where Daniel slept the night before. On the way, Cassidy paused to coax Daniel to come along.

Miss Oneida pulled back the duster on a billowy day bed, still smartly made, to reveal a small, black gym bag. Cassidy looked at her, puzzled.

"He had it with him," she said. "He wouldn't let me look inside it, God bless him. I made up this room for him, but he slept on the floor last night. Gibberish all night long! It's been so hot, without the rain, you know. He must have had terrible, terrible dreams, the poor boy."

Daniel sat cross-legged on the floor at the end of the bed, again facing the wall. Miss Oneida uncrumpled her handkerchief while Cassidy rummaged through the bag. He found three pairs of cheap, new undershorts and a pair of mismatched socks—he glanced at Daniel's ankles and saw he was wearing their mates. There were also a few dozen old letters neatly bound with long ribbons of dried grass, and some scraps of delicate paper with incomprehensible words he took to be Vietnamese.

And beneath it all, almost hidden on the bottom of the bag, lay an overstuffed white business envelope.

Cassidy sat on the bed and gently untied the old letters. He instantly recognized the handwriting on the soiled envelopes as his own, and his father's. The postmarks all dated back to the war.

"Can you believe this? He kept all his letters from home," Cassidy said aloud. "Nothing else."

He glanced at Daniel for some clue, not even sure which mystery he should try to solve first. He got no help.

Cassidy fished the newer envelope out of the bag. It was already open.

Just then, Daniel turned toward him and spoke to Cassidy for the first time in more than twenty-five years.

"*Thien-than*," he rasped in a sand-paper voice, pointing at the envelope. "*Thien-than. Tom... Tom.*"

Cassidy let the gym bag slip to the floor and knelt to face Daniel. He watched Daniel intently, mystified.

"I don't understand," Cassidy told him. He tried to look directly into Daniel's eyes for some clue, but his brother turned away. "I can't understand what you mean."

"*Thien-than, thien-than*," Daniel repeated. He pointed out the window, high into the sky.

"What... an airplane? Sky? I'm so sorry, Daniel, I just can't..."

Daniel fluttered his hands dreamily through the air like two wings.

"A bird? Do you mean a bird?" Cassidy asked, his voice rising. "Rain? A butterfly? An airplane? Jesus, Daniel, I just can't understand."

Daniel withdrew, almost as abruptly as he'd spoken. He turned his face to the wall, whispering the words to himself over and over again as he rocked. "*Thien-than... thien-than.*"

He slipped away to another world, right in front of them. Cassidy touched his shoulder, and Daniel jerked away.

Cassidy looked at Miss Oneida, who fussed with her hankie in a rocking chair beside the bed. The morning sun streamed through the window, enough to see her eyes welling up with tears. Miss Oneida was bewildered, too. It was as if they stood on one rim of a wide canyon, and Daniel stood on the other. They saw only his shadowy outline in the distance, heard only his echo.

Cassidy picked up the envelope in his lap. It was plain white with a cancelled Thai postmark, addressed to Archie's old house on Ithaca Street. "Addressee Unknown" was stamped in two places on the front, and the envelope had been slit open.

Assuming it had been returned to its sender, Cassidy peeked inside, uncertain what might spill out.

It was a long, typewritten letter on the stationery of a Bangkok hotel, folded crisply around Daniel's dog tags. Cassidy leafed through the pages. At the bottom was a hand-written post-script, but he started at the beginning:

26 May 1995
Bangkok, Thailand
Archie McLeod
302 Ithaca Street
West Canaan WY

Dear Mr. McLeod:

I have the pleasure of delivering what must be the most remarkable news you've ever had: your son Daniel has been found alive in a remote sector of central Vietnam.

I am a retired Marine colonel who has devoted himself to hunting evidence of American POWs and MIAs, living or dead, still in Vietnam. My son was killed there in 1969 and his body has never been returned.

Last month, during a classified visit in-country, my translator and I were eagerly approached by some peasants in Quang Tri Province. They claimed they carried a message from an American soldier who'd been living for many years in a small hamlet deep in the jungle. One of them reached into a small cloth bag and handed us a set of dog tags, not those of a soldier, but of a civilian correspondent named Daniel McLeod, stamped *bao chi* to designate him as a reporter.

The remote village was called Noi Chuoc Toi, they told us, more than forty kilometers up the Diem Vuong River through dense jungle terrain. They would take us there, they said, and two days later we reached Noi Chuoc Toi.

Information of this sort almost always comes with a price and isn't always accurate. The U.S. government has known for some time that living American POWs or remains of American personnel are often held jealously by *an kuop*, a low-grade local Mafia. Hundreds of these small-time warlords operate throughout the country in small regions, usually only a few nearby villages at any one time, controlling certain economic trafficking, such as drugs, medical supplies or black-market trade goods.

Based on intelligence collected over the past 10 years, I believe these *an kuop* are still holding several living American soldiers (they call them "pearls"), in addition to remains of others who might have died during or after the war in their custody, in anticipation of their being "purchased back" by the American government. It was a trick they learned during the French war: Western countries will pay considerable sums of money, millions in fact, to ransom their soldiers. In short, prisoners became money in the bank for the *an kuop*.

But these men who came to me, obviously poor farmers, asked for nothing. They only carried the message for their American friend.

Upon reaching Noi Chuoc Toi, we were taken to an unguarded hutch on the edge of the village, where we were introduced to a Caucasian man, approximately in his mid- or late-50s. He lived in the hutch with a Vietnamese woman and was somewhat startled by our arrival.

The woman told us he had been a newspaper reporter long ago, and his name was Daniel McLeod. She had been his translator, then became his lover in Danang during the war. She told us she brought him to her village in the summer of 1971 when he first became ill.

Throughout the time we were there, Mr. McLeod never spoke. The woman retrieved a stack of letters and a few pieces of paper from a hiding place in his hutch, then sat on a mat by the door. It was as if he'd expected us to take him away.

Of course, getting out of Vietnam would prove more difficult than getting in. We were detained by a loud, swaggering Vietnamese pipsqueak who was driven around the countryside in a rusted-out Rambler. He was a lieutenant to the local warlord, who had quickly learned of our presence. He demanded that we compensate his boss's "expenses" for Mr. McLeod, a sum of one hundred thousand dollars. Without it, they would not release him to us. Furthermore, they threatened our safety if we attempted to leave without paying the so-called "expense" money.

An kuop have often demanded as much as one million dollars for a pile of charred bones. We can only assume that they were aware Mr. McLeod had been a civilian and would not command the same price as a living American soldier. Or perhaps they believed his mental state made him less valuable. Either way, we had no intention of paying them.

We escaped that night. Sometime around 0300 on 22 May, with the aid of Mr. McLeod's female companion and some of her brothers, we slipped out the rear of the hutch through a slit in the dried grass. We were led a few kilometers in total darkness to a jungle road. After a few hours on foot, we crossed back into Laos and we were able to contact an American helicopter support unit to retrieve us.

I should tell you that we made a considerable effort to convince the woman to return with us to Bangkok, where she could be processed as a political refugee for aiding our escape. I regret to tell you that she refused. I cannot know what her fate will be if and when she returns to Noi Chuoc Toi, but I can guess. She said her good-byes in Laos. I am sorry.

Within 24 hours, we returned to the U.S. Embassy in Bangkok to meet with officials in the Joint Task Force-Full Accounting, primarily to confirm Mr. McLeod's identity and to arrange for his repatriation. Using classified government sources, JTF ascertained and conveyed to us that Daniel McLeod, a *San Francisco Chronicle* correspondent, was presumed KIA on 18 July 1971 in a Marine ambush in the Ashau Valley. Neither his body nor his identification were recovered by Marine personnel. What happened to him during and after that ambush remains a mystery to me. However, by what we can ascertain from his female caretaker, it is likely that he left the patrol under cover of darkness sometime before the firefight.

Although extremely withdrawn, Mr. McLeod's health was evaluated in Bangkok by several doctors, including an American psychiatrist. Aside from being slightly malnourished, they found his physical health to be acceptable under the circumstances for a man of his age, but his acute mental state troubled them. They believe he suffers from post-traumatic stress that has gone untreated for more than twenty years.

In the meantime, the brass at JTF classified Mr. McLeod's case as being outside its mission to account for military personnel in Vietnam. I believe that once they understood the depth of his mental illness, they knew they had plausible deniability if his case were ever made public. Quite simply, his presence in Vietnam would be explained officially as either a civilian desertion or, in a worst-case scenario, a sick man's fantasy.

Why? You must understand that the American government, in its infinite wisdom, continues to spit-polish its foolish policy that no living Americans were left in Southeast Asia after the war. To admit their intelligence had failed our fighting men would have disastrous consequences, not to mention ruin a few political careers. Even though I believe their moral task is to prove otherwise to people like you, they remain unwilling to acknowledge the possibility that a single American could have disappeared from their scope.

At this point, I cannot do more than to tell you that, through several private contacts with sympathetic personnel inside the U.S. Embassy, Daniel McLeod was discreetly provided with a new passport so he could return home. "Friendly" sources inside JTF also provided the phone number for a brother in San Francisco, California; your address was taken from letters Daniel currently has in his possession.

Mr. McLeod and I hope to board a plane here at Don Muang International Airport in Bangkok within the month, when proper travel papers are approved by Thai officials. We will enter customs in Los Angeles and after a connecting flight to Denver, we'll travel by car to West Canaan.

I hope my letter finds you well. For reasons of my own, I have decided to personally take him home to Wyoming. A father should know first. Daniel is not well, but I am looking forward to delivering him to you. My organization will pick up the costs. I don't know how much more I can do.

I am proud to play a part in his return.

Col. Thomas W. Marrenton, USMC (Ret.)

Lake Forest, Illinois

At the end of the letter, in a rushed scrawl: "I am sorry. This letter was returned and I have been unable to contact any other family members of Mr. McLeod's. I have an urgent family emergency in the States, and will be unable to accompany Mr. McLeod past Denver. I will see that he has proper and safe transportation back to West Canaan, where I am hopeful he still has family. Again, I am sorry. TM"

Cassidy laid the letter on the bed and wove his fingers in the cold, stiff chain of Daniel's dog tags. Their metallic tinkle had the distant sound of rain.

Daniel curled toward the wall, covering his ears to keep out the sound.

The POW hunter couldn't have known their father was dead. Marrenton wanted only to return another man's son from the grave, maybe as he'd dreamed it would happen for him someday.

He couldn't have known...

"He doesn't know about Dad," Cassidy said to Miss Oneida. "Daniel came here thinking he'd find him. I've got to take him over to the house. I'll have to show him."

He helped Daniel from the floor, while Miss Oneida fetched a set of old brass keys from a cracked sugar bowl on the kitchen window sill.

The three of them walked the one block back to Ithaca Street, where they'd come together a few hours earlier. The morning had blossomed into a green, dry heat that seemed to rise from the earth in waves. Along the street, a few children were playing in their yards or riding their bikes in the street. Some of the houses belonged to ranchers who sent their wives and children to live in town during the school year, but during the summer, they sat mostly empty.

On the corner, Daniel stopped at a towering cottonwood. He looked up into the canopy of fluttering leaves and pressed his palm against its rugged bark, searching for the pulse of an old life.

Cassidy went ahead to the sidewalk in front of his father's house. It was suddenly smaller than he remembered. Boarded windows and doors made it look like a big, weathered shed. Except for Miss Oneida's flowers painting the margins of the place, the house was colorless. Not at all like the picture of it he had tucked away in his mind years before.

They all stood in the front yard, assessing the damage of Wyoming's seasons, of nine thousand empty days and nights. Memories are sometimes difficult to keep up.

Cassidy walked toward the side yard and wrestled back the overgrown lilac, revealing two small handprints in the path beneath it. Archie had scratched the year, 1955, in the wet concrete with a nail forty years before.

Cassidy beckoned Daniel to stoop closer. Kneeling together at the edge of the smooth slab, they laid their hands—Cassidy's right, Daniel's left—against the shallow depressions in the sidewalk, the rain-worn touchstone of their past. Fingers overlapped their fading reflections, touching one another. Two little boys entwined, two sad men followed along, out of step.

Cassidy tried to embrace his brother in the shade of the lilacs. He leaned to kiss his head, but Daniel pulled away.

Cassidy found a rusty hammer in the tool shed out back, and yanked down the weather-beaten, gray planks that barred the front door to their father's house.

Outside, Daniel retreated to a corner of the empty, weathered front porch.

Inside, the mustiness was overpowering. A thick layer of dust had settled everywhere, and cobwebs draped from the ceiling like faded, crepe-paper prom decorations. Cassidy propped the heavy front door open with a kitchen chair and went around back to pry the boards off the back door, to air the place out. Daylight seeped in.

The fresh stream of air stirred up the dust, which sparkled like morning stars in the first sunlight that had shone there in twenty-three years. Bright little stars from a long-dead universe.

Everything—the furniture, his father's books, the family pictures scattered on walls and shelves, even the umbrellas in the stand by the front door— was just as he'd left it, though cloaked in dust. He and Miss Oneida wandered through the house without touching anything, as if it were a holy place. The floorboards groaned here and there, and the air was lifeless, old.

"We've got our work cut out for us," Cassidy told Miss Oneida, who was whipping her pudgy hand in front of her, trying mightily to shake a sticky cobweb off her fingers.

"Don't you worry about a thing," she said. "This old place'll clean up real nice."

Then he found what he'd come for. On the mantel over the fireplace was a faded photograph of their mother and father in an ornate gilt frame. He took it down, blew off a layer of dust, and rubbed it gently across his shirt sleeve to polish it up. He was startled at the resemblance between Daniel and his father, between himself and his mother. Maybe it was just the light or the moment, he thought, but the dark eyes, the smiles, the shapes of their faces...

He went out to the front porch and sat on the cracked steps. Years of rain and snow had stripped away the paint and the wood was bare.

Soon, the day was hitting its rhythm, and children played in the street while a mower hummed somewhere down the block.

He held out the old photograph to Daniel, who came just close enough to take the picture, which he held close to his face and carefully examined. His eyesight was failing.

Cassidy touched his finger to his mother's face and tried to make eye contact with Daniel.

"She's gone, Daniel," he said. Almost without thinking, Cassidy pointed toward Mount Pisgah Cemetery, a few blocks away. He lingered on that word, *gone*. He'd never been able to say it right out, that she was *dead*.

"Do you remember? She's gone."

Daniel looked at the photograph again. His face was still blank, no hint of recollection.

Cassidy then touched his father's face in the picture.

"He's gone, too, Daniel. A long time ago. He's with Mama now. In Heaven. Gone. Can you understand?"

Sweeping his hand again toward the cemetery, Cassidy choked back his own sadness. If death had once brought them closer together, it now was a wall between them.

Daniel stared blankly at the old frame. He was disconnected, empty. He traced his finger across his parents' time-worn, half-forgotten faces as if he were simply feeling the smoothness of the glass. He showed no sign that he cared, if he understood at all. No emotion.

"*Bo chet*," he whispered.

That was all.

He handed the picture back to his brother. *Bo chet.* Cassidy knew what it must mean: *Dead.*

Cassidy moved closer, but Daniel shied away from the possibility of being touched. He dragged himself back to the shaded corner of the porch, where he pulled the petals off the iris blooms that poked through the warped railing. Cassidy was on the verge of crying, but Daniel's face betrayed no emotion.

Suddenly, Miss Oneida screeched.

Cassidy leapt up and ran into the house. He found her in the back bedroom, sitting on a musty bed and facing the open closet. She was breathing laboriously and fanning her red cheeks.

"I just opened the closet and... well, I've never seen a rat that big in my life," she apologized in her tiny voice. "I'm such an old fool, don't mind me."

They laughed as Cassidy scanned the floorboards for the rodent, which certainly must have been as startled as Miss Oneida. He looked under the bed, but the only vermin he found were ghostly dust balls.

The room would have been his, but after his mother died, he and Daniel always slept in the same upstairs room, safe under the sloping eaves. Most nights, he crawled into bed with Daniel and was warmed by him, in both body and spirit. Daniel gave him courage, always.

So the little room Cassidy never used went for storage. In the closet were all of his parents' old clothes, just where he'd hidden them after Archie's funeral. Trousers, blouses, robes, dresses and shirts: they looked like salvage-store cast-offs.

The rat hunt petered out among the pile of old shoes in the bottom of the closet. Then Cassidy remembered something. He rifled through the pockets of some old pants until he found it: a tarnished silver half dollar.

"Look at this," he said, displaying the coin to Miss Oneida, who held it at arm's length to examine it. "Dad always had one of these for us when we came down to the paper. I found this one after the funeral and left it here."

"Well, I'll be..." she said, surprised by the discovery of such a treasure.

Cassidy hefted it, turned it over in his fingers, checked the date: 1954. He plopped down beside her on the old bed, raising a silent storm of dust.

He was both exhausted and exhilarated. He'd been awake since dawn the day before. His eyelids wanted desperately to close, just for a moment, an hour maybe.

It had crossed his mind that he was dreaming, and dawn would eventually draw him back to reality. For now, he was a little boy again. He fought back a yawn, and thought about his prodigal brother, home from war, from death. Where had time gone?

The new air drifting through the room smelled sweet and earthy, like freshly tilled garden soil and newly cut grass. Cassidy heard children laughing and shouting somewhere through the open window, a lawn mower's hum, a meadowlark's trill. He wanted to open up his father's house again, to live there while Daniel got better. The church bells called the good folk of West Canaan to God on a summer Sunday.

Cassidy surrendered. He closed his eyes and lay back on the bed.

"Do you think they still dip ice cream in chocolate down at the Dairy Freez?" Cassidy asked Miss Oneida, but she was not in the room anymore. She'd wandered out to the porch, to look after Daniel.

Images swirled in his head. Sunday ice cream. The memory of garden dirt sticking to his hands. Dew in the lawn that dampened the black dog's belly. The timbers of the east wall, ticking as they warmed in the first light. Dusty stars that eddied in an early-morning window...

Cassidy rubbed the coin between his fingers, absorbing its vague outlines, like Daniel had rubbed the glass on his parents' photo. He wanted to touch Daniel, but he didn't know how, any more than he knew how to touch the air that whispered through the room.

He reached out into it and fell asleep.

ORACLE
WEST CANAAN, JULY 3, 1995

A cool droplet of sweat trickled between Tia's breasts, dispersing in a tiny wet circle where it soaked into her blouse. The air in the *Republican-Rustler*'s morgue was dead and heavy, and smelled like damp lumber. The morgue itself was merely a wooden cabinet jammed between a coal furnace and a broken-down air-conditioning unit in a dark corner of the basement. The ceiling was low, its open joists waterstained and mouldered. A bare lightbulb dangled by a frayed cord just a few inches over her head, hotter than the summer outside, and it threw off a waxy stink with its dim yellow light.

Tia Lazarus was neither big enough nor dressed for heavy lifting, but she lugged a few stacks of old papers out of her way. She piled other enormous hard-bound volumes on top of the ancient printing machinery that cluttered the basement, too heavy and large to scrap when it became obsolete. Old wooden letters, lead pigs and inky handprints were strewn all over. There were no working presses in the darkened basement because the *Republican-Rustler* hadn't printed its own paper since the daily over in Gillette, forty-three miles away, installed its new offset presses back in 1973. The place was half museum, half graveyard.

Like an archaeologist in search of ancient words, Tia dug down through the artifacts of old news toward the summer of 1957.

It was buried here, somewhere.

Every story in that haphazard pile of yellowing newsprint had a deliberate place among the billion or so words in the life of West Canaan. Like the seasons, they had a familiar cycle: birth announcements, school honors, wedding stories and obituaries. It was the most human of history: time meant nothing without place, and a place was nowhere without time.

Tia found 1957 shoved to the back of the cabinet, a hefty book with a stained leather spine and a cloth-bound cover with frayed corners. She cleared a place on a massive tabletop, a smooth stone where leaden pages were once pieced together. She searched the ceiling's open beams for another light fixture, but the socket was empty. So she tucked her shoulder-length brown hair behind her ears and leaned closer to the pages as she leafed through them.

After ten minutes, she cursed under her breath as she flipped through the newspapers brusquely, scanning the headlines and bylines for something, anything that looked promising. Frustrated, she slapped her empty notebook on the table and wiped her forehead with the back of her ink-smudged hands. The more she sweated and squinted in the niggardly light, the more pissed off she got.

This whole assignment rankled her. Retracing the route of her father's road opus, *The Clever Dogs*, hadn't been her idea, but *Rolling Stone* made an offer too lucrative to pass up. It was difficult to tell which had drifted further into the mainstream: the magazine or the Old Counterculture that now beatified its long war dead, including her father, as martyred saints to a cause that was truly lost. Tia often joked to friends that there'd soon be little plastic figurines of all the "saints"—Kerouac, Lazarus, Morrison, Abbey Hoffman, Joplin and all the other long-lost messengers who died never knowing where the hell they were going—pointing The Lost Way from the dashboards of every BMW, Volvo and kid-clogged Ford minivan in the whole, sick country.

Maybe she even believed it.

But she couldn't complain too much. As a writer, she'd always flourished in Jack Lazarus's shadow. Because of him, she wanted to be a writer and because of him, she prospered as a writer.

Jack Lazarus had been dead for ten years, but the name still had selling power. Rediscovered by Baby Boomers and *Rolling Stone*, he sold more books dead than he ever did alive. He died in 1985, before the chemistry of his fame and marketing excess reached critical mass—indeed, perhaps he needed to be dead to be the icon he'd become—but before long, somebody put his pallid, crooked smile on T-shirts and book bags. Soon, some Hollywood producer called Tia with his idea to film the story of her father's life, with one of the hot, young, too-beautiful actors at the time ("You know, like Charlie Sheen or maybe Tom Cruise," the producer bubbled) as the peripatetic Jack on his passage through the lost continent. More recently, some wretched soul even created a computer web site where other wretched souls went in search of the great man himself. The name drew them like the scent of lotus blossoms.

And Lazarus was Tia's name, too. She discovered its potency when she was still a teen-ager, when she sold her first magazine article over the phone to an editor who was more enamored of Jack Lazarus than anything she'd written.

At first, she wrote some magazine articles. Then she wrote a few books. The first was a novel inspired by her tragi-comic affair with Jeremiah Kipper. They'd met in New Orleans in 1985, a few months after her father died, when she was only twenty. Jeremiah, who was twenty-three, drove the bus named Desire. On that first ride, she plopped in the seat behind him as he drove and, up and down Desire, they discovered they shared the romance, if not the essential meaning of literature. Jeremiah was in love with stories, but had a singular knack for missing their message. He loved the sound and fury of words, and he was generally unemployed, so he became a knight errant in a quixotic quest for meanings that always evaded him.

Tia was the half-damsel, half-squire in his passenger seat, but never his wife. In the few short years they shared, they hurtled their red Corvette down Route 66, the Dust Bowl route to California; made love and fell asleep one rainy night in the shell of Jack London's burned-out Wolf House in the Valley of the Moon; swam naked in Walden Pond; floated down the last hundred miles of the Mississippi on a coal barge; and drank a bottle of wine on a Cannery Row dock.

Then in July of 1988, they flew to Spain and made a pilgrimage to Pamplona in a rented Fiat. On the seventh day of the seventh month, Jeremiah fulfilled his greatest—and last—wish. He ran with the bulls.

At least part of the way.

Tia wrote about a character who was not named Jeremiah, but who *was* Jeremiah, in her first novel. In the book, she described his end, which was Jeremiah's end, too.

"I am quite certain that had Hemingway written anywhere that Pamplona's town fathers required that the cobble-stone streets be hosed off in the early morning before the running of the bulls, he would have known the footing would be slicker than round stones in any big, two-hearted river," she wrote.

"He loved Hemingway, but of course, he didn't understand Hemingway, so it was as fine a death as a bus driver could ever expect. And I loved him, so I didn't understand him either. Maybe I still don't."

She wrote three more novels, and even fabricated her own road book to fill out her contract to a penurious little publishing house. None of her books compared to her father's, but they sat next to his on the shelf and sold well enough to maintain a comfortable life alone on her little farm, forty-five acres of forest near the Mendocino coast. She'd bought it five years ago with the small inheritance her father left her: three-hundred thousand dollars and his literary rights. It was the farthest place she could imagine from Queens, and from penetrating grayness. Tia saw her mother whenever she was in New York, which was always too much, even at once a year.

Now this shit. She told herself the only reason she took the job was to get away from her farm for a while. But in all these years, she'd never really gone searching for Jack Lazarus.

Now, she was all but lost on the blue highways where her father had unearthed his backroad masterwork, searching for signs of him where there surely were none after almost forty years. God damn *Rolling Stone* all to hell.

She'd already tracked his erratic route over six states and found, by and large, Jack Lazarus was a cypher in the enigmatic outback he both exalted and gutted like a trophy hunter. His impetuous plunge into the heart of America had healed over.

In 1957, Jack Lazarus was unknown. For two years he rattled around farm towns, river-bottom burgs, decaying pueblos, roadside tourist traps, mountain communities, backwoods enclaves, old mining camps, railheads and county fairs, looking for some lost civilization that he imagined had been built on a bedrock of innocence and naivete, an Eden about to be razed for a shiny new Gomorrah. He even wrote that way because he loved the texture of Biblical language.

Maybe he believed it, too.

On the road, he sustained himself by taking work when and where he could, slumming a few weeks at a time, usually writing for weekly papers along the way. He'd trade words for food and a place to sleep, maybe a tank of gas to get his skanky Buick down the next road.

From the notes he scribbled on napkins and matchbooks and odd scraps of paper, and from the rhythms of ten thousand road miles, Jack Lazarus laid down a masterpiece. Nobody had ever written a yarn like *The Clever Dogs*, a journey through and around fact and fiction, dislocation and homecoming, pain and deliverance, summer and winter. It sliced open a passage to the innards of both a living man and a living nation, and bled them out.

His was a new kind of fictional journalism, raw-edge stuff about a forgotten interior, by turns vulgar and poetic, but always piercing. *The Clever Dogs* was like a beautiful song in a strange new key.

So publishers rejected it.

Thirty-eight times. It frightened them.

Dispirited, Jack Lazarus fell to ground in the Arizona desert, living in a trailer near a desolate place called Oracle. He struggled to smooth the book's raspy, free-form edges but still the manuscript was returned with polite rejections. And he celebrated every one with a tequila and pot bender.

Then in the autumn of 1963, *The Clever Dogs* was finally published by a desperate little house in Chicago, and Jack Lazarus drank a three-day toast to his first book. Of all the stories he'd ever written, this was the one that validated him to Jack Lazarus, for he believed *a real* writer faced the first true challenge of telling a story that would survive him.

The little publishing house put out a thousand copies. Jack Lazarus used his one thousand-dollar advance as a down payment on a new old car and a lid of some good Mexican marijuana. He wept openly when he saw the first copy, an honest-to-God book with his name on the cover. Then he got drunk.

The Clever Dogs would have sunk to the bottom of the literary settling pond if the whole nation hadn't lost its innocence just six weeks later, on November 22, when a president was murdered in the Heartland. Later, when interviewers would ask what he was doing on that crucial day in his literary career when John F. Kennedy got shot, Jack Lazarus would say he was sleeping off a drunken orgy in the arms of a one-legged whore in a bordello in the tiny village of Ensueno, Mexico. It was the God's honest truth, though nobody ever believed him. After all, he was a writer.

By the winter of 1964, the gypsy-angel Jack Lazarus was anointed as a prophet, a visionary. Even if he had not foretold Kennedy's death in so many words, *The Clever Dogs* had described the stage for it, or so some said. The book was heralded as a prophetic vision of the struggle between decay and purity. Jack Lazarus never saw it that way, but in the interest of preserving his toehold in the day's literature, he never disputed it openly either.

So, in time, his work was blessed by even New York's fashionably unflappable literati as "seminal."

Tens of thousands more copies were printed.

Then hundreds of thousands.

Then somebody wanted to make a movie of *The Clever Dogs*, but it wasn't like any story Hollywood ever saw, so Lazarus was smiling when he cashed the check for the film rights. The picture was never made because time mellowed it, dulled its razor-sharp edges.

After fame came a wife. She was a caterer's assistant. They'd met at a lavish Manhattan party thrown by Truman Capote, where Jack, the son of a backwoods Missouri farmer who abandoned his land to find work in an Illinois shoe factory, was so uncomfortable he hid out in the kitchen and chatted up the help.

From then on, everything he wrote was published, but nothing he wrote was better than *The Clever Dogs*.

Maybe that's what killed him. Or maybe it was his wife abandoning him after four years, justifiably.

Or maybe something else. He never saw his book the way others did. Sometimes, when he was very drunk, he'd cast himself as a bit player in a Biblical tale, one of the unknowing characters who appears briefly and then is gone, like Lazarus himself, a mere plot device moving some post-industrial Gospel along. Maybe it was his destiny to toss that one great story on the heap and be called home.

Or, more likely, maybe it was the drugs and whiskey.

But in the haze between, he had a baby girl. She was born in 1965. They named her Tia, after a barmaid in Truchas, New Mexico, who, in a mescal haze, told him that clever dogs always chase the sun.

Now Jack Lazarus's baby girl was 30 years old, rummaging around the stifling basement of a podunk paper in the middle of nowhere, looking for her father's footprints.

The heat embraced her, smothered her like a fat lover. Tia glanced toward the stairs, then quickly lifted her blouse to expose her damp breasts to fresher air, fanning them with her notebook.

It was just too hot. She tucked her blouse back in her jeans, stuffed her notebook in her back pocket and headed up the basement stairs cradling 1957—at least as it appeared from West Canaan, Wyoming—in her arms.

"Find everything?" Sam Whittington, the editor, asked her as she trundled up the stairs.

She'd met him briefly when she first came in off the street, introducing herself and asking if the paper kept any back issues. He'd led her to the stuffy basement and showed her the cabinet morgue before he was called back upstairs by a visitor.

He was worth a second look, she thought: in his late forties, he had a smooth, deep voice. The rolled-up sleeves of his open-necked Oxford shirt revealed muscular, tanned forearms and a tuft of chest hair peeking out his collar. A yellow pencil behind his ear set off his disheveled dark hair, graying at the temple. He also wore a gold wedding band. Almost perfect.

"It's like a sauna down there," she said, thumping the hard-bound volume on the nearest desk, scattering a stack of loose papers. "I was getting claustrophobic. Where can a girl get a cold drink?"

"C'mon, I'll buy," Sam said, smiling. He tossed some copy on the desk and motioned toward the front door, propped open to ventilate the place.

It was mid-afternoon. They walked a half block to the Dairy Freez, a decrepit drive-in joint, and ordered a couple of Diet Cokes. A matronly woman wearing bright red lipstick and lavender perfume shoved two sweaty paper cups with plastic lids through the tiny walk-up window. The bent-up screen was stuck open.

"Thanks, Robbie. Keep it," Sam said as he slipped two dollars through the window.

Tia and Sam strolled across the empty graveled parking lot, back toward Main Street.

"What exactly are you searching for down in the cellar?" Sam asked her as she sipped her soda. It cooled her as it went down.

"My father passed through here in 1957. He was writing a book about places like this. I'm working on a magazine piece about it, and I thought maybe I'd find something in those old papers."

"So you're a writer?"

"I try to be. It runs in the family, I guess."

Sam was quiet for a moment, thinking it through.

"Wait a second. What did you say your name was again?"

"Tia. Tia Lazarus."

"Well, I'll be damned. That could only be Jack Lazarus." Sam beamed. "I don't think anybody else ever wrote about this place. Is he your father?"

Tia never tried to hide her relationship to Jack Lazarus, but neither did she flaunt it. As much as she hated being a writer who was the daughter of another famous writer, she was still proud to be *his* daughter when someone recognized the name.

"So you've heard of him? He was my father. I was beginning to think he'd never been to any of these little places he wrote about. Nobody out here seems to know the name."

"Know him? Hell, I wanted to *be* him," Sam said. In these parts, a relationship with a published writer qualified as celebrity. "I read *The Clever Dogs* in college, like everybody else I knew, but I'm sure there aren't many people around here who ever picked it up. A little too high up the tree, if you know what I mean..."

"That's what I'm here to find out, I guess," Tia said. Sam was the first person she'd met so far who'd shown any interest, much less read her father's book.

"I guess I never knew Jack Lazarus had a daughter. I mean, I never really thought about it..."

"That's okay. Sometimes he didn't know it either," Tia said.

They hadn't been close. She was only four when her mother divorced him and his binges and moved to California. The last time Tia saw him was the summer after she graduated from high school. She and a friend drove across America to find him: a caved-in little man watching TV all day in a flat on Chicago's Southside, consumed by his past and Wild Turkey.

When a vein in his brain burst in 1985, just two years later, Tia was in college. She clipped his obituary out of the *San Francisco Chronicle* and put it in the worn copy of *The Clever Dogs* he gave her. She didn't go to his funeral, the distance between them was too great. But she knew this trip, this long strange trip, would end at the untidy grave that always looked so small and confined to her. That part was *Rolling Stone's* idea.

Tia and Sam sat down on a weathered sidewalk bench in the cool afternoon shade of a dress shop a few doors down from the newspaper. The cracked front window, repaired with silver duct tape, advertised dowdy fashions that were long out-of-date. A layer of road dust collected inside the sill.

Tia popped the plastic lid off her soda and finished it. She let a piece of ice loll around her mouth as she glanced across the street at nondescript storefronts beneath soulless brick facades. A profusion of flags fluttered a day before the big Fourth of July parade, West Canaan's biggest social event of the year. Nobody missed the Parade, or the Elks Lodge free hotdog feed afterward.

The other side of the block was bathed in afternoon light. A few people drifted in and out of shops, waving to one another occasionally before ducking into the bank or the barbershop. Except for the rustling of a few people and a persistent breeze, the place seemed to her to be barely clinging to life.

Tia wondered secretly what made her father write about this barren place. Drought made it uglier, hotter. She caught herself wrinkling her nose and covered it by pushing up her sunglasses.

"Well, anyway, I loved your dad's book," Sam said as they sat there cooling off. "The summer after I read it, I got in my car and drove west until I fell asleep. I woke up and didn't know where I was, and for the first time in my life, I felt completely peaceful. I had nowhere to be, and nowhere to go. Then I just turned around and went home and never left again."

"My father was a gypsy. He told me before he died that he never felt more alive than when he was on the road. He had this fantasy that he would live as long as he had a story to tell. I guess he ran out of stories."

Sam smiled as if he knew about the life force that propelled a storyteller.

"Well, *The Clever Dogs* was a fine story. He saw this place the way we local yokels could never see it. You know, lots of times, I've fished in that pool on the creek, where he wrote that great line about 'surfing the Crazy Woman.' And he wrote about Archie McLeod, the old editor here. Hell, I'd never seen anybody or any place I knew in a book before, and there was Archie's name in that great book. It was like a snapshot of him, only words."

"You know Archie McLeod?" Tia asked. For whatever reason—and Jack Lazarus usually had one—Archie was the only character her father mentioned by name in his pages about West Canaan.

"I grew up in Sundance, another little town not far from here. I knew old Archie and his boys, mostly from sports in high school. When Archie died, his son asked me if I wanted to buy the newspaper and made me a pretty sweet deal, just so he could walk away and never look back. Been running it ever since."

"Well, there goes that," Tia said, a little crestfallen. She had hoped Archie was still alive, so she could talk to him about her father. "When did he die?"

"1972. A long, long time ago. Seems a lot longer some days."

A man wearing a short-sleeved white shirt and a wide brown tie came out of the barbershop and scooted past them on the sidewalk. A thin line of pale skin cut a swath from ear to ear, like fresh-scrubbed white sidewalls on an old car in the Independence Day parade. He smiled and flipped a little wave in Sam's direction. Sam raised a couple fingers in a lazy wave back, as if maybe they'd already waved earlier in the day.

Maybe they had. Tia, who caught a whiff of bay-rum as the man passed, suddenly imagined that everyone here knew everyone else.

"My father worked at a lot of these little papers when he was traveling, just to pay his way. Did he work here at the, uh... God, I'm sorry."

"The *Republican-Rustler*. Sort of trips off the tongue, doesn't it?" Sam teased. "But, yeah, he wrote a few things for Archie. I've seen a few of his bylines in the old books from the summer of '57, but I honestly can't remember any of the stories. Is that what you're looking for?"

"Partly," Tia said. "It's a little bit like listening for the echo of a tree that fell in the woods forty years ago. I'm not sure he ever made a noise here."

"Nicely put," Sam said. He rattled the ice around his empty paper cup.

"Is there anyone here who might remember him?" Tia asked. "Just point me in the right direction."

"I'm pretty sure he lived over at the McLeod place while he was here. Cassidy was just a little kid then, but maybe he could tell you something."

"Does he still live around here?"

"As a matter of fact, he's been here in town for a few days now," Sam said. He shook his head and ran his fingers through his graying hair. "That's a whole different story, believe me."

"What do you mean?"

Sam hadn't actually seen or talked to Cassidy, but told her what he'd heard on the street about Daniel, how he'd gone away long ago and returned from the land of the dead like some ghost. Tia was transfixed by a story that, to her, sounded implausible as hell.

"Nothing personal, but this just doesn't ring true. Some hot-shot reporter is missing in Vietnam for more than twenty years and he suddenly pops up again in his hometown? If it's true, why haven't I heard about it on CNN or Geraldo or something?"

"Tia, nobody cares what happens in a small town except the people in a small town. There aren't many stories I print here that folks don't already know. Sometimes I put it in the paper just so they know that I know, too. Nobody outside pays much attention. That's just how this little town is."

More like another world, Tia thought.

"So he's here now?" she asked. "Have you talked to him? This sounds like a helluva good story..."

"Well, I just heard it from somebody down at the coffee shop. I hear they're staying at their father's place, a couple blocks from here. Keeping pretty much to themselves, but they're good people. Cassidy is a writer, too, you know. He's written a couple books, pretty good ones, and he worked for a long time at one of the San Francisco papers. He might talk to you... about your father, anyway."

They walked to Archie McLeod's old house on Ithaca Street and knocked on the front door. Tia felt a nervous twinge.

Nobody answered. A sprinkler sputtered from one end of a hose in a corner of the patchy lawn, and a lace curtain fluttered in an open window, but the place was empty.

A little disappointed, Tia slumped against the porch's loose, paint-flecked railing and gathered her dark hair in a knot to cool her neck.

"Maybe tomorrow," Sam told her. "Nobody misses the Fourth of July parade. If we don't see them there, I know somebody who'll know where they are. It's a pretty small town. They can't go far."

Tia knew her father must have stood on this same porch almost forty years ago. Jack Lazarus was long gone, but she had finally crossed his true path. Maybe Sam was right: he couldn't have gone far.

"Sure," she said. "Tomorrow."

They left the empty house and walked back to the newspaper office, where Sam still had work to do.

"How about coming over for dinner tonight? My wife grew up here, she's the best cook in the county, and maybe she remembers something about your father. Sound good?"

"Well, if it wouldn't be an intrusion..." Tia said.

"Are you kidding?" Sam laughed. "My wife gets downright ornery if we don't sit down to a fancy supper once a week. And you probably haven't had a home-cooked meal since you hit the road. Say yes."

Tia accepted the invitation and agreed to meet Sam back at the newspaper office at seven o'clock. Before she left, Sam insisted she take the volume of 1957 papers back to her room at the Lazy U Motor Court.

Back at the motel, the clerk, a large woman with curlers in her hair, was sweeping pea gravel off the concrete path to the empty pool.

"Don't reckon there's much need," the desk clerk said, sweat dripping from her chin as she swept in the late heat. "Cain't fill no pool with water that ain't fell in two months."

Tia jiggled her key in the lock and bumped her hip against the obstinate door. She'd closed the blinds when she left, but the maid must have opened them and the room was stifling. She flipped a switch and the air conditioner clanked out of its deep sleep with a musty gust. She slipped out of her damp clothes into a cool shower where she washed off the heat and dust.

Refreshed, she stripped back the bedcovers and lay naked on the cool sheet, leafing through the old, yellow papers.

In a newspaper story published in the middle of June 1957, she found her father's byline. It was a story about a West Canaan man, only fifty-eight years old, who died from a heart attack while hunting deer the previous autumn. When they found his body a day later, one arrow was missing from his quiver.

After the funeral, his teen-age son embarked on a quest to find the missing arrow. For months he combed the forest and foothills where his father died.

The next summer, when the itinerant Jack Lazarus desperately needed a story to write, the young son found his father's lost arrow—piercing the rib cage of a magnificent eight-point buck that had fallen stone-dead in a dry creek bed.

"Dad loved to hunt," the son was quoted in the newspaper story. "He knew he only had one shot, and it had to be true."

Hunting or life? Tia wondered.

Didn't matter. The old drunk could write.

She closed her eyes and rolled onto a cool part of the sheet. She was like that boy, she thought, searching for something her dead father lost a long time ago, hoping to discover that he died the way he would have chosen, more than a forgotten bit player.

But it never happened that way.

Not anymore.

RHYTHMS
WEST CANAAN, FOURTH OF JULY, 1995

The only thing Flashlight Freddie Bascombe took more seriously than upholding the law against oversexed teen-agers who necked under the water tower on Mount Pisgah was leading the Fourth of July parade down the Main Street of West Canaan. It was a point of pride for the butt-sprung old lawman, waving from his sleek white squad car at all the smiling folks.

Hell, he'd seen most of their fish-belly white asses and nubile tits at one time or another in thirty-one years of Friday nights up on the cemetery hill. Now he tossed a few hard candies to their tow-headed children. He glumly accepted as evidence of a personal failure that some of them most assuredly were conceived up there.

And after shining his light on two generations of horny kids in West Canaan, he reckoned he understood the facts of life well enough to know that, like a game of crack-the-whip, instinct would fling these young-uns up that hill, too. All in good time.

Such were life's rhythms here: the children would grow up and go up the hill to make children who would grow up and go up the hill... and Flashlight Freddie Bascombe would always lead the Fourth of July parade down the Main Street of West Canaan, Wyoming.

Cassidy and Daniel sat on the sun-warmed stone wall that encircled the courthouse lawn. The ancient trees were filled with birds in song, and the smell of fresh popcorn drifted in the dry air. It hadn't rained in more than two months, and the town was bone-dry.

Four feet above the sidewalk, their backs to the shaded lawn, it was a fine perch for watching the big parade. And they were safe there on the retaining wall, away from the bustling curb where no one could accidentally brush against Daniel.

Or Cassidy.

Daniel wasn't easily moved anywhere. Cassidy occasionally coaxed him outdoors during the daytime, but at night, Daniel stayed away from doors and windows. When the sun went down, he grew more agitated.

Deep down, Cassidy knew the whole town must be aware of their presence, but he wasn't yet ready to be embraced by them. All in good time, but not today. He tugged the bill of his Giants cap lower and pushed his dark glasses tight against the bridge of his nose, concealing himself even more, hoping against hope his secret—Daniel's secret—would be safe a little longer.

Daniel fussed with the stiff sleeves of his new chambray shirt. Cassidy had given Miss Oneida his MasterCard and sent her to Starbuck's Boot and Saddle, a workingman's place but the only shop in town that stocked any men's clothing. She returned with a few pairs of jeans, some work shirts, underwear and a pair of boots for Daniel. For now, Miss Oneida was taking care of them again, just like she always had.

Every morning for almost two weeks, Cassidy helped to dress Daniel—a delicate task considering Daniel's aversion to being touched—and all day, Daniel, annoyed by the new fabric and leather against his skin, chafed.

Except for the cryptic words he uttered that first morning, Daniel hadn't spoken again. A few days after Cassidy arrived, the two brothers moved back into their father's house, but the change of scenery made no difference. Daniel remained a shadow in any room.

Cassidy grew more anxious at being unable to connect with his brother, whose nights and days were haunted by furies Cassidy could neither see nor understand. Daniel's body grew more tenuous, his emotions more numb, but his senses more raw. He passed the time in another consciousness, often sitting by the open window of the upstairs bedroom where, long ago, lace curtains swirled around him and his dreams were never so hideous.

After a few days, the euphoria of Daniel's resurrection subsided. Cassidy groped for answers. He still didn't know why Daniel had disappeared in 1971, why he was so desperately dislocated from reality, if he could ever be well again.

Daniel needed help, but the prospect frightened Cassidy. He'd picked up Miss Oneida's phone a dozen times to call the mental health clinic in Billings. Once or twice, the receptionist answered before he hung up.

Then he called a psychologist he'd met a few years before at a book party in San Francisco. The good doctor was about to make a killing with a glib little book about sex addictions, but over a glass of wine, Cassidy found him eloquent and serious. On the phone, he told Cassidy that unless Daniel agreed to be evaluated, there was little he or any other shrink could do. And treatment would be impossible if Daniel couldn't or wouldn't participate in the cure. The only real choice, he said, might be institutionalization. Confinement.

In the end, the doctor offered no substantial shred of hope.

"Nobody ever recovers from this thing," he told Cassidy on the phone that morning. "In the most extreme cases, they are changed profoundly. It's like somebody just turned out the light, leaving nothing but the nightmares."

The mental picture of Daniel locked in a cold, sterile nightmare, behind the fences and the deceptively peaceful lawns of the state hospital or a nursing home somewhere, blinded Cassidy. His logic became circular: if no hope existed, then there was hope. Hope that something other than being warehoused might yet work.

The hell of it was reality. Once, Daniel had been his hero. When the news of his death came in 1971, Cassidy again ducked out the back, escaping into the dead-end alley of his idealized memory. Seeking help now would be admitting the reality of Daniel's grave condition, forcing him to surrender his fantasy. Excruciating pain would rush in to fill the void.

Now, Daniel's resurrection wasn't so much a restoration as it was a loss. Cassidy faced it as he had faced his many other losses, with artful and poetic denial.

But in the end, no matter how confusing and painful his dilemma became, there remained one terrible possibility he didn't want to contemplate: some institution, maybe even the government, might take Daniel away from him again. Forever.

Yes, he rationalized, maybe Daniel's only hope of reconnecting was here in West Canaan someplace. Some memory might drift past for him to grab. Maybe Daniel wasn't as sick as he seemed, or was much sicker. Maybe the real Daniel—the storyteller and master rock skipper—was just hiding inside this pitiful man who whimpered in the dark every night, sometimes screaming.

In any case, he needed to be protected, not prodded and poked by shrinks, secreted away in the state mental ward, or hidden away like a dirty little secret from a dirty little war.

Not Daniel.

And it wasn't just the special stigma small towns attached to being crazy, which is what you were if somebody saw you coming out of the mental clinic and what you weren't if they didn't. One of the comforts in a small town is that somebody is always crazier than you. A fella could bay at the moon and copulate with goats and he'd merely be a "character."

But if, in a moment of clarity or weakness, he sought help for one or the other of his afflictions, he'd better do it secretly because in a place like West Canaan you're not crazy 'til *you* know it.

So Daniel wasn't crazy. He was just lost.

Once, a long time ago, he'd shown Cassidy the path around pain. Now Cassidy was a master at it and felt obliged to guide his brother the rest of the way. If Daniel was lost, Cassidy had only to find him. Nobody else would, or could. It might not take long, or it might take forever. But he couldn't bear the thought of losing Daniel twice.

In those first few days, Cassidy made a few other calls, too. To Marrenton, the POW hunter. A thousand questions, but no answer at the colonel's house for days. And to Barbara, whose voice mail said she was out of the office for a month.

"Mr. McLeod?"

A man's voice floated above the carousel of faces going past, all searching for a shady curbside to watch the parade.

"Mr. McLeod?"

A tall man in faded jeans came toward Cassidy and Daniel, a dark-haired young woman in tow. The man with a pleasant face was a little older than Cassidy, and vaguely familiar. A beat-up Nikon hung around his neck, a notebook poked out of his shirt pocket and a pencil was tucked behind his ear. He was no fastidious tourist. Cassidy, in whose veins ink flowed, knew at a glance: this guy was a newspaperman.

Cassidy smiled warily as the two approached, uncertain if he should even acknowledge them and surrender his anonymity forever.

But the two didn't look as if they were together. The man was rough around the edges and fit this small-town landscape like a latigo; she was smooth-cut, fresh and a little out of place in designer jeans and her West Coast white linen blouse, the collar turned up.

The man spoke first.

"You might not remember me, Mr. McLeod, but I'm Sam Whittington, the editor down at the paper," he said, thrusting his hand out. "We met a long time back, after your father died."

"Of course, Sam," Cassidy apologized, still a little uneasy. But he shook Sam's hand firmly. "I seem to remember we were both much younger then. I don't know if you ever met my brother, Daniel."

Daniel was unraveling a loose thread from his cuff, oblivious to his surroundings. Sam stuttered a handshake, but thought better of it. Cassidy wondered how much the newspaper editor—and the rest of the town—knew about Daniel's illness.

"I heard you fellas were back in town," the editor said. "I hope everything is going well for you... both."

"Fine, thanks, Sam," Cassidy said, then smoothly detoured around the subject, as always, with humor. "The place hasn't changed much. Still only two seasons, I see: winter and the Fourth of July."

Today of all days, that old chestnut was funnier than usual. Sam got a kick out of it, but Cassidy just smiled, watching the pretty woman who was watching Daniel. She was the kind of woman who always caught his eye: dark hair, casual, neither too young nor too skinny, and a plucky air about her. Not much makeup. He wondered if her eyes were brown, like her hair, behind her designer sunglasses.

He reached toward her.

"Hi, I'm Cassidy McLeod."

"Oh, God, I'm sorry," Sam said. "Cassidy, this is Tia Lazarus, a writer who's in town doing some research about her father..."

"Jack Lazarus," Cassidy quickly interjected, finishing Sam's sentence. His memory of the writer who lived with them on Ithaca Street in the summer of the water tower, as it came to be known later to him and Daniel, was as clear as spring water.

Surprised, Tia nodded. A faint, impressed smile drifted across her lips.

"Was that just a lucky guess?"

"I met your father a long, long time ago, when I was just a kid here. He stayed at our house a couple weeks and worked for my dad. Great book. So it's a happy coincidence meeting you, Tia Lazarus."

"Happy to meet you, too, although it's not such a coincidence," Tia said, extending her right hand toward him confidently. Her forearm was tanned and smooth. She wore no jewelry. "Are you always so perceptive?"

"Almost never," Cassidy said, taking her hand in his. Her grip was strong, her palm warm and damp. "But only one guy named Lazarus ever did anything worth researching in West Canaan, and you look a little like him, from what I remember. And, I must confess, I've read *your* work, too."

Tia beamed like a schoolgirl, a little off-balance.

"In that case, it's *especially* nice to meet you," she said.

Cassidy, a writer who was never quite certain himself how one should behave when recognized, sensed a little self-consciousness. He rescued her with a last introduction.

"Tia, this is my older brother, Daniel," Cassidy said. Daniel turned away from them all and lay on his side in the lawn that sloped down to the wall, just as Tia reached out to shake his hand. She glanced toward Cassidy, looking for a sign of what she should do next. He forced a smile and waved her off with a gentle shrug.

"I'd, uh, like to hear more about my father, Cassidy, whatever you can tell me," Tia said, sidestepping the awkward moment.

Discordant marching music, remotely akin to the *Washington Post March*, blared somewhere up the street. A bass drum pounded above it. Daniel curled tighter and covered his ears, but the others turned to see the parade beginning. Flashlight Freddie led the way, of course.

"Some things never change, eh, Sam?" Cassidy said. "Freddie's gonna die someday, but he'll lead the Fourth of July parade 'til they pry his cold, dead fingers off the steering wheel."

"That's blasphemy, Cassidy," Sam said. "Freddie's never gonna die. He traded his soul to the Devil for flashlight batteries. He'll just keep going and going and going..."

They all laughed. Freddie and his unholy flashlight had cursed more than one heavenly date for Cassidy in his younger days. True intimacy had never been his strong suit, but he could rub up against girls as warmly as the next guy. He had a natural way of talking to them that invited fantasy. He never fed them lines and he never lied. It was just his humor, a romantic spirit and a hint of his hurt that made them want to hold him close and make love.

A passing parade was still news in this little town. Sam fumbled with the lens cap on his camera and unconsciously touched his shirt pocket to make sure he'd brought his notebook.

"I've gotta take some pictures for the paper, guys, just so my gentle readers know I was here. Nothing ever happens in a small town, but it's amazing what you hear," he said. "Maybe I'll catch up to you all later. Nice seeing you again, Cassidy... " he paused, half a moment, "... and Daniel. Welcome home, both of you."

Cassidy shook his hand.

"Nice seeing you again, Sam. I'd like to drop by the paper soon, if that's okay with you."

"Anytime, really. I'd love it if you came down. I'm sure there's lots of memories down there still," Sam said, then blended back into the red, white and blue crowd.

On her own now, Tia hopped up on the wall next to Cassidy to watch the parade.

Flashlight Freddie was followed by the gray men of the Elks Lodge color guard and their faded American flag. A fat woman in a bulging tank-top heaved herself out of a lawn chair, covering her heart with her right hand and cuffing a little boy with her left. "Show some damned respect," she warned him above the racket. He dragged his baseball cap off his head and rubbed the spot on the back of his crew-cut head where she'd thumped him, giving her a sour look.

Then came the whole West Canaan Little League; the town's two fire engines; Miss Antwinette's toe-dance students; the high school rodeo queen on a tawny buckskin; the Damned Mayor and town council stuffed into an old Studebaker; eight Boy Scouts tossing candy to the kids; the local ambulance, which stalled every time Miss Antwinette's toe-dancers stopped to trip the light fantastic; the junior high marching band, comprised of three trombones, two trumpets, a baton-twirler, two snares, a bass drum and a tuba; a biker who only entered to show off his classic Indian motorscooter; and a flatbed full of the more alert residents of Homestead House Nursing Home— towed by a fume-belching diesel tractor that most certainly robbed those old folks of a few extra days on this earth.

The crowd applauded politely.

Then one of the parading Boy Scouts dropped his bulging grocery bag full of candy. The children of West Canaan swarmed over the luckless Scout and snatched every last Tootsie Roll off the hot asphalt in a matter of seconds, like sweet-toothed piranhas on a feeding run.

"Don't they feed the kids around here?" Tia jibed between giggles. She leaned sideways for a better view of the melee, her head almost on Cassidy's shoulder. He smelled sweet apples in her hair.

"Aren't Scouts supposed to 'be prepared'? I'll bet he wasn't *prepared* for that, huh?" he deadpanned, and they laughed together.

Cassidy remembered Independence Day parades long ago. Until he was too big, maybe six or seven, his father would hoist him on his shoulders so he could see above the crowd. Back then, the World War II veterans were still fairly young men, and they marched proudly to the drumbeat of another time. Now they rode in the back of a pickup.

As a child, he saw everything from his father's shoulders, looking down upon his small world. For a while, he was fascinated by seeing things from high up, whether from the tree on the corner of Ithaca or from his brother's second-floor bedroom window. Until he nearly fell off the water tower. After that, he stayed closer to the ground, even if he never lost the desire to see much farther.

"How long's it been?" Tia asked.

"Since what?"

"Since you've been back here. Sam says you've been away a long time."

"More than twenty years," he said, tugging a tuft of grass that sprouted between the fieldstones on top of the wall. "Twenty-three actually. But, you know, sometimes it's almost like I never left. So much is the same as when I was a kid here. My dad's place, the smell of morning, this parade. Then I look in the mirror and I'm not that little kid anymore. He's the only thing missing, and I'll be damned if I know where he went."

Cassidy felt a twinge of self-consciousness at that last little bit. He steered away from it, to other small talk. They talked about California the way expatriate Californians talk about the place, with longing and loathing. They talked about the weather the way everybody talks about the weather. But Cassidy let nothing more personal slip through his grasp, though he suspected there was another question Tia had not asked and he could not answer: *What's Daniel's story?*

"Tell me about you," he said, hoping to divert the conversation away from Daniel.

Tia gave a tired shrug.

"You want to know my favorite ice cream or something deeper and darker... like turn-ons and turn-offs?"

"Let's start simple," he said. "Where did you grow up?"

"After the divorce, my mother and I left Chicago and went back to Queens, where she grew up. When I was in third grade, she remarried. My new stepfather was a limo driver, but he took good care of us. One day, he drove some Hollywood producer who filled his mind with visions of fast women and faster money on the West Coast. He came home that night and told us we were going to Los Angeles."

"And you went."

"And we went. We rented a house in Pomona, then a few years later moved into Glendale. California was the other side of the earth from New York, and there was plenty of work for limo drivers around Hollywood, but my mother and stepfather eventually got tired of sunlight and people saying 'Have a nice day,' I guess. They preferred a harder edge to their lifestyle. They hauled me back to New York when I started high school in 1980."

Tia's unrooted childhood was far different from Cassidy's.

"At least you got to see a lot of the country. Until I left high school, I'd never been two inches over the state line," he said, then adding in his self-deprecating way: "Then I just went crazy... I went all the way to Missourah. Hoo-boy."

Tia laughed and continued.

"At least you were someplace you wanted to be. By the time we went back, I hated the idea of New York. I hated what they did to me by taking me away from my friends, from this perfect little place where it never snowed. Every minute after we left, I only wanted to get back to California, and things got pretty sullen around that dark little house in Queens."

"Same place you came from?" Cassidy asked.

"God, my parents didn't even have enough adventure between them to move back to a different borough. One day, I looked at them and they looked gray to me. Not the color of living skin and eyes and hair, but all gray. Then I looked at my own hands and imagined them turning their color of gray, too. It was the first time I ever remember feeling I didn't have my own identity."

"How was your relationship with your stepfather?"

"He was good to my mother because she was his trophy. He was married to *the* ex-wife of the great Jack Lazarus. He'd tell his poker buddies stories as if he had lived them, but they were just stories my mother told him once. It always struck me as very strange that he was almost prouder of my father than of my mother. As for me, he was detached and unemotional. We never connected, and it only got worse after we left California."

"So how'd you find your way back?"

"I applied at Berkeley. Some English professor recognized my name—or my dad's name—and pulled some strings to get me in. I still had no identity of my own. By that time in Berkeley, all the fires were out and the only radicals on campus were deep into Reaganomics. In the summer of my junior year, when my father died, I quit school and drifted around America."

"What were you looking for?" Cassidy asked her.

"Me."

She told him about Jeremiah Kipper, but not all the others. Except for Jeremiah, each one had set her back two steps in her search. She was harder now, but she never wanted to be gray.

"You want to hear a funny story about your father?" Cassidy asked her when the conversation and the parade lagged.

"Sure. That's why I'm here."

"I was in an American literature class at Missouri, where I went to school. It was one of those classes in a lecture hall with about two hundred students. I had a crush on the girl who sat next to me. She was the most beautiful girl I'd ever seen, thanks in no small part to her Southern drawl. Anyway, one day, she came to class with your father's book on top of her textbooks and I saw my chance."

"You didn't..."

"I did, absolutely. I told her I knew Jack Lazarus personally and I'd get the book autographed for her if she'd go out with me."

"Did she?"

"Hey, everybody loved Jack Lazarus. Of course, she did."

The Fourth of July parade just petered out, finally. Cassidy and Tia talked a while longer, as children hunted the gutters where candies might have bounced unseen. Flags were furled, and horses boarded back on their trailers. A couple of guys in coveralls scooped up manure with snow shovels. The street was opened to two-way traffic again, but everyone was afoot, ambling toward Town Park for the annual hotdog picnic.

The rhythms were strong and deep. They transcended the seasons, over which men had no control, but they were still in harmony with the seasons. Cassidy thought of Miss Oneida, who had never attended the parade because it was her custom, her rhythm, to separate one-fourth of her beloved irises every Fourth of July. Like her flowers, she drew strength from the earth and every day between the last and first frosts, she returned it to the earth.

Daniel rocked morosely. He drew his knees to his chest, rocking atop the courthouse wall, back and forth on the wide capstone. He was absorbed in his mysterious little world.

Cassidy slipped down from the wall and stood in front of Tia. "How about a late breakfast? My treat."

Tia glanced at her watch and looped the strap of her soft leather backpack over her shoulder.

"You cooking?"

"No, but I can vouch for the chef. She made sure I never had to mug a Boy Scout for candy when I was a kid. What do you say? We can talk about your dad."

"Deal," Tia said, smiling a little. "Maybe we can talk about Daniel, too?"

Cassidy had hoped she wouldn't ask. His back was to the street as he put his hands around her waist and helped her off the stone wall.

He never saw the little boy—the same crew-cut kid whose mother cuffed him for not saluting the flag—light a string of firecrackers and toss them onto the courthouse lawn just a few feet behind Daniel.

Cassidy flinched when the firecrackers unzipped in an earsplitting burst, like gunfire. He wheeled around to see where it came from, and caught a glimpse of the kid running up the street, laughing.

An unearthly howl erupted.

Daniel shrieked with all the force his lungs could discharge. Cassidy turned back to his brother, as if in slow motion, and saw terror in bystanders' eyes that wasn't caused by any fireworks.

Daniel was crawling across the lawn, away from the popping firecrackers, screaming. His eyes were bulging, wild. He scanned the sky and vomit gurgled down the front of his grass-stained shirt.

His body contorted grotesquely as he flailed at an invisible horror. Each time he struggled to his feet to run, he fell again, tangled around himself, like a dreamer fleeing a nightmarish monster. His screams were inhuman.

Cassidy leaped onto the lawn from the sidewalk and ran toward him, but Daniel fought him off. If Cassidy came close, Daniel shrieked. People were gathering on the sidewalk, watching in curious horror as Daniel clawed at his shirt and dived under the thick juniper shrubs that concealed the ground-level windows of the county courthouse basement.

Cassidy plunged into the hedges after him, but Daniel was like a shadow, gone. By the time Flashlight Freddie got the call, Cassidy had frantically circled the courthouse several times, but found no sign of Daniel. Except his new work boots dropped down a window well.

The fat gravedigger, Fakey Ducas, never went to war, but every Fourth of July, between dawn and dusk, he told war stories and swilled bottled beer at One-Eyed Jack's Bar. His flabby butt hung so far over the barstool, it almost looked like his anus had four legs.

These weren't the kind of war stories you'd hear over and over again until you knew every spit-spewing rat-a-tat-tat, mostly because Fakey never told the same story twice. About the only thing his lies ever had in common was the first few words, where the foreword for his violent fairy tales wasn't "Once upon a time," but rather, "Now this is no shit, boys..."

But it was always shit.

Fact was, Fakey never left the States during the Second World War. He'd been a chubby teen-ager who dreaded the rigors of infantry life and enlisted in the Navy. A lowly seaman who never learned to swim, he mowed lawns and tended the flowers for the officers' wives on Captains Row in Norfolk. He made his greatest sacrifice for the war effort when, during the desperate battle for Iwo Jima seven thousand miles away, he torpedoed a desperately lonely Navy wife, but he never saw a dead Kraut or stormed any pillboxes or landed at Normandy or liberated a bordello in a French town whose name he couldn't pronounce. Hell, he hadn't even been in the Army.

Most everybody in town knew they were lies, but like most liars, Fakey didn't know they knew. So he spun his personal mythology with relish and abandon. If he was crazy, he just didn't know it yet, which made him merely one of the "characters" of West Canaan.

Nonetheless, he had the second most important job in town every Fourth of July, Flashlight Freddie's being the first. At dawn, up on Mount Pisgah, he planted tiny American flags on the graves of the town's dead soldiers and sailors. And when the suppertime sun crept across the boot-scuffed dance floor of One-Eyed Jack's, up the wall to the splendid buck's head over the back-bar, it was time to return to Mount Pisgah and gather those flags before sunset. Such was Fakey's custom.

When the light was high on the saloon wall, Fakey swiveled his creaky stool away from the bar and poured himself off it. He clapped the backs of the smirking boys who bought rounds just to hear how tall his tales might grow. He slouched in a drunkard's march toward Pisgah, an imaginary carbine on his shoulder and the vulgarity of a half-remembered cadence on his lips. His besotted rhythm jostled the beer in his belly and he belched all the way down Main Street.

At the graveyard, Fakey set to retrieving the seventy-four flags that marked the old soldiers' graves, whistling, as the spirits moved him, *Anchors Aweigh* or *The Marine Hymn*. He didn't know the Army song, so he just didn't whistle it as he dropped each flag into the apple crate he carried.

When he bent down to snatch the flag from Archie McLeod's grave, the old gravedigger's thickened heart convulsed, squirting blood to the driest parts of his fleshy anatomy. He might have died but his urge to run was stronger than death itself.

It was a corpse, gray and naked. Its hand reached toward him.

Fakey had dug the holes for plenty of dead folks, but they always came secretly and safely stored in boxes. He stumbled backward over a sprinkler head, dropped his crate in a red, white and blue panic, and ran away from the cadaver.

Fakey didn't recognize the corpse. Of course, he didn't waste much time getting acquainted either.

But Daniel wasn't dead.

He was sleeping, finally, on the south slope of Mount Pisgah, where the sun was warm. His breathing was arduous, but rhythmic. For this brief moment, with Heaven and comfort so close at hand, his furies had fled.

Daniel lay in a fetal ball atop his own grave. He'd fallen asleep with his arm stretched across the wet grass so his fingers might touch his mother's headstone.

BORDERS
WEST CANAAN, JULY 12, 1995

Tia stayed in West Canaan, not just to listen for an echo of Jack Lazarus's voice but to listen to an inner voice, too. Like a prairie wind whispering in tall trees, the distant voice told her she was a messenger here, with a job to do. Maybe it was the same voice Jack Lazarus had heard in this place.

Tia's instincts had served her well enough in the past, so she stayed. Most days, she visited Cassidy and Daniel at their father's house, watching their dance of silence.

She moved out of the decrepit Lazy U Motel when Miss Oneida Overstreet offered to put her up in her spare bedroom, rent-free. In return, Tia kept the old spinster company and helped tend her prodigious flower beds, which were in glorious bloom despite the drought because she watered them by hand every evening, when the heat couldn't steal their succor.

Kneeling beside the old woman, turning the soil and pulling wild morning glories that entwined themselves among the flowers, Tia knew each flower in Miss Oneida's well-turned soil had some meaning: the sturdy, mustard-colored *achillea* given to her long ago by her only real beau, a high school Latin teacher who was killed in the Second World War outside the walls of an insane asylum in

Sicily; the aromatic, sleep-bringing lavender, descended from the seeds in blossoms that scented the bed linens her mother brought West with other stragglers on the Oregon Trail in 1883; the untamed lupine she brought down from the Big Horn Mountains in the summer they killed the last wolf there; and orange-scarlet honeysuckle she brought back on the train from her family's ancestral home in Virginia's Shenandoah Valley, where she took her mother's casket home to be buried beside her father in the Overstreet cemetery in 1953. That's the same year she got her new family, the McLeods.

Many more flowers flourished in Miss Oneida's beds, in all the gentle colors of memory. Some were gifts, some clandestine cuttings, and some had long ago shed their scientific names in favor of more personal ones, such as Gladys and Oscar's daisies, Old Ping's poppies and Archie's forget-me-nots. And on summer Sundays, the First Presbyterian Church's altar was always trimmed with baskets of flowers Miss Oneida cut herself.

"The white ones always smell the best," Miss Oneida told Tia, fanning the front of her work-worn garden apron with her gloved hand. She shaded her eyes against the unyielding sun and scanned the dense, colorful foliage for splashes of white.

"Like the white narcissus in spring, oh my. Or those white roses over there," she pointed them out. "It doesn't matter what flower, if it's white, it'll be as fragrant as the fields of Heaven."

But the irises, whose proud blooms had wilted in June, were her favorites. Their flags of peach, violet, yellow, sky-blue and luminous white stood watch over the gardens in late spring, giving hope and leading the way. By midsummer, all that remained were the hardy clusters of green swords. For sheer profusion of irises, her tiny yard was renowned in West Canaan.

"They're messengers, you know," Miss Oneida said, crumbling clods of dirt between her gloved fingers, which had grown stiffer and knottier every summer. "It's Greek mythology. Iris was the goddess of rainbows and a messenger, too. That's why I plant them all mixed up, all the colors together, like a rainbow. They come in the spring and, to me anyway, they bring a message that the rain is over. Then they're gone. Just like that. Isn't that just too sweet for an old fool like me?"

"You're not an old fool," Tia said, kneeling beside her. "I think you tended Cassidy and Daniel like these flowers, didn't you?"

"They were good boys, even though sometimes they were full of piss and vinegar, pardon my language. But they never got in real trouble. Their father was the best man I ever met, as honest as the day is long. He worried they might grow up incomplete, if you know what I mean, so he gave them everything he could. I don't mean money and such, but he gave them what he knew, how he saw the world. And I loved them almost as much as their own Mama loved them, with all my heart. And I did my best to see they knew it."

"What was Daniel like?"

Miss Oneida pushed back the floppy brim of her straw hat and smiled broadly.

"Oh my, he was the smartest little boy you'd ever hope to see. He could read before he started school, and when he was growing up, he read every book Archie had. He didn't just skim the words, mind you, he saw meanings in those books. You could ask him about anything and he'd likely know... or he'd go read a book about it. He was a wise young fella."

"He sounds like a little genius," Tia said.

"Daniel was that, to be sure. But he wasn't one of those smarty-pants kids who were afraid of their shadows, either. He loved his adventures. And he always had some wild exploit in his mind. You knew when he was up to something because his eyes twinkled like stars."

"What about Cassidy?" Tia asked, without looking up as she gingerly smoothed the dirt around a rose bush. It was Cassidy she really wanted to know better, but she didn't want to seem too eager.

"The newspaper kept Archie awfully busy, so Daniel sort of stepped in and took care of his little brother..." Miss Oneida shed her cloth gloves to reach down the cuff of the faded cotton dress she always wore in the garden. She pulled out a wadded Kleenex just as her voice broke. "It's so sad to see him like this now, the poor, broken boy. I feel so helpless..."

Tia understood that Cassidy and Daniel would always be little boys to Miss Oneida. She put her arm around the old woman's sloping shoulders.

"Don't worry, he's in good hands now. Cassidy seems to be dealing with him very well."

"Cass is still my baby," Miss Oneida said, regaining her composure enough to manage a little smile. "He was so young when his Mama died, he never really got to know her. And of all the foolish things you'll ever hear, I think he still blames himself for her dying, deep down inside. Of course, it's nonsense, but no little boy understands that. When he got a little older, he'd come by here on some summer mornings and ask me for flowers. He would take them up to his Mama's grave. It was the only time I ever saw him do something alone. These were always the ones he asked me to pick for him," she said, reaching out to a pinkish columbine that looked like a spray of shooting stars.

Kneeling there, Tia leaned on her hand shovel and turned the soil. A fat earthworm, a sign of life, wriggled in the loose dirt. Miss Oneida dug a shallow depression in the loose, dark earth, then covered the worm.

"When my father died," Tia said, "I felt guilty about never really knowing him. It seems like we beat ourselves up over so many things we can't control. It's difficult to get past it. I wanted my dad to be proud of me, but I always felt I never did anything to make him love me. To *deserve* him, if you know what I mean."

Miss Oneida laid her hand gently on Tia's forearm and reminisced.

"Once, I asked Cass what he wanted to be when he grew up. You know what he told me? He said he wanted to be whatever Daniel was. He's spent his whole life *deserving* his brother. They were always like two halves of the same whole."

"They must have been very close," Tia said.

"Oh, they were inseparable, went everywhere together. Even when they were so high, Daniel was a bright little man and Cassidy was like a cute puppy dog, but he was always a little sad. Everybody just wanted to hold him tight and make the hurt go away. I see it in him still."

Tia understood. She'd wanted to make him smile almost from the first time they'd met.

"It's funny to say, but Daniel took care of him way back then, and now Cass is taking care of his brother. If he can be saved, his brother will save him."

"Cassidy or Daniel?"

Miss Oneida paused to ponder her ambiguity.

"Dear, it might not matter either way."

Still no answer at Barbara's condo in L.A.

Her voice-mail message said she'd return on the twenty-fourth, but Cassidy hoped she'd get back early. His need to talk to her seemed strange to him, especially since they'd long avoided important discussions. He didn't even know what he'd say, or how much he could tell her about Daniel without sounding crazy.

He wondered where she'd gone for three weeks. Her machine didn't say it was business, and Barbara loved to visit her grandmother's house on Camano Island in the Puget Sound for a few weeks in midsummer, when the blueberries were coming on. The place was natural and slow, and its isolation comforted her. She'd taken him there when they first met, and Cassidy wondered now if she was alone.

He hung up without leaving a message.

Cassidy wandered through his father's house, looking for Daniel. He found him, lying still and flat on a braided rug that covered the dark wood floor in the living room. The afternoon sun was pouring through the front window, washing him in light. He looked thin and pale lying there.

"Daniel?"

The sound of it echoed in the quiet house.

Cassidy spoke his brother's name a hundred times a day, hoping it would spark a reaction just once. It never did.

Daniel just turned his face toward the wall.

Cassidy sighed. He shuffled back to the kitchen, where he got a beer from the clunky old refrigerator and sat down at the dining table, which was still cluttered with breakfast dishes.

The phone company had hooked him up a few days ago, but the old rotary-dial phone on the wall hadn't rung since they left. He hadn't gone out since the parade because Cassidy was suddenly afraid of how Daniel might react to the slightest stimulus. He kept the doors locked tight to prevent Daniel's escape. And it grew increasingly clear that even if Daniel were to speak, he no longer spoke a language that Cassidy understood.

He felt alone.

Except when Tia was around. Since they'd met, she'd come for lunch at Archie's house almost every day. They'd sit on the porch and talk until dinner. They'd eat and she'd walk back to Miss Oneida's house alone.

Cassidy didn't know why she'd decided to stay in West Canaan, but she pleased him. She was good company, and beautiful. It seemed to him they genuinely liked each other, although not so much as a goodbye kiss had passed between them.

His beer can sweated in the afternoon heat. Cassidy took it out to the back porch steps, where he sat with his back against one of the freshly whitewashed four-by-four columns. The still, hot air made him prickle, and he rolled the cool can across his forehead.

White moths flirted with the blossoms on the tomatoes and squash in the little vegetable garden Miss Oneida tended in the backyard. A sprinkler made a scratching sound in the next yard, but the air around him was dry.

A list of tasks swirled in his head: paint the south wall of the house, where the sun had laid the wood bare. Cut back the lilac hedges that had overgrown the edges of the yard. Paint and fix a couple of drooping shutters. He thought he might start writing again, if he could contact Barbara and have her run up to The City to ship his laptop computer and a few other things he left behind in his confused rush to return to West Canaan.

He thought about calling the Pentagon and telling them they sent home somebody else's remains in that little metal box, not Daniel's.

He felt only spite for the military just now, not only for its errors, but for its sins. They'd buried some other grunt's pieces on Mount Pisgah that gray autumn day in 1971. Maybe in the military's coldly methodical and systematized zeal to account finally for the dead, other parts went some place else just to make the numbers add up. He couldn't be sure that they wouldn't come looking for Daniel, hunting him down for some stupid reason that would sound righteous to the military brass in the name of national security.

And if Cassidy called someone now, they'd only compound their first error by dumping the unknown soldier some place else, perhaps not as warm as the south side of Pisgah. He decided he'd wait until a saner moment, when his anger and fear had subsided.

And he thought about Tia.

She always wanted him to tell the old stories. He'd told her all about Archie and Annie, about Daniel and his yarns, about growing up in West Canaan, about summer and winter, about that old black dog named Shadow that had run away but always lurked on the edge of his consciousness, thanks to Daniel. She loved dogs, she said, and the story touched her.

Occasionally, she took some notes, but mostly she just listened intently. And when she spoke, she spoke with the passion of a writer. She laughed sweetly, almost shyly. Sometimes, she twirled her hair around her finger while he talked, and he secretly wanted it to be him that she was touching. Her dark eyes must see right into him, he thought.

He didn't know if she had gotten what she came for, but he was happy she was still looking.

A tiger swallowtail butterfly floated over the cool grass and landed on one of the marigolds Miss Oneida planted in the vegetable garden to repel caterpillars. Cassidy thought about it for a moment: what changes inside? The butterfly was nothing more than a metamorphosed caterpillar, but something fundamental, something more than its sense of smell, must have changed.

Had he changed? He didn't think so.

In a dream a few nights before, Tia came to him. He lay in his old bed, watching the stars through an open window, whose curtains wept softly in the night breeze. Without speaking, she touched his face lightly with cool fingers and then kissed his eyes.

Her hair fell around his face, hiding him in the scent of sweet apples. He kissed her tenderly on the lips, then felt a tear fall from her cheek onto his neck.

"I can't stay," she told him in the dream.

"I know," he said. "Nobody stays."

INTERIORS
WEST CANAAN, JULY 14, 1995

The morning was calm after a night of thunder.

The rain fell far to the north, and far too little to do any good there. It settled the dust in the air, but a feathery tan smoke hovered over the high prairie from grassfires sparked by lightning.

The night before, sitting in the eave-window seat in Daniel's old room on Ithaca Street, Cassidy kept his nightly vigil over Daniel, distracting himself by measuring the distance of the most spectacular flashes across the boiling black northern horizon. A long time ago, Archie had taught Cassidy to count the seconds between the flash and its low-rolling growl... *one Mississippi, two Mississippi, three Mississippi*... a mile for every count. None came closer than *eight Mississippi* before the storm blew off to the east, sometime after midnight. The stubborn drought that besieged West Canaan for almost three months now had fought off the rain for another night.

But the lightning ripped through Daniel's heart. Piercing flashes across the night sky had filled Daniel's eyes and the guttural thunder shuddered down through the restless air into ancient layers of rock and back up through Daniel's spine. It sliced up through him, lodging in his brain.

Cassidy could only watch over him as he trembled in a dark hollow behind the bureau, his face flat against the wall, his hands sealing his ears from the primal drumbeat. So far, every attempt to connect with Daniel had been futile. Muddled by frustration, Cassidy fell asleep there on the window-box. He didn't awake until the 5:35 freight train braked to a slow, iron-scraping stop at the depot three blocks away, its boxcars lurching forward against one another in a brotherhood of rolling thunder. His neck and back were stiff from being folded awkwardly there all night, and his mouth tasted like stale beer.

Cassidy stood slowly, seducing out the kinks while he stretched his arms over his head. The blood thumped in his ears, making him a little light-headed. He looked around the floor for his tennis shoes, glancing toward the bureau.

Daniel was gone.

Cassidy quickly scanned the room, looked under the bed, in the closet. He called Daniel's name and, even in his growing panic, wondered why.

He leaped down the cranky stairs, three at a bound, watching for any movement. The hallway was bathed in morning light, empty. The front door was still locked from the inside. The tiny den, where all their father's books mouldered on the shelves, was too spare to hide anyone. Cassidy checked the closet in his father's bedroom, but he knew Daniel had avoided it since the first day. The back bedroom was empty, too.

The cluttered kitchen rang with the chirping of the morning birds outside the open window, their songs echoing off green tile and worn linoleum. A few days of unwashed plates and silverware overflowed the sink, the dining-table chairs were turned outward, as they'd left them last night. The floor was smooth and cool, almost soothing, under Cassidy's stockinged feet.

Daniel was not there.

Cassidy checked the door to the back porch, the only other way out of the house except windows that stayed open on muggy summer nights. He turned the unopened deadbolt and walked out to the backyard. A scant dew from the night's watering seeped through his socks. Softly, he called again for his brother, so as not to wake the neighbors. A dog barked back at him.

The tool shed door, as always, stood open. Cassidy pushed it wider and waited for his eyes to adjust from the bright morning to the dark interior.

Nothing but junk.

Cassidy breathed deeply. He tasted faint grassland smoke in the air. He tried to stave off a panic, tried to reason it through. *Think. Where could he go?*

The cemetery. Because Daniel had run there after the firecracker incident, it was the first place to rush through Cassidy's mind. But still, he thought, Daniel hadn't left the house through either door.

Cassidy walked around the house, checking the screens on the windows. They were fastened from the inside, and all were intact.

Daniel could only be inside the house.

He went back in, locking the porch door behind him in case Daniel was waiting for a way out. He tugged a string and the pantry light came on. The ranks of pine shelves were nearly empty, except for old pots and pans, so he turned off the light and closed the door.

The cellar.

He'd missed it. When the pantry door was open, it hid the cellar door. Archie's house had been built on concrete piers over a dirt hole that naturally became the cellar. Long before Annie McLeod died, they'd stored root crops down there, potatoes, carrots and the like, so it always smelled like cold, wet earth and musty vegetables. But because the earthen walls were shot with small coal seams and tended to erode into filthy piles that rubbed off on anyone who went down there, it had been off-limits to hide-and-seek when they were children.

So the boys stayed away from the cellar, even when a champion hiding place was required. Although it would have been spacious if empty, it was more like a dark, dirty cave than a room in a civilized house. In the hottest summer and the coldest winter, regulated by the insulating earth and the house above, the cellar's temperature remained crisp, like a constant autumn.

Cassidy hadn't been down there since his father died, but even then he'd only ventured in long enough to stack a couple boxes of old shoes and kitchen items in the corner nearest the steps. The place still retained its forbidding ambience.

The plank stairs were split and warped by time. Cassidy tested the top step with his foot, leaning on it bit by heavier bit, fearing he might fall through. He leaned into the cool darkness and called Daniel's name.

Silence.

He knew a bare lightbulb hung down there somewhere in the blackness, unlit for almost twenty-three years. Cassidy ran his fingers along the two-by-four stud plate inside the cellar door and found the box of wooden kitchen matches that his father had kept there to help him find the light string in the dark. A few remained.

Cassidy scratched one of the old matches across the side of the box, expecting it to sputter, but it flared wildly. He walked slowly down the stairs, holding the burning match high as he moved into the layer of low-lying chilly air. Stooping slightly to keep from bumping his head on the short ceiling, he stepped onto the earthen floor as the light from his match flickered dimly in a small circle around him.

Old crates and file cabinets, rusty coffee cans filled with rusty parts, spider webs, broken picture frames, tumble-down chairs and dented coal buckets surrounded him. Awkward stuff he couldn't recognize from any time in his life. Thick oak beams held up the floor above him, like a dry, naked forest supporting a low, brown sky criss-crossed with a cumulus of old pipes and cables. He tugged the string on the bare bulb, but the light inside must have waned long ago.

The dirt floor was loose but in the fine dust, presumably undisturbed for years, there were bare footprints. They led toward a shadowy corner of the dark hole.

"Daniel? Are you here? Daniel?"

No answer.

The match burned down to his fingers. He shook it out, struck another. As it danced to life, something moved behind a three-legged dresser that tipped forward where its missing leg would have been. An empty drawer fell open and an old set of antlers—a six-point muley buck Cassidy shot when he was 15—tumbled to the dirt floor from a precarious perch on top.

It was Daniel, hiding.

Relieved, Cassidy moved closer, slowly. Daniel was curled in his sad, fetal position, covering his head.

"Daniel. It's okay. I'm here. It's okay. You're safe," Cassidy reassured him in a calm, soft voice, but took care not to touch him. He'd begun to read Daniel, to know how close he could come, how loudly he could talk without startling his brother. He took pains to avoid sudden noises and movements, or flashes of light. It didn't take much. One morning a few days before, a whiff of smoke from the garbage cans in the alley agitated Daniel so much that he hid under a bed upstairs all day.

Sleep wasn't sleep for him. It seemed to be little more than a fitful consciousness, as if Daniel were floating, eyes barely closed, just below unsettled waters. He was the victim of his own torture, shackled by dreams and memories that had no name. Daniel never spoke during the day, but he talked endlessly, incoherently in his restless sleep, sometimes out of fear, always in Vietnamese.

Chilled by the cellar air, Daniel shivered. Cassidy was learning, day by day, that Daniel moved of his own accord, in his own world and time. It was unlikely he could be coaxed out of the cellar if he was frightened, so Cassidy struck another match and searched for something to warm his brother until he decided to come upstairs into the daylight. He yanked on a dusty, moth-eaten bedspread covering a bulky pile of boxes and laid it loosely across Daniel's shoulders.

He'd uncovered something he didn't remember seeing before. Ever.

An enormous and exquisite trunk. Not the kind that accompanied olden travelers on trains and ships, but the kind that families passed down through generations. Cassidy wiped some of the dust away and saw that the trunk was inlaid with polished mahogany and cherrywood, with handmade brass latches and handles. A timeless garland of delicate leaves and blossoms was carved on each cornice. Sturdy oak gussets, sleek and strong with subtle grains, reinforced its heavy lid and box. In a sense, it looked as if it hadn't been built as much as it had been nurtured into existence by some mysterious but faithful artisan.

Cassidy measured the massive chest in his mind. It looked far too heavy for him to lift alone and, even if he could find help to move it, almost certainly too heavy for the decaying cellar stairs. He lit another match and held it close to the latch. It was locked and there was no key.

Cassidy was puzzled. How could a naturally curious child have missed seeing something so grand and, most of all, so secret, for it must have sat in this place since before he was born? Where would his father have hidden the key to such a treasure—indeed, why hadn't he ever mentioned it at all? And what could it contain?

"Nhung con ma."

The words—or rather their proximity and peculiarity—startled Cassidy. The voice was out of time, raspy and breathless.

Daniel was suddenly, silently beside him, tracing circles in the dust on the trunk with his finger. Cassidy started to speak, but the match singed his fingers and expired.

In the fumbling moment it took to strike another, Daniel was gone like a shadow.

EVENSONG
WEST CANAAN, JULY 17, 1995

The missing key might unlock more than the extraordinary trunk in Archie McLeod's cellar. Cassidy believed it would unlock the enigma that his brother had become.

He'd been up since dawn, sitting at the breakfast table in front of the big south window, just where his father always sat to watch the morning finches playing tag in the hedges. Daniel had eaten some dry toast, then wandered off toward the back of the house, where the sounds of the day were muffled. After Daniel spoke in the cellar, Cassidy went to him, but whatever door had been opened by the sight of the trunk quickly slammed shut again.

The key and the trunk obsessed Cassidy. He barely slept.

He checked his watch and glanced toward the phone on the wall, then checked his watch again. Still too early.

For the past three days he had searched the old house. He'd closed it up in 1972 almost as Archie had left it on the morning of the day he died, so Cassidy knew the key must still be wherever his father hid it. But where?

The first place he looked was Archie's old bedroom, in the old chest of drawers, shoeboxes, the dresser that was an antique even when Archie was using it. He found dustballs and mouse turds, but no key.

Cassidy found a set of keys in Archie's ancient rolltop writing desk—a labyrinth of secret drawers and tiny treasures, such as his great-grandfather's pocketwatch—but none came close to fitting the chest's ornate lock.

He hunted behind the books that lined one wall of the front room, the pockets of old coats in the hallway closet, in every nook and cranny he'd known as a boy. He even checked the fieldstone fireplace for loose rocks that might conceal a trunk key, just as the loose brick at the *Republican-Rustler* had always concealed the backdoor key.

After showing Tia the remarkable wooden chest a few days ago, he recruited her to help him search. Together, they scoured the house while Daniel hid in the back bedroom.

More than once, he'd risen in the middle of the night and hunted for the key in places it would never be hidden. One night, long after midnight and long after fingering the hidden margins of every ledge and every sill in the kitchen, he found himself staring blankly at the inside of the refrigerator. He gave up and went back to bed, unfulfilled.

"Are you sure he would have hidden this key at all?" she asked as they sat on the stairs after the first few hours of hunting. They were both out of ideas. "I mean, what could be in the trunk that he'd want to hide from you?"

"I don't know," Cassidy said. "But he never said anything about the damn trunk. If it wasn't deliberate, why wouldn't he mention it? I never knew my dad to keep secrets from us, but there must have been something he never told us about this trunk."

"Apparently he did, if you really believe the trunk was down there."

"Right," Cassidy said. "That's why I think he would have hidden the key."

"What about the newspaper office? Would he have taken it there? If he was hiding something, wouldn't he put it where you might never find it?"

They arranged to meet Sam Whittington at the *Republican-Rustler* the next day, a Saturday. Even though Cassidy had removed all of his father's personal items after he died, the three of them rummaged around the cluttered office, emptying old coffee cans onto tables, feeling behind desks and over door jambs, in the hidden spaces behind desk drawers.

Nothing.

On Sunday, Cassidy dragged all the rusting junk from the backyard shed onto the lawn. He found the key to the padlock that nobody ever locked, but nothing else. He foraged through the house all day and into the night, and finally gave up.

Cassidy glanced at his watch once more. It was nine in the morning on a Monday. California was an hour behind Wyoming, so he sipped his lukewarm coffee and waited.

"How do you spell that?" de Sales asked. His sandpaper voice was made more scratchy by West Canaan's obsolete long-distance connection with San Francisco.

"I can't spell it, I only know what it sounds like: *Noong kohn mah*," Cassidy explained. "That's pretty close. I'm sure it's Vietnamese. Can you find some immigrant shopkeeper down in Chinatown and find out what it means for me?"

The request was a little too sketchy for the old reporter.

"For Christ's sake, Cass, how the hell am I supposed to do that? Just walk up to some Oriental-looking guy and pop the question? What the fuck kind of word is this? How do I know it's not some fuckin' insult and this guy won't kick my ass with one of them kung-fu doohickies?"

"It's not an insult. I don't know what it means, but I don't think it's anything bad. I just *need* to know. Nobody within a thousand miles of here speaks Vietnamese, and I don't know who else to ask. Can you help me, Frank? For old time's sake?"

De Sales groaned.

"Sure, kid. For old time's sake. I can check it out for you today. It's not like they give me the big stories anymore. Just tell me, what's this all about anyway?

"I can't tell you right now, but if you'll just help me out on this, you'll get one hell of a story to go out on. I promise."

Cassidy heard the old reporter sigh amid rustling papers on his desk.

"Yeah, right. Last time somebody promised me I was gettin' a big story for doin' a favor, I got a dose of the clap and an all-expense-paid weekend in the Seoul jail. Just say the damn word again, so I don't make a fool of myself."

"The phrase sounds like *noong kohn mah*. That's the best I can do. I really appreciate this, Frank."

De Sales grunted a jaded laugh.

"Just buy me a beer when you get back from Montana or whatever fuckin' foreign country you're in. What's the number there?"

Cassidy gave de Sales the new number that he had taped to his old phone and they hung up.

He knew de Sales. The old reporter only pretended to be spent and unchivalrous. But he was one of the old knights, stalwart and proud, and he wouldn't come back from this quest without his grail, the first key to the trunk's mysteries.

Miss Oneida dressed in her Sunday church dress and brought pork chops for dinner. Tia came with her. The three of them ate on the back porch as the sun went down, before the bugs came out. As usual, they left a plate for Daniel on the kitchen table and it went untouched.

When the Little League's night games started, they heard the incoherent electric hum of the PA announcer's voice and car horns honking in the distance.

"Somebody got a big hit," Cassidy said. Tia looked puzzled. "Some parents sit in their cars in the parking lot behind the outfield fence and when a kid hits one out of the infield, they honk. They've been doing it since beer was outlawed in the stands."

Tia smiled.

"Cass was the star player on the Legion team when he was in high school," Miss Oneida piped up. "He even made the regional All-Stars who beat those cock-sure boys from Denver that year. He hit a home run they still talk about."

Cassidy put both hands over his face, concealing his smile, but not the blush that settled across his face.

"Oh now, Miss Oneida, it wasn't the shot heard 'round the world. To hear you tell it, Tia would think I was Bobby Thomson or Mickey Mantle. It was a lucky hit on a bad pitch, a high fastball right on the sweet spot. And I don't think anyone still talks about it."

But Miss Oneida wouldn't let him escape his own small-town legend so easily.

"Your father was so proud of you. He kept that home-run ball around here for years. The whole town was so proud, like you showed them city folks what they never would believe about a little place like this, that we had heart."

Cassidy listened for the distant cheers and heard it all again. He moved a pork chop bone around his plate, then wiped his mouth with a napkin.

"I think back to my dad sitting there in the stands or taking pictures for the paper, and I can't imagine he was prouder of me than I was of him. I remember the first time I ever hit a home run. I was about ten or eleven. I didn't think I hit the ball that hard and it surprised me to see it go over the centerfield fence. That one was for me, because it wasn't supposed to happen. After that, I tried to hit one for my dad and I struck out, swinging for the fences. But I never stopped trying to hit one out for my dad."

Tia gathered up the plates and took them inside. She came back to the porch and stood in front of Cassidy, hiding something behind her back.

She was wearing white shorts, the kind that made her tanned legs look darker and luminous. He looked up to brown, smiling eyes that hinted at a surprise.

"Are these yours?" she asked, revealing two old baseball gloves. They were dark brown with old oil, and limber as puppies.

Astonished, Cassidy sat upright. The old leather was still supple, and the webs bore the names of the gloves' long-ago owners in faint black hand-lettering: *Cassidy M.* and *Danny M.*

"Where'd you find these?" he asked as he pursed his fingers into his old mitt and popped his fist into its deep well. In his crumpled Giants cap, he looked as if he was ready to come off the bench, if only for an old-timers' game.

"Under some pillows in the window seat. I found them when I was looking for the trunk key this morning. I hope you don't mind."

"I haven't seen this glove since high school. I started using Daniel's my senior year and put this one away. God, it's still so soft."

From the ballpark, the public-address announcer's voice hummed something, lilting at the end as if something wonderful just happened. Cassidy couldn't make it out, but smiled as he recalled old days on the smooth grass.

"Will you take me there? To the ball park?" she asked, extending her hand to him.

Cassidy wanted to go, but hesitated. He hadn't left Daniel alone since he arrived. Miss Oneida waved them along.

"I took care of that boy from the time he started standing up to pee. I think I can watch over him well enough while you walk off your supper. It'll do you some good."

Cassidy rose from the steps and brushed off the seat of his khaki hiking shorts. Tia looped her arm through his and tugged him across the lawn, toward the bright lights of the ballpark a few blocks away, shimmering like the Northern Lights over the old cottonwoods.

Up tree-lined Ithaca Street, they strolled past the houses, old places Cassidy knew by long-ago names. He rubbed the leather glove and its magic conjured images he'd laid aside once.

A white picket fence a few doors down still tempted him to leap over it into the cool grass on the other side, Twin Tommy Ganneman's yard.

Cassidy told Tia how Twin Tommy had been his best friend all the way through school, and on summer nights when kick-the-can was played, together they leaped over the waist-high white pickets of Twin Tommy's yard and hid beneath the barberry hedges, waiting and watching for the chance to sprint free.

Twin Tommy's brother—the kids all called him Twin Sammy— died of polio when he was nine. Each replicated the other so exactly, their mother parted their wiry chestnut hair on opposite sides to tell the difference. Once they knew her secret, they switched and, forever after, nobody was certain which was which—maybe not even the twins themselves. Even if it was Twin Sammy who died, Twin Tommy died a little himself and never cared which part lived on. He knew he was both somewhere inside.

"Whatever happened to him?" Tia asked. Still arm in arm, she walked close enough to Cassidy that her hips brushed his.

"He went north."

"Canada?"

"For a while. Back in 1967, right after we got out of high school. Tommy's dad was a leatherneck who fought on Guadalcanal. He sat on the county draft board and Tommy had a low number. No way was his old man going to pull strings."

"That must have torn him up, to have his son bail out like that."

"Yeah, but he was only gone a few weeks. While he was gone, his girlfriend found out she was pregnant. Tommy came back. He married her, then joined the Marines and went to Vietnam."

"Where is he now?"

Cassidy looked at the sidewalk, then beyond the ballfield lights into the night. They passed a tiny house where an old man and his wife sat on the porch. The man raised just one finger in a subtle wave to Cassidy, who smiled and waved back as they kept walking.

"Up on Mount Pisgah."

"He was killed? Oh, I'm sorry. I didn't know..."

"No, Tommy made it home well enough. In fact, he did two tours and came back all in one piece. Got a few medals over there, too. A goddammed hero. He was a better soldier than his father ever dreamed he'd be, than he himself ever dreamed."

Cassidy walked past a few more of the quiet houses of his memory. The old places drew him along. Someone was barbecuing steaks in the backyard and the smell drifted between the houses. Children were playing back there, laughing.

"How did it happen then? Him dying, I mean," Tia asked.

"How does it ever happen? Some piece is missing somewhere. There's a tear someplace, a hole in your defenses. Like a gene missing its shield against cancer. Or a flaw in the wall of a vein that bursts. Or maybe a tiny gap in the survival instinct. I really don't know, but if you think about it, it comes down to that most of the time."

Tia stayed in step with him, then spoke softly and watched his face. He felt warm with her.

"What was Tommy missing?"

She understands, he thought.

"Time, I think. He was missing time. Like it was his destiny. He shared the first half of his life with a perfect twin, like splitting every moment, every experience perfectly in two. It was as if he'd only lived half a life until then, and could never get that time back. I know this sounds like some California bullshit, but after Twin Sammy died, he never really talked about it, but he'd say things like that."

"Like what?"

"Well, he had this idea that when they were conceived, their essence was mixed together. Long before they became two separate people in the womb. From one, two. So he always felt as if a part of Sammy lived on in him..."

"And that a part of him died with Sammy," Tia said, knowing.

"He came back from 'Nam to a wife and a child he didn't really know. He took a job on the railroad and they all lived in a trailer house on the edge of town. They even had another kid. Maybe he lost his way for a while. But in the end, he knew his way home."

"What happened?" Tia asked.

Cassidy knew what she meant.

"Tommy came home off a long haul late one night. He got a beer out of the 'fridge and drew a hot bath. While he soaked, his wife and her lover sneaked in and blew his head off with a 12-gauge shotgun. That was it."

"Oh my God... she killed him?"

"She killed him," Cassidy said, "but part of him was already dead."

To Cassidy, the old houses on Ithaca Street had faces. Their deep, dark eyes watched him pass, following each step. Porches like thin, serious lips pursed beneath sober faces. Their brows were knitted with birds' nests and creased by bent rain gutters.

Houses, like faces, hide all kinds of memories.

Moses Field was a green patch of Elysian grass, a well-lighted field in the shadow of Mount Pisgah. The incandescent floodlights, erected since Cassidy's playing days, thrust blue-white into the Wyoming sunset, so brilliant in the dry sky they must have drawn moths from the next county.

It looked smaller now. The fences were not so far, so unreachable. So mythical.

Cassidy and Tia stood against the chain-link fence beyond the home team dugout, where little boys in blue caps clowned around while their frazzled coach tried in vain to seat them on the bench in their proper batting order.

The smell of wet, new-mown grass was the same as it had always been, the same as Cassidy remembered in his dreams. It was watered from the tower that stood over all in West Canaan, the monument from which life poured. The dust of the infield, unsealed by dry days and drier nights, rose and fell like a calm sea when the breeze or a baseball coursed through.

A few parents sat in the splintered bleachers behind home plate fanning themselves with magazines and ball caps, but many more sat in cars parked outside the fence on both foul lines, drinking cold beer and soda pop from coolers. Some rolled down their windows to talk to the parents parked beside them, others backed up their pickups and watched from lawn chairs unfolded in the back, like a poor man's box seat.

Cassidy leaned against the fence, breathing in a pleasant memory. Out of habit, his fingers rested on the steel fabric of the fence—an old ballplayer would never entwine his fingers where a blazing foul ball might crush them. The game never leaves you, he thought.

"You love it, don't you?" Tia asked.

"This game? Sure. Who wouldn't love a place where you never have to grow up? It's like life itself, when you think about it: you start at home and head out. Life is treacherous out there and you can be put out anywhere between the bases. You're always moving back toward home. It's the only place you're really safe. That's the Zen of the Yard."

"Zen, huh? The Tao of the Full Count?" Tia teased him. "That's a great way to think about it, though."

"Hell, little boys know fun, not philosophy. Old men like me make this stuff up because we can't be out there."

"You're not old. Did Daniel play, too?"

"He was beautiful when he played. I'd come to watch him play and he was my hero. He was left-handed, so I always tried to be left-handed, too. I'd always volunteer to be the batboy so I could sit by him on the bench. Even when he was young, he swung his bat in a true and perfect circle, so smooth you thought the night-air must be on *his* team."

A little boy in baggy pants stepped up to the plate and ripped a ball through the shortstop's legs. The horns honked as he and his trousers flapped toward first. Flouting his coach's wild entreaties to run past the base, he slid. Smiling as bright as any arc-light, he rose, brushed off his pants and pulled his cap down so his ears splayed out like wings.

Cassidy chuckled.

"Daniel told me a story once. He said there was once an old ballplayer named Moses who came to West Canaan on the train and went right into the nearest bar. He challenged any nine men to a baseball game, and he'd play on the other side with any eight players they picked. So they chose up sides right there in the bar, laid their bets under a whiskey bottle and went out to a pasture to play ball.

"First time Moses came to the plate, he whacked one deep into the alfalfa and streaked around the bases for a home run. When the home team finally got his side out, Moses pitched so skillfully, they never got a hit. All afternoon, Moses scored every run off the flustered home-boys and then pitched them down one by one.

"In the ninth inning, Moses came to bat again, but the hometown pitcher, who'd been embarrassed all day by this itinerant ringer, cocked his arm and hurled a beanball right at Moses's head.

"Whether he never expected such a throw or had finally found his way home, nobody knows. But Moses stood in and the ball hit him squarely in the temple, killing him instantly."

Startled by the death of Moses, Tia's eyes widened as she covered her open mouth reflexively.

"This really happened?"

"Daniel said it did, and we believed him. Anyhow, the hometown boys, whose poor play was rivaled only by their poor sportsmanship, were so distraught and embarrassed that they took the ante they'd rightfully lost, and they arranged for Moses to be buried in a fine applewood casket in that cow pasture where they played."

"Where exactly was it?" Tia asked.

"Right here. This is it. Moses Field."

"No way..."

"Daniel told us that the old ballplayer is buried right under second base. And if you play here, you've got to tip your hat during the game to old Moses, who was never bested by the hometown boys."

"That's a wonderful story! Do you think it's true?" she asked.

"Does it matter?"

Cassidy bought her a soda pop and they sat on the bottom plank of the rickety lumber bleachers. Tia sipped it and watched the little boys on the field until, finally, one of them tugged the bill of his cap unconsciously.

"See there, he's saluting the old man," Cassidy said.

Tia giggled like one of the schoolgirls who kept watch on the infielders from the bleachers. Always the infielders.

"Daniel was right," she said, laughing as she pulled the curled bill of Cassidy's crumpled Giant cap over his nose. "He must have been a wonderful brother. Was he a good player?"

Cassidy took off his cap, and leaned backward, reminiscing. He ran his hand through his peppery hair.

"We'd play in the sandlot all day, and Daniel would clobber the ball. He was the only kid we ever saw hit it clean over the Johnsons' house. It'd land in their garden, maybe shatter a cabbage when it hit. We never shattered a cabbage, so we had to be in awe of him."

"He was the local slugger, huh?"

"Not just that. He was the best at whatever he did and we all knew it. We all wanted to be just like him. Especially me."

"And you became like him..."

Cassidy shook his head. He didn't look up.

"Maybe I got good at some things, but never like him."

"You're very close to him." Tia pushed her hair back and watched Cassidy's face.

"All you see now is a gray, withered, pitiful man. But I see a little boy who saved my life and told astounding stories and imagined better places. I see a little boy I always feared would fly away and leave me alone."

They walked around the edge of the outfield grass, in the shadows beyond the advertising signs that beckoned in the dreams of little boys who'd never play anything but right field. Out there, where the long balls rolled into the high grass while proud parents honked, Tia slipped her hand into Cassidy's.

It had been a long time since a woman had held Cassidy's hand. Her palm was as soft and warm as a Wyoming summer night. If he'd missed the old feelings that welled inside him now, it was his own fault, he knew.

Now he fought off the urge to seal himself off from Tia, to stay safely distant.

"Why didn't you ever have children?" Tia asked him.

"What makes you think they'd have me?"

Cassidy winked at Tia and grinned. She shook her head and gently punched his shoulder.

"I think you'd be a good father if you weren't such a smart ass. Try to give me one straight answer. So why didn't you?"

As they walked, Cassidy watched the rightfielder, a kid maybe seven or eight. He was looking between his legs, trying to read a sign, upside-down, on the outfield fence.

"I love kids. I love the idea of children. But maybe I was afraid."

"Of what?"

"That I was too much of a child myself. That I couldn't do it right, be a good dad. That something might happen to them. That I couldn't be there when they needed me the most. Take your pick. I really don't know and it really doesn't matter, I guess."

"Sure it matters. It seems too bad that you don't have a son to teach baseball and tell all these wonderful stories," Tia said.

"My first wife wanted children, but we just never got around to it. My second wife just wished that I'd had kids with my first wife. Barbara was a professional woman and it's hard to give birth if your policy is to never let them see you sweat. She would have preferred to lease a baby... with an option to buy."

Tia smiled but said nothing.

Beyond the fences, around the other side of Moses Field, they sat side by side on the rocky edge of the Pond. Without rain, its shore was wide and the water low. Cassidy found a flat stone between them and skipped it across the small water, surfing at last into the reeds on the opposite bank. The V of its wake purled over the surface.

"What are you going to do... with Daniel, I mean?" Tia asked.

"I don't know. I wish it were just a dream sometimes. Maybe it is. I've had dreams like this before, where he was alive and everything seemed so real. Every time, I am betrayed by my dreams. I just don't know where I'll wake up this time."

"Is Daniel missing something, like Tommy?"

The night was quiet, except for the ballpark.

Cassidy had learned Daniel's lessons well. When pain approaches, seek refuge in fantasy. But it was getting more difficult, because pain was coming in waves these days and there were too few places to run.

"Only Daniel knows that," Cassidy said.

The night sounds filled his silence.

Another hit. Horns blared beyond the trees. The announcer's amplified voice seemed to come from the sky: the ball rolled under the fence, a ground-rule double.

Tia reached over and turned Cassidy's head toward her. She looked at his eyes for a moment, then kissed him. A summer kiss, gentle and slow. He touched her cheek as their lips met, then gently wove his fingers through her dark hair. Tenderly, he kissed her mouth and cheek, letting his lips drift softly across her face.

Starlight played on the water as Tia nestled closer, turning her back to Cassidy's chest. Cassidy wrapped his arms around her and, again, smelled sweet apples in her hair.

"I'm sorry," she said. "I've wanted to do that for a long time."

Tia rested her head on his shoulder and they sat in the darkness a while longer, listening to the frogs and a late-inning rally at Moses Field.

A quarter-moon hung over the ballpark, far beyond left field, near the part of Heaven where the announcer's sonorous voice echoed.

"Whatever happened to the ball you hit out of the park against the Denver team? Is it still around?" she asked him.

"After my dad died I took it back to The City. It's still there..."

The next word lodged somewhere between his brain and his lips. It had fallen to earth like a pop-fly third out dangling in the night sky, waiting to be caught. Cassidy closed his eyes and let his arms slip from around Tia as he lay back on the smooth, cool stones.

"How could I be so stupid? Jesus..."

"What? If it's the kiss, I'm..."

"No, the ball. Or not the ball, but the key. I took some of my father's belongings home with me after he died. One of the things I took was a box of personal things, like cuff links and watches and rings and stuff. It had a tray with a hidden compartment under it. Jesus, I can see it sitting on the shelf in my study. The key must be in it. C'mon, let's get back."

He helped Tia up and they walked briskly back to Ithaca Street. Daniel had fallen asleep in the back bedroom, and Miss Oneida was rocking in the front porch swing sipping an iced tea as Tia and Cassidy came up the walk.

"There was a phone call while you were out," she said.

"Who was it?" Cassidy asked.

"A man. He just said you'd know who he was. Then he said he found your word, whatever that means."

"Did he leave a message or a number where I can call?"

"No, he just said to tell you one word. He said you'd know what it meant."

Cassidy leaned toward her.

"What did he say...?"

Miss Oneida shrugged, oblivious to the mystery that she was about to complicate. She fussed with a crumpled grocery sack full of the just-washed dinner dishes, delivering her brief message with all the energy of an old woman kept up past her bedtime:

"Ghosts."

DISPATCHES
WEST CANAAN, JULY 22, 1995

The package arrived General Delivery from San Francisco, no return address. Herman Searcy, the postmaster, phoned Cassidy a little after nine in the morning to tell him it had arrived.

The post office was only three blocks away, but Cassidy drove, partly because he didn't want to lug the box back home on foot, mostly because he couldn't wait to open it. He phoned Tia to stay with Daniel while he went to pick up the box.

"Planning on stayin' a while, Mr. McLeod?" Herman heaved the bulky, plain cardboard box onto the glass countertop and slid it into Cassidy's anxious hands. A postal clerk somewhere had scrawled its weight just above the address label: twenty-eight pounds.

"Maybe so, Herman," Cassidy said. "We'll see."

Herman Searcy smelled of wet paste, like stamps just licked. From his scuffed wingtip shoes to the feathery tufts of unruly gray hair that sprouted over his ears, he had the look of a disheveled bachelor who never gave a second thought to retirement because he had no place else to go, even after thirty-two years in the postal service. He loved his work. He'd been appointed postmaster in West Canaan twenty-two years after he started working there as a clerk, surviving by quiet perseverance and the monthly promise of a surreptitious peek at all manner of brown paper-wrapped nakedness. He read everybody's postcards and nobody ever complained.

Herman knew a good deal about everyone in West Canaan, just from reading the envelopes, postcards and packages they received. He knew who was celebrating a birthday, who was claiming bankruptcy, whose kin were vacationing in exotic places, and who hoped beyond hope that ten million dollars could be won by merely ordering magazines. Herman believed it was his job to know such things, because he steadfastly believed he was the True Messenger.

But he couldn't know what Cassidy's box contained, which vexed him. So he pried, in his obsequious way.

"Hope she's all there, Mr. McLeod," he said. Secretly, he hoped Cassidy would open the box from San Francisco right there.

"I'm sure it's just fine, Herman. I'll let you know if there's a problem."

"Just sign right here. She's insured, you know. Any problems, you just fill out a claim form and we'll try to make it right for you. You can check the contents here, if you'd like. Wasn't anything that can't be replaced, I hope...?"

Even though they were separated by the postal counter, Herman Searcy walked toward the door with Cassidy, peering curiously over his glasses.

"It'll be fine, I'm sure of it."

"I'll be here all day, Mr. McLeod. You just call me if there's anything you need. You'd be surprised what people stick in the mail these days. My Lord, you just can't imagine what folks send to each other."

"I'll bet." Cassidy smiled and took the box. "Nice to see you again, Herman."

He turned his back to the glass doors and a rush of air-conditioned government air swept him into the morning heat. He tossed the box on the front seat of the Taurus and hurried back to Ithaca Street.

Tia waited on the front steps. Cassidy sat with her, the box between them. He used his car key to slit the packing tape and unfolded its flaps.

Digging through wadded clumps of the *San Francisco Chronicle*, he uncovered his laptop computer case, some books, a small valet box and a bottle of California merlot.

"De Sales thought of everything," he chuckled, handing the wine to Tia.

Cassidy had called the old reporter back the night he got de Sales's message. He sent the key to his house on Russell Street with instructions to gather up a few specific items and send them to Wyoming. The whole exchange took five days by mail because none of the overnight shippers served West Canaan, where anything or anyone who moved too quickly was immediately suspect. Besides, none of the trucks came within eighty miles.

It was the antique valet, a fine, handcarved, dark-oak case the size of a shoebox, that Cassidy desired most. He set it gently on the top stair of the porch, opened its latch and raised the lid.

A tarnished snarl of his father's tie tacks, cuff links, rings, watches and collar stays lay jumbled in the top tray. He sorted through them with his finger, but there was no key.

He lifted the tray out of the box, uncovering a hidden space beneath it. There, he found Archie's war medals, some old coins, his father's beloved Buck knife and athletic pins... and a key ring with a dozen odd keys.

One of them was an ornate skeleton key, cold and iron black.

"It must be this one," he said to Tia as he lifted the keys out of the clutter of treasure. Tia picked up the valet box as Cassidy scrambled up the steps toward the house.

Cassidy stopped short. Daniel stood in the doorway, inside the screen, watching them. His arms hung like strips of rag at his sides. Cassidy sensed he must have been standing there for the last few minutes, but he showed no emotion.

Cassidy paused on the other side of the door from him. He tried to meet his eye, but Daniel turned away.

"Let's see what ghosts are in your trunk, Danny," he said. As he opened the door, Daniel melted back into the shadows of the hallway. Cassidy followed him, showing him the key.

"*Noong kohn mah*," he said to Daniel, repeating what he had heard his brother say in the cellar more than a week before. "Ghosts."

Daniel met his eye briefly and was strangely calm.

"Come with me, Danny. Let's go see the ghosts together."

Cassidy waited for some reaction, any sign of recognition. But Daniel slid down the wall into a puddle of sunlight and turned away. The mysterious door that separated the sunny rooms from the dark corners of Daniel's mind closed behind him, shutting Cassidy out.

Cassidy turned to Tia. He hurt inside and the look on his face showed it. She closed the front door and shoved the deadbolt into place, as a precaution.

"Give him time," she said. "He came out once and he'll come out again. Let's see what's inside the trunk. Maybe it will make more sense then."

"Sure," Cassidy said. "Let's try it."

Cassidy flipped the light switch and they went down the stairs into the cool cellar. He lifted a water-stained bedspread that covered the trunk and laid it on the dirt floor where he could sit. Tia crouched behind him, her hands on his shoulders.

His hand shook a little as he sorted through the old keys. The black iron skeleton key seemed the likeliest match, he thought, given the apparent age of the trunk and the shape of its keyhole. Cassidy slid it to the top of the ring and slipped it into the latch.

A key and its lock transcend time, even lives. The match is forever, the fit immutable. This one fit.

With a quarter-turn to the right, the faithful lock clicked open for the first time in at least twenty-three years. Cassidy unbuckled the two side-latches and lifted the trunk's heavy lid. Its hinges keened like an old dog stretching after a long nap.

The trunk's lid was lined with fine silk that still shimmered in the dim light as Cassidy opened it. A subtle mustiness was stirred up, not so much the smell of decay but of the past. Antiquity and old lavender.

It was filled with three generations of treasure, packed deliberately and precisely.

An upright oak box, polished and fitted with a brass handle on top, took up a fourth of the chest's volume. Its dovetail joints were the mark of an elegant woodworker, perhaps the same one who built the trunk itself. A miniature brass padlock hung beneath a small inscribed plate: DQM.

"That was my grandfather, Darius Quarrie McLeod," Cassidy said, tracing his fingers across the initials. "This must have been his."

Cassidy wormed his hand along the side of the box and lifted it slightly, admiring the handiwork. The wood had been sanded so finely, the last pass over it must have been no more than a puff of air.

"He was quite a man. When he was about fifteen, his father got a young neighbor girl pregnant in Glasgow, but rather than admit it, he forced my grandfather to take the rap. So Darius McLeod left Scotland and sailed to New York in 1895. He got off the boat and caught the next train west. By the time the train got this far, his money had run out, so he homesteaded a place out south of here."

"Pretty brave for a young boy to make such a long journey alone," Tia said. She looked deep into a photograph of Darius, finding catchlights of some distant genius that was vaguely familiar.

Cassidy spread another blanket on the dirt floor beside the trunk, then gently hoisted the elegant oak box out of the trunk by its brass handle. He felt its exquisite smoothness, its balance. Its joints fit as if they'd grown quite naturally together. It wasn't exceptionally heavy, even for a hardwood box the size of a picnic basket. He knew his grandfather had been an inventive tinkerer, but this box was the work of a skilled artist.

"It gets better. He ran a few cattle on his homestead and took a dollar-a-week job in a local feed store to make a little money. Before long, the owner high-tailed it back East and sold him his rundown store for a buck and half, not even two weeks' pay. He was only about eighteen at the time."

Cassidy examined the little padlock hanging on a tarnished hasp. He saw no key anywhere.

"Here we go again," he joked to Tia.

"Maybe it's with the other keys."

Cassidy groped in his trouser pocket for the ring of odd keys. Almost hidden among the hefty iron keys was a small brass one. It fit the little padlock.

Inside the box, he found an odd machine and some papers in an envelope. He unfolded them gently. They were government patent papers and schematic drawings, presumably of the machine that sat in the box before him.

"I never knew this," he said to Tia. "My grandfather had a patent for some kind of invention. This is it."

He read the official patent certificate further.

"It's a kind of lantern that doesn't use liquid fuel. He patented it in, let's see, 1933. There's his signature. It uses sticks of coal dust that have been bonded somehow. This is just unbelievable. I never knew. My dad always said he only tinkered around with stuff that was foolish, that nobody wanted."

"Back then, maybe it was foolish," Tia said. "In the Depression, who was going to invest in something like this?"

Cassidy lifted the peculiar machine from its box. It had a vented glass globe the size of a cantaloupe, covering some brass fittings that sprouted from a small metal casing. A pagoda-like housing covered it and a bail handle curved gracefully around the globe, anchored in a black cowling at the base. Protruding from the cowling was one small button.

"The plans say this is the starter button," Cassidy said. "When you push it, it lights an oiled wick that, in turn, lights the coal stick. You can see it down there."

He held the globe so Tia could see the intricate workings inside.

"Do you think it still works?" she asked.

"Are you brave enough to try?"

She gave it a little thought, then said, "Sure."

Cassidy read a few more of the handwritten directions, made a couple of adjustments and set the lantern on the top of the three-legged dresser he'd propped up with a couple of hat boxes. He pushed the starter button twice, but nothing happened.

"I bet it's been at least fifty years since this thing's been used," he said, fiddling with a few more buttons.

He pressed the starter button again and the lantern flickered. Tia stepped back, just in case the machine was more volatile than it looked.

Once more, he pressed the button. A soft light glimmered inside, then grew in intensity as the coal fuel caught the spark. Soon, the lantern glowed steadily like a warm fire, its heat scattered by the little pagoda on top. It threw off the faint pungency of coal smoke, something Cassidy hadn't smelled since he was a boy.

Both of them stood back and admired Darius McLeod's life work, smiling. It illuminated the old man's dreams as much as the dark cellar.

"What a wonderful thing. It must have frustrated him to know it wouldn't ever be used," Tia said.

"For dreamers, it's the dream that matters," he said, never taking his eyes off the glowing globe. "He didn't die unhappy."

Cassidy turned a dial that snuffed the flame, then carefully returned the lantern to its beautiful box, which he set on the stairs. He left the lock open, so they could come back to Darius's magnificent invention later. Now, there were other dreams to sort through.

He stooped in front of the chest again. Some loose papers, letters, photographs, clothing and small boxes were tidily arranged in the bottom of the trunk, frozen in time by their perfect formality. To disturb them would be to disrupt a careful order.

Cassidy lifted a few framed photos from the top of the pile. He recognized his father and mother among them, and a few ancient glass-plate photos of his grandfather, protected in gilt frames. In one, he stood with his arms folded across his chest, wearing a high collar and a silk tie. He sported a marvelous mustache, waxed to lissome curls at the ends, a Scotsman's sparkling eyes, and a hint of his devilish smile.

Among the photos were newer baby pictures. The infants in them could have been Cassidy or Daniel. He wasn't sure, even as he studied each one. Later photographs showed them together, Daniel always taller and always smiling.

The next layer contained three packets of letters tied with faded red ribbons. One stack was very old, their envelopes in a woman's handwriting, addressed to Archie. Another, older still but smaller, contained letters to Darius himself, addressed in a flowing, ornate style, in ink that had faded to a rich brown.

The third bundle was newer, less brittle and yellow. Cassidy peeked under the wide ribbon and saw they were letters from Daniel. He fanned them quickly, looking at the return addresses: San Francisco and an APO in Saigon.

"These are Daniel's letters home after he started working at the *Chronicle*. Most of them are from Vietnam," Cassidy said. He wanted to read them right there, but the mystery of the trunk drew him to it.

An unmarked manila envelope, tucked between a child's drawings and an ancient Bible, contained photographs of Daniel in Vietnam—the same black-and-white images delivered by the *Newsweek* photographer at Daniel's funeral.

"He was so young and beautiful," Tia said. She looked at each one for a long time. "So young. These photos... his eyes are so alive."

Not like now, Cassidy thought.

He dug deeper. Here was a delicate lace wedding dress wrapped in tissue paper; a Marine officer's dress tunic and trousers with the captain's bars still affixed, a Silver Star still pinned on its breast; some old property deeds in a tan envelope; his parents' marriage certificate; and an inscribed book of young Rupert Brooke's poetry his mother had given Archie on his birthday in 1953, the year she died. One page was marked with a delicate red silk ribbon. It was a poem called "The Wayfarers," and Cassidy read part of it aloud:

> *... Do you think there's a far bordered town, somewhere,*
> *The desert's edge, last of the lands we know,*
> *Some gaunt eventual limit of our light,*
> *In which I'll find you waiting; and we'll go*
> *Together, hand in hand again, out there,*
> *Into the waste we know not, into the night?'"*

Tia smiled, but said nothing. Cassidy closed the book and handed it to her. "For later," he said.

There was more in the trunk. Three wooden boxes, each as handsome as the larger, unopened one, were arranged neatly on the bottom. They contained something he'd never seen, his mother's jewelry: rings, brooches, necklaces and baubles she must have cherished.

Jammed tightly between them and the side of the trunk was a book, its spine obscured. Holding the boxes in place, Cassidy levered the book free.

"*The Clever Dogs*," he said in astonishment. It was in almost perfect condition. "I'll be damned. Your father signed it for my dad. Look."

He showed her the inscription over the bold, unmistakable signature of Jack Lazarus: "*In time, the road leads back, my friend. In time.*"

Even in the dirty light of the cellar, Cassidy saw a tear in Tia's eye. He stroked her hair, and she smiled.

"Would you like to have it? Please, take it," he said. She closed the book and looked at her father's familiar photo on the back cover, then handed it back to him.

"No, thanks, really. It meant something to your father or it wouldn't be in this trunk. And besides, I've got one just like it somewhere. Maybe a couple. You're sweet to offer, though."

Cassidy set the book on a spindly stool and opened his arms to Tia. She nestled into them and laid her head on his chest. His heart was strong and reassuring.

"You belong here," he told her. "I don't know why or how, but you belong here. And I am glad you're here, too, in case you didn't know."

For the rest of the morning, they read the brittle letters of Archie and Darius McLeod. They were about love and home and dreams and people long dead.

After he finished with each letter, Cassidy handed it to Tia.

Most of the letters to Darius were from his mother in Scotland. Most contained news about family and friends in Glasgow and acknowledged the young boy's many homesick letters. And each ended with every sad mother's last word to her son: *"I love you dearly, my good boy."*

But the last letter in the parcel was from Darius's father, dated in 1918. It was a laconic message, barely ten sentences long, that his mother had died from influenza and was to be buried in her childhood village on the Isle of Skye.

If any more letters were ever sent, Darius McLeod kept none of them. From the detached tone of his father's last news, Cassidy presumed that Darius never heard from his family again, and perhaps never wrote to them either.

"My granddad married a local shopkeeper's daughter, Lucinda Quinn, sometime before the First World War, when he was already in his late thirties," Cassidy said, finishing the unwritten story of Darius McLeod. "He'd waited a long time because he still lived in a hovel out on the homestead and he didn't think a woman should have to live like a coyote. When his feed store finally became more profitable, he moved to town and took a wife. My father was born two years after this last letter, in 1920, when Darius was fairly old, about forty. Then Granddad died in 1947, before I was born."

Tia listened raptly, surrounded by the fading letters and photographs and lives of men she almost knew. These men's lives were tangled together in subtle ways, each in the other, their journeys and their dreams. And their eyes.

Cassidy turned to the second packet. Archie's letters were from Annie MacKenzie, Cassidy's mother. There were maybe four dozen well-traveled and water-stained envelopes, most posted to a military address in Hawaii during the war and forwarded to wherever he was bivouacked.

Among them were letters Archie had written home and Annie had kept. Annie's letters were plain-spoken and lonely, her handwriting as beautiful as she had been. She wrote of her desperate nightmares about Archie and her conviction that he must return to her.

"We have sons to make," she wrote.

Cassidy felt a familiar pain rise in his throat.

Archie wrote back, though less often because he got four and five of her letters at a time. There was no hint of where he was fighting on the non-descript V-mail envelopes or in the censored sentiments he scribbled on government-issue stationery, but his letters were consumed with images of death and dying, confusion and fear, losing friends and finding faith... and homecoming.

"I dream about you and Wyoming, always together," he wrote to Annie in the summer of 1943 from an unknown island in the Pacific. "The heat here is oppressive, the water foul and the nights full of fear. Wyoming is none of those things. It is home and you are home. And I dream of growing old with you. I promise you will see me again and we'll go to the mountains where it is cool and we can lie beneath the pines and sleep and dream together."

Their last letter passed between them in September of 1945, a month after the Japanese surrendered. Captain Archimedes McLeod, USMC, wrote to tell her he was coming home, and he did. They never wrote another letter to each other after that because they never parted again until Annie died in 1953.

It was past noon. Cassidy couldn't go on. He needed a break from the memories, and wanted to look in on Daniel.

"Let's come back to this later," he said to Tia. "Let's see if Daniel will eat some lunch with us."

They went back upstairs. Cassidy found Daniel awake but withdrawn in the back bedroom. While Tia made sandwiches, he sat for a while in the rocker beside Daniel's bed, letting his mind drift off to Scotland, and the Isle of Skye, and to another mysterious, fetid island somewhere in the Pacific, places out of time that nonetheless fit somehow into his circle. A long time ago, he imagined West Canaan to be an island, too, surrounded by a vast sea of grass and sky and emptiness. Now it was his comfort.

And Daniel was stranded on his own island, isolated by furies and unknown memories.

Time was the ocean between them. Their islands drifted in a stream that flowed through generations, with no way off.

Except, perhaps, to be carried away in an old trunk, on a current of forgotten words.

After lunch without Daniel, who remained unstirring on his bed, Cassidy returned to the cellar alone and retrieved the packet of his brother's letters. He and Tia poured tall glasses of iced tea and wandered out to the back porch to read them.

At the top of the stack were letters from San Francisco. They began in 1967, the year Cassidy graduated from high school and Daniel went to The City, where Daniel often wrote home about the magical sounds and the feverish streets and the rain. Always the rain.

Daniel knew about rain.

He knew about magic, too. Long before he disappeared, a dozen summers before the circle was broken forever, Daniel wove the story about a boy who could run between raindrops. The story not only soothed Cassidy, it gave a voice to his own wish that pain could be avoided, and his knowing that it couldn't.

No matter how hard he tried, no matter how wide the gaps may be between raindrops, there was no way to avoid being splashed by it.

Daniel lived to tell stories, and his letters were filled with the life he saw around him. That's why it seemed perfectly natural that he followed in his father's footsteps and became a newspaperman. In high school, he'd hang around the *Republican-Rustler,* not cadging half dollars for ice cream, but writing up the spectrum of small-town life: birth announcements, school honors, wedding stories, the Main Street buzz, and obituaries. It wasn't long before the townfolk with newsworthy items sought out Daniel, sometimes waiting for him after school at the tiny writing desk Archie gave him in a corner of the newspaper's cluttered office.

Nothing could have made Archie prouder of his son than his affinity for newspapering. Archie had long ago determined that his sons would go to college at any cost, and when the time came, he'd saved enough to send Daniel to the best journalism school of his day, the University of Missouri in Columbia.

Daniel graduated with honors in 1967, with a low draft number and a reporting job at the *San Francisco Chronicle*. He covered a crime beat at night and spent his days puttering around The City in his moribund Karmann-Ghia, hunting for stories he could drag back to his dyspeptic city editor, a newsroom crustacean who seemed to float in a mephitic fog of cigar stink. He became so much a part of Daniel's early reporting, the old man was never listed by name in his letters, merely as The City Editor, respectfully capitalized.

That's how Daniel discovered the Haight Ashbury, its frenetic colors defying him to cage them in black and white.

For a boy who grew up knowing the smell of snow coming, this new bohemia was redolent with the raw scents of lovemaking, revolt, pot, anger, cheap food, rock 'n' roll, loneliness, wine, sometimes death.

Daniel rented a one-room flat that he first shared briefly with a lost girl from a small town in Oregon and thereafter with other lost girls who shared everything but the rent. He loved them all, and was gentle with each one. They were seduced by his tales, like musk.

Once the quicksilver of the Haight had suffused Daniel's mind, it seeped into his ink. His stories caught its spark in a bottle. Even the old city editor, chewing the mossy stump of his cigar, would thumb through Daniel's copy and send it down to the desk for the next edition, with almost no changes. That was the old boy's highest compliment.

But by 1969, the Haight's colors had dissolved into the violent greens of Vietnam, the all-purpose apocalypse. When Daniel asked to go there, to become a war correspondent, nobody was surprised, least of all his father.

"There's a madness I want to taste," he wrote to Archie just before he left the States. "I have never been harmed by what I could touch, only things I could not. I am afraid, Dad, but I am more afraid of staying here and never touching it."

It.

He never touched Vietnam in the same way it touched him. It nourished, frightened and smothered him. In the end, it swallowed him.

Daniel was a homesick country boy in a jungle town, taking on madness one grain at a time. Into 1971, he was still holding it together, yearning to be home, but he could never find his equilibrium. Just when he tipped   toward some balance with existence, another grain of madness was added on the other side.

Then, Ba Troi.

Only one letter came after that, postmarked 15 days later. It was short and peculiar. Several yellowed clippings about the massacre from the *Chronicle* were enclosed, with a half sheet of crackly rice paper bearing six lines of Vietnamese writing. It looked like a poem, even if Cassidy could not recognize the words. They used a familiar alphabet, but were embellished with all manner of accents and exotic markings. Beneath the alien words, in the same hand, but in English, was a date: *"First Day of Tet, 1971."*

The bottom of the page was torn off.

"Tet is the Vietnamese New Year," Cassidy said. "This date looks like Daniel's writing, but I can't understand the rest."

He handed the news clippings and the rice paper note to Tia, who read them carefully.

"I remember when this happened, this massacre," Tia said as she read Daniel's horrific account of the killings at Ba Troi. "We weren't supposed to be the bad guys over there."

Cassidy sat with the scattered pile of Daniel's letters in his lap, unable to see how they fit into the puzzle his brother had become.

"It starts there, at Ba Troi," he said. "I know it, but I can't figure it out. We thought he was killed. Maybe he wanted us to think he was killed. Something changed him. If I knew, maybe I could connect with him."

"Maybe you already have," Tia said. "You were all he had a long time ago, and he was all you had. My God, the stories alone. I've seen you talk about him. Maybe you understand him now better than you understand yourself. He told you everything you need to know."

Cassidy sipped his tea, then leaned back against the top step of the porch. The sun warmed him and he closed his eyes.

"Would you read the last letter again?" he said, handing Tia the
envelope. She gently unfolded the one-page, typewritten letter and
began.

"'Dearest Dad: Bad air tonight. I can hear the birds
coming in and going out. The diesel fumes mix with the
heat and the night here is like a rank, suffocating body bag.
It's hard to breathe and to sleep, so I lie awake almost every
night until the air settles. But some nights it doesn't settle
and the light comes before sleep. But the birds keep flying,
thumping all night in the distance and fouling the air, like the
boatman Charon beating the black water as he ferries the
dead across the Acheron and goes back for more. ~~Falling~~
Maybe you already understand. I've been out of the war for
about two weeks, but will go back soon, when I can face it
again. I got your last letter today. I'm sending some things I
wrote. I love you and need to hear from you. Daniel.'"

Finished, Tia searched Cassidy's face for a reaction. His eyes
remained closed.
"He loved... he loves... the old myths," Cassidy said, not moving.
"He knew them all. To him, they touched something common in
people. It was like a rhythm that pulsed in every story that was ever
told. Every story *he* ever told, anyway."
"So he thought all stories were connected somehow?"
"Yeah, sort of. They had a core of the same stuff. The heroes
were the same and the quests were the same and they all wanted to
know the same things: Who am I? What happens when I die? Can I
get back home? And there was always a journey to be taken, whether
from Troy or Camelot or Valhalla or Eden. The stories Daniel made
up were all like that, too."
"Like Daniel's own journey..." Tia said. "Just let me think out
loud for a second: he grows up wondering what's out there in the
world. He sees every event, every moment, every sound like it's
happened before. He grows up like a young hero, goes off to war and
is resurrected from the dead before he mysteriously returns to his

hometown twenty-three years later. His own life has been like a damned myth, so maybe he's right."

Cassidy opened his eyes and looked at her. Her face was soft, angelic. Her hair absorbed light and reflected it in her words.

"It sounds crazy, I know, but maybe he sees past all the little cruelties of time," she said, moving closer to Cassidy. "Maybe that's the only way suffering has any meaning. Or maybe this is all horse shit and he's just crazy. What do *you* want to believe?"

"Okay, let's play out your theory. In the old stories, the hero always returns with something, a fleece or a grail or some greater wisdom. Daniel came back with a fucked up mind, some cheap clothes and a pocketful of puzzles."

Cassidy heard the mounting frustration in his own words. Almost a month had passed and, outside of the two times he had spoken, Daniel showed no sign of improving. Daniel ate when he was hungry, but usually only with Cassidy's help. Half the time, he urinated wherever he was when his bladder filled, and hid for most of the day and night. Cassidy's hope was flagging.

"Would Daniel remember any of those old stories?" Tia asked.

Cassidy pondered the thought. He raised his eyebrows slightly, as if he wanted to hear more from her.

"I mean, he's not completely out of it or he wouldn't be here. If he was right about the old stories, that they're all connected, maybe they're the key to unlocking his"—she stopped, seeking the word that allowed for the most hope—"his sickness."

"Tell him his own stories? The ones he used to tell me?"

Cassidy leaned toward her. Maybe she had something.

"Nothing else has worked. A few stories couldn't hurt, could they? For three weeks, I've listened to you tell the most fascinating tales, but they were *his* tales. He told them when you needed to hear them. Did you ever think they were stories you'd need to remember someday? To tell again to ease some pain? Maybe his pain..."

Cassidy looked at Daniel's letters in his lap. Maybe Tia was right about the stories. Telling them again couldn't hurt. They had been more than words to him once. The ballplayer Moses might rise up and play once more. The old black dog named Shadow watched. Pledger Moon would live again, the way he always had.

Moon. The stories were still fresh, at least the ones Cassidy had put so far in his abortive memoir. Moon's journey had never ended, not back then and not now, but maybe he was nearer than he'd ever been.

Cassidy gathered Daniel's letters and re-tied them with the faded red ribbon that had bound them for more than twenty-three years. And for a moment he thought about Herman Searcy, the True Messenger, who had probably delivered every single one.

Now he knew what Daniel had meant about "ghosts." One still haunted him: Daniel's Tet poem, if that's what it was, remained elusive, but he resolved to decipher its mysteries, too, in due course.

As they sat on the back porch before supper they gathered the letters, clippings and photos to repack them in the trunk for a new journey.

Cassidy didn't see Daniel watching, listening to them from the open bedroom window above.

Later that night, while Daniel and Tia sat with him in the living room of his father's house, Cassidy told the first story he could remember, hoping the threads of Daniel's yarns might bind him up whole again.

He began it properly, too. *Once upon a time...*

PLEDGER MOON
WEST CANAAN, JULY 23, 1957

The midges rose from the wet lawns of West Canaan every night in summer. By the time The Whistle blew, they swirled in intoxicated clouds beneath porch lights.

Darkness was at hand. The boys abandoned the sandlot and the tiny gnats' nightly dance had begun.

It was Wednesday, press night at the *Republican-Rustler*, so Archie wouldn't be home until after midnight. The boys wandered through their dark, empty house to the kitchen. Daniel flipped on the light and scooped up the plate of oatmeal cookies Miss Oneida left for them on the kitchen counter. Cassidy followed him out the screen door to the back steps.

Midges swirled around them, as if mopping up the dim light that spilled onto the porch.

"They only live through the night, you know," Daniel said.

Cassidy swatted at the nearly invisible swarm while he held his breath for fear of sucking one in.

"Good." He had no particular love for gnats of any kind. Too small to see and too trifling to swat, they didn't play fair.

"No, really," Daniel said. "Their whole life is one day and one night. That's all. These were born this morning and by tomorrow morning they'll be gone. By breakfast time, there will be others to take their place, and tomorrow night when The Whistle blows, they will only have a few hours to live, too. It's like a circle and it keeps going 'til the days turn cold."

"Well, at least they all go together," his little brother said off-handedly, swiping at his ear when a midge darted past like a winged ripsaw in high gear.

This talk about life and death, seasons and circles... it was too much for Cassidy. In truth, for a little boy, he had already thought a lot about dying, and he didn't like the deep-down ache that seemed to suck inward. To him, it was something living apart from him, but inside. Something black and evil. When he nearly plunged off the water tower more than a month before, the Black Thing sucked even harder at him, as if trying to turn him inside out. They never told their father about the water tower and Cassidy preferred the lingering pain in his shoulder—and maybe the threat of a spontaneous implosion—to whatever pain his father might inflict if he found out.

"Do you think they, um, get to know each other before they, you know... die?" he asked Daniel. He tried to focus on the living, ephemeral fog over his head, but he couldn't.

"The midges you mean? Maybe so," Daniel said, watching one that lighted on the back of his hand. He didn't slap it; he shook it off. "C'mon, let's go in the shed, away from the bugs."

An open padlock hung like a drunken spider on the shed's latch. Neither boy ever recalled seeing it locked, nor knew where the key might be hidden. Daniel unhooked the padlock's shackle and hung it on a crooked nail where a knot of old baling twine dangled.

The shed was dark and musty, cluttered with garden tools and Mason jars full of nails and screws, cobwebs, hoses, an old tire swing, dried out lumber and greasy car parts in ratty cigar boxes. The smell of tire rubber and rusty metal hung in the dark. Annie McLeod's pie tins, packed in two unmarked wooden apple crates, were shoved up on a rough-hewn pine shelf above them, beyond the mess, out of reach.

In the dark, Cassidy pulled a milk can from under the bench and sat on it. Daniel turned over some buckets and scrambled high enough to scoot one of the apple crates within his grasp. He reached in gingerly—black widows thrived in the dark spaces of West Canaan's backyard sheds and cellars—took out one blackened pan and climbed back down.

He handed it to Cassidy, who raised it to his face and breathed in. It smelled only of dust and old metal, like the rusting rail of the water tower, although perhaps he imagined that it was seasoned with a faint scent of an apple pie. Or was it pumpkin?

"Pecan was my favorite," Daniel said.

"What did I like, Danny?"

"Cherry, I think. You'd smear it all over your face and Mom would laugh at you. Then you would laugh back. Pretty soon, everybody was laughing."

"Was she pretty? Tell me again."

"Yeah, Cass, she was pretty, especially when she laughed. You were her baby and you made her laugh. Right before she... she would sing to us at night. Lullabies. You'd always fall asleep and I watched her kiss you, then she'd kiss me and smile. She was very pretty."

It was quiet, except for the crickets outside.

Daniel could not see, there in the shadows, that his brother was crying, but he knew. He stood in the doorway of the shed in the delicate light of a pale half-moon and a billion stars.

"The moon is out," he said after a while.

Cassidy still sat quietly in the darkened shed, trying to keep from sobbing out loud. The Black Thing inhaled some of Cassidy's guts, so he cinched his knees tighter to his chest, trying to squeeze it out of him.

Daniel sensed the pain rising in his brother.

"Cass, did you ever think that somebody else in a place far away is looking at the moon right now? Do you think the midges see the moon and try to fly toward it, like it was some big porch light? How far would they fly, do you think, before they turned back? Just think what we could see from there..."

It was a tender and intentional allusion. The Black Thing exhaled a little. Cassidy looked up to see his brother's silhouette in the shed's doorway.

"Tell me a Moon story, Danny, would you?"

The summer was waning, and school was only a month away. The night breeze, a constant on July evenings, was like warm silk. Lonely crickets marked time. The flapjack-sized leaves of the giant cottonwoods soughed, hushing the night. There wouldn't be many more stories.

Daniel sat down on the shed's dirt threshold, his back against the door jamb. Cassidy still could only see his shadow against the dim light outside.

Daniel had conceived the story of Pledger Moon in early summer, as the two of them lay naked in the sun on the bank of Crazy Woman Creek, where it slowed to a wide and flat flow on the outskirts of town. When the midday sun was high and the trout stopped biting, they stripped off their jeans and underwear and leapt into the cold, clear crick with a shrill war whoop.

The Crazy Woman, being snow-water from the very highest crags of the Big Horns, offered only fleeting succor: their bodies clenched in its iciness after just a few seconds. They scrambled up the loamy shore and fell into the sweet prairie grass, where they watched clouds in the big sky and shivered until the sun warmed them again.

That's where Pledger Moon was born.

Daniel cooked him up from the simmering sunlight and sweat and branch water on the banks of the Crazy Woman. He was a fantasy, to be sure, but he wasn't just another of Daniel's yarns, not really. Moon's story was still unfolding and it was mostly a mystery to his callow young brother, as Daniel intended it to be.

The way Daniel told it, Pledger Moon was a black man, born to slaves in Mississippi, wherever that might be. To be honest, as it often was when Daniel told his tales, Cassidy was never absolutely certain if it was a real place or an imaginary place like Camelot. He didn't know much about slaves and he'd never seen a black man in West Canaan, but either way, he accepted as plausible that much of the story, as he did any story Daniel told.

Daniel spun a yarn as beautiful as any he'd ever told. It had a history to it, a rhythm, as if it had been told before. Their father read books to them about other heroes from different times, about

Odysseus and Gawain and David, but Moon was real because he once lived where they lived now, and looked at the same sky.

Daniel delivered unto Moon this history: as a youth, he fled the plantation and never saw his family again. He sought his fortune in the new West, becoming a trapper in the Rockies, surviving on what he could take from the high mountain streams and meadows and sell to traders in the frontier forts.

Before the Civil War, Moon returned to the East and settled down as a farmer for a while in West Virginia, another faraway place with a melodious name Cassidy didn't fully comprehend.

When the rebellion started, Moon became a soldier the only way he could: he rode his roan mare to Kansas and signed up as an honest-to-God, blue-belly Yankee in a volunteer regiment, the only one that would take a black man when the war started. He dreamed of wading into a sea of gray and killing rebels all the way to Mississippi, where he'd rescue his family from slavery and be happy with them again. He got his chance to fight, all right, with other Negroes in the First Kansas. But when he finally got to Mississippi, when the war was all but finished, the old plantation where he had been reared was abandoned and the slave quarters burned. He never knew what happened to his mother and father and his brothers and sisters.

When the fighting stopped, Moon went West as a scout in the Twenty-fourth Infantry, the famed Buffalo Soldiers sent to clear the Great Plains of hostile Indians. When his time was done, he wandered through life and the frontier as a sometime cowboy, sometime prospector and mountain man, sometime freelance scout for the Indian fighters. And for a time, he worked on the rails as a gandy-dancer, driving spikes into the fertile soil on the way West across the prairies and mountains.

He learned from the Indian scouts how to find his directions in the heavens. Every night he found the North Star and fell asleep facing east, toward the rising sun and the home he missed so much. But as much as he yearned to return to West Virginia, to his farm beside Solitude Creek, Moon never did. Adventures distracted him and his place eluded him, at least in Daniel's stories.

There was only one place Cassidy's heart could imagine: West Canaan, Wyoming, where only three roads led out of town and one just ended. Where the Crazy Woman Creek spread wide and bent southward toward the Powder River. Where his mother had sung him lullabies.

At eight years old, Cassidy wasn't even entirely aware of his own existence, and certainly had not yet begun to consider that he, too, would leave this place someday.

And when Daniel told him, as they lay in the warm grass along the Crazy Woman that first day, that Moon fought in the Civil War on the side of the Yankees, Joltin' Joe DiMaggio and Babe Ruth skipped through his mind like flat rocks on the surface of an undisturbed pool. Cassidy knew about baseball and he knew his father had fought in a war, but he had no idea how they were entwined, except that fistfights occasionally erupted at the sandlot when the need arose, quite naturally, to settle whether a hit had drifted foul or a runner had beaten the tag. That was all he knew about baseball and war.

But young Cassidy understood this well enough: after whatever war the Yankees played in, Moon became a gandy-dancer—a poetic title bestowed upon the railroad spike-drivers whose clanging cadence of metal and muscle was nothing if not a graceful, rhythmic dance—who helped build the Northern Railroad across the Powder River, the great water in these parts.

Then Moon got lost, in a way, and he never got home.

Not yet anyway. The story wasn't over, and Cassidy hoped it would never end. He liked Moon very much and worried greatly that he'd never find solace, but he knew if the gandy-dancer ever truly found his way home, the story would end.

The journey was the story, the way Daniel told it, and Cassidy wanted it to last forever.

"Where is Moon now?" Cassidy asked from his dark corner of the tool shed.

"Not far."

"You mean he's almost home?"

"No, he's got a long way to go still, like you and me."

"Jeez, Danny..." Exasperated, Cassidy slumped against the workbench in a pout.

"Hey, you wanted the story. You want me to tell it or not?"

"Well what is it?" Cassidy demanded. "Is he close to home or is he far away?"

"Both."

"Aw, crud, Danny..." Cassidy sulked.

"Remember how it looked from the water tower that day? We saw things way off, but they didn't seem so far? Same thing. It's all how you look at it."

Cassidy rested his chin on his knees, waiting for the story to start.

Daniel was quiet for the longest time. He sat in the dark and watched the sky.

"You know how the railroad tracks go off toward the Big Horns?" Daniel asked.

"Is this the start of the story?" Cassidy piped up.

"Yeah. This is the start. But just think about the tracks for right now..."

"No, don't start it like that. C'mon, Danny, you know..."

"Oh, for Pete's sake," Daniel acquiesced, then inserted: "Once upon a time..."

Cassidy smiled in the dark, and closed his eyes.

"Satisfied? Great. Now, you know how the tracks head toward the mountains, then they bend off in the direction of the Flats?"

Cassidy murmured that he did. The Dead Swede Flats were the baddest badlands, a hardpan that couldn't keep ticks alive. He'd been on the edge of them, hunting with Daniel and his father, but there was no reason anyone would venture farther on foot. Even the wild animals avoided it. It was a dead place the old Indians said was haunted by the souls of rattlesnakes.

"Pledger Moon helped lay those tracks when he was a gandy-dancer, like ol' man Flaherty when he had two legs, only a long time before..."

"Why do they call him that—a gandy-dancer?" Cassidy interrupted, as he was prone to do when Daniel told his stories. "Did he dance?"

"Ol' man Flaherty says it's because they looked like they were dancing as they hammered the spikes into the railroad ties. They did it in a rhythm, like a drum beat. One would hit the spike, then the other... clang, clang, clang, clang," Daniel pounded one fist against the other. "And they used tools made by some guy named Gandy, I guess."

"Ol' man Flaherty's creepy, with that one leg. Twin Tommy said he saw the stump-bone poking out and..."

"Cass, you wanna hear this story or not? I'll just stop right here if you don't," Daniel scolded. "Dad'll be home soon anyway and he'll kick our butts for being out here. And there's no stump-bone."

"Yessir, there is. Twin Tommy said..." Cassidy caught himself, clapping his hand over his mouth. "Sorry. Keep going."

"Like I said, Moon helped lay those tracks. They built the railroad across the Black Hills and the Crazy Woman Crick, then down into the Flats. From there, they crossed the mountains and hooked up with the Pacific Northern on the other side.

"It was the end of summer, in September, and most of the men went back to their homes when the job was done. Except Moon. He knew the country and, for the extra pay they offered, he stayed on to help the first trains cross the Divide.

"Moon took work on a special passenger train that carried all the railroad bosses from Chicago. They were headed to San Francisco to celebrate the new railroad. At night, they smoked big, fat cigars and drank whiskey from crystal goblets and played poker for money, and during the day they shot buffalo and deer from the train for sport, like they didn't care that they were killing them for no reason. Folks with money don't care much about such things, I suppose.

"Anyway, on a night like this one, clear and dark, the train rumbled onto the Flats. Moon was playing rummy with the brakeman when all of a sudden the train slowed down and, in a few minutes, was at a dead stop.

"Moon and the brakeman leaped out of the caboose and ran toward the locomotive engine. The muckety-mucks from Chicago leaned out the windows of their fancy car, all confused and demanding to know why the train had stopped so suddenly.

"The engineer jumped down from the kitchen of his great engine and wiped the sweat from his frightened face with his grimy sleeve, then pointed to the west.

"There was a train headed straight for them. At the edge of the Flats, where the edge of the Earth met the sky, they could see its headlight, a tiny but bright light aimed right at them on the main track. It was like the point of a brilliant needle coming right at them.

"If the unknown engineer was asleep at the stick, he'd plow head-on into the boss-men's train, and that'd be the end of him and plenty more, to be sure.

"Of course, by now, the rich old boys from Chicago were praising the Lord and their engineer for his watchfulness over them. They left their fancy railroad cars and ran beside the tracks in the clear, black night to shake his hand and to clap him on the back and to give him cigars from the big cherrywood boxes they'd brought with them. They were laughing and crying at the same time, because he had rescued them from certain death. It was sort of like the tent meeting where everybody was hootin' and hollerin' amens and blubbering when they saved Bimbo's mom from the Devil."

Cassidy remembered the traveling evangelist who came to town last summer, but wasn't sure what his friend's mother had been saved from exactly, although she was known to have gentleman callers at odd hours of the night. Maybe she was saved from them. It didn't matter, though. Whatever questions he had could wait, for he didn't want to interrupt Daniel's story, so he settled back against the rough edge of the tool bench and listened.

"But there was still danger in the night. What if the other train never saw them parked there? There were no sidings for a hundred miles, Moon knew. There'd be a big, spectacular wreck if the engineer didn't see them in time, they were all sure of that. Anticipating a collision of biblical proportions, Moon began to wonder where he'd run in the dark.

"It was dead quiet on the Flats that night. Not even a cricket chirped while they all watched the headlight. All the big bosses and all their railroad men just stood in the dark, their eyes fixed on the bright headlight of an approaching night-train.

"Half an hour passed, but the light was no closer. Had the engineer seen them and stopped his train? Maybe he had, they all reckoned and they were mighty relieved.

"But Moon was a clever man and he began to think on it. From the nights he spent in the wilderness or on guard pickets listening for Texas marauders, he knew how men's minds played tricks in the dark. Soon enough, he peered up into the autumn night sky and with the width of his palm, measured down the heavens from the North Star to the western horizon.

"There in the blackness, safe from those who might see, he went to the big bosses' engineer, who leaned against his hot engine and smoked one of the rich men's fancy cigars, proud as a peacock. Moon nudged him away from the men and they walked around to the dark side of the locomotive. So the others wouldn't hear, Moon whispered something to him.

"The old fella cursed under his breath, then scuffed the dirt. He squinted his eyes again at the approaching headlight and, in a mighty huff, turned his back to the oncoming train, like he was taunting it to hit him and deliver him from his misery."

Daniel paused as he lay down on the grass outside the shed door. The silence was too much for Cassidy, who couldn't contain his curiosity. He fidgeted and stewed, then finally bubbled over.

"What? What did he say, Danny? What happens?" Cassidy clamored.

Daniel loved it when his tales reached such a dramatic point. He lifted his palm in a sort of sideways wave to the sky and measured the heavens by the width of a little boy's palm. There was so much to know, so much he didn't.

"Look at the moon, Cass. Think about those midges flying higher and higher toward it, fooled into thinking it was the brightest porch light they'd ever seen in their short lives."

"What did Moon say, Danny? Please tell me. *Please.*" Cassidy was annoyed. He begged.

Daniel teased him further.

"We're just like them, you know. You and me, and the midges. Just little specks kind of swarming around for a short time, aiming toward some light we don't really understand."

"I'm telling Dad you called me a bug."

"No, Cass, I said we're all like the midges."

"They're bugs. And I'm telling if you don't tell me what Moon said."

"Well, that eastbound train never came. And it was sometime after midnight when the boss-men's Chicago Special got up its steam again and headed west toward San Francisco Bay.

"They arrived safely in a few days, and Moon never saw the broken old engineer again. The old boy just left the train in the yard and disappeared. And none of those working hands ever spoke about the near-wreck on the Flats again, because the boss-men all agreed they'd never tell what happened and they swore all the railroaders to keep the secret. They even paid them all an extra one hundred dollars to keep quiet."

"About what? I hate it when you do this. I'm just a little kid. *About what?*" Cassidy fretted, crossing his arms impatiently.

"About how they stopped the train on a warm fall night in the middle of Wyoming...

"And about how the boss-men cried out of fear because their bones might have been scattered like so much kindling on the Dead Swede Flats that night, and..."

Cassidy covered his eyes. Daniel smiled in the dark and drew out the ending as long as he could:

"About how they might have been killed for sure if a night train named Venus had not stopped to let them pass."

DOORS
WEST CANAAN, JULY 23, 1995

Cassidy dreamed he couldn't speak.

Couldn't hear.

Couldn't smell.

Couldn't touch.

The ghosts came to his bedside and looked down on him. Archie and Annie, the little boy Daniel, Jack Lazarus, Darius, old Moses and the black dog... all of them. He tried to speak to them, but no words came out. He willed his hand to reach out to them, but it wouldn't move. Finally he stopped trying and just stared back at them, silently.

He awoke sweating, the damp sheets on his bed stripped back. The wind had come up the night before, so he closed the window. Now, with the sun warming the east-sloping roof, the enclosed upstairs room was stifling.

He squinted at his wristwatch. It was after ten in the morning.

Muffled voices burbled downstairs. Cassidy smelled freshly brewed coffee. He sat up in his bed and listened for a moment, but couldn't hear the words, just the intermittent humming sound of conversation.

A man's voice was among them.

While Cassidy fumbled around for his clothes, he heard someone bound up the stairs, then a rapid knock at his bedroom door. Tia, almost hyperventilating, stuck her head inside, surprising him. The night before, she'd left after he told his story to Daniel, and Cassidy stayed up past two 'o'clock listening to his brother's haunted dreaming.

"Come down quick," she panted.

"What are you doing here?"

Tia was earnest and impatient as she closed the door, leaving Cassidy to dress.

"I'll explain later. Just come downstairs, fast."

A trouser leg was inside out and he nearly ripped the seam in his haste to put his pants on. Half-asleep, sweating and disoriented, he yanked on one sock and a T-shirt. His heart raced. He searched anxiously around the bed for the other sock and glanced out the eave window that looked down on the front yard. A dusty blue car he didn't recognize was parked in the driveway.

Barefoot and unsettled, he hustled down the old stairs, steadying himself against the thick banister, trying to rub the sleep from his eyes. Had they finally come to take Daniel away from him?

Downstairs, a barrel-chested, red-haired man was sitting in the den, drinking coffee and talking to Tia and Miss Oneida. He stood up when he saw Cassidy standing at the bottom of the steps.

"Mr. McLeod?" the strange man asked. Despite the late July heat, he wore a dark blue sport coat and a button-down white Oxford shirt, open at the neck. His gray slacks were creased, his leather shoes spit shined. He looked like a government man.

Standing, Cassidy could see he was a big man with broad shoulders and the dignified bearing of an old soldier. He looked to be in his late sixties as he made a few steps toward Cassidy, his big right hand extended. In the other, he carried a smart, black leather briefcase.

He was, in the military vernacular Archie so often used to describe the old leathernecks who commanded his respect, "squared away." And Cassidy was sure that the government had come to take Daniel from him for some kind of security reason.

"I'm Tom Marrenton."

Marrenton.

The POW hunter who'd found Daniel and brought him home. The name jolted Cassidy, then relieved him. He'd always visualized Marrenton as a grizzled, wasted old man in worn fatigues, more a casualty of war than a knight errant.

Now, as if still trapped in his dream from the night before, Cassidy couldn't speak, even as he met the retired colonel's firm handshake. He felt the strength drain from his arm as he held it out to the man. Standing before him was his brother's savior, and he was suddenly aware that his mouth was gaping open. His eyes watered.

"You must be Daniel's brother, Cassidy. I apologize for not calling ahead, but you've been on my mind since I got back to the States with your brother. I trust he got home safely, but it has worried me greatly. Is he...?"

Cassidy shook off his daze.

"Yes, yes, he's fine," Cassidy said, looking around the den and hallway for Daniel. He wasn't there.

"He's eating in the kitchen," Tia spoke up. She was standing behind Marrenton. "He was already up when we came over to surprise you with breakfast, then Mr. Marrenton pulled into the driveway. That's when I came up to get you."

Marrenton looked squarely into Cassidy's eyes. His chiseled face was clean-shaven and virtuous. And his eyes were profoundly green.

"I'm very sorry to hear about your father. I didn't know he'd passed away, or I would never have sent Daniel here. I hope you understand."

"I do understand. Thank you, for everything you did. Really, I'm grateful. But it's been a very difficult time, even though my brother has come home. He's terribly ill and hasn't spoken, except a couple of Vietnamese words. It's like he's in his own world and we can't get through to him."

"That's one reason I came," Marrenton said. "Maybe I can help. Can I see him?"

Cassidy led Marrenton to the kitchen. Sitting at the tiny dining table, his hair matted by restless sleep and his face unshaven, Daniel looked up from a small plate of toast as they came through the swinging door. Whether he recognized Marrenton or was simply surprised to see a strange face, his dusky eyes became intent. Marrenton spoke first, raising his hand in an unfamiliar greeting as he stood just inside the doorway.

"*Chao anh.*"

Daniel stared at him. His face remained indifferent, but for the first time since he arrived in West Canaan, his focus was captured by someone. Cassidy recognized the change in Daniel's usual detachment.

"*Anh co nho toi khong?*" Marrenton said, then spoke in an aside to Cassidy. "I asked Daniel if he remembers me."

Daniel nodded slightly. Under his breath, almost in a whisper, he murmured: "*Thien than.*"

He made a fluttering motion with his hand, like an autumn leaf falling to Earth. "*Thien than.*"

"Those are the words he spoke when he got here and he did that motion, too," Cassidy said as Daniel spoke. "What does it mean?"

Marrenton paused, then translated, never breaking eye contact with Daniel.

"It means 'angel.' To Daniel, I must have been an angel who came down from the sky to take him away."

Daniel's face was empty, but he watched the colonel as he sat slowly in a chair across the narrow kitchen table from him. Daniel's eyes remained fixed on him.

"*Can you understand me? Can you speak?*" Marrenton asked him in Vietnamese, translating for Cassidy as soon as he spoke.

Daniel breathed deeply, but didn't answer. His eyes searched Marrenton's face. Cassidy waited.

"*Do you know where you are now?*" Marrenton asked, again in Vietnamese. And again, Daniel just watched him, wary but unemotional.

After a moment, Marrenton spoke once more, but to Cassidy.

"After what he's been through, it's common for a man to withdraw from a world that he sees as full of demons. He's not really sure where reality ends and fantasy begins. For some, the withdrawal is almost complete. For them, only death would be a more complete escape," he told Cassidy. "To make matters worse, after almost twenty-five years utterly immersed in the Vietnamese culture, he might not speak English anymore, or even understand it very well. That might be half of the problem here."

"What do you mean by 'what he's been through'?" Cassidy asked.

Marrenton flattened his broad hands on the dinette and splayed his fingers wide across the scarred tabletop. On his left hand, there was a simple gold wedding band; on the right, an ornate class ring from Annapolis. The skin on the back of his hands was tanned and tough, but fraught with spots and veins, and his knuckles were beginning to knot.

Marrenton collected his thoughts. After a moment, he looked up at Cassidy.

"Son, men do crazy things in war. I've been there when they did. We have these ideas that it's all about glory and courage, and it's all a bunch of crap. War is about insanity. Maybe that's why we have heroes, and damned few of them. They're the ones who never knew."

"What happened to my brother?"

"*War* happened to him. Daniel waded into it up to his neck and saw a horror he never imagined could happen. He couldn't get around it. Maybe he even understood it, and that's worse than never understanding."

"Ba Troi," Cassidy said, seeking answers without a question.

Marrenton pressed his thin lips together and nodded without looking up.

The words were barely spoken when Daniel whimpered like a frightened pup and looked at his own half-clenched fists, as if an answer was folded in them. He looked distressed by the mere mention of the long-dead village.

Sensing an opening in Daniel's consciousness, Marrenton quickly shifted his attention to him again.

"*Anh co nho Ba Troi khong?*" he asked.

Daniel's hands began to tremble. He rubbed them together, as if he were desperately trying to cleanse them. He grew more agitated, but made no sound.

"What happened at Ba Troi?" Cassidy pressed Marrenton, who watched Daniel intently. Ever since Daniel's funeral in 1971, when the photographer, Adams, said Daniel was fragged for his stories, Cassidy had believed Ba Troi to be the moment Daniel's fate was sealed forever.

"I just asked if he remembered Ba Troi. You know what the papers said. It was a night raid, nothing unusual for long sweeps. Those boys had been out for a week and they were tired. They probably were juiced up for the night operation and when you're juiced up, every shadow is Charlie. A kid was killed in a booby-trapped hootch and his buddies went nuts. It all went to Hell, fast. They wiped out the whole village, about 98 men, women and children. Those boys were consumed with hate and they wanted to punish those villagers for killing that boy. But it wasn't their fault. What the soldiers did... your brother saw everything."

"Yeah, but he wrote about it. His stories damn near won a Pulitzer Prize. He couldn't have been like this when he wrote it. Something else happened to him," Cassidy said.

"I said he *saw* everything, but he didn't *write* everything for the paper," the colonel said.

"What do you mean?"

Cassidy felt his stomach knot. He wasn't sure he wanted to know Marrenton's secret.

"Ba Troi was worse than any of us knew at the time. Many times worse. Far worse than the stories your brother wrote. Even by the miserable standards of an insane war, this was pure butchery. He saw it all. If you witnessed young girls being raped and old men's eyeballs being carved out of their skulls, would it change you?"

The thought repulsed Cassidy, pushing him back in his chair. His fingers traced through his beard as he tried to imagine the terrors Marrenton described, as if they were scenes in a movie, safely removed from reality.

"How do you know?"

Marrenton looked down at his hands on the table. After a long pause, he answered.

"I went back there."

"To Ba Troi? When? Why?"

"Two weeks ago. I wanted to see for myself. I found it on some old field maps. There's another village nearby and some of the farmers took me to where Ba Troi had been. It's an empty corner of the jungle now, overgrown with elephant grass. They won't plant anything there because they fear the ghosts of the dead would be disturbed, so the jungle is slowly reclaiming it. The villagers showed me where the soldiers threw the bodies, and they told me what Daniel's stories never said. It just confirmed what I already knew."

"What more was there to know?"

The tough old Marine colonel gathered himself. He swept his hand across the tabletop, clearing a spot where he could lay out years of anguish.

"I'm sorry, but this is tough stuff, son. I don't know how it will help, if at all, but you should know."

"Tell me."

Marrenton recounted in grisly detail how the American soldiers slaughtered the villagers at Ba Troi, terrorizing them in the end by setting fire to a baby girl and throwing her out of the chopper. He told Cassidy how they dumped the bodies in a shallow, muddy grave nearby and left Ba Troi to rot in history.

Cassidy still had questions.

"The baby... that wasn't in Daniel's stories. Why wouldn't he write about such a sick thing? How do you know this happened?" Cassidy asked. "And how did Daniel just disappear? Everybody thought he was dead."

Marrenton lifted his black briefcase from the floor to his lap. He leafed through some papers inside and pulled out a leather-bound journal. It was scuffed and stained, many years old.

"This is your brother's," he said, handing the weathered book to Cassidy. "It was among his belongings when we found him in Noi Chuoc Toi. After reading a few pages, I decided to keep it safe. At first, I wanted to let the world know about Ba Troi. I wanted to cleanse myself as if it were my own burden. But it isn't. It's Daniel's and I wanted to deliver it personally. That's why I came here. Nobody else knows about it. It contains the *real* story of Ba Troi. Maybe it explains why Daniel is like this now."

Cassidy riffled the pages and recognized Daniel's familiar, crabbed handwriting, the same he'd seen in his letters the day before. The dates on each page started in 1969, shortly after Daniel landed in-country, and ended in late 1971. Cassidy avoided reading further, for fear of upsetting his understanding of the painful journey Daniel surely described. He wanted to start at the beginning.

Marrenton spoke again to Daniel, while Cassidy absorbed the existence of his journal. The colonel leaned across the table and looked straight into Daniel's eyes. Daniel hadn't yet allowed anyone else so close, but he didn't recoil from Marrenton now.

The old soldier spoke softly, solemnly:

"*Su chet tha thu cho anh.*"

Cassidy looked up from the pages in his hand. Daniel was still watching Marrenton's lips. The silence was plaintive.

"What did you say to him?"

Marrenton stood to leave, looking somber. His eyes were misty and his jaws clenched as he gathered himself for his long journey back home. As quickly as he'd appeared in West Canaan, he'd be gone again.

"I told him, 'The dead forgive you.'"

RIVERS UNKNOWN
WEST CANAAN, JULY 24, 1995

Marrenton wouldn't stay.

After a breakfast of coffee and Miss Oneida's poppy seed muffins, he drove away from West Canaan before Cassidy thought to ask him the meaning of the strange words on the torn rice paper.

Cassidy spent the rest of that Sunday, the eve of Daniel's forty-ninth birthday, engrossed by the Vietnam journal. He read late into the night. The words resonated like a distant storm and filled him with the rage and fear Daniel captured there.

Daniel had written in it almost every day, sometimes several days at a time from notes he took in the field. The early entries, through the last half of 1969 and into 1970, were Daniel at his philosophical best, writing about war and courage and his observations of men under fire. His world was alive with the colors and smells of life co-existing with war, or in spite of it.

But after the summer of 1970, the entries grew darker, poisoned by the fear of dying and horrors he'd seen but never imagined.

On August 26, 1970, he wrote about a Vietnamese boy he'd befriended on the street outside his hotel. The child was eleven or twelve and would sell Daniel pieces of fruit for a few American coins.

"Nguyen was his name, but to him, I was just Joe, the name the Vietnamese gave all Americans in their country. I came to know this friendly little boy so well that I gave him a small Christmas gift at the end of 1969: a half-pound box of See's Candies left in my room by a foppish *London Times* reporter from Saigon, all soft-centers I never liked.

"I told him 'Merry Christmas' as he fingered the chocolates. He didn't know anything about our holiday, but he grinned like a child on Christmas morning. Careful not to disturb any of the candies, he replaced the lid and stuffed the box in a satchel he always wore slung across his shoulder. He then fetched a ripe mango and handed it to me, emulating the best he could the words he'd heard me say: "Numbah won, Joe... mai kissmaa.'

"Since then, on the mornings when I've been in Da Nang, Nguyen has waved to me when he saw me and, showing his mouthful of crooked teeth, he has greeted me with words out of time: 'Mai kissmaa, Joe.'

"This morning, before I'd gotten out of bed, the hotel was rocked by an explosion. Like all the other guests at the downtown hotel—most of them other correspondents, some military people, a few mysterious businessmen who traded on the misery of war, and some AID 'spooks'—I rushed down to the street from my room, in case the hotel was under attack. I'm not certain why the street might be safer, but if there was something to be seen, I knew I'd see it there.

"The front of the place opens onto a narrow cobbled street. At this time of morning, it's usually alive with people on their way to market or to their work in the small shops that cannot close merely because there's a war raging around them.

"But the street was clear, except for a few dazed passersby and wide-eyed hotel guests lingering in a small circle outside the front door.

"The blast had crumbled part of the building's facade near the front glass door, which was shattered around us. As I stepped across the debris toward the street, I saw Nguyen's demolished fruit stand, normally set up about fifteen paces south of the front door. In the pulp-spattered chaos of splintered crates and shredded canvas were parts of a half dozen American Marines' bodies, their bitter gore and guts flowing down the gutter with pieces of ripe fruit in bright red rivers. The sharp stink of sulfur and blood mixed with the sweet smell of oranges and mango. Two of the soldiers didn't have heads, and the others' naked torsoes were stripped completely by the blast, leaving only a few strands of cloth to soak up the blood that welled out of them. A passerby found one of their heads beneath a pedal cab parked across the street.

"Then I saw Nguyen's skinny little legs at the epicenter of the blast, connected only by a bloody fillet of meat at the groin. Nothing more.

"The boy had been a breathing bomb, waiting for his killing time. That time had come when these six American soldiers walked up to his fruit stand in the innocence of morning, their caution at low tide. He must have smiled as he pulled the pin on a satchel of grenades, and they would have smiled back, never knowing how they died.

"Death walks among us. Some days, he's even good company."

Marrenton was right about one thing: the journal's last entries contained more of the horror of Ba Troi than Daniel's newspaper stories ever revealed. And after he wrote his stories about the massacre, he never wrote again except in this book.

His style became sparer and sloppier than ever before. Sometimes single, seemingly unconnected words appeared in the midst of half-thoughts, which in turn were punctuated with unusual misspellings and incomplete thoughts. But they all described the taste of violent death in his mouth and the way the sound of buzzing flies droned in his head for weeks after the massacre. He wrote about the endless beating of helicopter rotors that haunted him back in Da Nang, pounding out the sound of the racing heart in his chest when "the birds" flew too near to his tiny room.

And they gave a name to Daniel's private horror as Daniel wrote down what happened to him in the aftermath of the raid. It was Mastema.

"What was dying? It didn't feel," Daniel wrote, describing the brutal encounter with the gunnery sergeant in a scrawl that drifted across the page, ending not with a period but a trail of ink that fell off the page. "Part of me was already dead. Greased. They would fill the hole with me, too, and cover me up. Make the hole all the way thru find what's inside"

The last entry was written two days before Daniel was reported killed in the Ashau Valley. It gave no clue to his real fate, but it had an air of haunting finality nonetheless, as if he knew he'd not write again.

"The crying dosn't end in nites. Mother is gone now. The fire might be burning still / its inside," he wrote.

The last words Daniel ever put on paper were printed letter by letter, no capital letters and no punctuation, by a shaking hand at the bottom of the final page:

"*angel fire*"

On the morning of Daniel's forty-ninth birthday, Cassidy sat across the silent breakfast table from his brother, trying to parse out his enigma. Daniel had confronted a horror that starved for his soul, but escaped. He'd done his job, writing about Ba Troi in his flawless prose for the *Chronicle*, then lost his mind. Cassidy could not begin to know why, and it hurt him.

"Happy birthday, Danny," Cassidy said, watching and waiting for any reaction. Daniel stopped chewing his toast and averted his unfocused, red-rimmed eyes, still caked with tiny flecks of sleep.

Cassidy searched his brother's face for clues the way he'd once searched his father's aging face for hope that life would never end.

What he saw was an old man. Daniel's tortured sleep left him with dark folds beneath his eyes, which flickered to every shifting light but reflected dim, perhaps dead, emotion. They were not the eyes of the little boy and young man he knew so long ago.

Daniel's subtle expressions were as impossible for Cassidy to translate as the frightened words he heard his brother mutter almost every night in a stranger's voice. Skinny arms protruded from the dirty T-shirt he slept in and his pale, blue-veined skin hung loose on forearms that once bore the golden bronze promise of summer. His fingers were skeletal and nervous, like bony talons clawing against one another. And he smelled like the doddering old folks they'd known in their childhood, who'd reeked of dust and old urine and were now long-dead.

He tried to elicit the reaction he'd seen the day before, with Marrenton.

"Ba Troi," he said deliberately to Daniel, but there was no response. Not even a flicker of memory appeared. Daniel kept his eyes turned away.

For the past three nights, Cassidy retold some of Daniel's old stories and longed for a sign of Daniel's recovery. By morning, when the hope of the previous night came unraveled, he was frustrated again. He wanted to believe Daniel had died and he was merely ministering to an ageless soul that had risen from his dead flesh in the Ashau Valley and wandered home. It would be easier if it were true, but even Cassidy's penchant for detouring around his pain couldn't make it so.

Daniel was alive.

And this was his forty-ninth birthday. Cassidy wanted it to be a celebration of survival, not part of a long goodbye, so Miss Oneida was baking the cake Daniel liked most as a child, dark chocolate, for a quiet party in the house where Daniel grew up. Tia's gift was a velvety velour shirt she found in a forgotten bin at the men's shop, hoping it wouldn't chafe Daniel as much as the stiff work shirts that still hadn't softened enough in Miss Oneida's ancient Maytag.

Cassidy had two gifts for his brother. The first was to be his father's gold-plated pocketwatch. Archie had been a practical man, so seldom wore it except on special occasions, such as christenings, weddings and funerals, when he felt obliged to scrub his inky hands and dress in his finest dark suit. Darius had given it to Archie when he married Annie, and the date of their wedding was engraved in it: January 5, 1942. Cassidy reasoned he would have wanted Daniel, his first-born son, to have it. Most of all, he'd want Daniel to receive it on such an occasion as his first birthday after rising from the dead.

The second gift was Daniel's to begin with.

Just before sunset, the party was to begin.

Cassidy and Tia carried the old wooden breakfast table out to the backyard and covered it with an embroidered cloth, festooned with bright daisies and grape hyacinths, from his mother's pantry. They positioned it carefully in the shadow of the big cottonwood. The branch where they once suspended a tire swing was thicker than a man's leg, and blocked the stinging rays and the dying heat of the setting sun across most of the lawn. Without rain, even the loving landscape of the old backyard was oppressive in midsummer.

The table's centerpiece was Miss Oneida's three-layer chocolate cake, dark and deep as night. It was dappled with blue rosettes and a chain of sugary ringlets around its rim of tawny frosting. Its looping sentiment was lovingly written in simple white icing: "Happy Birthday, Daniel."

A yellowjacket hovered around the cake as they set out plates and silverware for dinner. Miss Oneida carried a platter of home fries and fat, greasy burgers she'd cooked on the stove inside. She set it in the center of the table and shooed the wasp away with her apron.

"Let's eat before the yellowjackets come to carry it off," she said, leaning across the table to smoothe the cloth.

Cassidy tried as best he could to herd Daniel through the kitchen toward the backyard, but he'd go only as far as the screen door, held open for him by Tia. Daniel hadn't been outdoors since the Fourth of July parade, but it hadn't occurred to Cassidy that his brother's furies might have confined him more than his own fears for Daniel's safety. All along, he feared his brother might escape the old house and hurt himself. Now Daniel appeared to be a prisoner of his dread that something terrible waited for him out there.

Worse still, every time Cassidy was looking for some ray of hope to shine through the dark clouds that surrounded Daniel, his brother turned darker.

Cassidy nudged him gently, but Daniel wouldn't move farther. He jammed his hands against the door frame, bathed in the last waves of sunlight that washed across the threshold. He grunted as he stiffened his arms, and Cassidy stepped back.

"It's okay, Danny," he said, trying to calm his brother. "You can go outside and eat. Nothing will happen to you. Come sit with us."

But Daniel abruptly turned and slipped past him. He slung his elbow across Cassidy's chest and ran scared into some safe room deep inside the house.

Cassidy sagged against the kitchen wall, rubbing his temples. In a fit of frustration, he kicked a grocery sack of garbage on the floor, strewing potato peels, greasy butcher paper and empty soda cans across the kitchen floor. Cassidy stood there in the mess, his shoulders slumped, not knowing whether to cry or sleep. Neither was easy these days, though more and more, he wanted to do both.

Tia, who'd watched from the porch, tried to comfort him.

"He'll have something to eat later, when he's hungry," she said, still holding the open screen door. "I'm sorry. I know you wanted this to be a special day for him. Let him go for now."

Cassidy was rattled, rendered almost incoherent by his confusion and anger.

"I locked the doors because I thought he might sneak out. Goddammit. That was the last place he wanted to be. I just don't get this... this crap at all. Maybe he needs help, maybe I can't do this. Why won't he talk? Why can't I touch him? What the hell is this all about? I can't think anymore..."

Tia said nothing for a moment, then tried again to settle him. She came inside to pick up the trash, and stood next to him. She touched his shoulder while he contemplated his fear.

"I don't know and you don't know what's going on in Daniel's head. But it's not your fault, so don't let it spoil this day for you. We can all come inside for supper and it'll be just perfect again. Didn't your dad say 'you don't know what you don't know'? Come help us move everything back inside. You'll feel better."

Cassidy knew he wouldn't. Every day, he grew more bewildered by Daniel's illness. Nothing worked. It wasn't just a matter of inside or out, day or night, loud or soft anymore. Daniel's fears lurked deeper in him.

He sat down on a small wooden stool in the kitchen and took a small box with a thin red ribbon out of his shirt pocket. He turned it over and over in his hands, then tossed it onto the sideboard Miss Oneida had left open when she prepared the meal.

"He's missing time," Cassidy said softly, staring at the gift he intended for Daniel. "And I think he knows it."

After supper, Cassidy found Daniel in his upstairs bedroom. He was sitting on the floor at the end of the bed, huddled in a dark spot under the sloping eave. A sharp prong of sunset cut through the brittle yellow shades, slicing imperceptibly deeper into the opposite wall. The day was almost over.

Cassidy lay across the other bed, which he'd moved upstairs to be closer to Daniel at night. He leaned back against the wall, watching his brother.

They sat there in silence for a long time, maybe a half hour, before Cassidy spoke. One gift remained.

"I want to tell you a story, Danny," he said.

For a fleeting moment, Daniel looked at him through the bars at the foot of his old bed, as if he were imprisoned by his past. Cassidy wanted to see longing in his eyes, but saw nothing.

The story began.

"Once upon a time..."

THE TEN STONES
WEST CANAAN, AUGUST 7, 1957

With only a week until the County Fair, when all the ranchers' children were fleshing out their prize animals for the big show and the slaughter afterward, the town boys were cashing in soda-pop bottles, practicing precision penny-pitching with bottle caps on a checkerboard, and dreaming about fabulous victories on the carnival midway.

The best bottle hunting was along the county roads that led nowhere in particular, because that's where most people went. The barrow pits were full of tin beer cans, empty shells tossed by midnight plinkers and sign-shooters, and every kind of glass container known to the drunken drivers and drinking lovers of West Canaan, Wyoming. Except maybe milk bottles. They never found any of those.

With a yard of baling twine he stripped off his father's bundling spool in the garage, Daniel tied a milk crate to the rear fender of his brand-new Schwinn, a birthday gift from Archie just two weeks before. And Twin Tommy hung a mildewed canvas saddle bag across the handlebars of the bike he shared with his brother, Sammy, who couldn't ride along because he had broken his arm when he fell out of the neighborhood tree house three days before. The wire basket on Cassidy's balloon-tired, hand-me-down Black Phantom was large enough to hold almost a whole case of big-boy beer bottles. Two pieces of Dubl-Bubl were in each boy's pocket. The hunters were ready for the hunt.

On a good day, at a penny a bottle, they could clear a dollar down at Godbolt's Market, the only grocery in town. Godbolt's sold them back to bottlers at two cents apiece for a handsome profit, and the end of summer, when lawn jobs grew tiresome, was the high season for young bottle-hunting entrepreneurs.

The routine was inviolable. They'd stack their booty in empty crates beside the back door. There, Art Rexford, the peevish butcher whose hands shook with a palsy so severe that it seemed a miracle he had all his fingers, counted each one, checking scrupulously for cracks and chips that would preclude any profit. With a violently trembling hand, he'd scribble something illegible on the back of a scrap of butcher paper and send them up one of the four dark, narrow aisles to the cash register at the front of the store. The dark hardwood floor, mottled and bowed by water that seeped through the roof every spring, creaked under their feet.

Vera Gwynne, the clerk at Godbolt's Market who wore cat-eye glasses and a beehive hairdo piled at least a foot over her tiny face, would look at the chit, turn it sideways, pop her gum and redeem their bottles. If it was slow, which it almost never was on Wednesdays, she'd even count out their bounty in equal piles of pennies, nickels and dimes for them.

"It's like finding money on the ground," Daniel always said as they walked back through the store, which smelled of raw meat and the fresh-turned earth that was washed from new produce that came on a truck from Rapid City every day.

He understood the alchemy. The filthy treasure they scavenged from rural roadsides, alley trash bins and the beds of pickup trucks parked outside the Little Chief Diner turned magically into silver in their pockets. And bottle hunts relieved the boredom of August, when the roadsides reached the height of their clutter.

This day, the hunt started after breakfast, as they had planned. They met at Twin Tommy's yard and pedaled across Main Street, turning south on David Street, which eventually petered out into a rutted dirt road. After a couple miles, the road known simply as Mine Road ended at the town's coal pit, a grimy gash in the prairie that fed the boilers at the courthouse, the jail and the two school buildings every winter. The road was seldom maintained and even less traveled, except by teen-agers who'd been chased off Mount Pisgah by Flashlight Freddie on a Friday night, and the occasional poacher.

And to the irresolute folks of West Canaan, it went without saying that the search for riches always finished on a dead-end road. But for boys who dreamed of brighter lights and bigger midways, a dead-end road was the best place to start.

"Remember, just the soda bottles and the beer bottles," Daniel hollered instructions to his two companions as they rolled off the smooth pavement onto the dusty Mine Road. "They won't take anything else, and we couldn't carry all the booze bottles anyway. Leave 'em for target practice. And watch out for rattlesnakes."

They bicycled over the next hill, a few hundred yards farther, then laid their bikes in the dry, yellow grass and wild alfalfa that thrived in a thicket tangle beside the road. A meadowlark trilled, then watched silently from its perch on a telephone pole. The day was already blazing, not a single cloud marring the deep azure of Wyoming's late-summer sky. Cassidy felt a trickle of sweat dribble down his spine, tickling his tailbone as it slipped beneath the waistband of his trousers.

Daniel scouted the sagging barbed-wire fence line that separated the orderly and inviting alfalfa fields from the wild roadside. He found a long stick, a stout shard peeled from a decaying post, and he handed it to Cassidy.

"Don't reach down into the grass if you can't see what's down there," he lectured Cassidy. "Whack the brush with this when you walk, and if you see a rattler, holler out."

"You don't need to worry about that," Cassidy said, already searching the ground around him. "I'll holler plenty."

He hated snakes. All snakes. Almost as much as he hated bugs, which he knew to be, for the most part, innocuous nuisances. Not snakes. To him, they were death lurking on the path. He'd heard the stories the grown-ups told about sleepy housewives shuffling into their kitchens to find rattlers wrapped around the cold steel of their faucets. He'd even seen them on the trail into Outlaw Hole, on the banks of the creek, even in town. Once, he'd nearly stepped on a rattler coiled beside the push mower in his own backyard. That's when he knew snakes might be anywhere, and he took no wild place for granted.

The three of them scoured the barrow pit for two hours, thumping the weeds with their sticks, dodging squadrons of fat grasshoppers, emptying warm rainwater and flat beer from the bottles they picked up. Along the way, they also found an old cowboy boot, which they fitted upside-down on a fence post; a headless antelope carcass, bloated and festering with maggots; three hubcaps; a rusty tailpipe; and a pair of women's panties, trimmed in lace and draped daintily on a fully erect Canadian thistle. They hadn't been there long, maybe overnight.

"How could somebody lose a good pair of undershorts out here?" Cassidy asked, marveling at the smoothness of unsoiled silk between dirty little fingers that smelled like stale rotgut and ninety-proof pondwater. He sniffed the panties and wrinkled his nose.

"Yuck. Perfume."

"That's what you get for sniffing other people's underwear, you dork," Twin Tommy said, laughing. He wiped his hand across his sweaty white T-shirt before snatching them away from Cassidy.

"You're a dork yourself, you dork," Cassidy retorted, flustered.

They hung the panties on a strand of barbed wire for anyone who might be looking for them and resumed their hunt for bottles. By lunchtime, they'd found eighty-three pop and beer bottles on the west side of Mine Road alone.

"Let's take these down to Godbolt's now," Daniel said, finishing the count. "We'll come back after lunch, okay?"

They were hungry. They knew Miss Oneida was baking cookies for them when they left and Daniel's mouth watered just thinking about warm chocolate chip cookies dipped in cold milk. And they were all eager to have carnival money jingling in their pockets.

"Wait a sec. How many more 'til we got a dollar?" Cassidy asked.

Daniel had already figured it for himself, but right now he craved cookies more than money. He was hungry and hot.

"Seventeen. But we can come back after lunch. It'll be a cinch to get that many... but let's do it after lunch."

He walked to his bike, expecting the two smaller boys to follow close behind. They didn't.

"Seventeen ain't much. Let's just find them now and get a buck," Cassidy argued. "It's like finding money on the ground, right?"

"Yeah," Twin Tommy said. "Nobody ever got two bucks worth of bottles in one day. No way. Let's go for the record."

Exasperated and outvoted, Daniel rolled his eyes and lowered the kickstand on his overloaded bike. He backed away from it slowly, expecting it to topple, but it didn't, thankfully. They didn't redeem broken bottles at Godbolt's Market.

"Okay. Seventeen, then we stop," Daniel said. "That's a buck. But you guys get thirty cents each and I get forty for staying. Deal? Just seventeen and then we scram, right?"

Cassidy and Twin Tommy glanced at each other and quickly agreed. Daniel found and carried more of the bottles, so it was a fair deal. Thirty cents was a windfall for an eight-year-old anyway, good for one cotton candy and a whole two-bits' worth of nickel games. And the day wasn't done.

They crossed the road into the unexplored barrow pit on the east side. Cassidy waded into the tall grass and found three beer bottles right off. Rather than make another trip to his bike, he threw away his snake stick and lifted the front of his T-shirt to make a pouch for the muddy bottles.

"Got three here," he yelled.

Twin Tommy had jogged up the road, ahead of Cassidy, and Daniel beyond him another fifty yards. They called out every time they found another bottle.

"Four... five... seven," Twin Tommy yelled, bending so deep into the tall grass he disappeared completely. Wherever he moved in the grass, he kicked up a small dust storm of grasshoppers.

"Eight... nine," Daniel said, farther up. "Ten."

Cassidy shuffled along, parting the grass with his free hand and dodging the 'hoppers that ricocheted all around him in a frenzied buzz. They were all colors of green, their tender thoraxes sheathed in spiny armor. They clacked and whirred in eccentric arcs as they leapt out of his path.

A long one, bright green, clung to his shirt and he brushed it off, leaving a tiny brown stain of "tobacco" where it had perched.

"Eleven," he heard Twin Tommy yell somewhere up ahead, fully engulfed in the weeds.

Cassidy spied a clear soda bottle through the dense cover and bent to pick it up. A droning flurry of grasshoppers took flight past his ears and one smashed against his face like a hard-shelled, six-legged hailstone, startling him. Already in a half-crouch, he spun sideways and stumbled over a rusted-out muffler hidden by the grass and trash. He fell on his left shoulder, the same one he injured at the water tower almost two months before. His bottles scattered around him as he unconsciously muttered a cussword his father favored.

The stiff grass prickled. The grasshoppers had fled away from him, but the buzzing didn't stop as he lay there collecting his wits and brushing invisible insects away from his face and neck. His shoulder ached. The hum was different now, more sustained and sinister.

Cassidy turned toward the sound. Barely two feet from his sweaty face, shrouded in the trampled grass, a rattlesnake curled.

He couldn't make a sound. He stiffened grotesquely, his hands frozen across his belly. The diamondback's coils reflected gray-green in the surrounding foliage. Its tongue flickered wildly, tasting Cassidy's fright in the air.

"Twelve... thirteen," he heard Daniel shout far up the road.

Cassidy tried to inch away but the overgrown grass was like a wall behind him. He was lying on his hurt shoulder and pain pulsed through it every time he tried to rock slightly away from the rattlesnake. He wouldn't be able to use his left arm to push himself to safety. He knew any sudden move or sound might cause the snake to strike.

"Fourteen," Twin Tommy hollered.

The snake rattled at him more angrily.

Inside, Cassidy was erupting with fear. It flowed through him like hot springs. He began to whimper, but he didn't move. Until Daniel and Twin Tommy had found the last bottle, the seventeenth, he knew they wouldn't even miss him.

"Fifteen," somebody said. Cassidy couldn't make out the voice. It seemed to be moving away from him. "Two more to go."

Time stood still. The rattlesnake coiled tighter. Its malignant eyes were fixed on Cassidy. He tried to breathe but his throat and chest were too tight. If the rattler struck, he knew it would hit him in the face. But if he waited until he saw the snake move, it would be too late to try to deflect the bite with his hand.

"Sixteen," Daniel shouted. He sounded miles away, too far to hear Cassidy's heart throbbing, muffled by the heat and the grass. "Who's gonna get the last one? Hey, Cass, you gonna find it? You only got three so far."

Cassidy wanted to scream, but couldn't. He dared not take his eyes off the rattlesnake, which dared not take its eyes off of him. Every muscle was taut. The adrenaline surged through him and he began to tremble.

He felt something move on him. Some living thing crawled on his cheek. A grasshopper. He prayed that it wouldn't jump. The snake would strike at any movement.

"Seventeen," Twin Tommy hooted. "Wahoooo! Let's get out of here and eat! Hey, Cass, I got it. Let's go!"

The rattler buzzed manically, its rhythm desperate and menacing. Cassidy was close enough to count its rattles, but couldn't. He waited to hear their footsteps on the road. *Where were they?*

The grasshopper on his cheek prowled closer to his eye. He felt its prickly legs clinging to his face, pinching his skin to keep its clawhold.

The rattler feigned a strike, thrusting its head toward Cassidy as if to warn him one last time. He jerked his hand instinctively toward his face and closed his eyes, waiting. The bite never came, but the buzzing rattle resumed.

Cassidy heard voices on the road. They were near, maybe only fifteen or twenty yards from where he lay. He wanted to shout for help. He dismissed the idea of tossing one of the bottles that lay near his hand, or slowly raising his foot above the foliage. Too much movement.

More than anything right now, he dreaded dying in the weeds along Mine Road, and was paralyzed by his fear and by the pain in his shoulder.

Daniel called to him. His voice was angry, impatient.

"Cass, where are you? Cass, quit farting around. We're getting hungry here. We're leaving without you if you don't quit pouting and come out."

The grasshopper crawled closer to his eye. If it cleared the rise of his cheek and peered down into his eyeball, he knew he'd panic. Yet, if it jumped, he feared it might spook the snake into striking. *Where was Daniel?*

He whimpered softly. A thin strand of spit hung from the corner of his mouth.

Twin Tommy yelled for him again, but his voice was farther now. *"I'm here! I'm here!"* Cassidy wanted to scream, but couldn't. His throat tightened, squeezing out a tiny, desperate sob.

The snake raised its head to strike. Cassidy's neck began to ache. He closed his eyes and waited to feel the rattler's cold fangs slice into his face.

The air whirred. A hollow clang shook Cassidy and his hands instinctively flew to his face. Another clang sounded. Then another.

"Move!" Daniel yelled from above him. Cassidy tried to roll away through the thick hedge of weeds, but could only turn his back to the snake.

Daniel flailed at the rattlesnake with the rusty tailpipe. Before the wounded snake could slither away, he pinned its head to the ground with one end of the pipe and fished his pocketknife out of his jeans.

The snake writhed as he bent down close. In one clean slice, Daniel lopped off the rattler's head, even as its fat, cold-blooded body coiled around his arm, sounding its death rattle. The jaws on its disembodied head flexed, still pinned by the tailpipe. Daniel stabbed his knife through it, staking it to the ground.

"Cass, are you okay?" he said urgently, kneeling beside his brother and looking for bite marks. "Did it bite you? Cass?"

Cassidy turned over slowly, holding his left shoulder. He was startled to see the snake flexing around Daniel's arm, its buzz fading. Twin Tommy stood quietly behind Daniel, his face pale.

"It's all right," Daniel reassured Cassidy, still looking for wounds on his brother's body. "It's dead. The head's cut off. It can't hurt you now. Are you okay?"

Cassidy just nodded, then began to cry. His tears dripped in dirty streaks down his cheeks. Daniel tenderly stroked his hair. His own heart was racing.

"Help me bury the head and we'll go," he said, helping Cassidy to his feet.

Twin Tommy found a shot-up Folger's can and dug a shallow hole in a clear patch of dirt. With the rattlesnake's head still skewered on his pocketknife, Daniel examined its pink maw and deadly fangs before scraping it off into the hole. He kicked the dirt back into it and the three boys spit on the grave.

"What took you so long?" Cassidy asked as he collected his three spilled bottles from the spot where he fell. Daniel stood on the edge of the road, counting the buttons on the snake's rattle. There were ten.

"What do you mean?" Daniel asked.

"Seventeen. That last bottle. It took you too long to find it. I had to lay there 'til you did."

Daniel laughed a little and shook his head. The snake's muscles still rippled, but he stepped on its bloody neck and stretched its twisted corpse up from the ground to his chest. The rattler had been more than three feet long.

"Seems to me we found that bottle just in time," he said, admiring his diamondback. "Sort of like the Holy Grail. It was where it was always supposed to be, I guess. The time was right for it to be found. Not sooner and not later."

Without talking anymore, they mounted their bikes and churned over the hot road back toward town, one hundred bottles and three hearts clamoring until they reached the smooth asphalt. They stood on the pedals to balance the extra weight better.

Down at Godbolt's, Vera popped her gum and cashed them out. They took the afternoon off to nap in the shade of the cottonwoods beside the Pond.

No matter. Nobody ever found two hundred bottles in one day anyway, and nobody ever would.

That night, a warm breeze billowed the curtains in Daniel's upstairs bedroom. Cassidy lay in his brother's bed, awake long after midnight, just watching the delicate drapes dance in the full moonlight. He smelled rain in the air and heard distant thunder, but it was too far to promise any respite from the dog-day mugginess.

The ten-button rattle lay on the nightstand, a kind of talisman against whatever other evils lurked in their small world. Daniel had skinned the snake and pegged its slimy hide to a long plank in the garage. He poured table salt on it to prevent rot.

It was press night at the *Republican-Rustler*, when they flew the presses for the weekly edition. Archie still wasn't home.

"It's hot," Daniel said, kicking back the sheet.

Cassidy said nothing.

Daniel propped himself up on one elbow, facing the back of his brother's head. He tickled his fingers lightly on Cassidy's bare back.

"That snake was more afraid of you than you were of him."

Cassidy huffed.

"Yeah, sure. He wasn't rattling at me, he was just shaking from fright. He thought I was gonna bite him."

"Well, he didn't bite you. He could have, but he didn't."

The Black Thing stirred in Cassidy's belly.

"If he bit me, would I die?"

"Aw, Cass. He didn't bite you, so..."

"I mean it. Would I have died if he bit me?"

Daniel was quiet for a long moment before he spoke.

"Maybe. But he didn't."

Cassidy heard the enormous cottonwood leaves rustling in the trees outside the window. The curtains swelled, then poured in a graceful wave to the wall, casting lacy shadows across the wall.

"If I went to Heaven, how would I know her?" he asked.

"Who?"

"Mom. How would I recognize her?"

"You'd know."

"But how?"

"You'd just know. You were born knowing and you'll die knowing. That's the way it is."

"I don't remember her." Cassidy began to cry. "What she looks like, I mean. I'm afraid I won't know her. What if I died today and I went to Heaven and I didn't know her?"

Daniel rolled out of bed and crept through the dark room. Cassidy heard him go down the creaky stairs, then return. He turned on a bedside lamp and handed Cassidy a photograph in a silver frame. It was a picture of their mother, taken not long before she discovered the cancer that killed her.

Cassidy wiped his eyes and runny nose, and sat on the edge of the bed looking at her.

"She'll look just like that," Daniel told him. "The way you always knew her. But it won't matter. When the day comes a long, long time from now, you'll just know. We'll be old men, you and me. She'll be proud of you and you'll know her face when she smiles."

"Maybe she won't recognize *us*," Cassidy fretted.

"Don't worry. She'll know."

Cassidy put his mother's picture on the nightstand where he could see it, and Daniel turned off the light. Their mother watched over them in the moonlight, smiling.

"Tell me a story, will you?" Cassidy said.

"It's late. We should sleep. Dad will be mad if he gets home and we're still up."

"No, please. Just a short story? About Pledger Moon? Then we'll sleep."

Daniel turned his pillow to its cool side and lay back on the damp sheet. He stared at the low ceiling and folded his forearm across his mouth, tasting a sheen of salty sweat with his tongue. The sinuous curtains whispered to him.

"A long time ago..." he began.

"Danny, not that. You know," Cassidy said.

"Okay, okay," Daniel said, feigning exasperation. In fact, he enjoyed his innocent joke every time. "*Once upon a time...* jeez, now let me tell the dang story."

Cassidy smiled in the dark and cozied down into his pillow.

"Once upon a time, long before the Old Ones settled in this place, and far from the safety of the railroad towns, Pledger Moon wandered. Sometimes, he turned toward his home, the West Virginia farm he left behind when he went off to the Civil War. It had been almost fifteen years since he slept in his bed, listening to the song of Solitude Creek.

"From the day he left his farm and joined up with the Yankees, he'd been sickened by the horrors of war, followed the setting sun toward the great Western sea, fought with white men against red men, and worked the rails as a gandy-dancer to draw his pay. And he grew old, nigh on fifty near as he could reckon, and he yearned to settle down. But he never went home."

"Not never?" Cassidy interrupted, turning his head toward the sound of his brother's voice beside him.

"Not so far anyway," Daniel answered.

"So where is he now in this story? Is he in Wyoming? Is he a cowboy or a gandy-dancer still?"

"If you'd shut up, I'd be able to tell the story."

"Well, you're not telling it," Cassidy fumed. "Hurry up and get to the good part."

"It was the winter of '78. Moon had grown too old for the hard work on the railroad, so he became a buffalo hunter. The new railroad trains made it easy to get buffalo hides to market and everybody in the East wanted buffalo robes, so sharp-shooting hunters were paid well. Moon went north, to the grassy plains of the Powder River Basin, to kill as many buffalo as he could.

"He camped alone on the Crazy Woman Crick and hunted the buffalo until he had enough of their hides to haul to the railhead in Laramie. Then he'd return and hunt some more.

"In the winter of that year, on a lonely night when the moon was full and icy cold overhead, Moon climbed a hill above the crick and looked out across the drifted prairie. The snow glowed under the moonlight, sparkling like a great ocean in front of him, all around him, spilling off the edge of the Earth somewhere far away. He felt like he was on an island, all alone.

"Then, far off, he saw a small, dark figure walking across the sea of snow. It came toward him, but it wasn't a man and it wasn't a buffalo, or any other animal. As it came closer, he could see it was a young Cheyenne woman, wrapped in a buffalo robe.

"Moon lay down in the snow and watched as the woman walked ever closer. He held his Sharps buffalo gun close to him, and as the woman came closer, Moon cocked its hammer. Maybe the woman didn't see Moon, or maybe she did, but when she came within a stone's throw, she stopped.

"There in the bright moonlight, the woman shed her buffalo robe and spread it out on the snow. She was completely naked beneath it, except for a medicine bag around her waist. She was the most beautiful woman Moon had ever laid eyes on and he felt his heart pounding. He watched as she reached into her bag and took something out, which she then laid on the robe."

"What was it? Was it like a sacrifice or something?" Cassidy asked. He loved Daniel's little mysteries, but they churned in him until he knew the answers.

"Moon couldn't see what it was. The woman turned and walked back into the distance, against the far mountains where the moonlight faded to gray. Then she disappeared."

"But what was it?" Cassidy demanded.

Daniel continued.

"Moon waited until morning, then went out to where the woman had laid her buffalo robe. On it was a stone. A smooth, black stone unlike any other Moon had seen. It was the size of a peach pit and perfectly round. Its surface was so luminous, he could look deep inside of it, but not through it."

"Was it like the obsidian we found at the Buttes? 'Cept maybe like a marble?" Cassidy asked, peeking through a circle he made with his index finger and thumb, pressing for more answers. "That's black and clear and..."

"Cass, you wanted me to tell the doggone story, didn't you?"

"Go ahead."

"Anyway, Moon followed the woman's footprints in the fresh snow until they just vanished. He took the buffalo robe and the black stone back to his sod house by the crick and thought about it no more.

"But a month later, on the morning after the next full moon, again Moon found a buffalo robe and on it, a perfectly round black stone. And again, a woman's footprints led away toward the mountains, then simply disappeared. Moon decided he would hide and watch for the woman on the next full moon.

"And he saw the woman again. Once more, the woman disrobed and left one of the mysterious stones.

"Six more moons, six more stones. Through the spring and early summer, when the snow gave way to a sea of buffalo grass, the woman came and left her latest gift. Moon kept all the stones in an empty flour tin, and although he often studied them and believed they must have been intended for him, he could not know their meaning.

"In August, on a night like this when the moon was full again and the air was hot, the woman came. As always, she laid her robe on the ground, took something from her medicine bag and laid it on top of the robe. Then she walked away. But this time, after a short distance, she turned back toward Moon and raised her hand. It seemed the woman knew he was there, so Moon waved back. The woman smiled and walked into the darkness.

"Ten stones now, and Moon was no closer to understanding this mystery than that first winter night. He decided he would speak to her when she came again."

Daniel turned his pillow over again and settled into it. He glanced at the clock on the table and saw it was nearly one o'clock.

Despite the lateness, hours past his bedtime, Cassidy waited anxiously for the story to resume, wide awake.

"But after that, the woman never came again. The hunter's moon passed with no sign of her. Moon looked for her until the first snow, then knew in his heart the woman would never return. Had she been a real woman or a ghost? Where did she come from and where did she go? And what did these ten stones mean? Moon didn't know, and he was sad.

"Then in a dream, the woman came to Moon, just as she had before. She walked across an ocean of snow bathed in bright moonlight, spread her buffalo robe out and sat upon it, completely naked. Her smooth, brown skin seemed to soak up the light and reflect it through her eyes. Then she spoke to Moon in his dream.

"'These stones are memories,' she said. 'They must never be thrown into the water or a memory will be lost. Each one is a memory you must keep forever.'

"'But what memories?' Moon asked her.

"'The first is your mother,' the Indian woman said in his dream, then counting each stone but the last. 'The next stones are your father, your brothers and sisters, your childhood, your home, your past journeys, your dreams, your pain, and your sins.'

"'And the tenth stone? What is it for?' Moon asked her."

Daniel paused to see if Cassidy was still listening. He was.

"What? Come on, what was it?" Cassidy asked, sitting bolt upright in bed and facing Daniel.

"'The tenth stone,' the dream woman said, 'is for memories you have yet to know. It is for the journey still ahead. That stone is the most valuable.'

"Then the Cheyenne woman rose from the robe and walked toward the mountains, never turning back once, until she faded into the darkness at the edge of the moonlight."

Cassidy waited for more, but there was no more.

"That's it? She just walks away? No smooching or anything? He has ten neato rocks and he can't even throw 'em in the crick? That's not even a real ending."

Through the open window, Daniel heard Archie's heavy footsteps on the front porch. The front screen door squeaked on cue and a light came on somewhere downstairs, shining up through the stairwell.

"Dad's home," he whispered. "Better fake it if he comes up."

Archie padded up the stairs to Daniel's room, certain after finding Cassidy's bed downstairs empty where they'd be. He stood in the doorway for a moment, then came to their bedside. They both pretended to be asleep, but they smelled cigar smoke, sweat and lead fumes as he bent to kiss them both. Cassidy wrinkled his nose.

"Good night, boys," he said softly.

"Good night, Dad," they said at the same time.

FAREWELL APHELION
WEST CANAAN, JULY 26, 1995

Calvun LaForge, the local mechanic and sometime lounge singer down at the Elks Club despite his imperfections, wiped his hands on a greasy shop rag and squirted a fat brown gob of tobacco spit on the McLeods' gravel driveway.

"She's gonna need some fresh hoses, a new carburetor and battery, maybe some gaskets and filters," Calvun said. "I seen an old Mustang once that sat in a shed for twenty years and her transmission bearings was flatter'n roadkill from jes' settin' there in gear for so long. She run purdy damn rough, but she run."

Calvun grew up fixing things. He was a few years younger than Cassidy, born with only half of his left foot. His disability made him the last choice when sandlot teams were being chosen, and he soon preferred to sit on the sidelines rather than suffer the ignominy of always being the least and the last. But while he sat there in the grass watching, he repaired the other boys' mitts, their bikes or fishing reels. He took his pay in ice cream or soda pop, and before any of the rest of them, he found his place in the world. In that, he was chosen first.

Not long after he realized his own mechanical intuition, his mother ran out on him and his father, who operated the town's only filling station. It seems his dad hadn't risen sufficiently high on the town's social ladder for his mother's worldly airs, and Calvun always believed she was secretly ashamed of his handicap anyway. When she left, the only person in West Canaan chagrined by Calvun's shortcoming was gone. He blossomed.

Calvun started work at his father's gas station while he was still in middle school, pumping gas and breathing life into pump motors and lawn mowers that sat idle all winter. He never left. In time, he came to know better than anyone what made machines run and what made them stop running. Before he graduated from high school, he was known as the best mechanic in three counties. In time, LaForge and Son became the only garage most folks would take their cars and, more importantly, their tractors.

Calvun either knew machines better than people or people better than machines, for he never married. He just fixed cars—and sang Elvis songs when the spirit moved him, usually on Saturday nights at the Elks. That's what he was good at. Cars anyway.

He was under one, a cherry-red '68 Stingray, when Cassidy found him down at the garage the day before and asked him to come over to check out his father's antique half-ton Ford, Old '46. The faded Greenfield green pickup hadn't been out of Archie's garage in at least twenty-three years, probably longer. Even in its day, the temperamental V-8 was only used for longer journeys into the countryside, not around town. Archie usually walked, for no place in West Canaan was too far from anywhere else.

There it sat, its rust-flecked hubs settled in the dirt as if, in time, it might be swallowed up by the earth entirely. A thousand generations of spiders had festooned its toothy grille in cobwebs, between two beady headlights. Enormous side-view mirrors jutted from its chassis, and low-slung running boards rested on the hard ground of the garage floor. It looked like a tubby, earthbound bug. Indeed, to Cassidy, the green heap looked like a moribund steel grasshopper too fat to hop, too stubborn to die.

Calvun leaned on his good foot, mauling his chew. He lay across the front fender, wiping a pappy crust of congealed oil and dust from the engine block.

"What about the oil?" Cassidy asked.

"Ohl was here before us and it'll be here after us." Calvun grinned, exposing his crooked brown teeth and a mossy glob of chaw in his cheek. A wet fleck of snoose clung to his bottom lip. "Ohl don't git old."

Cassidy casually walked around the faded rear bumper and knelt beside the back rear wheel well. He rubbed a layer of dust off the cracked, rotten rubber of the long-flat tire.

"This was the first new vehicle my dad ever owned. Bought it after the war, when my mom was still pregnant with Daniel," Cassidy said, speaking as much to himself as to his mechanic. "Eleven hundred bucks. Can you believe it? That was a big commitment in those days and he hated to drive it around for fear he'd use it up. He wasn't real mechanical."

"My daddy says if it has tits or tires, someday it's gonna give you trouble," Calvun said.

"We'll damn sure need tires," Cassidy said.

Calvun poked his head around the front fender, a goofy grin on his face. His ball cap, advertising Elephant Brand manure, was cockeyed on his greasy blond head.

"I got some old tires down at the shop. The old boys 'round these parts like to put 'em on horse trailers, so we keep a few around," Calvun said, spluttering another dollop of juice on the ground between his feet.

"So you think you can get it running again?" Cassidy asked, careful not to cross Calvun's line of fire.

"She's a beaut. Ain't got but forty-three thousand miles on 'er. Aluminum pistons. Holley carb. Still might run like, oh I'd say, about a hunnerd horses at thirty-eight-hunnerd ar-pee-ems. Hardly a growed-up woman yet. Hell yeah, we can git 'er runnin' again, though I don't s'pose either one of us can think of a good reason to disturb the dead."

Calvun guffawed at his own joke, then nearly choked himself by sucking down a chunk of chaw. He coughed violently.

"Are you okay?" Cassidy asked.

Calvun waved him off, speaking—finally—in a half-throttled stage whisper. His face was chokecherry red.

"Hell, that happens all the time, 'specially when there ain't no rain and a feller don't like to spit so much. Why don't we jes' git us some fuel and find out what this gal's made of?" he asked, wiping some brown spittle from the corner of his mouth with his sleeve.

Calvun hobbled down the driveway to the truck parked in the shade of the house, "LaForge and Son" hand-painted on the passenger door. He hacked a couple more times, spit on the dusty drive and came back with a plastic milk jug full of gasoline. Cassidy wrestled with the gas cap, which was cemented in place by time and a corroded gasket.

Ever helpful, Calvun dug a can of WD-40 and a hammer from the mammoth tool box in the back of his truck, but Cassidy finally persuaded the gas cap to come peacefully. They dumped the gas in the dry tank, pumped some into the leaky carburetor and turned the ignition over. The recalcitrant engine shooed them away with a grumble. Somewhere in its bowels, metal grated against metal, and a noxious belch of bluish smoke came out.

"She's got some life in 'er!" Calvun hollered. "Give 'er another little kiss."

Cassidy turned the key again and tapped the balky accelerator. The old Ford's engine wheezed and sputtered and smoked.

"Keep the pedal on the floor!" Calvun yelled from under the hood. Cassidy could only see the greasy back pockets of his jeans, barely clinging to his skinny ass as he hung over the front fender, rapidly fingering hoses and wires and fittings as if he were tuning a long-lost Stradivarius.

Suddenly, the engine bellowed to life. Calvun emerged from a pungent haze with a broad, brown smile and pumped his greasy thumb in the air. The truck backfired, but the engine kept running like low thunder.

"Hoooo-boy. She don't smell too purdy now, but she'll clean up real nice," he said. "Let 'er run a few minutes and I'll see where the ol' gal leaks. I'll go down't the shop and git all the parts and fix 'er up right here in the garage this afternoon. We'll git some clean water in her radiator, check 'er belts and change the ohl. Shouldn't go more than four hunnerd, countin' labor. Sound like a deal to ya?"

"Sounds damn cheap to me," Cassidy said, pleased. The cost of reanimating a memory, he thought, is always worth it. They shook on it through the open window.

As he got out of the truck Cassidy caught a glimpse of something moving on the passenger-side floorboard. A mouse had dropped from under the dashboard and scurried beneath the seat. He opened the glove box and found an oily nest of shredded paper and a crusty leather glove gnawed down to the knuckle of each finger.

"Oh, yeah, I shoulda told ya," Calvun said. "There's gonna be mice in them seats. I'll bring my cat back this afternoon. He don't charge by the hour."

Tia and Miss Oneida came for supper. Daniel had stayed in the upstairs bedroom since morning, and hadn't eaten at all. So after the dishes were done, Cassidy took a portable radio and went out to the driveway to wash Old '46.

Calvun had ripped out decrepit hoses, rusty brackets and rotten gaskets, strewing parts and vulgarity up and down the gravel driveway. When he was done, he filled the radiator from the garden hose, fetched his overfed cat from the cab and started it up so quickly it might have just rolled off the assembly line. He drove the old truck down to his garage for some last adjustments, filled it up with gas and brought it home. He left the keys and his bill for three hundred forty-eight dollars on the front seat, now vermin-free. Across the bottom, in an almost childish scrawl, he wrote: *"Take good care of her. She's a grand old lady who must love you a lot. If you ever want a good home for her, call me first. Cal."*

Cassidy wanted to make her shine. He backed the truck out of the garage and sprayed years of dust off with the hose. Tia brought two sponges and a bucket of soapy water, and they washed her from bumper to bumper, then waxed her to a brilliant shine that reflected the setting sun.

"She's really beautiful, a classic," Tia said. "Will you take me for a spin?"

"It's going to be night soon. You sure you want to tempt fate by taking her out in the dark?"

"What good is a beautiful truck if you can't tempt fate in it?"

Cassidy laughed. He dumped the bucket of dirty water on the strip of knapweeds that grew beside the driveway, then told Miss Oneida he and Tia were going for a drive.

"You kids go on and have a little time to your own selves. We'll be just fine here, me and Daniel," she said, then hustled Cassidy out the door. He grabbed the radio from the back porch and opened the driver's door for Tia. Calvun had even oiled the hinge so it swung open like new.

"Where are we going, sir? I should know your intentions." Tia asked, smiling.

"Ice cream first. Then maybe up Mount Pisgah where all the kids make out. No dinner, no movie. It'll be like a real proper date in West Canaan, Wyoming," he kidded her.

Cassidy adjusted his pan-sized sideview mirror and backed out of the driveway onto Ithaca Street. He horsed the steering wheel hard to the right and ground the gears before the Old '46 lurched forward and died, farting off a backfire in protest. Sheepishly, Cassidy restarted it and, showing more respect for the pigheaded clutch, coaxed the truck down the street.

"This is why God made power steering," he said.

Already, dusk had filled the spaces between the old cottonwoods and the street fell gray in the twilight. The Whistle blew as they passed the old sandlot, and the children began moving toward home.

On a Wednesday night, even in the hottest days of the driest summer, the Dairy Freez was empty. Cassidy swung the lumbering Ford into a space and pushed the button on the speaker. A woman's voice crackled back and asked for his order.

"Two chocolate dips, that'll be all, thanks," he said loudly through the car window toward the tinny speaker hanging on a bent post.

"Welcome home, Cass," the voice came back.

Cassidy pondered the vaguely familiar sound of her words for a moment.

"Robbie? Jesus Christ, I don't believe it. You're still here," he said, genuinely surprised.

"I'm always here. I own the place now. Near forty years I been here," the voice in the little box hummed. "Lots of things change, but folks always want ice cream."

"How'd you know it was me?"

"It's Wednesday, ain't it?" she said. "You're late."

"So it is," he said, resting his chin in the crook of his arm on the driver's window. "Are you still pretty as ever?"

"If you don't count old and dried up, sure I am," the voice said. "I heard you were back and when I saw your dad's old truck pull into the lot, I sort of suspicioned it was you."

"Ah, you cheated," Cassidy teased. Tia, who saw the familiarities of a small town as utterly charming, couldn't contain her amusement. She laughed quietly beside him at the small world she'd entered.

"No, Cass," Robbie said. "It's Wednesday, after all."

A teen-age girl with braces and bright red lipstick delivered two chocolate-dipped cones in a flimsy cardboard tray. Her young, dark eyes, Cassidy could see under the fluorescent glow of the drive-in awning, were as deep as a memory and inviting as a long-ago summer afternoon. Beads of sweat glistened on her forehead.

"Grandma says it's just fifty cents," she said.

It was Wednesday, after all.

Mount Pisgah rose above the streetlights, and on its far side, opened onto the black prairie of night. There were no cars when Cassidy rolled to a stop at the edge of the lonely dirt road where the high school kids usually parked. He turned off the headlights and the rumbling engine, then reached under the seat for the battery-powered radio.

The warm night and soft music from a far-off oldies station embraced them, with only a few stars beginning to shine through the reflected light of a distant sunset as it bounced off the Earth into the western sky. A barely discernible sliver of the moon rode high; tomorrow it would be new and invisible.

"I wish it would rain," Tia said, dabbing her slender throat with a drive-in ice-cream napkin. "Miss Oneida said it's been dry since spring and no rain in sight. How does she know?"

"Lots of ways," Cassidy said, counting the folk ways of rain watchers. "The dandelions close up their blossoms, for one. If there was a moon, you'd see a ring around it. And those manure piles out back will start to smell real strong when rain is coming. Let's see... my dad said the robins will go to their nests and stay there. And if there's a fair wind blowing, you can smell the rain coming. I bet Miss Oneida's been watching those dandelions and sniffing the air like some old hound dog."

Tia inhaled. The air was empty, but the notion of smelling the weather appealed to her as she watched the western skyline for thunderheads that weren't there.

"Where's Venus?" Tia said, searching the dark expanse through the windshield.

"You can't see Venus at this time of year. She's hiding, like the moon. In the fall, she will be right over there, just above the horizon," Cassidy said, pointing to the western skyline just above the mountains.

"How do you know so much about the stars? Your father?"

"Daniel. He showed me. He started by teaching me how to find the North Star, so I'd always know true north. Once you know that, he said you should be able to find your way home, even at night. We were kids and we'd never left our own backyard. I didn't know it wasn't true. When we finally left, we couldn't find our way back."

Tia put the radio on the dashboard and scooted across the cracked leather seat to be next to Cassidy, who leaned his left arm out the open window.

"I haven't thought about home since I've been here," she said, leaning her head on his shoulder. "No matter where the North Star is."

"One thing I learned is it's not about stars," Cassidy said. "It's about saying goodbye. It sounds funny, but leaving is the key to coming home. A star can't really guide you to a place you've never been."

"That sounds like something my father would have thought up on a good drunk. He knew about leaving, and he always had a way of doing it. He was a pro."

"People leave, Tia. You can't stop them. Your father went on a journey that will last forever, and you're following him. You can go your own way now, because he's not coming back. They never come back..."

"Daniel came back... you came back."

Cassidy was quiet. Had loss so consumed him that he was beyond restoration? Certainly the same Daniel who went away hadn't come back, and he still felt a sense of having lost him. The same Cassidy hadn't come home either. It wasn't the fault of the stars, but the journey.

The radio's dial glowed green against the horizon, the only light they could see. The darker the night became, the more stars came out and the stronger the signal from somewhere in Oklahoma, light years away.

"Show me some more stars," Tia said, nudging Cassidy out the door.

He took her hand as they got out of the truck, leaving the door open and the music playing. He eased his back against the Ford's grille and she leaned backward against him, looking up at the black palette of sky sprayed twinkling white with a billion ancient lights. He searched the sky for her perfect star.

"Okay, we've got to start at the beginning. Over there, to the north, can you see the Big Dipper? Homer called it the Great Bear. Sort of a big, bright square with a long handle?"

Cassidy placed his hand over hers. Pointing for her, he traced the constellation, his face next to hers to sight a straight line.

"If you follow the line of the first two stars on the ladle, up about two widths of your hand, you'll come to a bright star. That's Polaris, the North Star. Mariners used it to navigate, and Plains Indians could orient themselves every night to the rising sun."

Tia pressed against him, holding his hand against the sky. A train sounded its whistle on the far edge of town, and a dog howled a mournful reply.

"And over there, high in the southwest, a little higher" —he raised her hand higher on the sky—"that bright star is Arcturus, probably one of the first stars ever named and if you were born under it, the Greeks believed you would be rich. Over here... the Hyades, the rain bringing sisters, aren't up yet. They'll rise in the early morning behind us, in the east. And straight up above us right now is Vega. It's part of the Lyre of Orpheus."

Cassidy traced her finger around the beautiful seven-stringed instrument made of flirtatious little stars.

"Orpheus sang songs so beautiful they enchanted stones. The old myths say he played so beautifully that he even attracted rows of oak trees to the barren coast of Thrace."

"What did he do to deserve a place in the sky?" Tia asked.

"His wife, Eurydice, stepped on a poisonous snake and died. Heartbroken, he went to Hades and while he played his lyre, he asked permission for his wife to return to the world with him. Hades was so enthralled he granted Orpheus's wish, on the condition that they dare not look back until they reach the sunlight. So he played his music to guide her through the darkness, never looking to see if she followed. Finally, uncertain that Eurydice was behind him, Orpheus looked back just as they emerged from the Underworld. He watched his wife slip back down into the depths of Hell."

"That's too sad. Are there any cheerful stories up there? Any happy endings? Surely there must be one among a billion stars," Tia said.

Cassidy hugged her close and they faced straight out from where they stood.

"In the western sky, up about halfway, you'll see a charming little vee of stars. That's Berenice's Hair. A long time ago, the wife of a king promised the gods she'd cut off her blond hair if he came home victorious. When her husband finally returned from war, she cut her locks and laid them in a temple. After a few days, they disappeared. A sympathetic astronomer in the king's court looked at those stars and told the sad queen that her hair had become part of the heavens. She was happy again."

Tia rested her head against Cassidy's shoulder and pulled his arms around her.

"I've never seen the stars so bright as they are tonight. The sky is almost white with them," she said.

"For a long time after I left, I dreamed about seeing the stars like this. I missed sleeping outside and waking up in the middle of the night under Andromeda. It was completely quiet, except for the crickets. In the city, the lights drown out the lesser stars. The haze and humidity filter the light from all the rest. But I guess we don't see anything as well as when we're home."

Tia turned and kissed Cassidy, something she hadn't done since the night they walked beyond the ballpark. He had missed the taste of her, hoping she'd kiss him again. He felt like a little boy again, getting his first kiss.

"I asked Daniel once, why do the stars go away? He told me they don't go away, they just wait..."

A gentle river of starlight flowed around them. The radio hummed in the cab, but the rest of the night was silent.

"I saw you with him one morning as you slept," Tia said.

"With Daniel?"

"Yes. In the upstairs room. I came over in the early morning expecting you to be up already, but you weren't. You were asleep up there, together. I watched you for a moment. It looked like you were both dreaming the same dream."

"Maybe we were," Cassidy said. "Once, we did."

The first few mellow guitar chords of The Rolling Stones' *Wild Horses* wafted out of the silence that surrounded them, glancing off the invisible atmosphere toward their little hill.

"I love this song. Will you dance with me?" she asked.

Cassidy extended his hands to her, stepping close to her, his hips against hers. She smiled into his eyes as he slipped his right hand around her waist and let his fingertips rest on the smooth skin just beneath the waistband of her jeans. He held her hand against his chest, and felt her lightly run her fingers across the back of his neck.

They turned slowly there in the dark, stepping tenderly in time with the slow rhythm of music from far away. Cassidy sang some of the words to her, pulling her close. She squeezed his hand, tucking it against her breast, and kissed his neck.

He wanted her. Not just her body, but her essence, too. He smelled her, like rain coming from far away. Tia was good company. He wanted to understand the nature of her ways, the way Daniel once understood the nature of deep trout streams. She came nearer to him than anyone ever had and he wasn't pushing her away, like he had all the others. It seemed like it could go on like this forever.

The radio drifted in and out, its music filling the emptiness between them like a night breeze that drifts between two lovers.

She kissed him again, and gently searched his lips with her long fingers. He tasted sweet chocolate.

"Can we dance any closer?" she asked, her breath warm and insistent. She yielded to him. Cassidy drew her tighter until he felt her heart beating against him.

"We dance close in Wyoming," he said, "because there's no place else to go."

The music, the stories, the stars and the last heat of day swirled around them, between them, inside of them. They didn't need to speak.

The melody faded away and a new song came on the radio. Something slow and sweet drifting out of his past. Tonight, Oklahoma was a distant star shining music just for them.

They danced a while longer in the dark of the moon, then made love across the old leather seat of Old '46 while the stars waited and watched.

LAST GOODBYE
WEST CANAAN, JULY 29, 1995

The grass in the McLeod backyard had been perpetually unkempt for more than forty years, but the time had come, at last, for mowing.

Cassidy had dutifully dragged a stammering sprinkler around it four times a week since he arrived a month before, but the drought had slowed the lawn's growth dramatically. Patches of barren earth still showed through and the heat braised some spots, but the hardy bluegrass his father had seeded had deep roots and began to thrive in broad, unruly thatches.

So did dandelions. They sprouted boundlessly, launching their seeds in tiny parachutes that carried on evening breezes across vast open spaces, going to ground wherever the wind ends.

The push mower was leaned against a wall inside the garage, its swirling blades crusted with rust. It yipped like a wounded dog as Cassidy shoved it into the hot morning sunlight. With an old paintbrush, he slathered the blades with a pinkish glop of rust-busting phosphoric acid he'd found down at Thorson's Hardware Store. After a few minutes, he wiped it off with a red shop rag, revealing the gleaming silver blades below. He untangled a piece of old string from the axle, oiled the bearings and wheeled it along the sidewalk until its screeching racket mellowed to an efficient slicing flutter.

The blades whirred like a flight of doves. It was a sound straight out of his childhood.

He rolled the ancient machine off the concrete onto the lawn. It shaved through the thick grass like a hand-cranked combine, spewing clippings behind. Unlike those multi-speed modern magical mulcher mowers that skimmed over the grass with electric efficiency, the push model turned sweat into energy and left evidence of its labor to be raked and contemplated before it became mulch in the garden.

Cassidy could have borrowed Miss Oneida's mechanized mower or hired one of the neighborhood boys, but this was the only mower he'd ever used in his life—having never owned any home with a lawn in The City—and it was a matter of conscience that he should use it now. Besides, when oiled properly, it rolled as quiet as Sunday morning and allowed for the kind of meditation that a mower of lawns seeks.

So quiet did it run that when Cassidy had mowed most of the backyard, he heard the phone ring inside. He finished the short swath he'd cut under the trees and hustled through the back door to the kitchen to answer it.

"Hello?"

"Hi, Cass. It's Barbara. I just got your message that you were back in Wyoming. What in the name of God is happening? Is everything okay?"

She sounded as if she were trying to keep her agitation in check. Barbara hadn't changed.

In the message he left on her machine weeks ago, he hadn't told Barbara about Daniel's resurrection, just that he needed her to call him in West Canaan. Maybe it sounded desperate. But she knew how painful the place was for him and that he hadn't been there since his father died in 1972. And she knew nothing short of a personal cataclysm could draw him back.

"Fine, fine. I'm okay. It's nice to hear your voice. But you won't believe what's happened here."

"Oh my God, Cass, I'm so sorry I didn't get back to you earlier. I went up to Camano Island for a few weeks, then went straight on from Seattle to New York for a meeting. I just got back early this morning on the red-eye."

He heard Barbara's fatigue in her voice. She almost sounded as if she'd cry, but was doing her best to sound politely worried. Cassidy tried to settle her.

"Barbara, it's okay. I sort of figured you went to the island. L.A.'s hot in July. No problem. I just didn't know who else to call."

"What's wrong? Your message sounded strange. I can still tell by your voice when something's not right."

"Nothing's wrong. Not really. I mean... well, I really don't know where to start this story. It's so strange and wonderful."

There was a long pause before Barbara spoke.

"Is it a woman?"

Cassidy laughed. She'd walked out on him and now she sounded ever so slightly jealous. Her guard was down because she was tired. If she felt anything for him still, it was good, because part of him still loved her, too.

"No, Barbara," he said, seeing a chance to tease his way into breaking the news. "It's not a woman. It's a man."

"Oh my God..."

She sounded as if she'd hang up on him.

"Barbara, I'm kidding."

"You son-of-a-bitch. You'd think I'd know you by now. I can't see your eyes. I could always see that twinkle. So don't fuck around, Cass. What's really going on?"

"It's Daniel. My brother. He's alive and he's here with me."

Barbara didn't speak.

He listened closely for her voice. The phone cord was too short for Cassidy to sit at the breakfast table, so he sat on the tile counter next to the phone. When she didn't say anything for a moment, he began Daniel's peculiar story.

"They found him alive in Vietnam and brought him back here. It's been twenty-four years since... well, since he died. But now he's not dead. This all sounds so goddam weird. Anyway, I've been home about a month with him. He's very sick and I don't know what to do."

Barbara was astonished, her voice shaky.

"My God, I can't even... your brother Daniel? How? I mean, he's alive? Jesus, Cass, I can't even talk."

"Yes, he's alive. He's here. But he's sick. I thought I could help him, but nothing is working."

"Sick how?"

"Mentally. They say it's post-traumatic stress from the war, but it's bad. I've never seen anything like it. He's almost like a zombie. He can't talk, not English anyway, and he's out of it most of the time. I can't get through to him. He's already freaked out once, and I'm afraid it could happen again at any moment."

He told her how Daniel had been delivered back into the World from the land of the dead, how he found him that first day, the horror of the parade incident and the sleepless nights, full of nightmares and ghosts. He told her about the POW hunter Marrenton and Daniel's journal and the letters in the trunk.

Barbara's voice still sounded a little tremulous.

"Cass, I don't know what to say. I really don't. I want to tell you to take him to a doctor, but I know you must have already thought about that. I'm just... I don't know, just speechless. They said nobody was left there, didn't they? I've never heard such a wild story in my life."

"I know the feeling. Confused. Excited. A little scared. I'm thrilled he's alive, but sad, too. He's not the same as he was. It's all gone, all the genius, all the stories. All gone. In a lot of ways, he's not back at all. It's certainly not the way I always dreamed it."

"Who else knows about this?"

"Not many. Please don't say anything 'til I sort it all out. I don't want to deal with all that quite yet."

"No problem, Cass. I won't breathe a word. What are you going to do now?" she asked.

"I don't know. I'm not ready to lose him again. I guess I just wanted to talk to somebody. To you."

The line was quiet, no sign that his affection had hit its mark. He pictured her face, her eyes. Then Barbara spoke, stronger than before.

"Cass, I know this is a hard time for you, but we need to talk soon about us. Not now, but soon."

She didn't sound touched at all. She sounded ominous.

"Now's fine for me, Barbara," he said, masking his own disappointment with characteristic humor. "Is it about the divorce? I thought we agreed on something simple, amicable. Nothing extravagant. A quiet little affair with just a few close friends and a judge. Is that it?"

"No, Cass, that's not it," Barbara, who had always been too serious, laughed uneasily. "But now isn't a good time for either of us to talk about it. You've got way too much to deal with. We can talk another time, really."

"It's another woman, isn't it?" he asked, teasing.

He loved to hear her laugh. It rippled gently like water over rocks. She never did it enough when they were together, especially toward the end. If there was any chance for them, he thought, she'd laugh again.

"No, Cass, that's not it either."

She didn't laugh.

"Dammit, Barbara, what is *it*?" he said, finally exasperated. "We're not little kids here. You don't need to talk in code. If it's not the divorce, then what are you talking about?"

"Cass, I really don't want to get into this right now. You need to focus on what's going on there. On Daniel."

"And you, Barbara. Even if it's just for a little while longer, I need to think about you, too. Just tell me."

Cassidy settled back against the cabinet, bracing himself. He knew what was coming.

"I've met someone, Cass. That's all. I wanted you to know."

He was right, if only because he both feared and deserved to hear it.

Cassidy closed his eyes and tried to imagine her face again. Then he saw a man in the background of his imagination. He knew she was crying, even if he couldn't hear it. She tried so hard to hide her emotions. Breathing deep, he reminded himself that he'd lost Barbara long ago and she was never coming back. Maybe she'd even laugh, but she wouldn't come back.

"Good for you, Barbara. I'm happy for you, really. You deserve someone who... hell, I don't know. Sorry. I'm no good at being alone. I just hope it works out for you."

"Cass..."

"Hey, I'm okay with it, really," he lied. "Don't worry. I had my chance, right? You're a big girl now. I'm sorry about all this other stuff with Daniel, but I figured you'd want to know where I was and what I was doing. I'll keep you posted, okay?"

"Oh, Cass, please..."

"Barbara, honest, I'm all right. I understand how it is. We'll talk again soon, I promise. You be good to yourself, will you?"

He wanted to get off the phone, to lick his wounds privately. But Barbara wasn't ready to let him go.

"Cass, I don't want to hurt you. Believe me, please. Maybe we stopped being lovers, but we didn't stop being friends, and the last thing I would do is hurt you. I need you to believe me."

He hurt anyway. It was like some old moth-eaten sweater that he knew he must discard eventually, but he had fooled himself momentarily into believing he still needed it.

"I always believed you, Barbara. I understand. It only hurts for a minute, then I'll be fine. Okay? Look, I'll call you soon and you can tell me all about him. No hard feelings, all right?"

"Cass, I don't think I'll stop loving that about you."

"What's that?"

"Whatever it is that lets you sidestep around pain so gracefully. It's like a perfect little dance. I wish I knew how to do it. I just keep blundering into pain. Sometimes I hurt so much."

"Practice, practice, practice," he said, trying at first to be blithe, then sympathetic. "You know I'd give you anything, even that, if it took away the hurt. But I've got to go now. The lawn mower is still running. You take care, okay?"

Barbara surrendered.

"I will, Cass. You, too."

Barbara began to cry. They said their goodbyes, both knowing they'd probably never talk again.

His stomach knotted by yet another loss, Cassidy finished mowing the lawn. He raked up the clippings and scattered them between the vegetables to hold down the water and weeds. He retraced his relationship with Barbara, from the beginning to the end, counting up the memories of times they'd made love on the beach or in the mountains, the walk in the vineyard where he proposed to her, the day they bought sandwiches and two bottles of wine and hired a boatman to drop them on their own uninhabited island in the Gulf Stream. He regretted now never bringing her back to Wyoming.

In due course, the leaves would decay and replenish the soil. The mower's swirling blades would conceal themselves in rust again. He wouldn't hurt anymore. As with everything else, like memories, regrets and getting over love, it takes time.

Daniel stayed in the upstairs bedroom all day. The windows were closed and the shutters drawn to keep it cool, but still the heat rose through the house and collected there. There was no air conditioning. Cassidy looked in on him every hour or so. Each time, he found Daniel lying still in the same place on the floor, half naked and sweating.

It had been almost three months since the last rain fell on West Canaan. Early May might as well have been a hundred years ago, to listen to the ranchers talk down at the Little Chief. That's when the last of the spring storms had drenched the prairie, giving false promise to the tender shoots of young buffalo grass and buckwheat. It was almost August and the prairie grasses had been sucked dry by the heat. They waited for wildfire to end their season.

In time.

Watching the sprinkler feather its precious water across the lawn, Cassidy drifted. The afternoon air was close, hot. He swung aimlessly on the front porch swing, a cold beer between his legs, going nowhere in his mind. Barbara had every right to go on with her life, even if his seemed stalled. Tia would leave too, eventually, he knew. They all leave.

Cassidy let his head fall back and stared at the dusty cobwebs in the porch eaves. Dry sprigs from an abandoned bird's nest sprouted from a nook above one of the weathered gray joists. He thought about painting, but he didn't know how much longer he could stay in his father's house. He feared his memory and poor carpentry skills would fail to restore it properly. He needed to get back to work on the book, but more importantly, maybe he needed to get Daniel some real help. Maybe back in California, where he could be close, for occasional visits. Maybe...

"Hey, stranger."

The woman's voice floated across the lawn.

Cassidy looked up, shielding his eyes against the bright sun. He felt sweat beading on his neck. Tia stood beside her car parked at the curb, holding a grocery box. Her dark hair fell across her tanned shoulders as she came up the walk. She wore a white, form-fitting dress that rippled around her calves as she walked toward him.

He rose from the swing and met her on the steps with a kiss on the lips.

"Is it hot out here or is it just me?" he said, taking the cardboard box from her. "You look so fresh."

"I bear gifts, and that always makes me glow," she said, tapping the box. "This is for you."

"For me? My birthday isn't for six months yet. Should I shake it and try to...?"

The box shook itself.

Cassidy's eyes widened. He set it on the porch and unfolded the interlocked flaps. A black, wet nose erupted through the opening, followed by floppy black ears, four outsized black paws and a fat black ball of fur with a long, happy black tail.

"A puppy!" he said. "It's a good thing I didn't shake it, huh? Look at this little, um..."—he quickly peeked under the dog's hind legs—"this little guy, black as ink. Hey, little fella, what do you say? Nice to be out of that box?"

Tia took off her sunglasses and smiled while Cassidy cuddled the pup.

"He's a black Lab, two months old. I got him at a ranch just north of town this morning. You told me you had a black Lab once that ran away, but Daniel always told you it was out there in the dark watching over you. Well, maybe she's in this one somewhere."

Cassidy released the puppy to explore the porch and hugged Tia. They sat together on the swing and watched the little black ball of fur sniff around, then squat to pee. His yellow puddle spilled through the decking.

"It's official now," Cassidy said, laughing with her. "He owns the place."

"Now the hard part. What will you name him?" Tia asked.

"There's only one proper name for this black dog," he said, improvising some religious sign of christening. "He shall be... Shadow."

"Yes, I was hoping that would be the name you picked," she said, obviously pleased. "That's why I got him for you. Shadow, it is. A perfect name for this little black silhouette of a dog. Do you think it might jar something loose in Daniel?"

"I don't know, but let's hope this pup knows the way home better than his namesake did," Cassidy said.

The newly christened puppy plodded clumsily to the top of the porch steps, unsure whether to try to descend onto the inviting green grass that spread out in front of him. He wagged gleefully at the notion of making a run across the green expanse, but if the idea was appealing, he still didn't trust himself enough to try. Some journeys must wait.

"I have something else," Tia said.

"More? Better than slow-dancing with me under the stars and a black dog to keep me company in my old age? What else is there?"

He glanced around. She'd brought nothing else with her.

"I want to make love again," she said. "Now."

"Right here?" he teased, testing the sturdiness of the porch swing.

Without saying more, Tia stood and held out her hand to Cassidy. He smelled her soft lavender and took her hand. It was warm and moist in his as he stood to kiss her.

She led him inside, the puppy padding mirthfully in tow. Hand in hand, they went to the back bedroom, where the air was coolest, and quietly closed the door behind them. Tia raised the window sash for fresh air, then turned to Cassidy with the reflected light of day behind her. Long lacy curtains drifted lazily, almost imperceptibly, behind her.

He came to her. They kissed, pressing themselves against one another. He slipped her dress off her shoulders and pulled it gently down the length of her body to the floor. She stood there in her silky panties, her skin warm under his fingers.

Cassidy kneeled in front of her, kissing her smooth stomach and letting his hands glide softly down the back of her legs. He kissed her tanned legs and brushed his face in the sweet musk of her.

Tia held his head, her fingers curled in his thick hair. The black puppy watched, his head cocked sideways.

Tia moaned softly, then slid her fingers below his bearded chin so his eyes rose to meet hers. Her lips beckoned him. Cassidy stood and she lifted his T-shirt over his head, then unbuckled his jeans while he kissed her neck. He tasted the sweat and lavender at the soft curve of her shoulder as she gently touched him.

She moved with Cassidy as he turned her toward the bed and laid her across the fresh coverlet he'd put there the day before. It was cool against her skin.

They giggled as the old box springs screeched under them with every move.

Cassidy let his hand float down across her breasts, along the swale of her hip, to slip beneath the lace of her panties. She parted her thighs slightly, allowing him to find her wetness before he slipped her panties down her long legs and dropped them on the bed beside her. She closed her eyes and arched her hips toward him.

He slipped his pants off and they lie there together, naked, in the bedroom where he grew up. Laying beside Tia, he kissed her breasts, teasing her nipples between his lips while her hand softly stroked him.

In the light, she was even more beautiful than he had ever imagined. Cassidy fell into her brown eyes and her liquid smile. Watching her, seeing how her dark hair spread across the pillow and her legs bent toward him, he wanted their lovemaking to go on all afternoon. He let his fingers trace the outline of her breast, across her tummy to a dark, secret triangle.

Tia slid her hand beneath his hip, gently entreating him to get on top of her. She spread her legs and guided him into her. Slowly, he filled her, moving his hips in time with hers while she entwined her legs with his. He clasped both her hands tightly in his, spread her arms out beside her.

"You're so beautiful, Tia," he whispered to her, kissing her cheek. He moved slowly.

"I wanted you for so long. Please come inside me," she told him, breathing harder now. Her face glistened with sweat. "Oh, God..."

Tia shuddered repeatedly with an orgasm, burying her face against his shoulder and biting him hard on the chest. Before she was done, he felt his semen spilling through him, past the point when he could control himself any longer, and he could only let it surge into her.

They sagged against one another, rolling to one side while still holding hands and kissing. Cassidy stayed inside her for a long time, until he grew soft and sleepy.

"Thank you," he said, kissing her shoulder. "That was the best gift of all."

She smiled and turned her head away from him, toward the wall.

"What is it?" he asked. Then he felt her hand tighten and her chest heave a little. She was crying. "Tia, what's wrong?"

Biting her lip, Tia turned her face toward him, her eyes filled with quiet tears. One trickled across her cheek and fell to the pillow.

"I have to go," she said.

Cassidy worried that he'd taken her for granted in some way, overlooked some need. He kissed the palm of her hand.

"I'm sorry, if it was me. Will you come back for dinner?" he said apologetically. "We can talk then."

"No, I mean it's time for me to get back on the road. It's been a month, an extraordinary month, but I have to do this thing. I thought maybe I'd find him here, but I haven't. I found you, and Daniel, and Miss Oneida, and all the others, but not my father. It's not about this goddam *Rolling Stone* story anymore and maybe it never was. It's about me... and him. He never knew me and I never knew him. But I want to, even if he never did."

Cassidy lay back on the pillow, confused and hurt, as much for her as himself. No day was good to lose a love, but he wasn't sure he could absorb any more pain on this day, of all days. A delicate wind rose, teasing the lace curtains, while he groped for any answer that would keep her here where he could touch her, maybe save her, too. She was the only thing that seemed real to him now.

"That's what he found here. Just people and stories and another place beside the road. You've always been looking for the wrong thing. You're looking for a ghost who passed through here once, and you keep thinking you're going to find something he left behind, like some shadow that he never missed as he blew out of town. Let me tell you, he left damned few memories, one book of words... and you. In fact, he slept in this damned bed right here, but you're no closer to him than when you got here. That's the truth. Tia, everything you need to know about the memory and dreams of Jack Lazarus is here inside you," he said, laying his hand across her soft breast. "Besides, you can't leave. I need you more than he does now."

Tia didn't speak, so they lay there on the bed, naked and sad, for a long time. When the puppy whined, Tia got up and dressed. Cassidy watched her, finding it almost as erotic watching her dress as it had been undressing her.

"If you knew you were leaving, why did you do this?" he asked.

"Are you sad it happened?"

"Not at all. But it makes it hard to say goodbye."

"Maybe so. I guess I wanted a part of you that nobody else could have. I don't know."

The puppy whined a little more.

"The dog will be sad if you go," Cassidy said, hoping to make her smile... and to stay.

Tia bent down and lifted the new puppy, cradling him against her breast. She rubbed his stomach and let him lick her face where her salty tears had fallen.

"Can I call you sometime?" she asked Cassidy without looking at him. She sat on the edge of the bed. "I'll leave my number. I really want to stay in touch. Will you look me up when you get back to The City, maybe come up to the farm and see me?"

Cassidy was losing her and he knew it. He might love her, but he couldn't say it. Suddenly embarrassed by his nakedness, he covered himself with his T-shirt. He wanted her close to him, forever, but he couldn't find it in him to embrace her that way. As if the Fates were drawing her away for her own good, he felt powerless to stop her before she went out the door.

They all leave.

"Sure, Tia. But won't you please stay? I mean, you've kept me sane in all this insanity. Can't we talk about it?"

"I can't."

Tia turned to Cassidy and touched his face, as if she were trying to memorize it. She bent over him for a last kiss and he smelled sweet apples in her hair as it fell around him.

"It's funny. I was going to ask you to come with me, but I knew you couldn't ever go," she said. "I was going to say you were looking for a ghost who once lived here, that maybe you were wrong to expect to find a shadow that he left behind, and maybe everything you needed was already in your heart. I guess you understood completely. Good spaces, Cass. Please call me."

She said goodbye and left him alone again.

After the sun went down, Daniel crept downstairs from the bedroom under the eaves. He found the air cooler and he was hungry.

Cassidy, who'd been reading in Archie's den, was startled to see him standing by the doorway, half hidden behind the wall. He looked at his wristwatch. It was after 9:30 already.

He went to the kitchen to make sandwiches, and to wonder where Tia would spend the night. He wasn't sure which direction she'd headed from West Canaan, though it's likely she'd gone east, toward the Badlands. He hoped she'd call.

Daniel ate a few bites of bologna and cheese, and drank part of a cup of tea, then went to Archie's bedroom and lay down on the bed, staring at the ceiling.

Cassidy put the dinner dishes in the sink and went to him. He sat in the rocker at the foot of the bed, where their father had read almost every night before bed. Some nights, as children, he and Daniel would crawl into Archie's bed and he'd read to them until they fell asleep. Rather than move them, Archie got in beside them and tried to keep them warm all night.

Every night for the past week, Cassidy had told one of Daniel's old stories, the best he could remember it. Not once had his brother shown any recognition, any sign of emotion, any suggestion of healing. Their therapy hadn't been without its benefit, but only for Cassidy, who'd begun to see the wandering Pledger Moon as Daniel's prophecy of his own fate. Neither tale was finished.

"Let's try again," he said aloud to Daniel, who didn't move at all. *"Once upon a time..."*

SANCTUARY
WEST CANAAN, AUGUST 25, 1957

The only things that living and dying in West Canaan, Wyoming, had in common were Mount Pisgah Cemetery and the threadbare, purple-velvet chairs at the Wigwam movie theater. And maybe the loneliness of it all, but having chosen this place to live and die, one understood the consequences.

And by far, the abstract principle of aloneness in death (or in life, for that matter) was of less consequence than whether the Wigwam had booked an Elvis Presley matinee on the day of one's funeral.

That's because Nub Carlile and his son Emory owned both the funeral parlor and the movie house. The undertakers were notoriously frugal businessmen who knew the value of a monopoly on a priceless commodity: escape. More to the point, if you needed a picture show or a casket in West Canaan, the Carliles were going to take your money.

They were so cheap that when they opened the Wigwam Theater back in '42, they bought just sixty folding chairs, all cushioned in purple velvet, from an alcoholic traveling salesman out of Denver whom they likely cheated. The gaudy fabric matched the purple velvet curtains that hung beside the screen, and the purple carpet runners that sloped toward the flickering light, and the purple velvet

cordons that hung from tarnished brass posts in the snack bar—a
package deal from the same drunken peddler who was never seen
again in these parts. Though everyone in town knew the Carliles to
be shrewd, even dishonest, horse-traders, many wondered who
skinned whom in the bargain but didn't care much in either case.

The chairs' rickety wooden legs could be locked together with a
sliding brace, like bow-legged cowboys in a three-legged race, to
make six straight rows of ten seats each. Even buttressed against one
another, the whole row of chairs squawked and shuddered when
someone so much as shifted his buttocks on one of the thinly padded,
uncomfortable seats. So after the lights went down, most polite folks
just sat quietly, never moving until someone else moved, to minimize
the untold mayhem that undisciplined sitting could cause. (It was
years later that Emory had the idea of moving an old sofa into the
place, down front at the foot of the stage, mostly at the urging of the
hemorrhoidal Damned Mayor.)

But for more than fifteen years, on those solemn occasions when
the funeral parlor needed chairs, the indiscreet Carliles would carry
them across Main Street and set them up at their mortuary in ten
straight rows of six chairs each. The interior design of death varied
slightly from that of a movie house, like a dark mirror. At any rate, it
meant the theater was temporarily without its furniture.

And that's how Cassidy came to know two things: funerals
always had the faint aroma of buttered popcorn, and there were never
matinees on burying days.

There were two synergistic flaws in Nub Carlile's greed. He
scrimped on everything and he didn't think like a little boy anymore.

The former induced him to build his Wigwam Theater with
homemade cinder blocks that began to disintegrate into a fine powder
almost as soon as they were set in mortar. Within a few years,
hastened by uneven settling in the porous soil that underlay all of
West Canaan, immense cracks opened on every wall so fast that Nub
had a standing monthly grout order at Thorson's Hardware. In time,
his walls were more putty than block.

The latter prevented Nub from reckoning how the walls of his crumbling movie house would shift just enough to skew a door casing. And if a balky movie house door that never closed properly happened to open onto a dark alley cluttered with shopkeepers' ash bins, no little boy worth his salt would forgo a chance to see a free picture show.

They didn't sneak in every time, but Daniel and Cassidy knew the way well enough. Their father wouldn't approve of their fraud, but to them and their friends, there was a kind of honor in cheating the penurious Nub Carlile and his sour son, Emory. In the imaginary world the Carliles themselves helped create for them, it was the privilege—maybe even the duty—of heroes to be crafty when villains were the dupes.

For the last matinee on the last Sunday afternoon of summer, the day before Little Powder Elementary School started its new fall term, the Wigwam was showing *The Searchers*, a new John Wayne picture. Actually, it came out the year before, but the Wigwam almost never showed movies when they were really new. Suffice it to say, the movie was new to West Canaan, which was accustomed to being at least a year removed from anything that was conceived on either coast.

Daniel and Cassidy cut across Main Street, past the movie house fifteen minutes before the three o'clock show. Delphina Stueben, the high school girl who allegedly once took a dollar to show her breasts to some of the older boys behind the outfield fence, was selling tickets in the little glass booth. Emory Carlile himself was tearing stubs at the door. And Frankie Good, the plump teen-age usher who could grow a mustache by the time he was in the eighth grade, was behind the snack counter. Not counting the projectionist, it took just three people to run the theater and they were all accounted for. The coast was clear for sneaking in the back door, so Daniel and Cassidy ambled around the corner to where the alley spilled its gravel onto the paved sidestreet.

"You got your ticket from last time?" Daniel asked. Cassidy dug deep into one hip pocket of his jeans, then the other, before showing Daniel a torn red stub. The Carliles were too cheap to change the color of their admission tickets, making it simpler for the back-door boys to appear to have gained legitimate admission by flashing their stub if a curious usher challenged them. Nobody ever checked the numbers.

"Good. I'll go first and see if anyone's watching," Daniel said as they walked up the alley toward the defective back door of the Wigwam. "You stick close and don't say a word 'til we get to our seats."

"Don't sit so close this time," Cassidy complained. "It hurts my eyes."

Daniel gave him a look.

"Well, it does," Cassidy offered lamely.

They moved some ash bins away from the door, which stuck out from its skewed wooden frame like one card askew from the rest of the deck. Its knob wobbled in its socket. There was at least an inch of space between the top rail of the door and the jamb, and a perfect arc scraped in the dirt where the bottom rail dragged on the ground when the door was opened.

Daniel spread his feet wide and heaved up and back on the door with a grunt. It rasped against the ground, but opened enough for them to squeeze through before Daniel yanked it closed again.

Inside the theater, the back door was hidden by the long, purple-velvet drape on one side of the screen. Once the door was closed behind them, they tarried there behind the curtain to let their eyes adjust to the darkness, perfectly still to avoid rustling the long, pleated fabric that concealed them. Daniel peeped through a gap until he was sure nobody would notice them in the dim light of the theater, then they walked in stiff-legged haste to the closest seats, which tilted at an awkward angle and squeaked grotesquely as they slid into them.

It was the front row again, but they were safely inside.

Daniel smiled at Cassidy. Cleverness and wile had certain rewards beyond a little boy's economy. They occasionally produced tiny victories worth savoring.

Cassidy couldn't wait to celebrate.

"Go get us some taffy, the kind in the box with the little prize," Cassidy said.

"Here's a quarter," Daniel said, fishing in his pocket and making the seats squawk. "You go up and get some yourself. I hate that stuff anyway."

"Come with me."

"You can't do it yourself?"

"I can, but I want you to come with me."

"I'll save our seats. You go get taffy for us. And a soda pop. Otherwise, you get nothing 'cause I'm not going."

Cassidy craned his neck toward the darkened projectionist's booth. Only a few people, mostly other kids, sat in the theater. No sign of the usher, who'd be busy popping corn and jerking sodas in the lobby.

"What if they figure it out that I didn't come in the front door?" Cassidy asked. A few more people came through the dusty purple curtains that separated the Wigwam's sixty rickety seats from its tiny foyer.

"Every time, you worry about the same thing, but have they ever figured it out? They haven't got a clue. Just go up and ask for the taffy and the pop and pay Frankie and come back here. It's easy."

It sounded hard. Cassidy pondered his brother's instructions for a moment.

"What if I have to go to the bathroom?"

"Do you have to go to the bathroom?"

"No, but what if I did?"

"You'd go into the bathroom and pee. Or did you forget how?"

"But nobody pees *before* the movie," Cassidy reasoned. "They might think something's up."

Daniel rolled his eyes and shook his head. Before he could say anything, somebody sat down behind them. He fixed a steely glare on his little brother.

"Wait here," he said, rising from his seat and heading toward the light leaking into the darkness at the back of the theater.

Alone, Cassidy fidgeted. He slunk down in his seat and looked straight ahead. He never liked the guilty feeling after they sneaked into the theater, even though the raw adventure of it was thrilling. If their father ever found out—and they did nothing without assuming he would—they reckoned he'd tan their hides but good, although neither of them could recall ever experiencing even one "moment of clarity" that Archie occasionally threatened.

Daniel got back to his seat just as the lights dimmed and the cartoon began. He handed Cassidy a small box of taffy, which he tore open for the mysterious toy inside because he was never particularly fond of the salt-water taffy wrapped in wax paper inside. Unable to see what it was in the dark, Cassidy held it up in the flickering, reflected light from the screen: a tiny plastic Indian chief, no more than an inch tall.

After the cartoon, the movie started. Its theme music swelled to fill the little theater.

"Are there girls in this movie?" Cassidy asked.

"Sure. There are always girls in movies. There aren't any movies without girls," Daniel told him.

"I don't know why there has to be girls in a cowboy movie. They just gotta have cowboys and Indians and cavalry guys and horses and John Wayne. Girls ruin all the movies."

"Shhhh. Just watch."

"Or war movies. Don't need girls in a war movie. They just wanna kiss and stuff. Yuck. I hate the kissing parts."

"If you don't shut up, I'm moving to a different seat," Daniel warned Cassidy. "Unless you want to sit by yourself, clam up."

Cassidy pouted until John Wayne appeared on screen, which never took long. There he was, taller than all the rest, with broad shoulders and a heroic gait. He was larger than life up there on the screen, more than just light and shadows glimmering on a sheet of cheap white cloth. To Cassidy, he wasn't just any hero. John Wayne was invincible and Cassidy took solace in knowing that whatever happened, whatever flaws he might have, he'd never die. John Wayne *couldn't* die.

He didn't die this time either. He saved the girl from the Indians, although once he also threatened to shoot her dead. Of course, there was also lots of shooting and fighting. And throughout the whole movie, Cassidy only spoke once, when Duke's character, the bitter

Ethan Edwards, told one of his fellow searchers, "I'll meet you on the far side."

"What does he mean?" Cassidy whispered anxiously to Daniel. "Far side of what? Where's he going?"

"Some place bad," was all Daniel said, working a piece of taffy in his jaw.

The far side of someplace bad was a place only a great hero could find, Cassidy thought. Like John Wayne.

When the picture ended, they walked out the front door among the rest, bold as ever as they went past Emory Carlile, who was counting the afternoon's money and didn't look up.

It was after five o'clock and Sunday supper would be waiting for them, so they crossed Main Street and ran all the way back to Ithaca Street, astride fearless cavalry mounts and taking potshots at imaginary Indians who lurked in the lengthening shadows cast by weary sunlight on the last day of summer vacation.

They killed like heroes.

Just like John Wayne.

Sunday nights were for bathing, in the same way that Sunday mornings were for baptizing. The regularity of bath time in the McLeod house led Cassidy to believe there was some holy connection between the Sabbath and personal hygiene, some reason the Lord wanted his flock cleansed behind the ears before every Monday morning.

As the enormous, claw-footed tub filled, Daniel and Cassidy peeled off their clothes and stood naked beside it, splashing their fingers in the hot water. The perfect temperature lingered somewhere between three fingers and purification: if Daniel couldn't submerge three fingers in the water for a ten-count, it was too hot for Cassidy and too tepid to disinfect.

Daniel sunk his hand in the clear, swirling water and began to count. Sitting on the lip of the tub, Cassidy studied his dark arms and neck, bronzed by summer. Daniel's hips were strong and the muscles in his young legs were beginning to show subtle, powerful lines where they met his knee and his rump. A faint line of blond fuzz trickled from his navel toward his penis, where Cassidy spied a darker, barely visible tuft that had somehow escaped his notice before.

"You've got hair on your ding-dong!" Cassidy blurted, pointing at his brother's groin.

Daniel's face flushed and quickly covered himself with both hands, bending double in an unnatural crouch.

"Quit lookin' at my privates, you little pervert," he said, angry and embarrassed at the same time. "I'll kick your skinny little butt if you say anything to anybody. I mean it, you dork. Now look the other way."

Giggling, Cassidy turned his head toward the wall but not enough to suit Daniel.

"All the way. I don't want some perverted little kid staring at my privates."

He cuffed Cassidy's head then leaped into the privacy of the water. Cassidy rubbed the back of his head and followed, slipping into the tub with his back to Daniel, but not before he looked down at his own penis to see if any hair had sprouted there, too.

"This is too hot," he whined to Daniel as he settled indelicately beneath the surface, holding his tender testicles and penis tightly as insulation against the hot water. He exhaled several pained gusts as he let the water trickle slowly between his fingers.

First, Daniel washed Cassidy's back, then they swiveled in the tub and Cassidy washed his. They washed their hair with the fat bar of soap Miss Oneida had left on their towels, then scoured their ears with a twisted washrag. When they were done, Cassidy pulled the stopper and the gray water made a sucking sound as it curled like a tornado down the drain.

Daniel dried himself off, modestly turning his back on Cassidy, then put on the new pajamas that Miss Oneida had laid in the hallway outside the bathroom door. Cassidy patted himself with his towel and dropped it on the floor before dressing.

School started the next day, and the last night of summer was almost as special as Christmas Eve. While they bathed, Archie laid gifts on their beds: unsharpened pencils and crisp folders, fresh gum erasers, arrow-straight wooden rulers with a metal edge, new white socks, dark blue jeans and collared shirts wrapped in plastic, each one festooned with a hundred straight pins. And new patent leather dress shoes that shined like a pool of oil.

The first day of school always smelled like new broadcloth, pencil shavings and butch wax. It itched around the neck, pinched at the toes and sang like new corduroy. Pants were cuffed and belts overlapped with the promise of a year's growth. Empty pages waited to be filled.

Cassidy was entering second grade, Daniel the sixth. Little Powder Elementary School was the only grade school in West Canaan and this was the last year the two brothers would spend under the same leaky tar-paper roof.

"What's second grade like?" Cassidy asked, sniffing a new eraser.

Daniel sat on his bed, trying to find all the pins in his new plaid shirt.

"It's really hard," Daniel said. "They make you do division and multiplication, and you have to read books this thick." He spread his index finger and thumb three inches apart.

Cassidy continued counting his pencils and said nothing. For all his protests and interruptions, he believed almost anything Daniel told him.

The Whistle rose and fell in the summer night. Nine o'clock. Bedtime. Its wail hadn't drifted away when Archie came upstairs to tuck them in.

"Dad, what's division?" Cassidy asked.

"It's a kind of math where you find out how many parts you can break a number into," Archie said, sitting on Daniel's bed. "Like these ten pencils. Division helps me find out how many equal piles of two pencils I can make. Do you know?"

Cassidy counted them off, two by two, then counted his piles on the nightstand.

"Five."

"That's division. Splitting apart."

Cassidy smiled.

"That's good. I thought it was gonna be hard."

Archie kissed his boys goodnight and turned off the light.

"You have a big day tomorrow, so get your rest tonight. No monkey business up here. Sleep tight..."

"And don't let the bed bugs bite," they said in unison.

Archie stood in the doorway a moment, the light behind him. He was slumped, uneven around the edges. Cassidy traced his outline, from his baggy pants to the rumple of empty shirt that hung over his trousers. His neck looked skinny, his hair shabby.

Reduced to a shadow, even without the troubling details Cassidy saw in the daylight, he still looked old.

Cassidy wanted to tell his father how much he loved him, but he didn't. He loved his mother and she died. He didn't want to lose his father, too, so he kept it a secret.

"Good night, boys," Archie said, then closed the door.

The night was perfectly still and they heard a train in the distance, coming in. After a while, they heard Archie on the porch, gently rocking the bench swing in time with the crickets. The moon was bright. In another month, the air would be too cold for an open window, the crickets would be gone and there'd be a ring around the moon before rain, maybe snow.

Summer was almost over.

"Danny, you awake?" Cassidy whispered.

"Yeah."

"It was a good summer, wasn't it?"

"Yeah, it was good, if you don't count almost falling off the water tower and then almost getting bit by a rattlesnake. Otherwise, it was pretty good. What was your favorite part of the summer, other than that?"

Cassidy thought about it.

"Fishing, I think. That was the best part. That was some fish."

"Yeah, Cass, some fish."

"How 'bout you? What was your favorite part of the summer?"

Daniel sat up in his bed and rested his chin on his knees. To him, summers were end-to-end days of cool branch water, baseball, blue sky and the prickle of sweat. Days tasted like dust and new mown grass, nights like prairie vapors. The light was brighter and fell from higher in the sky. He knew he was changing, starting some important journey that frightened and exhilarated him a little. But what was best?

"I don't know really. It was a good summer all the way around," he said.

Cassidy wasn't satisfied.

"No, you have to say something. One thing that was good. That's what favorite is: one thing, not everything."

"I can like whatever I want. And I liked it all. The whole summer."

"What about Pledger Moon? Don't you like him?"

Over the course of the summer, Daniel had told more than a dozen Moon stories to his little brother. He'd come to understand how the tales distracted Cassidy from thoughts that hurt him, like their mother's death. But summer was ebbing away and the stories would end.

"I like Moon fine, but it's just a story. You know, maybe the stories were my favorite part of summer."

"Tell another one, would you? The last one?" Cassidy asked, rolling onto his stomach to listen.

"It's too late. It's after ten. We gotta sleep."

"Just one last story?"

"I'm still mad about you looking at my privates."

"I won't say a word, I swear on a stack of Bibles. Cross my heart and hope to die. Please?"

Cassidy wasn't dealing, he was begging.

"Never?"

"I double-swear. Honest."

Daniel stretched his legs across the sheet and lay back against the cold iron bedstead. At first, it chilled his skin, then soothed it in the dead, hot calm of late August.

"Moon was getting old..." he began.

"No, no, no," Cassidy piped up anxiously. "That's not how it starts, and you know it."

"Not every story starts like a fairy tale, dang it," Daniel snapped.

Cassidy pouted.

"Oh, jeez, all right then. *Once upon a time,*" he said with a dramatic flair.

Their father's voice rumbled from below the window.

"Hey, pipe down and get to sleep," he said in a stern tone. "Don't make me come up there..."

They said nothing for a moment, then Daniel continued in a whisper.

"Once upon a time, on the first morning of autumn, Pledger Moon stood by the Powder River, washing himself. It was 1899, the last year of the century. The sky was deep blue, but the sun raced lower across the sky. The leaves on the trees around him were changing to yellow, red and orange, looking like a prairie fire. The river had carried all the winter snows away and it was time for the cycle to start again.

"Moon looked down into the pool and saw his own face reflected there. He saw that he was no longer a young man. He was like the river, which had flowed deep and forever and touched many shores, but the time had come for him to go home.

"By now, all the men he'd known in his life had either died or were grandfathers. They had been soldiers once, or farmers, or gandy-dancers. Some were trappers in the high meadows, some were sod-busters. Some were outlaws and brigands, some traders, some Indian warriors and renegades. Some had been rich and some poor. Some had gambled and some had lost. He'd buried a few of them, mostly after the ground thawed in the spring for easy digging. So many years had passed, he couldn't remember every place where he laid a friend to his final rest, but a few he'd never forget.

"Moon was a wanderer who had lived on the brink of the frontier for most of his life, just beyond the clinging grasp of time and civility. More and more, the ranchers were settling the country, and he worked for them, moving on after drawing a season's pay. But he looked around him and saw no one who would bury him when his time came. His heart was heavy and his legs were tired."

Cassidy spoke softly.

"Is he gonna die?"

"We all die. Moon will die, too, when his time comes."

There was a long silence, then Cassidy spoke again softly.

"Will Dad die?"

"Someday, he will," Daniel answered. He brushed the back of his hand along his little brother's shoulder. "But it's a long, long time before he gets old. A long time. Don't worry."

"Will you die?"

"We all will die. Me, too. But not tomorrow, not even next week. We'll be old men, you and me. I promise. We got things to do before then."

"I'm afraid."

"Of what?"

"You'll go away. And Dad'll go away, like Mom. I'm afraid to be alone."

Daniel lay down on his pillow, looking straight into Cassidy's sad little eyes.

"We are brothers. I won't leave you because I am part of you and you are part of me. No matter what happens, that's how it is. But you scare yourself by talking crazy like this. Me and Dad aren't dying. We're not even sick. So stop fretting so much, you worrywart."

Cassidy pursed his lips and smiled bravely in the dark, then closed his eyes.

"So keep telling the story. Is Pledger Moon going home finally?" he said, burrowing deeper into his pillow.

"Moon wasn't even sure he had a home anymore. He never had a wife or children. He left his farm in West Virginia before the war, almost forty years before, and never went back. He'd wanted to return to his land, but there was never a fair wind blowing to the East, he always said, as if he could sail home if only he had a promising breeze at his back.

"Then while he studied his aging face in the water, the surface rippled. He looked up to see the flaming trees rustling, their brilliant leaves floating like little boats on the wind. They drifted east, toward morning. And he knew it was time to go.

"He gathered his few belongings and some food in a satchel made from a buffalo hide. He counted out the black stones again, placing nine of them in it. But the tenth, the stone the Indian woman told him many years ago was for a memory he had yet to make and a journey he had yet to take, he put in a medicine bag around his neck. He left everything else and started his last journey, toward home."

In the pause, Daniel felt Cassidy's sweet, warm breath against his face.

"Cass, you awake?"

There was no answer.

Cassidy was fast asleep. Daniel pulled up the sheet to cover his little brother's bare shoulders. The night was long and, before morning, it would turn cool.

So the Moon story was finished, forever. The next day, school would begin and nights would be shortened by homework lessons and early bedtimes. They would see new adventures ahead. Autumn would soon be at hand, then the first snows would come when the last roses were still in flower. There would be days when it was too cold to snow, when they longed for muggy nights, hot as a stone in the road. In time, shy spring would come around, tentatively at first, like a young man calling on his first girl. And then a new summer after that, when a little boy's life was renewed. There were new days ahead, new roads.

And new stories.

Daniel snuggled close to Cassidy. He wanted to hold him tight and make his fears go away, but it was too hot. Cassidy slept in the embrace of words that would never die. Soon, Daniel slept, too.

Anyway, it was the journey, not the ending, that mattered most.

CROSSWINDS
WEST CANAAN, AUGUST 28, 1995

Mount Pisgah was, at its essence, a place of hope.

When the time came for the Old Ones to bury the first among them to die, a stillborn baby birthed a few days after they encamped on the nearby Crazy Woman Creek, the menfolk dug a grave at the top of a timid hill that was slightly closer to Heaven than the rest of their new landscape. Since they had hardly shaken off the dust from their two thousand-mile exodus, they knew how easy any journey became the nearer one got to his destination.

By the same token, a few years later, when a notorious bandit from the Wild Bunch was lynched by justice-minded but impatient townfolk after murdering two innocent men at the livery, they dug his hole eight feet deep in the potter's field, a little closer to hell than most.

The town grew up around Mount Pisgah, a humble rise where Heaven, Earth and Hell rubbed up against one another. In time, all the Old Ones went up there to the top, perhaps hoping they were right about getting closer to Heaven. But by that time, they were beyond hoping, beyond praying, beyond caring. They were dead and buried beneath the cottonwoods, whose thirsty roots most certainly entangled their bones and sucked them dry. If there was a

Heaven, or if there wasn't, what was left of the Old Ones rose up through the veins of those ancient trees and into their leaves, absorbing the sunlight for a couple seasons, then falling back to earth. Dust to autumn dust.

So, it was hope that made a holy place out of a prairie hill. That was maybe the only miracle that ever happened in West Canaan, Wyoming.

And at the center of it all, the water tower rose like a steeple. It was just a common water tower, the likes of which stood guard over arid towns all over the Great Plains. This one had been approved by the West Canaan town fathers back in the Thirties and situated on the highest point in the municipality to facilitate the flow of precious water to the homes below. The highest point in the municipality just happened to be a graveyard.

And despite Flashlight Freddie Bascombe's best efforts to quell the mating rituals of West Canaan's horny youths, the back side of the cemetery became the favorite Friday night parking place for kids who littered the spot with empty beer cans, cigarette butts and used rubbers. More than a few of the town's children were conceived in fumbled and furious couplings beneath the shadow of the water tower. The odds would not be defied, even there. Maybe, *especially* there.

But if proximity counted for anything, as the Old Ones believed, Mount Pisgah was a crossroads where love, life and death passed in different directions.

Cassidy asked Miss Oneida to stay with Daniel for the afternoon while he went up to the cemetery.

He'd begun to understand at least one idiosyncrasy of Daniel's illness: Daniel had little difficulty going outdoors in daylight, but when evening approached, he grew frightfully uncomfortable and agitated. Even so, most days Daniel preferred to hole up in a dark corner of the house, not moving from his private world for hours at a time.

Daniel hadn't tried to communicate since Marrenton visited, but he also hadn't gone berserk. Cassidy was left wrestling with his hope that Daniel might miraculously recover by the sheer force of memory, but his hope was fatigued and twisted out of shape. And he knew it.

Miss Oneida brought him some flowers from her gardens and set them on the porch. There were a couple dozen white daisies overflowing a one-pound coffee can filled with water, and a single white rose in a polished pewter bud vase.

"These daisies were your father's favorites," she told him. "He'd always say nothing else in the world was so simple, yet so beautiful. And the rose is for your mother, because it's the most beautiful thing in my garden, period. You can leave them by the stones, and I'll fetch the vase later."

"Thank you, Miss Oneida," Cassidy said, sitting on the porch steps and smelling the rose. "One of the best memories I have of growing up is your flowers. I can still smell the fresh-cut lilacs you'd put in the middle of our dinner table every spring. Do you remember that? Whenever I smell good fried chicken or lilacs, my mind drifts back to those days."

Her thin lips trembling, Miss Oneida went fishing for the wad of Kleenex in her sleeve and Cassidy smiled. She dried her eyes and sent him away.

"You say 'hi' for me, now," she told him, then went inside. The screen door clacked closed behind her.

Cassidy walked to Mount Pisgah, past all the houses of his boyhood, past the old school, across Main Street toward the ballpark and the Pond, and through the black wrought-iron gates on the north edge of the cemetery. He followed the gravel path toward the top of the hill, where the Old Ones were laid to rest in the shade.

The names were familiar. They graced streets, parks and a good number of the local legends. As the son of a newspaper editor, he'd heard most of the stories over the dinner table or eavesdropping on late-night porch talk.

The headstones in this part of the cemetery were decorous, earnest. Except one. Cassidy and Daniel found it when they were children and they visited it regularly. It belonged to Hector Feeney, a bachelor farmer whose familiar nickname "Heck" was carved in the granite below his given Christian name. Heck Feeney never finished the third grade and so he never learned to read properly. But that alone didn't make him dumb. Heck had a special gift for stupid acts.

Heck Feeney stories abounded in West Canaan. Among them: one spring, he stumbled upon a den of rattlers in an outcropping of rocks on the badland side of his ranch. He rode three miles back to the homestead, loaded an empty fifty five-gallon fuel drum on his wagon and returned to the snake den. He positioned the barrel under the hole and built up a wall of stones so when the snakes came out of their hole, they'd naturally fall off the ledge into the barrel, from which they could not escape.

In a few days, Heck drove back to the outcropping and found his barrel nearly full of buzzing rattlers, large and small, writhing against one another in a most sinful spectacle. He poured some kerosene into the drum, then went back to his wagon for matches, which he'd forgotten to bring. So once more, he rode back to the ranch house to get matches and returned to the snake den.

Now, whether the snakes had churned up the kerosene fumes or the heat of the day had kept them close to the ground, nobody knows. But when Heck lit that match, the air over the barrel ruptured with a hell of a clap, then set off the fuel in the barrel like a cannon. Dazed by the shock and knocked to his ass as well, Heck sat there in the dirt for a split second before it started raining rattlers on him. He hightailed it out of there, and whenever the subject of rattlers came up among neighbors, Heck started shaking like he was palsied.

And that was just one of the stories. There were many, many more that described the dim-witted behavior of Heck Feeney.

But being an idiot was Heck's only flaw. It didn't affect his cosmic luck any. Back in the Thirties, some big oil company hit a gusher, then another, then more, on his ranch. Heck became the richest man within a hundred-mile circle around West Canaan— fulfilling some ancient prophecy that the dumbest man in any small town is also destined to become the richest. Small-town folks certainly prefer their neighbors to have more brains than money, but given their druthers, their *best* neighbors have neither.

As such, nobody listened much to Heck. He was rich and stupid. It wasn't proper.

But dumb and kind-hearted aren't the same thing. Heck Feeney was seventy-two when he died alone at his ranch house on February 16, 1952. Although he couldn't read a lick and almost nobody cared what he thought about anything, Heck left almost two million dollars to build and fill a proper library for West Canaan. The library was still known around town simply as Heck's Library, although they never stopped telling stories about him.

During his life, his money never earned him the respect it earned him in death. Right up to the end, nobody really listened to him. His headstone reflected the frustration of a lonely man who paid Nub Carlile two hundred dollars just to guarantee his epitaph would read:

"I told you I was sick."

Cassidy followed the gentle slope of West Canaan's society down toward the McLeod family plot.

Just off the path, where the trees thinned out, they were all buried. The graves of Darius and Lucinda McLeod, Cassidy's grandparents, were closest to the walk. His mother's pure white gravestone was a few steps beyond, bright as the sun that reflected off it. Archie's headstone was on one side, Daniel's on the other.

Cassidy laid one daisy on his grandfather's grave and one on his grandmother's. Lucinda had been much younger than Darius, but died giving birth in 1924 to a second child who lived only four days. Archie grew up alone with his father, and when he and Annie had their own son in 1946, they christened him with his grandmother's maiden name: Daniel Quinn McLeod.

Cassidy knew the story, but it dawned on him only as he read the dates on Lucinda's stone that Archie, too, had lost his mother when he was four years old. Maybe he knew all along what was in his little boy's empty heart.

He laid another daisy on Daniel's grave, or whomever's grave it was now. It still troubled him to see his brother's name there. Daniel was alive. Cassidy wanted to uproot the stone, to dig up the little box, send it back to the Pentagon and fill in the hole it left in his life. But the time wasn't yet right.

Cassidy kneeled at his mother's grave to pull a few tufts of crabgrass in the dry lawn. He wiped the dust off the stone, hot in the afternoon sunlight, and touched the simple block letters that summarized her life too simply:

Annie MacKenzie McLeod
Loving Wife and Mother
b. April 22, 1920
d. May 14, 1953

He placed the rose and its vase on a ledge at the base of the headstone. Against the smooth white rock, its delicate petals looked like porcelain. She would have been seventy-five now, maybe tending her own garden. He wondered what it would be like to call her on the phone and talk about nothing at all, just so she knew she wasn't forgotten.

Cassidy kissed his fingers and touched them to her name. "I loved you, Mom," he said softly, "and I never meant to hurt you."

With the sun at his back, he stood before the last grave, his father's. Its uncluttered inscription was in a familiar, honest typeface:

Archimedes McLeod
b. January 29, 1920
d. October 22, 1972
Newspaperman

In Archie's scrupulously tight writing style, it all came down to one word: *Newspaperman*.

A long time before he died, he'd set his epitaph in wooden type in the backshop of the *Republican-Rustler*, and for twenty-five years, it could be found with a little effort beneath the clutter of ad tickets, chicken-dinner news, hasty notes and photographs that covered the top of his desk. Archie always joked it was the best thing he ever wrote.

And it was a good word, Cassidy thought as he arranged the daisies in front of his father's headstone.

One good word.

"Hello," a voice behind him said.

Cassidy looked around, startled. The sun was low and blinded him at first. He shielded his eyes and stood.

It was Tia. Her hair looked thicker, windblown by miles on the road. Her arms were tawny. She looked rested, relieved.

"The road leads back, my friend," she said, holding her arms open to him.

"I'll be goddamned," Cassidy said, going to her. "Welcome home. I've missed you so much."

He held her tight, as if he'd never let her go again. He didn't feel alone anymore, and never wanted to again.

"Why are you here?" he asked her.

"I stopped at your house, but Miss Oneida said you came up here to bring flowers. It wasn't hard to find you."

"No, I mean why did you come back? Is everything okay?"

"The story's done and I wanted to see you again. I'm through chasing ghosts. I put eight thousand miles on my car and you know what? Jack Lazarus is still dead."

"Have you written the story yet?"

"It's done. I finished it in a Super 8 outside of Chicago last week. Four days. All these emotions just came pouring out. Stuff from when I was a little girl, the presents he sent. The last time I saw him. My loneliness. This road trip. You..."

"Me? How the hell did I get in this story?"

"You've always been in this story, since I first saw you. I've had a lot of time to think about this, but I think you're just like him. You're lost. Worse than me."

Cassidy said nothing, but turned and led Tia up the gravel path into the shade of the trees. Above them, the water tower shone in the afternoon sun.

"How is he? Is he getting better?"

"No. He's eating less now, and sleeping more fitfully. He hasn't spoken a word. Sometimes, he lets me take him outdoors for some fresh air, but his nerves are like raw meat. I don't think he's getting better. Maybe he's getting worse."

They walked past ranks of headstones, row upon row of them, each marking the spot where some soul just stopped to slough off its skin. Some were ornate, reaching toward Heaven in a last bid for attention; some lay flush to the lawn, like simple lives that needed no explanation, no celebration.

"I went to my father's grave in this shabby little cemetery on the South Side. It looked so small, with a flat little stone that just had his name and dates on it. Maybe a man is like a tree, you can't really take the measure of him until he's been laid out like that. His shadow was so immense, it kept me from seeing him clearly. He was always bigger than life to me, but he seemed smaller in death."

"He *was* bigger than life," Cassidy said. "He was a great writer. You can't take that away from him, and you can't change its effect on your life."

"But he wasn't a great father. Or husband. He was lost and he never found his way back. He never tried. Jack Lazarus came to the end of the road and just stopped."

"So if he wasn't a great father or husband and if I'm so much like him, why did you come back?"

"Because I loved him anyway. And maybe I love you anyway. But I loved him from a distance and I don't want to love you from a distance. I've made my peace with him by following his shadow down every back road he ever walked. I've read every word he ever wrote, slept in beds where he slept, touched people he touched. I'd wake up in the dark in some fleabag motel in some god-awful town and feel like his ghost was watching me. Jesus, I never once felt so close to him when he was alive. Now, I don't want to be on the road any longer, and I don't want to just stop, like he did."

"You're lucky."

"No, you're lucky and maybe that's what I came back to tell you. Daniel is alive. You've spent so much time worrying about what you've lost, you haven't protected and loved what you've got. You're so afraid of losing him, you don't really have him at all. Maybe you don't want to hear this, but I think it's time to take Daniel to a hospital. Don't lose him forever just because you never wanted to lose him in the first place."

Cassidy held her hand tighter as they walked. Up in the trees, they sat on a garden bench beside the path. The drought had freed the prairie dust to wander in tides of air close to the earth. Columns of light sliced through the high branches and the drifting dust motes, making them shine like rays of evanescent stardust falling on the Old Ones.

"When they buried my father, the preacher read from Genesis. He started at the beginning, about the Creation, because my father always said it was a damned fine lead for a story. I guess I'd heard it a thousand times, but I'd never really listened."

Cassidy reached down and plucked a dandelion that poked through a crack in the path at his feet. Tia rested her head on his shoulder as he continued.

"God decides on his little project and he says, 'Let there be light.' Of course, there *was* light and the Bible says, 'it was good.'

"But the preacher went on with his eulogy, through the first and second and third days, as God creates more of the world with land, water and plant life.

"But on the fourth day, God creates the sun and the moon and the stars in the heavens. They were to separate night from day, and to provide a kind of rhythm to our lives. But something wasn't right. There I am, about to watch my father's casket go down into the earth and I'm puzzling out this little religious mystery."

"What do you mean?" Tia asked, puzzled herself. She brushed her hair away from her face.

"If God created the sun and stars on the fourth day, what was the light of the *first* day?"

"I never thought about it, I guess," Tia said.

"Me neither, but there it was. That night I read Genesis again, wondering what it meant. What was the first light?"

"What do you think it was?"

"It was good."

"I don't understand."

"The first light, it was *good*. It said it right there in the book. The first thing God created was something we could have faith in. There was no mystery and I'm no preacher, but I'd missed it all my life. Maybe my father missed it, too, even though he was the best editor I ever saw. It was *good*."

Tia's smile reflected the day. She settled against him, holding his arm against her.

"Hallelujah, Reverend McLeod, I have seen the light," she teased. "And it is good. Damned good."

She made Cassidy laugh.

"Okay, okay. Sorry. What I'm trying to say, very badly, is sometimes we don't see what's plain. Do we see light, or do we see what is illuminated? In this case, am I seeing Daniel or am I seeing a memory?"

"Cass, I didn't mean to criticize. I mean..."

"I know. You just said what I've known for a long time." He smiled at her, then looked down at the dandelion between his fingers. "I thought he had come home for some mystical reason, to rescue me or something. I really wanted to believe it."

"There are lots of places in California where he could go. You'd be close. It wouldn't be as if you were abandoning him. They'd take good care of him, maybe make him well again."

"I know. I've already called."

"You mean, you're considering it?"

Cassidy paused, then looked off into the stream of light that flowed past them.

"No, I mean I've already made arrangements. There's a small private hospital across the Bridge in Inverness. It's secluded but close to The City. I can go up there on weekends and stay in a cottage. There's an opening in two weeks. That gives me time to close up my dad's place again and drive Daniel out there. I wish I could live here with him forever, but..."

Cassidy clenched his jaw to keep from crying. It hurt deep down in his center, as if he were burying his brother again. But he knew it was the only way. He'd put his life, such as it was, on hold for two months and it was time for him to assess the damage. He'd go back to the book and try to finish, although it frightened him to face it again. He was no closer to answers than before.

"Cass, it's the right thing," Tia said, holding his hand and trying to comfort him. "You did the best you could here. If it would help, I'll go back with you, if you'd like."

Standing, Cassidy took her by the hand and they walked back toward the gates. On the way, he stopped for a moment to look up through the trees at the water tower, rising fat and stoic over the hill. He felt a phantom twinge of pain in his left shoulder, which had healed quickly, furtively, almost forty years ago. For a moment, he was back in that time again, seeing the world beyond his little town, then suddenly seeing death, waiting for him beyond the safety of its limits. His near-fall from the tower had remained a secret between him and Daniel for almost forty years.

"Wait here," he told Tia as he walked quickly back down the path.

He came back a few minutes later, his eyes a little puffy and red. Tia was waiting for him on the cool grass.

"Where did you go?" she asked.

"I went back to tell my father something he never knew."

WATERS OF EDEN
OUTLAW HOLE, SEPTEMBER 11, 1995

Tia inched toward the edge of the canyon and looked down into its maw, as if a hungry tongue might dart up and drag her into its fathomless depths. She could hear the constant clamor of distant water cascading somewhere beneath the rim of the gorge, but she couldn't see it.

"We're going down *there*?"

For the first time in the brief time he'd known her, Cassidy thought, she sounded like a city girl. The Monday morning sun was high in the sky. Already, the early autumn heat was more sympathetic than summer's. A cool breeze tumbled off the mountain, soothing them as they prepared for their long hike to the water below.

The next morning, they would close up Archie McLeod's house on Ithaca Street, say goodbye to Miss Oneida, and begin their long journey west. Daniel was expected at the Inverness hospital on Friday. This pilgrimage to Outlaw Hole would be the last for him and Cassidy knew it.

"It's all right," he reassured her, looping the strap of a fishing creel over his Giants cap. The new black puppy cavorted awkwardly at his feet, eager to begin whatever journey lay ahead. "Just watch out for Big Phil."

"Big Phil? Who's Big Phil?" Tia asked. She pulled her sunglasses down far enough on her nose to casually scan the tree line for something or someone that might be even more dangerous than she imagined her imminent hike into this wild country would be.

"Big Phil Gardner. He's a cannibal who lived in Outlaw Hole a long time ago. They say he liked human flesh better than venison. He only ate a couple fellas, but you know how word gets around. Nobody knows what happened to Big Phil after he disappeared into the Hole."

Cassidy enjoyed the raw fright value of the old stories, the same ones that once scared him silly. And like Daniel, he couldn't resist adding a grain of drama in the retelling.

"Yeah, and it's a good thing I've got you to protect me, right?" Tia shot back.

"I'll do my best but if he gets me first, just play dead. He prefers to eat *live* meat," Cassidy teased her.

Daniel still sat in the cab of Old '46. He'd ridden between Tia and Cassidy on the way to the Crazy Woman Creek, staring straight ahead or into his lap. After some difficulty coaxing him to get into the truck, Daniel pinched his shoulders and knees together to keep from touching either of them. His baths were more dependent on his mood than regularity, so the smell in the cab was rank; Daniel covered his ears against the roar of the highway wind past their open windows.

Of course, he didn't speak on the head-bumping and gear-grinding drive through the Hole in the Wall to the trailhead, now grown over with skunk bushes. As much as they could, Cassidy and Tia spoke around him, almost shouting over the keening engine and the sound of the road, but the trip was mostly silent.

Now ready to start their descent into the Hole, Cassidy gestured to Daniel to come out of the truck. Finally, Daniel slid cautiously across the seat and stepped into the sunlight as if he were sticking his toe into cold water, shielding his eyes. His skin looked pale and his wrinkled clothes hung limp on him as he stood beside the truck, looking at the rocky ground. Shadow sniffed around his feet, his enormous tail swinging in a joyous three-quarter circle around him.

Daniel didn't look like he once looked, a part of this landscape. He now appeared to be a wasted vagrant who wandered into a wilderness.

It was impossible to know what might send Daniel into a hallucinatory frenzy, but Cassidy was determined that he couldn't cage his brother in their house forever. He was getting desperate to see some change in his brother's consciousness. Maybe the fresh air and the sun splashing on the creek itself might rekindle some old memory. The ageless solitude of the Crazy Woman held few surprises and, except for the sounds of the water, was as quiet as Eden on the first day.

Nonetheless, Cassidy rummaged around the bed of the pickup, behind the gas can he'd filled as a precaution. He came up with a brown bag from the hardware store, from which he pulled what looked like a blue tangle of rope. Tia watched as he looped one end of the thin blue nylon strap around his waist, the other around Daniel's, as a tether to keep him near and safe. There was plenty of strap between them, maybe twenty feet, but the rugged landscape of Outlaw Hole was no place to lose Daniel. As the Wild Bunch proved long ago, a man who intended to be lost could find no better hiding place.

"I'll lead the way," Cassidy told Tia. "You walk between us and hold the rope so it doesn't snag on rocks or bushes. Daniel will follow, if we're lucky. The puppy will keep up. Go slow and watch where you step. There are rattlesnakes."

"Oh, great. Welcome to Wyoming. Just walk off a cliff, watch for cannibals and don't step on any snakes," Tia said, sneaking a look at the ground around her running shoes as she walked toward the trailhead. "Just another shitty day in paradise, eh?"

"Shhhhh," Cassidy warned as she muttered a good-humored but nervous curse at him under her breath, "or the grizzly bears might hear you."

At first, Daniel fought the tether, leaning backward against it like an old gelding being led to his last pasture. He stumbled on the steep trail a few times, but struggled to his feet before anyone could help him up. Then he'd stand unmoving until the motley parade started downhill once more. One of his hands was badly scraped on the rocks and seeped a spatter of blood, but he didn't favor it or wipe it clean. It just dripped on the trail and his pant legs until the bleeding stopped on its own.

Cassidy found a thin, straight pole in a deadfall and stripped away its sharp, dried limbs so Daniel could use it as a walking stick. But rather than lean on the stick for support, he merely towed it down the trail, snaring it a couple times on some shrubs and stones while Shadow playfully chased after its dragging, bumping end.

In time, as they dropped deeper into the canyon, they arrived at a mammoth fir tree that shaded the path. Cassidy stopped and walked around it, searching for something. He knew the tree, but the rope they'd once tied around it to belay themselves down to the water was long rotted away. Without it, the descent to the creek was too steep and treacherous, even for the most able-bodied hikers.

"We've got to go farther down the trail," he told Tia, who sweated and shifted her day pack to ease the ache in her neck. Already, the back of her shirt was soaked with sweat. Daniel stood at the end of his tether, a few yards away. "Near the end of it, there's a little meadow by the crick where we can stop. We'll eat there, then we'll try to catch some fish. Sound like a plan?"

They trooped down the trail a few hundred more yards, until it opened into a small patch of wildflowers, bounded on one side by the steep southern flank of the gorge and the cold, clear water of the Crazy Woman on the other. The trail just ended there. To Cassidy, the last best place on Earth.

Tia sat on a log and let her day pack slip from her tired shoulders. Cassidy untied the tether around his waist and knotted it to a nearby stump while Daniel lay down in the warm grass and wildflowers. The little black dog waded in a shallow pool, lapping the cold water with his pink tongue, whipping his tail in wide, happy swaths.

"This is a beautiful spot. It's worth the walk," Tia said. She poured some water on her paisley neckerchief and patted it on her face to cool down. Deep inside the Hole the air was still, but the slow evaporation refreshed her.

"We used to camp right in here," Cassidy said, turning in a lazy circle, his arms outstretched. "Nobody ever came down this far. We'd wake up in the morning and there'd be deer all around us. Dad would already have caught our breakfast, and it tasted so good. Those were great times."

Tia rummaged in her pack for the tuna sandwiches and apples they'd packed that morning. The sourdough bread was soggy, but the lunch tasted good after the long hike. Even Daniel took one from her and ate it while he hid alone in the high grass, leaving a scrap for the puppy to steal.

When they'd finished, Cassidy rigged his old bamboo fly rod and went down to the water's edge. The stoneflies had long ago taken wing, so he tied a dry fly to his leader and unfurled a cast into an eddy beneath an overhanging stump. His fly floated in the backwash, swirled and slipped downstream. No trout rose to it.

He cast a few more times into the bracing water of autumn, pools he hadn't fished in half a lifetime, but got no bites.

"Would you like to try this?" he asked Tia.

"I'm not coordinated enough," she demurred. "And I don't want to touch the fish."

"I'll teach you," he said. "Come over here. Don't worry, you can't hurt anything unless you snag the hook in your neck or your butt. I can tell you from experience: that hurts."

Tia rolled her eyes and stood with her hands on her hips like a little girl fending off second-grade suitors. Cassidy smiled and beckoned to her.

"You'll do just fine. Come on."

Tia waggled the rod stiffly. The line hung, almost annoyed, from its tip. Cassidy stood behind her, gripping the rod with his right hand over hers and gently guiding the translucent line through her left.

"I know about you horny fishermen who lure innocent girls to the river with your wily promise to teach them how to cast," she said. "So watch it, buster."

"Hey, it always worked before," he said, then kissed her on the back of her neck.

"I see what you mean. You'd better keep your eyes on the water," she said, a feathery tingle running up her spine.

Cassidy drew her right arm back to start the cast.

"Okay, to start with, you're too stiff. Loosen up. Just let your body follow mine. Nice and easy."

Tia let her shoulders and arms go almost limp as he moved against her. He began the rhythmic casting motion with one hand and pulled the line with the other, then let the fly drift silently across the water into a deep pool on the other side of the creek.

"That was nice," he said. "You try it on your own now."

Tia dug in, her feet spread wide. She tried to repeat the motions he'd led her through, but ended up snagging the line in some grass behind her. She tried again, and again. Finally, she sailed the fly gracelessly into the passing water and the current dragged it downstream.

"By George, you've got it! You're a natural," Cassidy said, applauding. Tia curtsied, spreading an imaginary skirt to the sides of her blue jeans while she held the pole in one hand.

Suddenly, the rod bent backward like a willow in a windstorm. A furious silver burst erupted in the middle of the stream and the whole rig flew from Tia's grasp. She let out a tiny startled scream and ran away from the bank.

Cassidy's rod slithered through the grass and rocks on the creek bank, dragged toward the water by the fish Tia had hooked. He scrambled toward it, but it flew into the water. He leaped into the cold stream after it and searched the bottom where it went in. Groping under the water up to his shoulder, he found it entangled on a snarl of roots.

As he lifted it from the water, he felt a great weight pulling against it. The fish was still hooked, but had run downstream into churning water where the sheer weight of the current might sever the line and save him.

Cassidy stood in the chill water, taking up the slack line and working the fish upstream into easier water. He tried to move down the creek a little, but his way was blocked by a juniper snag that jutted over the water.

Tia was in shock. She couldn't believe she'd actually hooked a fish, much less one that fought so valiantly. She edged back up to the creek bank to watch the fight.

Dripping wet, Cassidy kept his line taut and his tip high, the way Archie had taught him. The trout rose a few times, then went deep, darting across the stream in a deep pool and refusing to be landed by a fisherman who was not among the Chosen.

Tia began to root for Cassidy, cautiously at first, then more energetically. Then the puppy began yipping, running up to the water's edge, then retreating. Creation might have been the last din heard so loud on the Crazy Woman.

"I saw him! I saw him! Pull him up!" She was hopping up and down like a cheerleader at the big game. Shadow barked more frantically.

Cassidy sidestepped along the slippery stones of the creek bed into deeper water, angling to draw the trout through a softer pool where he could get him closer to the bank. He leaned toward the swifter water, dipping his rod across the flow, reeling slowly.

The fish plunged deeper into the Crazy Woman, seeking salvation on the bottom. For a moment, the line went slack and stopped its frenetic traverse back and forth across the stream. The whole canyon fell silent. Cassidy's heart sunk a little, until the fish hit the end of the line again and made its final, desperate lunge for freedom.

Cassidy maneuvered the fish to the shallows and, overcome by the thrill of her catch, Tia and Shadow leaped into the water at the same time. She lifted the fat rainbow out of the stream while the dog snapped at it. He was easily twenty-four inches long.

Tia whooped and Cassidy waded back to shore with her, still holding the fish by the slender line that was its fate. The dog scrambled onto the shore and shook an excited spray of water on them.

At first, they didn't hear it over the sound of the water. Then they heard it. It didn't emanate from the river or the mountain or the trees. It was an off-beat slapping sound and it came from the meadow behind them.

They turned to see Daniel, standing in the tall grass, surrounded by wildflowers and the last butterflies of summer. He was clapping.

A crooked smile bobbed across his dry lips, then was gone.

They released the great fish back into the Crazy Woman, where it belonged. His resolve had earned him mercy, albeit at the cost of some of his life force.

By the time he shimmered back into the cold water, the puppy had fallen asleep in the bright sun and Daniel had lapsed back into his strange little world. Sleep and madness have no perfect place or time.

"But he rose to the surface for just long enough, just like that trout. I wish I knew why," Cassidy said as they prepared for the long walk out of the canyon. He was frustrated and overjoyed at the same time. These brief bursts of lucidness made Daniel's catatonia the more painful for him.

Tia tried to comfort Cassidy, rubbing her hand on his back. She began to share his bafflement.

"It will happen one of these times and he'll never go back. I'm sure of it. Be patient."

Cassidy retied the nylon tether around his waist and walked over to Daniel, who sat cross-legged and empty in an inviting patch of wild yellow violets and blue flax. Cassidy tugged gently on the strap and Daniel rose. Cassidy watched for any shadow of recognition to drift across his face, but saw none. Daniel merely looked away, toward the water.

They started up the trail, past the old fir that once anchored their journey to the waters. The trail rose up the rocky hillside to the spine of a small hogback ridge. A natural cairn of rocks, exposed by a million years of erosion, marked the trail's passage over the ridge. They sat there to rest.

"The Crazy Woman smiled on us today," he told Tia.

"She did. She smiled." Tia laid her head on Cassidy's shoulder.

"Let me show you something," Cassidy said, kneeling beside the trail. Shadow wormed his way into the small space where Cassidy moved some stones from a pile. The dog sniffed around, then peed on it.

Daniel stood at the end of his tether facing away from them, toward the lowering sun.

"Come see," Cassidy said, motioning Tia closer.

Out of sight in the dust under the stones were a handful of old coins, mostly dimes and nickels. A passing hiker, even a curious one, would never have moved the rocks to find the money unless he was divinely directed, for there was no more reason to explore this natural-looking cairn than the billions of stones in the canyon.

"It's like a hidden treasure," Tia said.

"Every time we came up here, we'd leave a coin or two for the Crazy Woman, sort of a sacrifice. Or maybe it was just a gift, I don't know. It was Daniel's idea. At first, I was scared I'd be cursed or something, then it just sort of became a tradition for us."

Cassidy stood and dug in his pocket. He withdrew a half dollar, a tarnished Franklin, the same coin he'd found in his father's trousers after his funeral. He tossed it on the scattered coins already concealed beneath the stones, as he'd intended to do since he decided to return to his sacred waters.

"May the Crazy Woman smile on us. Just once more," he said as he replaced the stones and scattered dirt to hide it again. "Maybe she already has. I'm very happy you came back."

Tia couldn't speak. She felt a lump rise in her throat and she put her arms around him to keep from crying where he might see. They stood on that ridge a while, watching the dying sun's light gild the orange and yellow walls of Outlaw Hole with its last inspiration. The steep cliffs rose above them like a painted sky.

Below them, the water whispered this part of forever, just as it had on the first day.

Cassidy shielded his eyes against the low afternoon sun. A thunderhead boiled in the north, reflecting the violent colors of a dying summer. It was still too far off to hear its thunder but he could see lightning in the silent space between Heaven and Earth. The air tasted electric.

"Look. You were right," Tia said, crouching beside the path. A clump of dandelions had closed up its yellow blossoms, as if battening down its hatches for a squall.

Cassidy smiled and looked far off to the north a last time. A long trail lay ahead and they must now race the storm home.

But, finally, rain was coming.

RAIN
WEST CANAAN, SEPTEMBER 12, 1995

By the time the sirens sang, it was after midnight and blood was trickling down the window pane.

They'd found him, even though he'd hidden well and never spoke for them to hear his voice.

The death angels had hunted him down at last.

Daniel covered his ears against the unbroken thumping of their wings in the night air outside. Since he'd returned to this place, he knew they'd been searching throughout the big sky of his childhood for him, but he never believed they would find him in his father's house.

Now they hovered over Ithaca Street, the only haven where he thought he could be safe from them. They must have followed him from the waters. But he knew the death angels would never come inside for him, because this was a sacred place of ghosts where they might be trapped in The Box forever, with all the rest. So they hovered in the trees and flashed their light to better see him through the dark windows.

He knew.

The time of the end was at hand. The words must be unsealed.

A bright light pierced the window and flooded the room, searing every corner. Ozone and sulfur stung Daniel's nose. He cowered against the wall under the eave, his knees pulled tightly against his chest. All the nights he'd searched the heavens, but never saw them. Now, if he moved, they might see him. He couldn't stop shaking.

Outside, they bellowed and shrieked as they searched for him, their wings beating faster and faster. They ripped at the sky and roared in their anger, their hounds squealing like frightened pigs and belching gray fumes. They heaved flares to light the blackness and to call forth other death angels to feast on him. They called his name and tried to trick him with their lies. The house trembled beneath their fury.

In every flash of raging light, he saw his little brother's face, sleeping peacefully beside him. And with every burst, Cassidy grew younger and younger, until he was a little boy again. But Daniel could not protect him any longer from the death angels. They waited for him, too.

The blood poured down the glass and the night grew blacker.

The time of the end...

Daniel heard his father's voice calling up to him from somewhere outside.

"We must go to the water, Danny," Archie McLeod said. "The waters will be good to us."

Then his mother sang a distant lullaby. Her voice was like the cool, clear water in a stream that ran past every place he'd ever fished and finally emptied into the Great Water that pulsed through his veins. He would see her soon enough, too.

And the Archangel, the moon-faced boy who only wanted to go home, stood on the grass in his white, flowing poncho and sang a hymn for Daniel that lasted twelve days. Days and nights passed and when he finished, they were where they began again, as if time hadn't passed at all, or had passed in a perfect and true circle. While the Archangel sang, he unbuttoned his fatigues and burrowed his fingers into the savage, putrefying gash across his belly and rainwater poured forth like a mountain cataract, hot and brown.

Then Daniel heard a baby wailing.

At first it seemed far away, then grew louder, closer. It kept crying, the way the siren called him home.

The baby cried louder, while the Archangel sang his endless song. The unholy water poured forth from his wound endlessly, rising like the Great Flood until it consumed him and all the rest on the ground.

... Except Mastema. He hovered over them all, above the boiling waters, the tempter and the executioner. He commanded the death angels and he dispatched the hot blood from the heavens. He laughed in thunderclaps and exhaled the smell of burning rot. Each time he flexed his terrible wings, he dispersed the smoke of burning grass.

The drumbeat of wings grew louder and the death angels' shrieking more manic, their hunger more ferocious.

The words must be unsealed.

Daniel could not escape the furies unless he could run between the bloody raindrops, the pain Mastema poured upon him. It marked him before and they found him by following its path. But the words must be unsealed at the time of the end. He must try.

The air was electric. When it burst, Daniel saw his brother's face, small and innocent, asleep in the bed beside him. He reached across the dark canyon between them and gently touched the little boy's cheek. It was as soft as he'd remembered.

Barefoot and naked except for his briefs, Daniel crept silently off the end of the bed, crouching in the dark so he wouldn't be seen. He crawled on his belly to the doorway and into the hallway beyond. Grasping the handrail in a stoop, he inched down the stairs and groped his way along the wall toward the back door.

Lightning ripped through the house, casting shadows of the long dead on the walls around him as he reached for the handle. They pointed the way.

It was locked. Daniel fumbled wildly with the deadbolt, yanking and twisting it until it clanked open. He turned the handle and the door was pushed open by a rush of stinking wind from the angels' wings. He stood there for minutes, maybe hours, watching the low, bleeding sky and searching the towering cottonwoods for them, but they did not show themselves. He watched the blood pour down, pitching off the porch roof in great gushes. He knew he must run.

There could be no misstep. He must avoid being splashed by the hideous rain, or death would surely follow more swiftly. The words would never be unsealed. When they were safe, Mastema could take him, finally.

So he ran.

Daniel leaped from the porch onto the unmowed back lawn and bolted across the yard toward the plank fence. The bloody rain still had not touched him as he scaled over it and ran through the narrow alley toward oblivion.

He crashed through some coal-ash bins and a dog barked in the night. A bolt of lightning illuminated his path like a flare as he ran toward the center, toward Source.

His lungs burned and his legs ached long before he came to the black iron gates of Pisgah. Blood pumped in his ears, pounding louder than the death angels' wings. But, still, he had not been touched.

In the dark, he crashed into a headstone and plunged into the wet grass. Blood flowed from a long, knife-straight wound across his shin, but he forced himself to move on against the pain, between the raindrops, toward the south side of the graveyard.

Daniel found the five headstones, clustered near the top of the hill and began digging with his bare hands in the wet earth. The rain came more furiously now, and soon it filled the shallow hole as he dug, loosening the soil as he went deeper and deeper. He flung the dirt down the hillside behind him like a mad animal.

Then the earth screamed. It reached out for him with rotting limbs, fingers choked in death. Their eyes were still open, searching for him that disturbed their death place. The stench of death enveloped him, like before.

Then the hole spewed blood in great arcs, drenching him. Their pain flowed still.

Soon, he was clawing through their entrails, slippery tangles of bowels and rotted flesh that made him vomit again and again while he scratched deeper.

His hands were raw, the skin sheared back by the unforgiving earth. But he knew the words were inside somewhere, in the safe arms of another angel, a good angel who never meant any harm.

Fatigued and grunting, he plunged through their guts toward their souls. The hole grew deeper and muddier. The sides dripped in bile and collapsed against him as he scraped handfuls of flesh and mud to the surface.

The digging had shredded his hands. Raw bone poked through his knuckles, but he rooted deeper toward the words. He descended toward Hell.

The metal box made a dull, hollow sound when he hit it. Daniel used a broken root to cut away the hard-packed soil around it, then to lever it free from the embrace of death.

The box was light as he lifted it out of the hole and slid it across the piles of mud that surrounded the gaping wound. The voices had fallen silent, but the rain still fell.

The box was sealed tight and he couldn't open it. He pounded on it with the root as he heard the drumbeat of death wings coming closer. Frantic, he clawed at the seal on the box, pressed even tighter by the weight of the earth on top of it. A flash of light bathed the cemetery in blue light and Daniel saw Mastema floating over the water tower, watching and laughing.

The crate must be opened. The words must be unsealed. He searched desperately for something to open the box, finally slipping in the mud beside his own grave, gashing his elbow against his headstone.

The headstone.

He wrenched the muddy stone free from the earth and dragged it through the mire. Nearly exhausted, he summoned his last ounce of strength to lift the massive stone waist-high and drop it on the metal coffin.

Daniel pushed the stone away. The blow had crushed one side of the aluminum box, popping its lid free. He dragged it free and kneeled in the black, slippery mud beside it.

A baby cried again, from inside. Daniel lay in the mud as he lifted her free from the box.

"Nam nghi di chau. Da den gio di ngu roi," he whispered aloud, comforting the child. "Rest, little baby. The time has come to sleep."

The baby's blackened bones were shrouded in a swaddling cloth of rotten rain poncho. Her skull, still flecked with leathery patches of burned skin, was tightly enfolded in a small opening at the top.

Rocking back and forth, Daniel cradled the baby in his arms, trying to soothe her crying.

Poor baby who died without its mama-san. We found a good mama for you, yes we did. Shhhh. You're almost home. They can't hurt you now, little one. They can't hurt you now.

That's why he'd gone back for her, to be sure she would be buried with a mother. He'd searched for her among the bodies, seven days dead and buried under the black earth of Ba Troi. The corpses of all the rest had all reached out to him, begging him to take them to Heaven with him, but he could not. Their bodies rotted and stunk, their guts uncoiled out of bellies split by bloat, their sunken eyes watched as he clawed through their decaying pieces to find the baby. The only one he could take to Heaven.

When he found her, deep under the restless dead of Ba Troi, he wrapped her in his slicker and hid her in a pack, knowing there was only one place where he could know that she'd be buried beside a good mother.

They had both died that night in Ba Troi. The dead owed something to one another. Daniel wasn't sure which one he was and, in the end, it didn't matter. They were all dead.

Now he kissed her tender face and smoothed her black hair. For a moment, her crying stopped and she looked into his eyes. She was such a beautiful baby. Why did they have to kill her like that?

The death angels drew closer and Daniel hugged her close, protecting her from them. He wanted to sing one of his mother's lullabies, but he couldn't remember. He couldn't remember. The sins of memory were his.

But she cried ever louder, frightened by the non-stop beating of death's wings. With one hand, Daniel tipped the crushed metal box toward him and felt through the morbid dust inside for something else, a small cartridge box he'd placed there before he had the crate shipped home. He knew if he sent it to Emory Carlile's funeral home, it would be buried beside his mother. The crate's size—and the gruesome clue its smallness gave to its contents—all but guaranteed it would never be opened before the funeral. Who would look at the rotted, anonymous meat inside? That's how he knew his words and the baby would be safe until the time of the end.

The cartridge box contained only a torn piece of paper with some writing on it. Daniel made sure it was safe and whole, then hid it beneath the uprooted headstone. He laid the baby gently in its cradle once more, replaced the bent lid on the little aluminum box and carried it back to the hole, where he covered it with mud again.

The words were unsealed.

The time of the end had begun.

Caked in mud, Daniel reached deep into the hole and wormed his fingers through the wet earth, until he touched the lid of the little box he'd reburied safely there. The death angels would not touch hallowed ground.

"*Chu se tro lai*," he promised.

"I'll be back."

Only one could protect the words.

The same keeper who had watched over them forever. The only one who knew.

The brother who had absorbed them like a living vessel. He could keep them safe from the death angels who would burn them in hell fires and scatter their ashes on the soul-sucking wind.

Daniel lifted the stone and retrieved the cartridge box and the paper inside. It was wet, but the words had not blurred in the sheeting rain. He held it tightly and raced back through the dark trees.

He ran faster than the rain and the wind and the lightning. It didn't touch him. When he came to the black, wrought-iron gates of Mount Pisgah, the boundary of hope and holy ground, he turned to see them, perched like shining vultures in the old cottonwoods. Flashes of lightning outlined them like shadows dancing across a flame. Their laughter boomed and echoed through the low sky, and the beating of their wings rattled in his chest.

He ran.

The death angels rose from the cemetery trees like a plague. Daniel heard them as he hurtled toward home. They sounded like the dust-off choppers that ferried the dead across the Styx. They came closer.

Daniel cut through Moses Field, propelled by a hot wind. His legs burned inside, his lungs felt as if they'd rip, but he ran faster, across Main Street in the dark. The movie house quaked under the angels' wings and its decrepit walls crumbled to dust, but the back door stood open, its frame standing alone in the ruins.

He went through it, clawing his way through the rubble to the other side. The angels shrieked over him, spraying the darkness with mortars of thunder.

While his furies erupted, Daniel reached Ithaca Street through the alley in back. He leaped onto the back porch and through the door. The rain had not touched him, but his mission was not yet finished.

On his belly, he crept back up the stairs to the room beneath the eaves. A fair-haired little boy slept in his bed, his breath sweet as a child's. Cassidy hadn't awakened in the din.

Daniel opened the cartridge box. He uncrumpled the delicate paper in his trembling hand and spread it flat on the night stand beside the ten-button rattle and ten perfectly round black stones. He touched Cassidy's cheek again, then kissed him and left silently.

Downstairs, he crouched along the wall toward the kitchen. He opened the cellar door and inched down into the darkness.

Voices came from inside the Box. The ghosts called to him to free them.

"Nhung con ma," he whispered reverently, caressing the dusty oak gussets of the huge trunk. At last, he lifted the lid and the voices took flight into the cool air.

The smaller box was meant for him, a gift across time.

DQM.

Daniel Quinn McLeod.

He yanked it out of the trunk and sat with it on the floor. The small lock was already unlatched, so he merely unhooked it and opened the box.

The machine inside was created for the end alone. Nothing more.

Daniel grasped the wire bail, holding the lantern against his bare chest, and went back up the cellar stairs as quietly as he could. He slipped out the back door again, hiding in the shadows, watching. The rain was pouring more furiously now, but he could not see Mastema and his horde, though he knew they were there. He could hear them breathing in the menacing clouds like choked horses.

He leaped from the porch toward the garage. The door was open.

The gasoline can was still in the pickup's bed. Daniel tried to heave it out, but on the way down it banged loudly against the hollow fender of Old '46.

The death angels must have heard. There would be no time. He ran as fast as he could out the garage door, into the darkness.

Something woke Cassidy in the downstairs bedroom. On this last night in his childhood home, sleep was fitful anyway.

In the netherworld between waking and dreaming, he couldn't be sure what it was, except that it banged like a distant drum. Maybe it was thunder, but it sounded closer, metallic. It had awakened the puppy, too, and he let out just one startled yip before retreating beneath the bed.

Tia was still asleep beside him, so he eased out of the old bed and pulled on his pants. He slipped his running shoes over his bare feet and began to search through the house.

Lightning illuminated the old windows and thunder rattled them. He turned on the light in the hallway, then the den. Their packed suitcases and boxes were stacked by the front door, ready to begin their early journey. They'd covered the furniture with sheets, to protect it against dust, so the den was full of squat little ghosts, bright and unmoving. The photographs on the mantel had been packed for the trip.

A front window facing the street had been left open, its curtain flailing helplessly in the violent wind. It must have blown something over inside the house, he thought, but it was too late to hunt for it. He closed the sash and locked it, maybe forever.

He turned back toward bed and, through the kitchen doorway, saw the back door standing wide open.

Cassidy's heart convulsed.

His body lurched toward the kitchen, but his mind reeled toward Daniel's room. He feared the worst. He threw himself up the stairs, two and three at a time, toward the cramped bedroom beneath the sloping roof where Daniel slept most nights, where Cassidy had seen him sleeping before he went to bed himself.

The sheets on Daniel's bed had been torn into shreds, and the furniture toppled. His room was empty.

Cassidy plunged down the stairs and woke Tia.

"He's gone. You've got to help me find him."

Tia dressed quickly, but Cassidy was already gone. He checked the cellar, then the other rooms. He was so frightened he could hardly breathe as he ran through the house.

Nothing.

Outside, he stood in the rain, lightning and thunder crashing around him, calling Daniel's name. He ran around the outside of the house, scouring the shrubbery and the dark spaces beneath the lilacs, then the tool shed. Soon he was drenched. A clap of thunder cracked overhead, almost before he saw the brilliant bluish flare of lightning.

Tia was beside him, her hands over her ears and a fearful shock on her face. She sprinted toward the garage for cover, then stopped dead in her tracks.

"Cass! Come over here!"

She'd found bare footprints in the muddy driveway. They were filled with water and led toward the alley.

"The cemetery!" Cassidy yelled.

They jumped into the truck. The ignition rasped, but didn't catch. Cassidy pumped the gas pedal furiously and turned the key. Old '46 just wheezed. Cassidy screamed an obscenity and pounded the steering wheel, but they didn't have time to make it work.

"Your car, do you have the keys?" he demanded from Tia, who sat dripping wet beside him, praying for the truck to start.

"No, they're inside," she said, trying to think exactly where she left them when she packed her bags the night before. "My bag, on the dresser."

"Go. Go. Go."

Tia ran inside. After what seemed an eternity to Cassidy, she flew out the front door, holding her car keys in front of her as she ran. He waited for her on the street, where she'd parked her car against the curb. She threw the keys to him and they spun a wide arc across the slick pavement as they made a U-turn in the middle of the night and rushed toward Mount Pisgah.

Daniel stared up the steel stairway of the water tower, into the angry clouds that swirled above it. The blood continued to rain down all around him, but it didn't touch him or the tower.

He climbed the ladder, clinging to the gas can and the coal lantern with one arm and pulling himself to each higher rung with the other. Step by uneasy step, he rose into the fierce maelstrom of fire and vomit stirred by the death angels, by Mastema.

Forty feet up, one of the rusty steel steps collapsed under him. His free hand locked on the rail as he plunged ten feet, slicing his palm until the sharp metal scraped across the bones and sinew in his hand. One of his legs had thrust through a lower step, breaking his fall. He struggled to right himself without losing his grip on the gasoline or the lantern. He needed them more than he needed the stream of blood that now pulsed from a great gash across his hand.

Daniel climbed higher, but still the bloody rain did not fall on him. The tower was a temple in the center where they could not touch him, but he could see them in the trees all around him, shrieking and laughing. Their slimy entrails hung in long loops from their abdomens, their red cocks hard and seeping, their serpent's eyes following him up the tower's precarious ladder. He knew he could not escape them this time.

The trapdoor onto the catwalk was rusted shut. He heaved against it until his head and shoulders were bloody. The whole ladder felt ready to collapse under him as he frantically struggled against it. Finally, it flew open and he shimmied onto the flat steel mesh walkway that encircled the tower's reservoir.

The sky erupted around Daniel like a volcanic nightmare. High above the trees, the air was energized. The razor-sharp odor of ozone seared him. His face was drawn, his eyes wild as he searched the boiling clouds for Mastema.

He unscrewed the cap of the gas can and held it above his head. The gasoline washed over him until the can was empty.

The baptism had begun.

Cassidy and Tia gunned the car across the cemetery lawn and along the pathway to where his mother and father were buried. Even in the torrential rain, they were horrified by what they saw in the headlights: Daniel's grave had been desecrated, with muddy earth scattered all around it as if a wild animal had burrowed into it.

Cassidy got out of the car and ran to the hole. Run-off spilled into it and he saw a piece of cloth floating in the grisly muck. He lay down at the edge of the grave and pulled on it, but it was stuck somewhere deep under the surface. He pulled harder, and it came free.

Cassidy screamed in horror.

He scrambled away from the hole on all fours, losing his footing twice as he clambered across the wet grass toward the safety of his headlights.

Tia rushed to help.

"Don't go over there!" he warned her, sucking for air. "Don't go..."

The downpour quickened until it seemed the air had turned completely liquid, threatening to drown them. Tia helped him back into the car, but he was still in shock.

"What was it?" she begged him.

Cassidy didn't speak. His eyes were riveted on the open grave, as if he expected something to spring out of it and come for him. He couldn't think straight, but for the first time, he knew it was no disembodied piece of unidentifiable soldier's meat they'd buried twenty-four years ago.

He began to shake.

A thunderclap stabbed through them as a lightning bolt cut across the sky. Through the rain-webbed windshield, Tia saw him first against the silver skin of the water tower.

"Up there!" she shouted above the din. "There's somebody up on the tower!"

Lightning ripped through the air again, and Cassidy saw him now, too. He exploded from his shock and ran toward the tower, Tia close behind.

Daniel fumbled with the ancient lantern, its wick protected by the glass globe. He pressed the ignition button a few times, but the fire wouldn't start. He shielded it with his body from the lightning and the sour wind that Mastema sent to snuff it out.

Daniel grew more frantic.

The fire *must* start. The lantern was left for this rite and it *must* work. He must be cleansed. The angel fire spoke to him and promised he could die when he'd shown the path to the Lost One. The path was shown and the Lost One had only to follow. He'd failed himself, but he knew the way. You couldn't go around the rain. Angel fire filled him, and he knew the way *through* the rain.

"Daniel! Stop! Don't move!"

The man's voice pealed behind him on the catwalk, which trembled under them.

It was the Lost One, the little boy, and there was fear in the strange words he spoke. The path must be lighted better, Daniel thought.

"Daniel, please don't move. Please," Cassidy implored him.

The little boy reached out to Daniel, but he inched away, farther along the sagging catwalk. He pressed the lantern's ignition button more furiously now. The path must be lighted.

"No, Danny, no. Please don't move. Just stop. Oh, God, please don't move," Cassidy said.

Suddenly, a steel support wrenched loose and the platform pitched sideways. Thrown off-balance, Cassidy grabbed the rail, slamming against it hard; Daniel jammed his bare foot against a stanchion and pressed himself against the tank. Cassidy tried to lift himself back onto the steel path, but his legs dangled lifelessly and his grip on the wet rail was slipping. He struggled, but the rain blinded him and the wind scoured his strength.

"Danny... oh, god."

Another bracket popped free. The whole catwalk beneath Cassidy collapsed, hanging only by two steel cables that ran under it.

Then, a hand grasped Cassidy's left wrist. In one smooth motion, he was lifted high enough to grasp a nearby rail. Despite the fire in his arms and shoulders, Cassidy got a foothold and dragged himself onto a safer section of the catwalk. Lying there, he vomited through the steel mesh.

He turned just as Daniel lighted the lantern. A look of calm washed over him. His tired eyes shone with relief. The rain had stopped. His journey was done.

In the glow of the old lantern, a dreamer's dream, Daniel turned to his little brother. There were no more stories to tell. The Lost One wasn't lost anymore.

Then Daniel spoke. His voice wasn't raspy, but soothing and soothed, and he looked directly into Cassidy's eyes.

"*Su chet tha thu cho anh.*"

They were Marrenton's words.

The dead forgive you.

He smiled and held the lantern close to his face. When he lifted the glass globe, a spark leapt across the silent, immeasureable space between life and death.

Daniel was engulfed in fire. He never screamed as he pitched off the catwalk, plunging more than sixty feet to the damp earth below.

The rain was over.

EPILOGUE

I'm all right now.

Pain is part of me, part of my comfort.

I spent a lifetime dancing around it, whirling fast enough to blur the ache. I still dance, but slow enough to feel the earth beneath my feet, close enough to know I'm not alone.

And I am not sad anymore.

Why? Because pain is the price we pay for memory. It's some kind of sin to forget what hurts, as much as it is to forget what makes you smile. Suffering has its meaning, and memory has its graces.

Daniel was buried, again, beside our mother and father on Mount Pisgah. We buried the baby with him, their ashes intermingled, as maybe they always had been. On the day of his funeral, a few days before the chill of autumn finally came to West Canaan, the first light shone bright and warm on the south side of Mount Pisgah. We eventually put up a new stone:

Daniel Quinn McLeod
b. July 24, 1946
d. September 12, 1995
Storyteller

And another preacher, a moon-faced Presbyterian boy fresh out of seminary somewhere in Missouri, read the words from Genesis again, the part where God promised that rain would always be followed by sunlight, and a rainbow would be the token of the sacred covenant between Heaven and Earth. And he spoke of another prophet who dreamed, even if he did not always understand:

"Go thy way, Daniel, for the words are closed up and sealed till the time of the end... go thy way till the end, for thou shalt rest..."

I will never know the horror that consumed my brother, but I know it was a pain too big for him. He couldn't get past it by imagining some place deep in his distance, where we had so often walked together. He'd walked me there so many times, but he'd never walked me back.

Until the end.

Some things are clearer now. At first, Pledger Moon was just a fictional character to a sad little boy. Daniel's stories carried me away from my hurt and fears, led me along the way his words led Moon on his fabulous journeys.

Then, as I grew older, I began to think maybe Moon was Daniel, a mystical wanderer who couldn't find his way home. When Daniel came home, it was as if he'd foretold his own redemption and resurrection.

I was wrong about that, like I was wrong about so many things. It was a fantasy that let me dance around the truth.

I am Pledger Moon. I know that now and, of course, the story isn't finished. When it is, I'll be past caring.

That long-ago summer ended and I never heard how Moon's story turned out, whether he ever found his home or died beneath his beloved stars. Perhaps Daniel intended it that way, for although he told many more stories after that, he never returned to Moon. Daniel grew up and left us, went off to Vietnam, told one last story and disappeared.

Daniel never came home. He died in Ba Troi. The fire inside him went out of control and the ashes of his spirit were thrown in a mass grave on the edge of the jungle with that baby, even though his body wandered for another twenty-four years.

Part of me wants to believe that he came home with a message. That he returned to teach me that the path around pain is narrow and treacherous, guarded by demons only he recognized. I want to believe he came to show me the way, to accept pain as part of life. I want to believe he knew, because he always knew.

But maybe Daniel came home for the simple reason that West Canaan was the source of life and, as such, must be the last best place to die. He knew the circle ended where it began, that heroes always returned.

So I'm leaving The City and going home to West Canaan tomorrow. It's where I belong.

I won't be alone. My wife, Tia, will join me. She is now writing a story that is completely her own, one from her heart. She rises before dawn and sits in my father's old leather chair, tapping it out in words she never knew she had inside her. Her words.

I should note, however, that mornings of late have been, well, unproductive. In six months, she will have a child, and our baby will be born in the house where I was born. Boy or girl, the child will be called Danny, and will hear all the old stories about the gandy-dancer Pledger Moon, the Crazy Woman, Moses the ballplayer, Twin Tommy Ganneman, Heck Feeney, Fakey Ducas, Big Phil, and dreamers like Jack Lazarus, Darius and Archie McLeod... and Daniel.

But this story is finished now. Other stories, new ones, wait to be told.

I know a place that's a little closer to Heaven than most. The way is every boy's idea of a proper path to the graveyard: a shortcut to the Dairy Freez corner window, past the balky back door of the Wigwam movie house, across the freshly sprinkled outfield grass, around the pond bank where the flat rocks grow, and through the wrought-iron gates of Heaven's own parking lot. On some summer night soon, I'll go there and look across forever, just to see what I missed before.

How far is it to Heaven?

A lifetime.

—Cassidy McLeod
San Francisco
May 1997

ANGEL FIRE

Toi o giua nhung thi xa, dan dan mat di nhung anh den.
Mot cuoc tham vieng vao dat cua su chet,
voi lai mot doan duong ngan bat qua.
Neu tat ca nhung con duong deu noi lien,
nhu la chung ta da moi thoi mo nhung con duong do nhu vay,
Toi se tro ve nha vao con mua ke tiep.

First day of Tet, 1971

I am between towns, losing the light.
An endless visit in the land of the dead,
with a short layover.
If all the roads are connected,
as we once dreamed they were,
I'll be home by the next rain.

Laughing Owl Publishing, Inc.

Call 1-800-313-7412 access code 71 to order by phone and use your major credit card. Or use this coupon for mail order.

___ **Song of The White Swan**   0-9659701-6-7 $10.00 US - $14.80 CAN
by Aleta Boudreaux (Historical Fiction) An epic tale of Celtic Brittany and the New World.

___ **Glencoe, A Romance of Scotland** 0-9659701-3-2 $10.00 US-$14.80 CAN
by Muireall Donald. (Historical Fiction) At the height of clan distrust, two ancestral enemies battle clan dishonor as they unwillingly fall in love during a bitter Highland winter.

___ **The Beloved** 0-9659701-4-0 $10.00 US -$14.80 CAN
by M.D. Gray (Occult Suspense) A tale of reincarnation, karmic reckoning and forbidden sensuality set in the Victorian South.

Credit Card: ___ Visa ____ Mastercard

Account Number _____ Exp Date____

Signature _____

Name_____

Address_____

State_____ Zip_____ Telephone _____

Please send me the LAUGHING OWL books I have checked.
I am enclosing $_____
Plus Postage and Handling $ 3.50 US / $5.00 CAN
Sales Tax (Alabama residents add 5%) $_____
Total Amount Enclosed $_____

No cash or CODs. Send check, money order, or credit card authorization to:
Laughing Owl Publishing, Inc.
12610 Highway 90 West, Grand Bay, AL 36541.
Prices valid in the U.S. and Canada only.
All prices and availability subject to change without prior notice.

™

To learn more about us visit our web site at
www.laughingowl.com